KU-032-418

# The Italian Woman

Jean Plaidy, one of the pre-eminent authors of historical fiction for most of the twentieth century, is the pen name of the prolific English author Eleanor Hibbert, also known as Victoria Holt. Jean Plaidy's novels had sold more than 14 million copies worldwide by the time of her death in 1993.

For further information about Arrow's Jean Plaidy reissues and mailing list, please visit
www.randomhouse.co.uk/minisites/jeanplaidy

### Praise for Jean Plaidy

'Plaidy excels at blending history with romance and drama'
*New York Times*

'A vivid impression of life at the Tudor Court'
*Daily Telegraph*

'One of the country's most widely read novelists'
*Sunday Times*

'It is hard to better Jean Plaidy . . . both elegant and exciting'
*Daily Mirror*

'Outstanding' *Vanity Fair*

'Plaidy has brought the past to life' *Times Literary Supplement*

'One of our best historical novelists' *News Chronicle*

'Spirited . . . Plaidy paints the truth as she sees it'
*Birmingham Post*

'An enthralling story of a grim period of history, told with
rare skill' *Aberdeen Press and Journal*

'Sketched vividly and sympathetically . . . rewarding'
*Scotsman*

'Among the foremost of current historical novelists'
*Birmingham Mail*

'An accomplished novelist' *Glasgow Evening News*

'There can be no doubt of the author's gift for storytelling'
*Illustrated London News*

'Jean Plaidy has once again brought characters and
background vividly to life' *Everywoman*

'Well up to standard . . . fascinating'
*Manchester Evening News*

'Exciting and intelligent' *Truth Magazine*

'No frills and plenty of excitement' *Yorkshire Post*

'Meticulous attention to historical detail' *South Wales Argus*

'Colourful . . . imaginative and exciting'
*Northern Daily Telegraph*

'Effective and readable' *Sphere*

'A vivid picture of the crude and vigorous London of those
days' Laurence Meynell

# The Italian Woman

## JEAN PLAIDY

arrow books

Published by Arrow Books in 2006

5 7 9 10 8 6

Copyright © Jean Plaidy, 1952

Initial lettering copyright © Stephen Raw, 2005

The Estate of Eleanor Hibbert has asserted its right
to have Jean Plaidy identified as the author of this work.

This book is sold subject to the condition that it shall not, by way of trade or otherwise,
be lent, resold, hired out, or otherwise circulated without the publisher's prior consent
in any form of binding or cover other than that in which it is published and
without a similar condition including this condition being imposed
on the subsequent purchaser.

First published in the United Kingdom in 1952 by Robert Hale Ltd

Arrow Books
The Random House Group Limited
20 Vauxhall Bridge Road, London SW1V 2SA

Random House Australia (Pty) Limited
20 Alfred Street, Milsons Point, Sydney,
New South Wales 2061, Australia

Random House New Zealand Limited
18 Poland Road, Glenfield,
Auckland 10, New Zealand

Random House (Pty) Limited
Isle of Houghton, Corner of Boundary Road & Carse O'Gowrie,
Houghton 2198, South Africa

Random House Group Limited Reg. No. 954009
www.randomhouse.co.uk

A CIP catalogue record for this book is available from the British Library

ISBN 9780099493181

Typeset by SX Composing DTP, Rayleigh, Essex

The Random House Group Limited supports The Forest Stewardship
Council (FSC®), the leading international forest certification organisation.
Our books carrying the FSC label are printed on FSC® certified paper.
FSC is the only forest certification scheme endorsed by the leading
environmental organisations, including Greenpeace. Our
paper procurement policy can be found at
www.randomhouse.co.uk/environment

Printed and bound in Great Britain by Clays Ltd, St Ives PLC

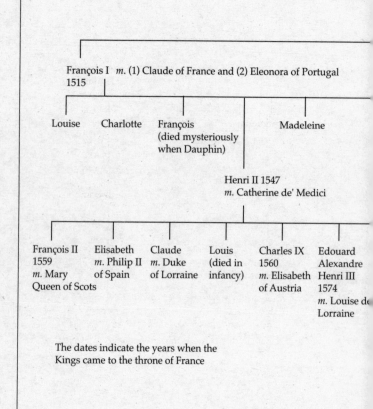

François I  *m.* (1) Claude of France and (2) Eleonora of Portugal
1515

| Louise | Charlotte | François (died mysteriously when Dauphin) | | Madeleine |

Henri II 1547
*m.* Catherine de' Medici

| François II 1559 *m.* Mary Queen of Scots | Elisabeth *m.* Philip II of Spain | Claude *m.* Duke of Lorraine | Louis (died in infancy) | Charles IX 1560 *m.* Elisabeth of Austria | Edouard Alexandre Henri III 1574 *m.* Louise de Lorraine |

The dates indicate the years when the
Kings came to the throne of France

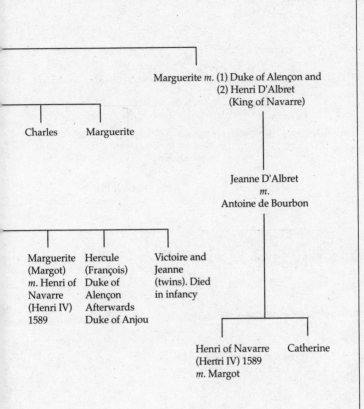

Marguerite *m.* (1) Duke of Alençon and
(2) Henri D'Albret
(King of Navarre)

Charles    Marguerite

Jeanne D'Albret
*m.*
Antoine de Bourbon

Marguerite    Hercule    Victoire and
(Margot)    (François)    Jeanne
*m.* Henri of    Duke of    (twins). Died
Navarre    Alençon    in infancy
(Henri IV)    Afterwards
1589    Duke of Anjou

Henri of Navarre    Catherine
(Henri IV) 1589
*m.* Margot

## ❧ CHAPTER I ❧

*I*n her apartments at the castle of Plessis-les-Tours a little girl knelt on a window seat and looked disconsolately out on the sunlit grounds. The sunshine out there, she felt, made the castle itself more gloomy by contrast. She hated the place.

'What am I,' she said aloud, 'but a prisoner?'

The lady who was stitching industriously at her embroidery, her back to the window and to the little girl, that the best of the light might fall on her work, clicked her tongue in answer. She had no wish to enter into a discussion of her wrongs with Jeanne, for although the child was only twelve years old, her tongue was so quick that even her tutor had learned not to enter lightly into wordy battles with her, since, with her logic and quick wits, Jeanne had a way of coming out of such encounters victorious. As for Madame de Silly, the Baillive of Caen and governess of Jeanne, she knew herself no match for the child when it came to an argument.

'I hear the wind howling through the trees in the forest sometimes at night,' went on Jeanne. 'Then I think that perhaps it is the souls of those who died in torment before they could make their peace with God. Do you think that is what we hear, Aymée?'

'Nonsense!' cried Aymée de Silly. 'You have just said it was the wind in the trees.'

'It is a prison, Aymée. Can you not feel it? Too much misery has been suffered in this place for me to be happy here. Think of those prisoners of my ancestor. Think of the iron cages in which he kept them . . . so small that they could not move; and there they remained for years. Think of the men who have been tortured in this dark and miserable place. Look out there at the lovely river. Men have been cruelly drowned in that river. When I go out at dusk, I seem to see the bodies of men hanging on the trees, as they did all those years ago.'

'You think too much,' said Aymée.

'How can one think too much?' demanded Jeanne scornfully. 'I am determined not to stay here. I shall run away and join my mother and father. Why should I be kept from them?'

'Because it is the will of the King of France. And what do you think would happen were you to run away? If – which, seems hardly likely – you were to have the good fortune to arrive at your father's court of Navarre, what do you think would happen? I can tell you. You would be sent back here.'

'That might not be,' said Jeanne. 'If my father, the King of Navarre, were there, he would hide me, since he at least wishes me to be with him. I know it.'

'But it is the will of your uncle that you should stay here. And have you forgotten that your uncle is the King of France?'

'That is something Uncle Francis never lets anyone forget.' Jeanne smiled, for in spite of her grievances against him, she loved her uncle. He was handsome and charming and always delightful to her; he was amused rather than angry when she pleaded to be allowed to join her parents, even though she knew it was his wish that she should remain where she was.

'When I see the little peasant children with their mothers, I envy them,' she said.

'You do nothing of the sort!' retorted Aymée. 'You only fancy you do. Imagine your feelings, my child, if you were told tomorrow that you were stripped of your rank! How would you like that?'

'Not at all. But all the same, I long to see my mother. Tell me of her, Aymée.'

'She is very beautiful; she is respected and loved by her husband, the King of Navarre . . .'

'And adored by her brother the King of France,' interrupted Jeanne. 'Do you remember that when I was very small, I used to make you repeat over and over again the story of how, when Uncle Francis was a prisoner in Spain, it was my mother who went to his prison in Madrid and nursed him back to health?'

'I remember clearly,' said Aymée, smiling.

'But,' went on Jeanne, 'do you think that a woman should love her brother more than she loves her husband and her own child?'

Aymée's face was pink suddenly; she pursed her lips as she frequently did when challenged with a question she was going to refuse to answer. 'Your mother is a great queen,' she said. 'She is the noblest woman in France . . .'

'I know, dear Aymée, but that was not the point we were discussing. Should a woman love her brother more than her husband and her child? That was what I said. And you dare not answer it. My mother could have had me with her, had she insisted. Uncle Francis would have given way had she pleaded, for he can deny her nothing. But she loves him, and because

3

she wishes to please him more than anything in the world, when he says: It is my wish that your daughter should be kept a prisoner at that most hateful, that most gloomy, that most miserable of all my castles . . .' my mother answers: "Thy will be done." She has no will but his. You yourself have said so.'

'It is very right and proper that all his subjects should obey the King, and even the Queen of Navarre is a subject of the King of France.'

Jeanne jumped down from the window-seat in exasperation. There were times when Aymée's method of skirting round a difficult subject infuriated her. Jeanne was vehement by nature; her temper rose quickly and subsided at the same speed. But how absurd it was to pretend things were not as one knew them to be!

'How I hate all insincerity!' she cried.

'And, Mademoiselle,' said her governess sternly, 'how I abhor such precocity! You know a good deal more than it is good for you to know.'

'How can that be when all knowledge is good to have? Aymée, you make me angry when you keep up this pretence. I am loved by my father and mother; my uncle has nothing but my good at heart. And yet, all these years when I have longed to be with my parents, I am kept from them. Now you will try to pretend, will you not, that my uncle, the King of France, and my father, the King of Navarre, are the greatest of friends. Let us have the truth. They hate each other. They are suspicious of each other; and it is because the King of France suspects my father of trying to arrange a match between me and Philip of Spain that he insists on my being kept here, so that he himself may be sure that I am not given to his enemy.' She laughed to see the dismay in the eyes of her governess. 'Oh, Aymée, it is

4

not your fault. You have done all you can to keep these facts from me. But you know how I *hate* pretence. And I will not have it here.'

Aymée shrugged her shoulders and went on with her embroidery. 'Jeanne,' she said, 'why not forget all this? You are young. You keep good state here. You have nothing with which to worry yourself. You are happy; and one day you will be able to join your parents.'

'Listen!' cried Jeanne. 'I hear the sound of a horn.'

Aymée rose and came to the window. Her heart was beating uncomfortably fast. It was a habit of King Francis when he was staying at Amboise to ride over to Plessis-les-Tours. Sometimes he came with just a few of his followers – a brief, informal call on his little niece. At such times Aymée was terrified, for Jeanne never seemed to remember that this magnificent and charming man, besides being her uncle, was also the King of France. She could be pert, disrespectful, and at times resentful. If the King were in a good mood he might be amused; but if he were not, who could know what might happen?

'Is the court at Amboise?' asked Jeanne.

'That I do not know.'

They stood for some seconds looking beyond the grass slopes to the trees of the forest; and then, as a group of riders emerged and came straight towards the castle, Jeanne turned to her governess. 'The King's court *is* at Amboise; and here comes the King to visit me.'

Aymée laid a trembling hand on her charge's shoulder.

'Have a care . . .'

Jeanne retorted: 'If you mean, tell him that I am happy here and pleased with my state, that I like to be kept from my

5

parents, then rest assured I shall *not* have a care. I shall tell no lies.'

⚜ ⚜ ⚜

In the magnificent hall, the King greeted his niece. This hall brought back memories to Francis; here he, as Duke of Valois, had been betrothed to Claude, the Princess of France; he had not been sure then that he would ever sit on the throne of France. His sister Marguerite, dearest of all women as far as he was concerned, had encouraged him in those days. What would his life have been without Marguerite? He thought of that always when he looked at Marguerite's daughter; and that meant that he must be fond of the child. He could not help but be fond of her for her own sake, since, with those blunt manners, that directness of speech, she was not without charm; and one grew weary of sycophancy. He wished, though, that Jeanne had inherited a little more of her mother's beauty. He wished that he did not see in her a resemblance to that sly old villain, her father, the King of Navarre.

She knelt before him and kissed his hand; and his lips twitched. He was remembering the tale Marguerite had told him of how this child had, in a fit of temper, once cut off the heads of the saints in her mother's tapestry and substituted for them the heads of foxes. That was a crime which had amused both Francis and his sister.

'Rise, child,' he said. 'You are looking well. The air of Plessis agrees with you.'

He watched the flush rise in her cheeks. He enjoyed teasing her.

'Indeed, Sire, it does not agree with me!'

He was aware of Madame de Silly, trembling in the

background, waiting in trepidation for what the child would say next.

'You surprise me, niece. I was about to congratulate Madame de Silly on your healthy appearance.'

'The air of Navarre – my native air – would suit me better, Sire.'

'When you hear the good news I have brought you, you will cease to fret for the air of Navarre. I have ridden over from Amboise with the sole purpose of imparting this news to you. What would you say if I told you I had a husband for you?'

Jeanne caught her breath in horror. 'A husband . . . for me, Sire?'

'I see that you are enchanted. That is well. You are growing up, my darling, and it is time we thought about a match for you. How does it appeal to you – the married state?'

'Not greatly, Sire. Unless, of course, it were with some great King.'

He frowned, and Aymée trembled. It would seem that Jeanne was daring to refer to the match her father wished for her – an alliance with the man who would one day be King of Spain.

'You prize yourself highly,' said Francis coldly.

'Unless there were great honour in a marriage I should not care for it,' said Jeanne. 'Many husbands give honour to women not their wives, so it is necessary for a wife to make a marriage which brings her honour, since she may not receive it from her husband afterwards.'

The King was always pleased with those who amused him; and the precocity of the child reminded him of his sister. His momentary displeasure disappeared, and he laughed aloud.

'My dearest niece, I have no fear that you will be unable to keep Monsieur le Duc de Clèves under control.'

'The Duc de Clèves!' she cried. 'What . . . do you mean, Sire?'

'That he is to be your husband.'

Jeanne forgot the homage she owed to the King, and her mouth hardened. 'You would give me in marriage to a duke of some small kingdom?'

'Oh come, child, the Duke of Clèves is not so insignificant as you appear to think. I can see that here in Plessis you do not learn things concerning the outside world. Now, on your knees and thank me for having your welfare so near my heart that I have arranged a match for you.'

'I fear, Sire,' she said haughtily, 'that I cannot thank you for arranging such an alliance for me.'

Madame de Silly stepped forward; the noblemen who had accompanied the King waited in dismay for him to express his anger. But it did not come; instead, he turned to them smiling.

'Leave me alone with my niece,' he said. 'I think it necessary for us two to have a talk together.'

They, with Aymée and Jeanne's attendants, bowed and retired.

Jeanne – terrified, though nothing would have made her admit that this was the case, and humiliated by her uncle's suggestion – tossed her head to convey that whatever the consequences of her boldness, she did not care.

When they were alone, the King said: 'Sit at my feet. That is right. Lean your head against me.'

He caressed her hair and, as she smelt the faint perfume of musk and Russia leather which clung to his clothes, she thought she would hate those scents as long as she lived.

'It grieves me, Jeanne,' he said, 'that I should be the cause of unhappiness to you. As you know, your mother is dearer to me than any living person; and because you are her daughter, I love you also. But, my child, it is not for us of royal blood to question the alliances which are made for us. As you are a sensible girl, you must know that. You are right to have your decided views and to show no fear in expressing them. I would not have it otherwise. But you know also that it is your duty to obey your King. You have nothing to fear. The Duke will be enchanted with you, and he is not without good looks.'

'Sire, am I not too young for marriage?'

'Nay. You are twelve years of age . . . old enough for a princess to marry.'

'But could I not have some choice in the matter?'

'Dear child, that is a privilege which is denied us, and you must console yourself that one husband is very like another. If you start with passion, you lose it quickly. And, dear Jeanne, marriage need not be an obstacle to the pursuit of passion. Moreover, happiness is sometimes found outside marriage, if it is not granted within. You are wise beyond your years, and I can see that I may talk to you as I do to your mother.'

'But . . . the Duke of Clèves! You promised me your son Henry.'

'Ah yes; but Henry has a little Italian for his wife . . . and you would not have liked Henry.'

'I liked him well enough.'

'As a cousin. Not as a husband. He is gauche and scarcely speaks. He is unfaithful to his wife. Poor Catherine! She is pleasant enough, but he spends all his time with Diane de Poitiers. You would not like Henry as a husband, my dear.'

'It might be that if he had had a French princess for a wife instead of that Italian woman, he would have spent more time with her.'

'You have been listening to gossip. So it reaches Plessis, then? Nay! Henry pledged himself to Madame Diane years ago; and he is faithful – dull and faithful. Do not regret Henry. And now, because I respect your courage, I am going to tell you why this marriage must be. There is trouble all about us, my little Jeanne. My Constable has been pursuing a policy which is not to my taste. I am sad to think that he works for Henry the Dauphin more than for Francis the King. You see, like you, I have my sorrows. The Emperor Charles has given the Milanese to his son Philip, and I am angry because the Milanese should be mine. You are too young for these politics, but you must try to understand. It is necessary for me to show my displeasure to Spain, and I want you to help me to do this through your marriage with this man of Clèves, who, in his rebellion against the Emperor, has become my friend. You see, we must keep a balance of power about us, and it is with the marriages of the young members of our family that we can do this. So you will be reasonable; you will agree to this marriage, and you will know that, in doing so, you are serving your King.'

'Sire, I beg of you, do not use me in this way. You are mighty. You are all-powerful. You can subdue your enemies without my help.'

'Not *all*-powerful, alas! And my enemies are legion. The greatest of these is the Emperor, with whom I must be continually on the alert. Then there is the sly old hypocrite of England. I am unsafe, child. That is why you, my loyal subject, must do all in your power to help me. Come, little Jeanne, a marriage is not all that important. Why, I have had two of them, and have managed to find much in life to please me. Both of my marriages were marriages of state – as yours must be. Did I complain? Not I. I respected my duty, and my destiny. First I married poor little Claude, who enabled me to do my duty to my country by bearing me many children. Then she died and, for reasons of state, I took a second wife. She is a very good woman and she troubles me not. Believe me, it is possible to live pleasantly and be married at the same time.'

'But I would not care for that sort of life, Sire. I wish my marriage, if I have one, to be a good marriage. I wish to love and serve my husband and I wish him to be faithful to me.'

The King lifted her in his arms and laid his cheek against hers. 'And you are right to have such thoughts. Rest assured that I will do all in my power to help you. Now you must prepare to leave Plessis at once. I want you to travel to Alençon, where you will be with your mother. That will delight you, will it not?'

'Yes, Sire, but . . . I do not wish for this marriage.'

He smiled with charming regret.

⚜ ⚜ ⚜

There would be a halt at Paris on the way to Alençon. Usually Jeanne looked forward with zest to her visits to Paris. She would enjoy the long journey which some found so tedious, riding with the procession of attendants with the baggage stacked on the backs of the mules. The magnificence of her uncle's court never ceased to amaze her; she enjoyed seeing her cousins; she was enchanted by the balls and masques; and the ceremonies of court were such a contrast with the dull life of Plessis-les-Tours.

But this journey was different, since behind it was a sinister motive.

Even the excitement of arriving at Fontainebleau could not make her forget her fears. Fontainebleau, she had always thought, was one of the most beautiful places on Earth. Its gardens, with that delightful mixture of the wild and cultivated, were such as she had never seen elsewhere; here were great rooms and galleries filled with the treasures of Europe which her uncle had taken such delight in collecting. Not that Jeanne was greatly attracted by art; it was the extravagance of the court which she admired. Then it was pleasant to renew old acquaintances.

She was disturbed, though, by her cousin Charles, who played unpleasant tricks. She had to be careful each night when she got into her bed to see that some hideous creature like a dead bat or toad had not been put there to keep her company. She was scornful of Charles, which was foolish of her, for Charles would not tolerate a lack of appreciation of his practical jokes, and those he played on her grew more boisterous and more unkind. But she refused to laugh when she did not wish to laugh; she would rather take the consequences than pretend to be amused when she was not.

Her cousin Henry was kinder, though he had very little to say to her; he had very little to say to anyone but his mistress. He had become of greater importance since Jeanne had last seen him, for then he had been simply the Duke of Orléans and now he was the Dauphin of France. She wished it had been possible to discuss marriage with him, for he had been married when he was very little older than she was; but of course, that was impossible.

There was Catherine, of course – Catherine the Dauphiness. Jeanne could never discuss marriage with Catherine, for there was something about the Italian which repelled her, although she did not understand what it was. Yet Catherine was a wife, and a neglected wife. There was a good deal of whispering about her because she had already been married six years and had no children. It was said that the fault was Catherine's because the Dauphin had, during the campaign of Piedmont, given a daughter to a girl whom he had temporarily loved during his enforced absence from his mistress. Poor Catherine! Jeanne would have liked to be friends. It was true that she was only twelve years old and that Catherine was twenty; yet they must both be, at this time, rather bewildered and unhappy people. But, it was not possible to be friendly with Catherine. Jeanne watched her receive Diane, smile and chat with her; there was no sign on those cold, pale features that she suffered the slightest humiliation. I shall never be like that! thought Jeanne fiercely. I shall never be meek. If this Guillaume dares to treat me as Henry treats Catherine, I shall leave him, no matter if all Spain and all France and all England go to war on account of it.

But when she heard the gossip which went on about Catherine she thought she understood why her cousin Henry was not in love with his wife and preferred the company of his mistress.

One of her ladies talked to her of this matter as she helped her disrobe at night: 'I like not these Italians, my lady Princess. They are well versed in the arts of poison, and their poisons are so subtle that none can be sure whether the victim has died of them or a natural death. It is said that Madame la Dauphine wished to be Queen of France, and for that reason she arranged that her Italian follower should first become the cupbearer of the Dauphin Francis and then administer the fatal dose.'

'You must not say such things!' cried Jeanne. 'If you were

heard saying them and it were brought to the King's ears, you would be in trouble.'

'It is others that say them, my lady. Not I. I merely tell you what I hear. The Dauphin's cupbearer was an Italian; that is all I say.'

Jeanne shivered. She would never like her cousin Catherine. How ridiculous she had been to imagine that she could ever confide in her!

Once in the gardens at Fontainebleau she met Catherine walking alone.

'Good day to you, cousin,' said Catherine.

'Good day to you, cousin,' answered Jeanne.

'So you are soon to be a wife.'

Jeanne could not help it if her lips tightened and the colour flooded her face; she was never able to hide her feelings. This was particularly irritating when she found herself face to face with one such as Catherine, who would never betray by a lift of the eyebrows or a movement of her lips what was going on in her head.

'You do not seem to be happy about this marriage, cousin.'

'I do not wish for it,' replied the little girl.

'Why not?'

'I do not want to go to a strange land. I do not want to marry.' Jeanne, as Madame de Silly often told her, never stopped to think what she was saying, and she went on impetuously: 'You will understand. Marriage is sometimes distasteful. Wives are neglected for other women.'

There was silence all about them. Catherine's face was quite expressionless, but the prominent eyes were fixed on Jeanne, and although Jeanne did not want to meet them, she found herself unable to avoid doing so.

She went on quickly: 'Oh, Catherine, I could not bear to be treated as Henry treats you. Everyone talks of him and Madame de Poitiers. Henry's eyes follow her wherever she goes! You must be unhappy.'

'I, unhappy? You forget I am the Dauphine.'

'Yes, I know. But to be so humiliated! Madame d'Étampes rules the King, but the Queen is still the Queen. It is hard to believe that Henry could be so cruel. I am glad I did not marry him. They were going to marry me to Henry at one time. I thought it was certain to come about, and I used to think that I should not mind marrying Henry, because he is my cousin and we have always known each other. But I would not, were I his wife, permit him to treat me as he treats you. I would insist. I would . . .'

Catherine began to laugh.

'You are good indeed to be so concerned with my affairs. How strange! *I* was pitying *you*. I am married to the heir of France, and you – a Princess – are to be married to a poor little Duke. It is you, dear Princess, who are insulted. I shall be Queen of France, so why should I care if the King has a hundred mistresses while I am Queen? And you will be a Duchess . . . a Duchess of Clèves . . .'

Jeanne grew scarlet. She had never before realised how deeply humiliating – as well as distasteful – was this marriage.

Catherine turned and left her standing there more bewildered and unhappy than she had been since the King told her she was to have a husband.

Jeanne was in disgrace, and the King was furious with her. She had met her future husband, who was twenty-four years old –

about double her age – and whom some might call handsome; but Jeanne had hated him as soon as she had heard his name, and she was unable to dispel that hatred. The King had implied that he was ashamed of her lack of graciousness; she in her turn was determined that she was not going to feign a delight she did not feel in such a marriage. As for the Duke of Clèves, he was bewildered by the behaviour of his ungracious little bride-to-be. The King's anger was largely due to the fact that he believed Jeanne's father to be secretly supporting her in her decision to do all she could to prevent the marriage; and this was something more than a little girl's repugnance for a suitor; it was deliberate rebellion of a subject against a King.

Francis wrote to his sister, and when Jeanne arrived in Alençon she was greeted by a stern mother; and this was yet another tragedy for Jeanne. She adored her mother; she had heard so many stories of her wit and beauty; it had been so long since they had met; and now, when at last she was allowed to see her, it was to find herself in disgrace.

Marguerite, gentle, living in a world of her own populated by the savants of her day – Ronsard, Marot, all the writers, painters and architects of the Renaissance era – was loth to tear herself away from the life of the mind to deal with the mundane business of a disobedient daughter. It never occurred to Marguerite to do anything but support her brother; she would do that, whatever he suggested, for his will immediately became hers.

There were long conversations during which Jeanne, sad and bewildered, yet retained her power to put her case clearly and pungently to her mother.

'The King must be obeyed,' explained Marguerite. 'Every command he gives it must be our joy to obey.'

'He can make mistakes,' countered Jeanne.

'Not our King, my child.'

'But he did. He made terrible mistakes. Have you forgotten what a mistake he made at Pavia?'

Queen Marguerite's beautiful eyes grew large with horror. 'Pavia! That was his misfortune. It was no fault of his. There never lived a braver soldier, a greater general.'

'But great generals are not defeated in war by lesser ones.'

'There are things of which you know nothing, and one of these is that a maiden should have no will of her own.'

'Then how is she to decide the difference between right and wrong?'

'Her parents and her King will guide her.'

'But suppose *both* her parents and her King do not agree?'

'You are being foolish. We are discussing your marriage with the Duke of Clèves. It is a good marriage.'

'How can that be? I, a Princess, who might have married my cousin Henry, who is a King's son, to marry with a Duke! The son of the King of Spain might have married me . . .'

'It is a good marriage because the King wishes it,' interrupted Marguerite curtly. 'And you, my daughter, must love and obey your uncle as I do.'

'But,' persisted Jeanne, 'this is not what I have been taught to accept as logic.'

Marguerite said sorrowfully: 'Jeanne, my dear child, do not rebel in this way. The King wishes your marriage; therefore it must be. If you do not agree, I shall have no alternative but to have you beaten every day until you do. Listen to me, my child. These beatings will be the severest you have ever received in your life. Your life itself might be endangered.'

'Is that so?' said Jeanne scornfully. 'I thought it was my marriage your brother wanted – not my funeral!'

Marguerite looked sadly at her daughter. She was proud of her wit and quick mind, but sorely distressed by her obstinacy.

She would not consent. She would not agree to this marriage. She would defy them all. She thought continually of the Duke of Clèves, and when she thought of him she remembered the smile of Catherine, the Dauphine. She knew she had spoken impetuously to the Italian, but Jeanne did not care for that. Catherine was quite insincere; she must be, to pretend that she did not care that her husband humiliated her, being so gracious to Madame de Poitiers that it was almost as though she were thanking her for being her husband's mistress. Jeanne had no patience with such insincerity; she called it slyness. She herself, in such circumstances, would have slapped Madame de Poitiers's face. And yet . . . she could not shut out of her mind the quiet sneer on Catherine's face which seemed to goad her, to make her more determined than ever to evade this marriage.

She decided to put on record her hatred of it, so that the world should know that, if she were forced to it, it would be against her will.

In her room she sat long composing the document, and when she had finished this is what she had written:

'I, Jeanne of Navarre, persisting in the protestations I have already made, do hereby again affirm and protest, by these present, that the marriage which it is desired to contract between the Duke of Clèves and myself is against my will; that I have never consented to it, nor will consent; and that all I may say and do hereafter, by which it may be attempted to prove that I have given my consent, will be forcibly extorted against my wish and desire, from my dread of the King, of the King my father, and of the Queen my mother, who has threatened to have me whipped by the Baillive of Caen, my governess. By command of the Queen, my mother, my said governess has several times declared that if I do not all in regard to this marriage which the King wishes, and if I do not give my consent, I shall be punished so severely as to occasion my death; and that by refusing I may be the cause of the ruin and destruction of my father, my mother and of their house; the which threat has inspired me with such fear and dread, even to be the cause of the ruin of my said father and mother, that I know not to whom to have recourse, excepting to God, seeing that my father and mother abandon me, who both well know what I have said to them – that never can I love the Duke of Clèves, and that I will not have him. Therefore, I protest beforehand, if it happens that I am affianced, or married to the said Duke of Clèves in any manner, it will be against my heart and in defiance of my will; and that he shall never become my husband, nor will I ever regard or hold him as such, and that my marriage shall be reputed null and void; in testimony of which I appeal to God and yourselves as witnesses of this my declaration that you are about to sign with me; admonishing each of you to remember the compulsion, violence, and constraint employed against me, upon the matter of this said marriage.'

When Jeanne had finished this document, she called to her room four of her attendants, and such was her eloquence and such was their pity for the little girl whose body was bruised with the violence of the whippings she had received, and such their admiration for her courage, that these four were bold enough to incur whatever punishment might go with the signing of such a document.

And then, having their signatures, Jeanne, fresh from the day's beating, seized an opportunity to take the document to the Cathedral, and there she demanded that the prelates read it; and she told them that she relied upon them to do what was right in the matter.

But alas, right for them was the will of their King, and so preparations went on for the marriage of Jeanne d'Albret with the Duke of Clèves.

✤ ✤ ✤

The King was annoyed by what he was pleased to call this ridiculously childish behaviour. For once Francis had failed to see the joke. His niece was a foolish, arrogant and obstinate little girl.

They had not beaten her recently because they did not wish to carry out their threat of killing her. Her gown was ready. It was made of cloth of gold and was so heavily embroidered with jewels that she could not lift it. She hated its jewels and its long ermine train.

How she envied everyone on her wedding morning! There were no exceptions. The women weeding in the gardens were happier than this sad little Princess; she envied the scullions, the meanest serving-maids; she envied neglected Catherine; she even envied Dauphin Francis lying in his grave.

Weighed down with the heaviness of her dress, pale-faced, sullen-eyed and broken-hearted, she walked in her wedding procession. She saw the great Constable, Anne de Montmorency, and she felt drawn towards him because she had heard whisperings that he was in disgrace; so her tragedy was, in a measure, his. He was blamed for the mismanagement of affairs with Spain, and after all it was due to that mismanagement that she herself was here, the bride-to-be of the Duke of Clèves. But Montmorency did not look her way; he was morosely occupied with his own disgrace.

King Francis, magnificent in white satin decorated with rubies and emeralds which made a perfect foil to his dark, sardonic face, was ready now to lead her to the altar. There was no kindness in his face to-day as he looked down on the little bride. He had been greatly annoyed by the document she had taken to the Cathedral. Had he not been concerned in it, he might have been amused by her originality, impressed by the courage which had enabled her to do such a bold action. But he was weary of her protests.

She felt his fingers on her arm; they pinched a little. But something within herself would not let her give up hope. There were still a few minutes left to her. She must look for a way out of this marriage. She would not yet accept defeat. She looked desperately about her, then she said faintly: 'I am unwell. I am going to faint. I cannot walk. The dress is too heavy.'

The King watched her through narrowed eyes. Then he gave Montmorency a curt sign.

'Carry the Princess to the altar,' he said.

For a moment Jeanne could put aside her own troubles for those of Montmorency, for at such a surprising order the Constable of France turned pale, and it seemed that he was about to answer to the King's curt command with an equally curt refusal. She knew that the biggest insult the King could have offered to France's greatest soldier was a command to carry a little girl to the altar. She wished fervently that she need not be the cause of his humiliation. But it was too late to do anything about it now, and after that brief hesitation, Montmorency lifted her in his mighty arms and marched forward with her. He would have been instantly despatched to prison had he not obeyed the King. He had had to accept disgrace as she must accept this marriage with a man she did not know, with a man she was determined to hate.

Jeanne was married . . . married to a strange man with an unpleasant guttural accent. He sat beside her during the feasting; he danced with her in the great hall. He tried to be kind, but Jeanne could not bring herself to smile for him. Her face was pale, her eyes like pits of glittering jet, her mouth set in a line of endurance. The King spoke kindly to her, and when she answered him coldly he did not reprove her; she even fancied that she now saw a gleam of compassion in his eyes.

The musicians were playing the gayest of tunes; there was a banquet, a ball and another banquet; but what Jeanne feared more than anything else was the night which would bring with it the solemn ritual of putting her to bed with her husband.

The King knew of her fears, and when he led her in the dance he tried to soothe her. As she had now obeyed him, all his anger against her was forgotten; she was his dear little niece once more.

He pressed her hand warmly in the dance. 'Smile, darling. It is befitting that the bride should smile. Monsieur de Clèves is not without his points. He can't be a worse husband than the Dauphin, and you might have had him. Smile, my little Jeanne. You have done your duty. Now is the time for pleasure.'

But she would not smile; and she was very ungracious to her uncle; yet he did not reprove her.

She did not know how she lived through the blatant horror of the ceremony of being put to bed. Her women tried to comfort her as they undressed her; her governess kissed her and Jeanne wondered whether she would be whipped if she refused to be put to bed with her husband, and who would do it. Would he?

Even now she was looking round for escape, and a hundred mad ideas came into her head. Could she get out of the palace? Could she cut off her hair and disguise herself as a wandering minstrel or a beggar girl? How she envied all wandering minstrels and beggar girls; they might be hungry, but none was the wife of the Duke of Clèves.

How foolish to think that escape was possible! There was no escape. She could hear the musicians playing softly. One of her women whispered that the King was waiting in the nuptial chamber to see her bedded.

They led her into the room, and when she saw her husband with his gentlemen she refused to look his way. And then, in sudden desperation she stared at King Francis, her lips trembling, her eyes pleading, and he with charming compassion and understanding came to her and, lifting her in his arms, kissed her tenderly.

'Why,' he said, 'your bridegroom is a lucky man, Jeanne. Faith of a gentleman! I would to God I stood in his place.'

And as he lowered her she fancied she saw a conspiratorial gleam in the darkness of his eyes. It was King Francis who led her to the bed. She lay in it beside her husband while her ladies and the Duke's gentlemen drew the costly coverlet over them.

Then the King spoke.

'Nobles and ladies, that is enough. The marriage has been sufficiently consummated, for we consider that the bride is too young for consummation to be carried further. She and her husband have been put to bed. Let that be remembered. This is a marriage as binding as any, but there need be nothing more until the bride is of an age suited to a more complete consummation. Ladies, conduct the Princess back to her apartments. And you, my lord Duke, go back to yours. Long live the Duke and Duchess of Clèves!'

With that impulsiveness of hers, Jeanne leaped out of the bed and kneeling, kissed the jewelled hand. Nor would she release it when restraining hands were laid upon her. She forgot that he was the King of France; he was her deliverer, the noble knight who had saved her from what she dreaded most.

The elegant, perfumed fingers caressed her hair. He called her his pet and his darling, so that it seemed that the uncle was the bridegroom, not the bewildered Fleming. But then how typical of Francis was this scene in the nuptial chamber. The King of France must be the hero of all occasions. He must even put the bridegroom in the shade; he must be the one to receive the loving devotion of the bride.

The year Jeanne was fifteen was the happiest she had known as yet, for two events, which she afterwards came to look upon as the most important of her life, happened during that year.

Since her marriage she had been living with her parents, sometimes at the court of Nérac, sometimes at Pau; and there had been one or two journeys to the greater court of King Francis. Jeanne had at last enjoyed the companionship with her mother for which she had always craved, and the three years had been spent mainly in study under the great sages, Farel and Roussel. Jeanne was quick and clever, although her lack of artistic taste exasperated her mother; she had not followed Marguerite's leanings towards the Reformed Faith and had remained a Catholic, as was her father. She adored her mother, but she was inclined to be a little impatient with her at times, for it seemed to Jeanne that Marguerite was too literary, too ready to see many sides to a question; her prevaricating nature was out of harmony with Jeanne's forthright one, and while idealising her mother, Jeanne found herself more in sympathy with the rougher ways of her father. Henry of Navarre had not the grace and charm which Marguerite had learned in her brother's court when she had reigned with him as Queen in all but name. Henry was coarse in manner and as forthright as Jeanne herself, so it was small wonder that his daughter had an honest respect for him.

As long as Jeanne lived she would never forget the occasion when he had come into her mother's apartment and found them at prayers. Roussel and Farel had been present, but they had been able to make their escape. Henry of Navarre's veins had stood out on his forehead, for he was very angry to find his daughter being initiated into the ways of the Protestants. He slapped Queen Marguerite on the cheek, an act which was later going to bring a sharp reproof from the King of France, and then he turned to Jeanne. He did not have to worry about the results of chastising *her*. He called for a rod and, while it was being brought to him, he told her that she was about to receive the severest whipping of her life, and that its object was to teach her never again to worry her addled head about the doctrines of religion. She would, in future, worship as he had worshipped and as his father had before him.

And there and then he threw her across a stool and belaboured her, while she lay, her lips tightly pressed together, forbearing to cry out, for she knew that if she did he would only lay on the more, since he detested what he called snivelling girls. But when he had tired himself he warned her that if ever he found her at such tricks again, though she were a woman by that time, she would be beaten to the point of death.

She bowed her head and said: 'I will remember, Father.'

After that her mother never tried to interest her in the Reformed Faith, though she herself went on with her studies.

Life during those years had been pleasant for Jeanne – so pleasant that she almost forgot that she was married to the Duke of Clèves; she had longed to live with her parents in her native Béarn, and for three years this joy had been hers.

And so she came to that wonderful year.

It was also a wonderful year for Catherine the Dauphine, for one bleak evening during its wet and gusty February, her first child was christened.

What a celebration there was at court, and how delighted was the King of France with the grandchild who was to bear his name! Prayers were said daily for little Prince Francis. His mother carried talismans for his safety in her garments; she had been consulting with all the most famous sorcerers and astrologers in the land. It was imperative for Catherine de' Medici that this child should live and that she bear more children. Jeanne heard the rumours about her which implied that she had come near to being divorced on account of her inability to bear children.

But Jeanne, the fifteen-year-old Princess of Navarre, was as happy as anyone on that day of the christening. She was in

Paris, and she loved Paris. Who at fifteen, if one were young at heart and loved gaiety and enjoyed masques and balls and festivities, could help loving Paris? She did, it was true, live in hourly dread of calamity. The war which engaged her husband's attention could not last for ever, and when it was over he would hurry to her side; then there would be no putting off that consummation from which her kind uncle had snatched her even as she had felt the warmth of her husband's body close to hers in the nuptial bed. She was no longer a child. She was fifteen, and others had been forced to face the marriage bed at that age. Catherine was one; Henry another. And now . . . they had their first son.

But she need not think of the return of Guillaume de la Marck, the Duke of Clèves, just yet. The war, she had heard, was not going happily for France; and that meant not happily for her husband, for was he not now the ally of France and the Emperor's enemy? Was that not why she had been forced to marry him?

He was involved in his wars, and here in beloved Fontainebleau was all the glory, pomp and splendour of a royal christening, and the christening of one who might well, when his day came, sit upon the throne of France.

Fontainebleau was beautiful even in February. The trees were wrapped in a soft blue mist; the air was cold and damp, but Jeanne was happy. Her women whispered as they dressed her for the ceremony. The candles guttered and her face looked almost beautiful in the great gilt-edged mirror, for the candle-light, soft and flattering as a lover, had smoothed out the hard line of her jaw, made more delicate the contours of her face, making her look slightly older than her years – lovely and mysterious.

Afterwards she told herself that she knew something wonderful was going to happen on that night.

Her dress was rich, even among the richness of other dresses, for as a royal Princess she was to lead the ladies, in company with the other Princesses who happened to be at court at that time. Jeanne was the youngest of the Princesses, and she wore her hair flowing about her shoulders.

She listened vaguely to the whispering of the women.

'Ha! Saved in time. *Mon Dieu!* We should have seen the back of Madame Catherine but for this little Prince, believe me.'

'God bless the Prince. I am glad he is here, but would it not have been a happy thing to have sent the Italian packing?'

'Hush! They say she hears through the very walls. Do you want to go into a decline? Do you want to drink a cup of water and say good-bye to life?'

'Hush! The Princess listens . . .'

'Let the Princess listen. She should be on guard. All should be on guard against the Italian woman.'

On guard! thought Jeanne. There was only one thing she feared – that her husband might come home from the war.

She could not stop thinking of that dire event even when she was passing along the route from the palace to the Church of the Mathurins, where three hundred torches lighted the way, bringing daylight to the night.

The scene at the church was such as Jeanne had never before beheld, accustomed though she was to the opulence of her uncle's court and its ceremonious occasions. The Crown tapestries and the ornaments dazzled her. The Cardinal of Bourbon stood on a round dais beautifully covered with cloth of silver, as he waited for the cortège to approach that he might baptise the little Prince.

Standing beside the Queen of France and Madame Marguerite the King's daughter, Jeanne looked about her with wondering eyes. She saw her father with young Charles, who was now the Duke of Orléans. Then came the wonderful moment when a pair of eyes belonging to one of the Princes met hers and held them. The young man smiled, and it seemed to Jeanne that never had she seen such a charming smile as that of Antoine de Bourbon, Duke of Vendôme. She was surprised that, although she had often seen him about the court, she had not realised before that he was the handsomest man in France.

The Bourbon Prince was standing next to Henry of Navarre, but Jeanne ignored the presence of her father. She did not care if his eyes were on her. It only mattered that Antoine de Bourbon was looking her way and that he seemed far more interested in the Princess of Navarre than the newly born Prince of France.

Jeanne heard no more of that ceremony; she saw no more. The walk back to the palace along the torch-lighted route passed like a dream; and as soon as the procession had reached the *salle du bal*, where a magnificent banquet had been prepared, she was looking for Antoine de Bourbon.

She knew of his importance at court, and that he was the elder of the Bourbon princes – as royal as the Valois family and next to them in the line of succession. Antoine and the younger of his two brothers, the Prince of Condé, were regarded as the two most handsome men at court; they were extremely popular with women, and it was said that they made the most of their popularity. But Jeanne did not believe the tales she had heard about Antoine; they were the sort of tales which would be attached to any man as beautiful as that Prince.

It was sad that, during the banquet, she could not be near

Antoine; it was sad that she could not do justice to the delicacies which were on the table; but later, when the banquet was over and the ball had begun, she found Antoine de Bourbon at her side.

'I noticed you in the church,' said Jeanne, subterfuge being completely alien to her. Jeanne said what was in her mind and expected others to do the same.

Antoine, handsome, profligate, ever on the look-out for fresh conquests, could not help but be impressed by the fresh charm of the young girl and by the amusing directness of her manner, which was in such vivid contrast to the coquetry to which he was accustomed.

'I am flattered. I am honoured. Tell me, did you find me of more interest than the most honoured and exalted baby?'

'Yes,' said Jeanne. 'Though I like babies.'

'I hope that you will learn to like me better.' He kissed her hand, and his bold eyes told her that he appreciated her neat little body in its elaborate gown.

They danced together. His conversation was racy and, although from others Jeanne might have disapproved of such talk, she was finding that everything about Antoine was above criticism.

In her downright way she said to him: 'The birth of this child will make a good deal of difference to you.'

He agreed that this was so. 'And it will make a great difference to Madame la Dauphine,' he added. He laughed slyly, for he enjoyed the gossip of the court, and he was going to enjoy still more startling this young girl, for, Princess though she was, the niece of the King himself, she was a country girl, brought up far from Paris, and there was about her the wide-eyed innocence and sincerity of manner which was rarely found at court. He thought her unusual and quite enchanting.

She was waiting eagerly for him to go on and, although Antoine was accustomed to the flattery of women, he had rarely found any so sweet as that which came from this child.

'How would you like to be in Madame Catherine's place, little Princess? Her husband has no feeling for her. His mistress has to force him to his wife's bed. How would you like to be in Catherine's place? Tell me that!'

Jeanne's eyes flashed. 'I would not endure it.'

'You have spirit. But, bless you, were you Catherine, you would have no alternative but to endure it.'

'*I* should beg to be released from such a marriage.'

'What! Leave the court of France, the company of kings and princes, for the misery of Florence and the company of merchants?'

'I doubt that Catherine suffered misery in Florence. Her family is rich – richer, some say, than the royal house of France. And I for one would rather forgo this splendour than suffer the humiliation which goes with it.'

'Don't waste pity on the Italian. Look at her. Does she need it, do you think?'

Jeanne studied the Dauphine. She seemed completely happy, but if Antoine was not aware of the cold glitter of her eyes, Jeanne was. Nobody at court understood what was going on behind the eyes of the Italian woman, and because they did not understand they were inclined to think there was nothing there to be understood.

'She has had good fortune,' Antoine continued. 'She has saved herself in time. There was talk of a divorce, you know. The King saved her from that.'

'The King is kind,' said Jeanne. 'He was kind to me when I needed kindness.'

Antoine came nearer. 'Any man would be kind to you, dear Princess. I would I had the opportunities of the King.'

It was court flattery; it was coquetry and flirtation. Jeanne was only fifteen, but she was fully aware of that. Yet, how sweet it was, and how magic were the words which came from the lips of Antoine de Bourbon, though she would be the first to admit that had they come from another she would have considered them insincere. To touch his hand in the dance was a sheer delight; to meet his eyes over a goblet of wine was enchantment; and later how hurtful it was to see him dancing with others, throwing his soft glances at them, and doubtless paying the compliments which a short while ago had enchanted Jeanne of Navarre.

This was the first event of importance which occurred during that year. Jeanne had fallen in love with Antoine de Bourbon even though she was married to the Duke of Clèves, whom her good fortune and a bad French policy kept at the wars.

As, during the eventful year, Jeanne followed the course of the war, never had this enforced marriage of hers seemed so distasteful to her. Thoughts of Guillaume de la Marck filled her with horror; she had magnified his shortcomings, and in her mind he was a monster, a menace to any happiness that she might have had.

When she was back at the court of her father, it was easy to dream. She would wander in the surrounding country, would lie in the castle grounds and dream of Antoine de Bourbon.

Being of a practical nature, she did not so much dream of Antoine the lover, caressing her, paying compliments which might be false, as of a happy marriage, a fruitful marriage, with Antoine and herself ruling Navarre together. She dreaded that summons which might come at any time and which she must obey – the summons which would order her to receive her husband and go with him to a strange land. It would be no use protesting; she had tried that before her marriage without success. Again and again she lived through the ceremony of being put to bed; she shuddered, trying to imagine what would have happened to her but for the intervention of her uncle. What great good luck that had been! But she must remember that Francis was only kind when he remembered to be or when being kind would bring no harm to him or his policies.

So during those months which followed the christening of little Francis Jeanne listened eagerly for any scrap of news of the wars which were being fought in Italy and the Netherlands. There was rejoicing when her husband defeated the Imperialists at Sittard, while the King and the Dauphin marched victoriously along the Sambre. Victory was on the way, and Jeanne was torn between loyalty to her uncle and her fears for herself, for she could not help knowing that as soon as the wars came to a victorious conclusion, her husband would demand her company. The Emperor Charles, furious at the turn of events, left Spain in the charge of his son Philip and went in full force to land at Genoa. His fury was directed chiefly against Jeanne's husband, the rebellious Duke of Clèves, for he looked on the Duke as his vassal, and a rebellious vassal must be immediately subdued and humiliated by a mighty Emperor. Jeanne heard of the appeals for help which her husband had sent to her uncle; but Francis,

33

notorious for hesitating when he should go forward and for over-boldness when discretion was needed, had now disbanded the greater part of his army and had no intention of making any military moves in a hurry.

Thus was sealed the fate of the Duke of Clèves, but his defeat meant the deliverance of Jeanne of Navarre from all she feared most. There was nothing for Guillaume of Clèves to do, when deserted by the King of France, but to throw himself at the feet of the Emperor and beg for mercy.

Francis sent for Jeanne and himself imparted the news to her. His eyes were smouldering as he told her, for it was typical of Francis's particular military weakness that, through his own negligence, having lost an ally who could have been valuable to him, he should choose to see the fault in what he called the perfidy of that ally.

'Jeanne, my child,' he said, 'I have bad news for you. We married you to a traitor.'

Jeanne felt her heart racing, her hands trembling; and she feared he would see the sparkle in her eyes.

'He has betrayed us, Jeanne. He has given himself up to our enemy. You could not love such a man. You could not want to be a partner in his miserable life.'

Jeanne was never one for diplomacy. She blurted out: 'I never wished to share his life. Had he been your friend, Sire, still I should not have wanted him.'

The King lifted his hand. 'That tongue of yours, my darling, will be the ruin of you one day. Curb it, I beg of you. My dear child, you have been sorely misused. You were married at a very early age to a traitor, for reasons of state which you very well understand, but I shall not allow you to remain married to such a man.'

Jeanne said with a lilt in her voice: 'No, Sire. I cannot remain married to such a man.'

Francis laid a hand on her shoulder. He said: 'I must therefore regretfully ask the Pope for an annulment.'

She seized his hand and kissed it; she knelt at his feet and kissed them. She thought the smell of Russia leather, which always seemed to cling to his clothes and which came from the trunks in which his linen was stored, the sweetest perfume in the world. She would never, she was sure, be able to smell it in future without emotion.

'Alas! Alas! This perfidious Duke has thrown away his dominions and his wife. I have lost one whom I thought was my friend; and you, my child, have lost a husband.'

He smiled down at her. 'Why, Jeanne, you shock me. You do not look so displeased as a wife should.'

'Oh, Sire, I have prayed for this.'

'What! Prayed that the King's friends might desert him!'

'No . . . not that. But I never liked him, Sire.'

The King kissed her. 'Ah, child, I rejoice. I would rather see the Emperor victorious than your happiness impaired.'

It was quite untrue, of course, but Francis had a charming way of uttering pleasant nonsense, and because he believed it himself – while he said it – he succeeded in making others believe it too.

So, in that eventful year during which Jeanne fell in love with Antoine de Bourbon, the kindly fates decided that her marriage with the Duke of Clèves – which had been no true marriage – should, by the wish of the King of France and the good offices of the Pope of Rome, be dissolved.

After her divorce, Jeanne went back to her comparatively quiet life at Plessis-les-Tours with Madame de Silly. She thought continually of Antoine de Bourbon; she listened avidly to all the news she could glean of his exploits in battle, which were considerable. He had become a hero to her and she idealised him as once she had idealised her mother.

She was growing up, yet there had been no talk of a new marriage for her. She saw less and less of King Francis, for his health had been failing for some time, and one February day, when she was nineteen years old, the news came that he had died at his castle of Rambouillet. Jeanne guessed that the death of her uncle must seriously affect her future, and she was right.

Her father, Henry of Navarre, sent for her to return to her home, for, on the death of Francis, she returned to the control of her parents. Her mother had changed. Since her brother's death she had lost all desire to live, and she spent much of her time in a convent, where she declared she was awaiting that happy day when she might join her brother; she longed, she said, to follow him to Heaven as she had followed him to Madrid.

There was a new King in Paris – Jeanne's cousin, whom she might have married – King Henry the Second; there was a new Queen, the Italian, Catherine de' Medici. It was not long before Cousin Henry sent an order to the court of Nérac, commanding that Jeanne should come to his court.

On her arrival, Jeanne was quick to notice how different was Henry's court from that of his father. Henry was more sober than King Francis had been; he was completely lacking in that gay charm. He had time for one woman only – Diane de Poitiers, whom he had now created Duchesse de Valentinois.

Jeanne knew that she had been summoned for a purpose,

and Henry, in his direct manner – not unlike Jeanne's own – lost little time in telling her so.

She knelt in ceremonial homage and kissed his hand. There were no caresses from her cousin as there had been from her uncle; there were no charming endearments. But Henry was kind, and he remembered his cousin with that mild affection which had not changed since he had become the King.

'Cousin,' said Henry, 'you are of an age to marry, and it is concerning this matter that I desired your presence here at court.'

Jeanne waited apprehensively; she had been driven to one distasteful marriage; now she wondered how she could hold off another. She had a feeling that, for all his quietness, Henry could be as obstinate as his father.

She said: 'I have been married, Sire, and my experience makes me feel that I should like to exercise a little caution. Having once married for state reasons, if I were to marry a second time I should like to have a little choice in the matter.'

There was no humour in Henry; he looked at her suspiciously.

'There are two gentlemen of the court who have expressed desire for an alliance with you. They are both of the highest rank, and I feel that either should find favour with you. One is Francis, Duke of Guise, and the other is Antoine de Bourbon, the Duke of Vendôme.'

'Antoine de Bourbon!' cried Jeanne, forgetting all formality for the moment. 'I . . . I remember him well. It was at the christening of the little Dauphin that I first became aware of him.'

'I would favour Monsieur de Guise,' said Henry. 'My cousin, he is a great Prince and soldier.'

'But . . . the Duke of Vendôme is also a great Prince and a great soldier, Sire.'

Henry did not like arguments. His mistress, Diane, had suggested the Duke of Guise, her kinsman through her daughter's marriage to his brother; if Jeanne of Navarre married Francis of Guise, a vital link with the House of Valois would be made to the advantage of the House of Guise and Lorraine. Jeanne felt a momentary horror, for she knew that if Henry's mistress wanted this alliance, then Henry would want it too; and being a sober young woman of twenty and not an impetuous girl of twelve, she no longer believed it possible to move the hearts of kings.

She begged leave to consider the matter, and asked the royal permission to retire.

Francis of Guise, the greatest soldier in France and the country's most ambitious man! There were few women who would not have been excited at the prospect of marriage with such a man. Beside him, many would say that Antoine, with his fastidious clothes and his elegance, was effeminate. The very manner in which he lifted his plumed hat when greeting a lady was the talk of the court. Henry would feel that Jeanne was a fool to prefer the gallant when she might have had an alliance with the strongest man in France. Declaring himself to be the most tolerant of monarchs, Henry gave her a few weeks to ponder the matter before coming to a decision, while he made it perfectly clear that the decision should be made in favour of the Duke of Guise. That, Jeanne knew, was the wish of his beloved Diane, for Diane was the enemy of the Bourbons, suspecting them of leanings towards the Reformed Faith; and every petty matter in France seemed to revolve round the religious controversy. Guise was a good Catholic; he was also

Diane's friend and relation through marriage. The King would certainly be willing to offer up his cousin in marriage to anyone whom his mistress chose.

Those weeks that followed were full of excitement and apprehension. Francis of Guise was sure of his success with the Princess of Navarre; he had not yet learned what joy Jeanne found in Antoine's company. Antoine declared to Jeanne that if the King threatened to give her to the Duke of Guise, he, Antoine, and she, Jeanne, would elope; and although Jeanne did not believe that he would be so bold, she loved him the more for making the suggestion.

Gradually Jeanne became aware of the Queen – the quiet Queen, so dignified, so calm, never showing by a look or a word that she felt herself slighted, charming always to her husband's mistress, grateful that Diane now and then spared her her husband that she might provide the heirs of France. And this woman, Jeanne realised, watched her closely. Often Jeanne would discover that the expressionless eyes were upon her, and she found it difficult to believe, as did the rest of the court, that the Queen was that mild and rather despicable creature who could smile when she was most slighted and accept with apparent unconcern the position of the most neglected and humiliated queen the French had ever known.

One day Catherine asked Jeanne to visit her, and when Jeanne went to her apartments she found the Queen was alone, having dismissed all her attendants.

Catherine dispensed with ceremony and bade her sit down. Jeanne obeyed, finding that she was unable to take her eyes from that cold, snake-like stare of the Queen.

'If you do not have a care,' said Catherine, 'they will marry you to Francis of Guise. I remember your marriage to Guillaume de la Marck, the Duke of Clèves. I remember the document you drew up. In those days you had courage, Cousin.'

'It did little to help me, Madame. I was married all the same, and it was the fortune of war which saved me from that marriage, not my own ingenuity.'

'Do you believe in miracles?' The mouth smiled slyly. 'Oh, I do not mean the miracles performed by our Lord Jesus, our Lady and the saints. I mean the miracles made by people like yourself.'

'I have never heard of such miracles, Madame.'

'They can be brought about. A miracle could save you from a marriage that you did not want. And if you were saved from this marriage you might have the man of your choice.'

'I do not understand.'

'Why does Francis of Guise want to marry you? Because he is ambitious. He wants to link himself with the King's cousin. He wants to creep nearer to the throne.'

'You are right, I know, but . . .'

'You could point this out to the King. You could say that in uniting Navarre with Lorraine he is making more powerful a man who, he would know but for the wiles of Madame de Poitiers, could be his greatest enemy. Remind him of his father's last words to him: "Beware of the House of Guise. The House of Guise and Lorraine is the enemy of the House of Valois." You could ask him if he has forgotten that.'

'You are right, Madame. But the King must already know this.'

'You would do yourself good to remind him of something which he may have been willed to forget. I have your welfare at heart. I should like to see you married to the man of your choice. Why do you smile, Cousin?'

Jeanne said frankly: 'I was thinking, Madame, how your desire coincides with my own. I do not want Francis of Guise for my husband. *You* do not wish it because Madame de Poitiers desires it.'

Catherine said coldly: 'I was not thinking of Madame de Poitiers. I was thinking of you.'

'I am grateful to you, Madame. I would like to say that, were I in your place, I should do the same as you do. I would do anything – anything to humiliate her.'

Catherine seemed to remember suddenly that she was the Queen of France and that Jeanne was her subject. She extended her hand.

'You may go now,' she said.

Jeanne realised too late that she had deeply offended the Queen. She had been tactless and extremely foolish; but how difficult it was to keep up such pretence in face of the obvious. She had only meant to convey that she understood and applauded Catherine's desire to score over Diane.

✤ ✤ ✤

Jeanne made good use of Catherine's advice.

When next she was summoned to the King's presence she was determined to point out to him what, according to Catherine, he had been willed to forget.

'What a princely man is the Duke of Guise!' said Henry. 'There is no other like him in the whole of France. Ah! You should be proud to wed such a man.'

Jeanne lifted her head haughtily.

'What, Monseigneur?' she said. 'Would you indeed permit

41

that the Duchess d'Aumale, who now feels herself honoured in performing the office of my train-bearer, should become my sister-in-law?'

She saw the angry colour rising in the King's face, for Madame d'Aumale was none other than the daughter of his beloved Diane.

But Jeanne, in her righteous indignation, swept on: 'Would you consider it meet, Monseigneur, that this Duchess, the daughter of Madame de Valentinois, should, through this marriage which you advocate, acquire the right to walk by my side instead of bearing my train?'

Henry was completely taken off his guard, and when this happened he was always at a loss for words. He did not often have to face a direct attack upon his mistress.

Jeanne seized her opportunity. 'Oh, Sire, Francis of Guise wants me for a wife – not my person so much as my royalty, my crown. Why, when his niece Mary of Scotland marries the Dauphin, and when he, through me, is King of Navarre, it would seem that there will be more than one King in France.'

Henry stared at his cousin incredulously. In his imagination he saw the dashing soldier; he heard the cries of the Parisians: 'A Guise. A Guise.' Francis of Guise was already the hero of Paris. Henry had some respect for the intelligence of his cousin. He himself was not intellectual, but that did not mean he could not admire those who were. He remembered that Jeanne's mother had been one of the most brilliant women of her day.

Jeanne went on: 'Have you forgotten the words of your father, those words he spoke on his deathbed? "Beware of the House of Guise . . ." Oh, Sire, your most gracious father understood the ambitions of this family.'

Henry was thinking that there was a good deal of truth in what she said, and although Diane wished for this marriage he would have to remind her of his father's warning and the danger of putting too much power in the way of the Guises.

He dismissed Jeanne without anger; and very shortly afterwards he announced that he favoured the marriage of his cousin Jeanne d'Albret of Navarre with Antoine de Bourbon, the Duke of Vendôme.

He had found a way out. Francis of Guise should have a bride who would please him as much as Jeanne would have done. He himself would publicly sign the marriage contract between Francis and Anna d'Este, the daughter of the Duke of Ferrara and granddaughter of Louis XII. That was a good marriage, a royal marriage; but not nearly such a dangerous marriage as a union with Navarre.

So Francis of Guise agreed with as good a grace as he could; and Diane, on this occasion, bowed to the will of her lover; consequently, Jeanne of Navarre was betrothed to the man of her choice.

❖ ❖ ❖

The happiest woman in France was being married. There had never been any, said her women, whom they had heard laugh so much. Jeanne explained: 'You see, I am a Princess and I am to marry for love!'

It was five years since the christening of little Francis, when Jeanne had fallen in love with Antoine, but what were five years of waiting now?

When her women awakened her on those mornings preceding her wedding, they marvelled at her happiness; she would sing and chatter and talk continually of her lover.

When, she demanded again and again, had a royal Princess had the good fortune to be allowed to marry for love? She was fortunate above all princesses. She liked now to think of that other marriage of hers – which was no marriage at all; she liked to recapture those awful moments when she had lain in the nuptial bed with Guillaume of Clèves. Oh, what horror! And what a miraculous escape! No wonder she thought of herself as the most fortunate Princess in the world.

Her mother laughed to see her so happy, but she was nevertheless displeased by the marriage. She had had higher hopes for her daughter. She might have been more actively against it had she not been so listless, feeling herself shut away from the world. Jeanne's father was also against the marriage, but the King of France had bribed the King of Navarre with an addition to his pension and the promise of an expedition to regain Upper Navarre, which the Spaniards had taken years before.

Jeanne marvelled that the consent of her father, that stern Catholic, who had beaten her for praying with her mother, could have been won over for his daughter's marriage to a Protestant Bourbon; but she had always known that his most cherished dream was the capture of Upper Navarre, that he might win it back to his sovereignty.

What great good luck was hers, then, and what did she care for the storms which might blow up through such a marriage! Let her mother be displeased with the match. Let her father be bribed. It mattered not. Antoine was to be her husband, and Antoine had declared that he loved her as he had never loved before.

Antoine, apart from one or two misgivings, was happy about his marriage. The Bourbon family had been out of favour for a long time; when King Francis had shown a fondness for the Count d'Enghien, who had died so tragically during a snow fight at La Roche-Guyon, it had seemed that the Bourbon family were about to see a rise in their fortunes; but with the death of the Count, favour had not been extended to the family, and the Guises were in high favour through Diane.

And now, Prince Antoine, head of the House of Bourbon, was to marry the cousin of King Henry. Antoine was pleased for that reason; moreover, being ardent and a deeply sensuous man, he could not help but be enchanted by his young bride. Not that she was so very young now, being past her twentieth year, but she was by no means old. There was another pleasant aspect of this marriage: it seemed almost certain that Henry of Navarre would leave no male heir, and that meant that Jeanne would, on his death, become the Queen of that province. Jeanne was not beautiful as the court of Paris understood beauty. She was indeed a little severe of countenance, but that spontaneous sincerity of hers was unusual, and Antoine loved novelty; and when her face was animated in conversation she was quite attractive. She was clever, and she was no weakling. Antoine, being weak himself, was attracted by strength.

He was therefore by no means displeased with the marriage that brought the Houses of Valois and Bourbon closer together. There was just a possibility that he and Jeanne might breed Kings of France. Young Francis – now the Dauphin – was a sickly little fellow. Catherine had another son, Louis, but it did not seem as if he were going to be long for this world. It would appear that King Henry and Queen Catherine were not going to have healthy children. Perhaps they suffered from the sins of the grandfathers, for both the paternal grandfather, Francis the First, and the maternal one, Lorenzo the usurping Duke of Urbino, had died of that disease which was called in France *La Maladie Anglaise* and in England The French Disease. Henry and Catherine appeared to be healthy enough; but it certainly seemed as though their children would not inherit that health; and if they did not . . . well, when the House of Valois could not succeed it would be for the legitimate Bourbons to take over the crown. The Guises might make a bid for it; but the people of France would surely never allow that. The Bourbons – next to the Valois – were the rightful heirs to the throne of France, and the cousin-german of the reigning Valois would be in direct line to the throne. Yes, it was indeed a good marriage.

His little Jeanne adored him; and he adored her. It was a fact that he had ceased to be interested in other women for many weeks.

But when he remembered that other marriage of Jeanne's to the Duke of Clèves, Antoine was disturbed. The marriage had not been fully consummated, it was true, but the pair had been bedded; and that, King Francis had said at the time, was sufficient to make the marriage valid.

King Henry had been against the marriage of Antoine and Jeanne at first and then, suddenly, he had changed his mind. Why? Madame Diane was bound to the Guises by the marriage of her daughter and their common faith. What if this were a diabolical plot to marry him to Jeanne of Navarre and, when their sons were born, to declare them illegitimate?

Antoine paced up and down his apartments. He loved his little Jeanne; he adored his little Jeanne; but not enough to jeopardise the future of his house.

So, on the day before that fixed for the wedding, Antoine begged an audience of the King, and when it was granted he expressed his fears that, as Jeanne had once been married to the Duke of Clèves, her marriage to himself could not take place.

✤ ✤ ✤

Jeanne never knew how near she came to losing her bridegroom.

By the time the ceremony was due to take place, however, the King and his ministers had succeeded in lulling Antoine's fears; and since this was so, Antoine was able to give himself up to love. This he did – being well practised in that art – much to Jeanne's delight and contentment.

'Let this happiness last,' she prayed; but she never really doubted that it would. She was completely happy; she could not stop reminding herself that she had been rescued from the husband she hated and given the man she loved. After such a miracle, she could not doubt that life would go on being wonderful.

Her father took her aside after the wedding. He smelt of garlic and there was wine spilt on his garments. His manners seemed rougher than they had before she had become so well acquainted with Bourbon elegance. Still, he was her father, and Jeanne had more of him in her than she had of her mother. He was a brave soldier, this King of Navarre; and if his ways were rough compared with those of the court of Paris, still, she understood him; and although she remembered the beatings she had received at his hands, she could not but honour her father.

He said: 'I want a grandson, girl. Nor do I expect to wait long for him. You've got a courtier for a husband – a dainty, pretty man, I doubt not. See that he gives you his children and does not squander them on other women, for by all accounts he's a man who can't do without a woman, although he has done very well without a wife until this day.'

Jeanne's eyes flashed and her stubborn chin shot up. 'He has led the life of a court gallant – that I know. But now he is a husband, Father; he is *my* husband. He has begun a new life with me.'

That made her father let out a guffaw and hiccup into his goblet.

'Don't ask for fidelity, girl. Ask for sons. *Ventre de biche!* Don't make me wait too long for a grandson, or, woman that you are and Bourbon that you may be, I'll take the rod to you.'

She smiled at him fondly. She honoured him for his bravery and, if he were crude and coarse, and his light love-affairs with women were numerous, he was but a man and her mother had never loved him deeply. It was not, she must remember, given to all men and women to love as she and Antoine did – for ever, most faithfully, ideally. Perhaps there had never been a perfect marriage before theirs.

Antoine agreed with her. 'I never dreamed,' he said, 'that the day would come when such happiness would be mine. Ah, sweet Jeanne, my dearest wife, how I wish I had led a life as pure as yours!'

Jeanne kissed him tenderly. 'The past is done with, Antoine. And the future is ours.'

Antoine went on lyrically: 'All women seem to have grown ugly in my eyes. Why is that, little Jeanne? There is no one else who has a trace of beauty. You have it all. Yes, all the beauty in the world is in that sweet face and form. I would barter all my fortune for one of your kisses.'

Jeanne believed him. As for Antoine, he had forgotten that a very short while ago he had had to be persuaded to continue with this marriage.

✦ ✦ ✦

Jeanne was a happy wife of two years' standing. The love between herself and her husband had grown deeper, for Antoine could not be insensible to her sincerity, to her steadfast belief that they would live in happiness for the rest of their lives.

During those two years Antoine had often been away from home; there had been occasions when it had been possible to accompany him to camp, but when it was not she would wait patiently for his return, and each time he came back there was a renewal of their ecstatic days together.

There had been sorrows. Jeanne's mother, having no wish to live after the death of King Francis, had died within a year.

The second sorrow followed quickly on the first.

In the September after her marriage, Jeanne, to her great delight as well as that of her husband, gave birth to a son. She wished to accompany Antoine to camp, and, remembering the devotion of her old governess, Aymée de Silly, the Baillive of Caen, she had put her son into this lady's care. Madame de Silly was a conscientious woman, determined to be worthy of the honour done to her, and she forthwith set about doing her best for the child. But she had grown feeble during the last years and her joints were so stiff that she found the least cold breeze increased her pains; she therefore had all windows sealed, and her walls hung with thick Arras, while fires burned in all the rooms of her house night and day. Heat, she declared, was necessary to good health, and what was good for her was good for the baby Prince of Navarre. He was accordingly kept in this bad atmosphere, never allowed out into the fresh air, and tightly swaddled in garments which were never removed. Under this treatment the little Prince grew frail and began to waste away, until at length his condition became so precarious that Jeanne was informed; and when she came to see her son, she was so shocked by what she found that she bitterly reproached her old governess and took the child away from her. Alas, it was too late. The little Prince died when he was just over a year old.

This was heartbreaking, but already she was pregnant again, and this time Jeanne vowed that she would look after the child herself. To her great delight, the new baby was a healthy boy and, under her care – so very different from that of the Baillive of Caen – he began to thrive.

And so, on this happy day, with the country temporarily at peace, she, Antoine, the child and their attendants travelled down to her father's castle, where they intended to spend Christmas.

Antoine was happy too. His thoughts circled about his wife, for he had never known any woman like her. She was, in her directness and that almost naïve frankness, enchanting; and she was, moreover, still wholeheartedly in love with him. Antoine was vain of his own personal charms; he was almost as fascinating to women as was his brother, the Prince of Condé, and of this fact he was keenly aware. Their high rank, their good looks, and the romantic lives they had led in the days before their marriages meant that they were subject to constant temptation. Antoine had written to Jeanne when he was away from her: 'I never dreamed that I could receive the courtship of ladies as I do now. I know not if it be the sweet winds that blow from Béarn which are the cause of this, or if it be that my eyesight has changed so much that it can no longer be deceived as it was before.'

The vanity of the little man! thought Jeanne fondly. So . . . he still received the courtship of ladies! Ah well, his profligate past was over.

So Jeanne continued to be delighted with her marriage; she was growing fond of her husband's family – in particular, her sister-in-law, Princess Eléonore, the wife of the Prince of Condé. And through Eléonore she came to be on familiar terms with Eléonore's relatives, the Colignys – Gaspard, Odet and Andelot. Jeanne and Eléonore had much in common; they were both in love with their husbands, and their husbands were brothers. Eléonore, it seemed to Jeanne, was a saint; Jeanne knew herself to be no saint, for she had not changed so very much from that little girl who had cut the saints' heads from their bodies in her mother's tapestry and substituted the heads of foxes; she was vehement and quick-tempered.

She was fired during those early years of her marriage by the religious devotion of her new friends. Her happiest days – when she could not enjoy the society of her husband – were spent at the Palais de Condé. Here came men and women of the new faith; some of them were refugees; there were rich and poor; some brought letters and others verbal messages too important to be trusted to paper. She met there Eléonore's uncles, Gaspard, Odet and Andelot; there was no one – except Antoine – whom Jeanne admired more than Uncle Gaspard de Coligny. He was a great man, a good man, a man who would die for what he believed to be right. Jeanne often felt that she would like to become closer to them, one of their community. But she realised that could not be as long as her father lived.

She remembered the beating he had given her when she had joined with her mother in her prayers. She was not afraid of beatings; in any case, her father could not beat her now; but it was laid down that a woman should honour her father, so how could Jeanne go against his wishes in this matter of religion? No! She would not forget her duty to her parent; she would confine herself to discussion, to discovering all she could of the new faith; but she would not accept it . . . yet.

Jeanne's father greeted them with pleasure. He was enchanted by his grandson, but he did not forget to reproach his daughter for the death of her firstborn. However, he was inclined to forgive her as she now had such a bonny boy to replace him.

He had arranged for a great hunting party to entertain his son-in-law and daughter, and he talked of little else. Of Antoine he was suspicious, noting the weakness of his handsome face, the dandyism of his clothes.

'Béarn is not Paris,' he reminded him grimly, 'but we Béarnais like things the way they are here.'

And Jeanne was amused to see how her father was just a little coarser in his manners than usual, determined to make no concessions to the finicky Bourbon.

She was very happy to ride out to the hunt, her husband beside her, her father riding ahead.

After the hunt, when they returned to the castle, the first thing Jeanne heard was the crying of the little Prince, her son. She sent for his nurse and asked her what ailed him.

The nurse, trembling a little, said: 'He is a little peevish, Madame. Nothing more.'

But all through the night the baby cried.

In the state bedroom at Fontainebleau, Catherine de' Medici lay thinking of Jeanne, and wondering why it should be that her thoughts kept returning again and again to the woman. As soon as she had seen Jeanne d'Albret at court, she had felt a strong repulsion for her; it was a strange feeling, an occult sense, which told her to beware. Why so? Jeanne was a fool, far too outspoken, possessing no diplomatic sense at all. Yet how strong she had been when they had tried to marry her to the Duke of Clèves. That declaration in the Cathedral showed power, while it showed a lamentable lack of restraint. Jeanne had hated the marriage they had planned for her, and well she might. The niece of King Francis, the cousin of King Henry, to be fobbed off with a foreign Duke-ling! Catherine could smile, well pleased in that respect with her own marriage, in which she could have been very happy if Henry had only made a pretence of loving her as Antoine de Bourbon loved his wife.

But what a foolish creature Jeanne was, not to realise that her happiness with her husband was fleeting. Was she blind? Did she not see the inherent weakness of her Antoine? At the moment he was faithful. At the moment! Catherine laughed that loud laugh which she often allowed herself when she was alone. How long did foolish Jeanne expect Bourbon Antoine to remain faithful? It was a miracle that he had remained so for so long. And when Jeanne's husband began to be unfaithful, the girl would be unable to hide her sorrow, for she had not been brought up in the hard school of a Medici. How would Jeanne d'Albret have acted had she been forced to witness her husband's infidelity with his mistress for nearly twenty years? Would she have smiled and bided her time?

No! She would have raged and stormed. Surely there was nothing to fear from such a woman. Yet Catherine frowned as once more she called to mind Jeanne's face, which, unformed as it was, showed as much strength as one ever saw in the face of a woman. She, Catherine de' Medici, would watch Jeanne d'Albret; every action should be noted; she would come to understand why it was that she felt this fear of her.

It might be because once Jeanne had been intended for Henry. How would Henry have liked his cousin Jeanne? Would she have been able to lure him from the everlasting charms of Diane de Poitiers? Was that it? Did that explain her feeling? Was it a strange, twisted jealousy of one who might have been more successful with Henry than she was?

She would have her latest child brought to her; her face softened with love at the thought of him. Her Henry, her darling, to whom, now that the contemplation of weaning her husband from Diane brought such despair, she was giving more and more of her attention.

What had she to fear from Jeanne d'Albret when she had three sons to prevent the crown of France being taken by a son of Jeanne's? Perhaps that son of Jeanne's was at the root of her fear.

Now she could no longer bear to be without her child. She wanted to hold him in her arms, to marvel at his beauty, to marvel at herself, that she, hardened each year with a thousand humiliations, grown cynical with much frustration, could love like this.

She called her woman, Madalenna.

'Bring my baby. Bring my little Henry to me.'

'Yes, Madame.' Madalenna hesitated. The girl had news; and it was news which she knew would interest her mistress.

'Speak,' said Catherine. 'What is it?'

'Yes, Madame. From Béarn.'

'From Béarn?' Catherine raised herself; her eyes were gleaming. News of Jeanne d'Albret. No wonder the woman had been so much in her thoughts. 'Come, Madalenna,' she cried impatiently. 'What news?'

'Sad news, Madame. Terrible news. The little Prince is dead.'

Catherine successfully hid her smile of triumph, for although this woman knew her perhaps as well as any did, she must not be allowed to know too much.

'Dead!' Catherine let out a croak that might have been a laugh or a sob. 'She cannot raise children, that woman. Two children . . . and both dead.'

'This Madame, was a terrible accident. It was his nurse's fault. She was talking to a courtier through one of the windows and, in fun, she threw the child down to him. It happened, Madame, that the courtier did not catch the child.'

'Ah!' said Catherine. 'So Madame d'Albret's servants are allowed to play ball with her son. No wonder she cannot keep her children.'

'Madame, the child's ribs were crushed, and the nurse, fearing her mistress's displeasure, tried to soothe his cries and said nothing of what had happened until the poor little Prince died; and when he was unswaddled . . .'

Catherine cried in sudden alarm: 'Go and bring my little Henry to me. Quickly. Lose no time.'

Madalenna ran off and very shortly returned with the child, which she laid in his mother's arms. Catherine held him against her breast – her love, her darling, her son Henry who would compensate her for all she had suffered from Henry her husband.

Now, with the child safe against her breast, she gave herself up to laughter at the disaster to the woman whom she continued to think of as her enemy.

✤ ✤ ✤

Jeanne was pregnant once more.

She had prayed each night and morning that she might bear a child which she would have the good fortune to rear. She was leading a quiet and regular life, visited by her husband's relations. Antoine came home from his camp whenever possible. He was as much in love with her as ever. Others marvelled at his constancy, but Jeanne considered it natural. They had their differences, their outbursts of jealousy, but these, Jeanne pointed out, showed only how deeply they cared for one another. The accident to their child – that terrible accident when the poor infant had lain for hours with the agony of broken bones tormenting him – might have ruined all Jeanne's happiness for a time if Antoine had not been with her to comfort her.

'Let me bear your grief,' he had said. 'I beg of you, do not torment yourself by remembering it.' And then he had added philosophically: 'For one that God takes away he can give a dozen.'

Her father had been furious; she had thought that he would do some injury to her, and she was reminded of that other occasion when he had beaten her into unconsciousness. He was a violent-tempered man. Now he called her inhuman; he declared that it was unlikely she would ever raise an heir and he himself would have to marry again. He threatened to marry his favourite mistress, who, although she might not be of royal blood, had a son by him and knew how to rear the boy. He would have him legitimised. He would see that Jeanne did not inherit his throne, for she was unworthy; she was inhuman.

They quarrelled violently, and Jeanne was very disturbed by the thought of what it would mean to any children she might have, if her father disinherited her.

However, before they parted, Henry of Navarre forgot his fury sufficiently to make her promise that, if she were ever to become pregnant again, she would come to his castle of Pau and have her child there where he might watch over her and it.

This she promised and they parted, smouldering anger between them.

Now she was pregnant once more. Antoine was in camp, so she lost no time in setting out for her father's castle, and when she reached Pau he greeted her warmly.

He had had her mother's apartments prepared for her, and these were the most magnificent in the palace. Exquisite paintings hung on the walls, and the splendid hangings of crimson satin had been embroidered by Marguerite herself with scenes from her life.

Jeanne's father watched over her during the next weeks, but he would not allow her to rest too frequently. He did not believe in the idle luxury of the court of the King of France.

A few weeks before the child was due, he talked very seriously to Jeanne. If she did not give him a grandson, he assured her, he would leave all he possessed to his bastard son, whom he would lose no time in legitimising.

'That,' he said, 'I would not wish to do, but if you, my daughter, are incapable of rearing children, then shall I be forced to it.'

He showed her a golden chain which was long enough to be wound round her neck twenty-five times and to which was fastened a little gold box.

'Now listen, girl,' he said. 'In this box is my will, and in this will I have left everything to you. But, there is a condition: when I die, all I possess shall be yours, but in exchange I want something now. I want my grandson. I fear that you will not give me the grandson I want. Nay, don't dare interrupt me when I speak to you. I tell you I want no peevish girl or drivelling boy. Now, listen. This boy must not come into the world to the sound of a woman's groaning. His mother must be one who does not groan when she is giving birth to my grandson. His coming into the world must be heralded as the great event it is. Is he not *my* grandson? So let the first thing he hears be the sound of his mother's singing, and let the song you sing be one of our own . . . a Béarnais song or a song of Gascony. No precious, drivelling poetry of the French King's court. A song of our own land. Understand me, girl? Let me hear you sing a song as my grandson is born, and in exchange you shall have all that is mine. Yes, daughter, the minute I die, all mine shall be yours – in trust for my grandson. You'll do it?'

Jeanne laughed aloud. 'Yes, Father. I will. I will sing as my son comes into the world, and you will be there with that little gold box.'

'On the word of a Béarnais!' he said; and he solemnly kissed her on either cheek.

'I'll send my servant,' he went on, 'my trusted Cotin, to sleep in the ante-room. And he shall come to me, whatever the hour, and I'll be there to greet my grandson and to hear you keep your part of the bargain.'

Jeanne was as happy during those waiting weeks as it was possible to be when Antoine was not with her. She walked with her father, for he insisted on her taking a good deal of exercise; he would rouse her if he saw her resting. He lived in a perpetual fear that she would give him a child like the sons of the King of France – 'poor mewling brats' he called them. They would see what a grandson he should have – a grandson who should be born into the world like a good Béarnais.

And when, in the early morning of a bleak winter's day, Jeanne knew that her time was near, she bade Cotin be ready for a call from her. When her pains began she remembered the agony which she had suffered twice before, and she wondered how she would be able to sing while her body was racked with such pain.

But sing she must, for her father's inheritance depended on it.

'Cotin,' she called. 'Cotin . . . quickly . . . go and call my father. My child is about to be born.'

The sweat ran down her face, and her body was twisted in her pain; but now she could hear her father's step on the stairs, so she began to sing, and the song she sang was the local canticle of 'Our Lady at the end of the Bridge':

> Our Lady at the end of the bridge,
> Help me in this present hour.
> Pray to the God of Heaven that He
> Will deliver me speedily
> And grant me the gift of a son.
> All to the mountain tops
> Implore Him.
> Our Lady at the end of the bridge
> Help me in this present hour.

Henry stood watching in triumph; and again and again, as the pains beset her, Jeanne chanted her entreaty to the Lady at the end of the bridge. Henry was content. That was how his grandson should be born.

And at length . . . there was the child.

Henry pushed aside those about the bed; his hands were eager to take the child.

A boy! Henry's triumph was complete.

'A true Béarnais!' he cried. 'What other child was ever born to the sound of his mother's singing? Tell me that. What are you doing with my grandson? He is mine. He shall be named Henry and he shall live to greatness. Give him to me! Give him to me! Ah . . . wait awhile.' He took the gold chain and placed it about the neck of his exhausted daughter; he smiled at her almost tenderly as he put the gold box in her hands.

Now . . . to his grandson! He took the baby from the attendants and wrapped it in his long robes. He went with the boy to his own apartments crying: 'My grandson is born. Lo and behold, a sheep has brought forth a lion. Oh, blessed lion! My grandson! Greatness awaits thee, Henry of Navarre.'

When she had recovered from her exhaustion, Jeanne felt the chain about her neck and tried to open the little gold box. But the box was locked. Her father had not given her the key; there had been no mention of a key.

Now she saw that he did not mean her to know what documents were in the box until his death. She did not know what she and her son would inherit; she had to be content merely with the prospect of inheritance.

She was angry; her father had duped her; but as she lay there her anger passed. The action was so typical of her father. He had trapped her while carrying out his part of the bargain to the letter. She could do nothing but curb her impatience.

Meanwhile, Henry of Navarre was gloating over his grandson. He rubbed on the little lips a clove of garlic – the Gascon antidote for poison. Then he called to his attendants, who had followed him to his apartments: 'Bring me wine.'

And when it was brought, he poured it into his own cup of gold and fed the newly born child with it. The baby swallowed the wine; and his grandfather, turning to his attendants and courtiers, laughed aloud in his pleasure.

'Here is a true Béarnais!' he cried.

✤ ✤ ✤

Henry of Navarre's interest in his grandson did not end with his birth. He had made up his mind that the boy was not going to suffer through too much coddling, and the best way of assuring this was to put him in the care of a labourer's wife.

With great discrimination, Henry selected the woman for the job, assuring her that if the child did not continue to remain a healthy boy, terrible punishment awaited her; he told her that the boy was not to be pampered, and that he, the King, and the boy's mother, his daughter, would visit him in private. Little Henry was not swaddled; in fact, he was treated like the son of a labourer, except that he was always assured of as much to eat as he could manage. Poor Jeanne Fourcharde, although terrified of the great responsibility which was hers, accepted it with pride – for she dared do nothing else when the King of Navarre commanded – and at least it meant that there was plenty of food for her family while the baby Prince was with them. It was no secret that this important little boy was living with them in that cottage, for across the doorway were placed the arms of Navarre and the words 'Sauvegarde du Roy'.

And so little Henry prospered and became sturdy and strong, coarse and rough – a little boy after his grandfather's heart; but his grandfather did not long enjoy him, for, less than a year after his birth, the King of Navarre died while preparing for a campaign against Spanish Navarre; he was a victim of an epidemic which was raging in the countryside.

Jeanne was now Queen of Navarre, and she lost no time in making Antoine its King.

It was now that Jeanne began to have her first doubts of her husband – not of his fidelity to herself, but of his astuteness as a statesman. Hitherto he had been perfect in her eyes.

Now that Navarre was ruled by a woman, Henry, the King of France, decided that he did not care to have a petty kingdom so far from Paris and so near to the Spanish frontier, so he planned an exchange of territory. For this reason he summoned Antoine to Paris, and when he was there, Antoine all but agreed to the exchange; and it was only when it was discovered that such must be sanctioned by Jeanne, in accordance with her father's will, that Antoine thought of consulting his wife.

When Antoine hurried back to Jeanne to tell her of King Henry's proposal, she was horrified; and this was the cause of their first real quarrel, for Jeanne could not restrain her tongue, and she called him a fool to have been so nearly tricked.

It made a coolness between them which was particularly painful to Jeanne; Antoine could quickly recover from such upsets. It was now that Jeanne discovered in herself those powers which were to make of her a clever diplomat. She travelled to Saint-Germain, where she met the King, although Antoine had warned her that this was a daring thing to do; for what was simpler than for Henry to keep her a prisoner while the exchange was made? But Jeanne, knowing her subjects would never submit to the King of France, by her subtle diplomacy made Henry believe that she herself would agree to the exchange if her subjects would agree to it; but she did not fail to point out that if they did not, he would find it impossible to subdue her territory. Henry saw the wisdom of this and sent her back to test the loyalty of her people. She had been right; she knew she could rely on that loyalty. How proud she was as she rode into Pau and witnessed the demonstrations of her people, who vowed they would accept none other than Jeanne as their ruler.

That was comforting, but she was sad, for she could not help feeling that Antoine, by his light regard for the kingdom which she loved, had betrayed her in some way.

Later there came a summons from Paris to attend the wedding which was being arranged between the Dauphin and Mary Queen of Scots; and it was during this visit that Jeanne had yet another glimpse of the impetuous folly of the man she had married.

When they reached Paris and before they had paid their respects to the King, they were approached by an old friend of Antoine's whose servant had been imprisoned. This friend asked Antoine to help him in effecting the release of this servant, and Antoine, flattered to be asked and eager to show his authority, promised to do what was requested of him. As his brother, the Cardinal of Bourbon, was Governor of Paris at this time, Antoine had very little difficulty in pleasing his friend.

When King Henry heard what had happened, he was furious at what he considered to be officious interference; and when Jeanne and Antoine came to pay their respects, he greeted them coldly.

He turned to Antoine and said: 'How, Monseigneur! Have I

not told you before that there is and shall be only one King of France?'

Antoine bowed low. 'Sire, before your Gracious Majesty my sun is in eclipse, and in this kingdom I am but your subject and your servant.'

'Why then do you presume to open my prisons without my authority?'

Antoine burst into floods of explanations, while the King's face darkened with fury. But at that moment, most unceremoniously, but as it turned out most propitiously, there ran into the chamber a small boy – little Henry of Navarre, the son of Jeanne and Antoine. He stared about him, his eyes bright, his cheeks rosy; and then without hesitation he ran straight to the King and embraced his knees. He did not know whose knees he was embracing; he only knew that this man had made an instant appeal to him.

King Henry could never resist children, just as they could never resist him. He hesitated for a moment – but only for a moment – and then he looked down into the bright little upturned face which was raised to his in genuine admiration and complete confidence.

'Who are you?' asked the King.

'Henry of Navarre,' answered the boy promptly. 'Who are you?'

'Henry of France.' The King lifted the boy in his arms and smiled, while the arms of Henry of Navarre were clasped about the neck of Henry of France.

'Why,' said the King, 'I think you would like to be my son.'

'That I would!' replied the boy. 'But I have a father, and that is he.'

The King was amused. He kissed the rosy cheek. He said:

'Methinks then that there will be no alternative but to make you my son-in-law.'

'That will be good,' said little Henry.

And after such a scene with the boy the King found it difficult to be angry with the father. The matter was dismissed. 'But,' said the King warningly to Antoine, 'you will do well to remember in future the rank you hold in France.'

Watching this scene, Jeanne's pride in her son was spoiled by her apprehension on her husband's account. It was a strange revelation to know that she must go on loving a man even when her respect for him had so sadly diminished.

How alien little Henry looked among the children of the royal household! He certainly looked more healthy than they, with his glowing cheeks and cottage manners. He himself was quite unconscious of any inferiority; and when Margot, who was a year older than he was, laughed at him, she soon found herself sprawling on the floor.

'He is but a child,' Jeanne explained, for Margot made the most of her injuries and carried the tale to her governess. 'And he has, as yet, learned little of court manners.'

Catherine heard of the incident and laughed somewhat coarsely. 'An old Béarnais custom perhaps, to knock down the ladies?' she asked; and Jeanne found herself gripped by that fury which Catherine seemed to be able to arouse in her more than any other could and which was out of all proportion to the incident.

But Henry learned quickly; he was soon imitating the manners of Catherine's sons and daughters and those of the little Guise Princes, who spent much time with the children of the royal household.

Jeanne felt that she could never be sure of these people who inhabited the court of France; they were not straightforward; they bowed and smiled and paid charming compliments while they hated. The royal children filled her with apprehension.

Poor Francis, the bridegroom-to-be, was so sickly and so passionately in love. He was continually telling young Mary how much he loved her, taking her into corners that he might whisper to her of his devotion. His love was his life, and he taxed his strength by trying to excel in all manly pastimes; he would ride until he was exhausted just to show the little Queen of Scots that he was every bit a man. His mother watched him, but showed no concern for his failing health; it seemed to Jeanne that Catherine regarded it with complacency. Surely a strange maternal attitude!

Then there was Mary herself, all charm and coquetry, the loveliest girl Jeanne had ever seen; though, thought Jeanne a little primly, she would have been more attractive if less aware of her own fascinating ways. Calmly this girl accepted the homage offered her; she seemed to think of little but her own charm and beauty. She even tried to fascinate Jeanne's little Henry, and he – the bold little fellow – was quite willing to be fascinated. Would he, wondered Jeanne, be another such as his grandfather and his great-uncle, King Francis the First?

Then look at Charles. Little Charles was only eight years old, yet there was something about him which was quite alarming. Was it that wildness in his eyes, those sudden fits of laughter and depression? It was disturbing to see the longing glances he cast at Mary Queen of Scots, his envy of his brother. At times, however, he was a pleasant enough little boy, but Jeanne did not like the gleam in his eyes. There was a look almost of madness in them.

Henry, Catherine's favourite son, was a year younger than

Charles. He was yet another strange little boy. He was clever – there was no doubt of that. Beside him, Jeanne's Henry seemed more coarse and crude than ever; but Jeanne would not have wished to possess such a son. He minced; he preened himself like a girl; he decked himself out in fine clothes, wept when he could not have an ornament he fancied, talked continually of the cut of his coat; he ran to his mother for her comfort if anything disturbed him; he begged her to give him ornaments to deck his conceited little person. And Catherine's attitude to him was extraordinary. She was quite a different person when she was with this son. She petted him and fussed him; although he had been christened Edouard Alexandre, she had always called him Henry after his father, whom there was no doubt she loved. Jeanne would never understand Catherine. This child, alone of all her children, did not fear her; and yet she had seen even the brazen Margot cringe before her mother; she had seen fear in that little girl's face merely at a lift of her mother's eyebrow.

And Margot herself? If Margot were my daughter, thought Jeanne, I would not spare the rod. For there was something about Margot, Jeanne was sure, which should be very closely watched. Margot was five years old now, and she would have been a lovely child but for the heavy Valois nose which she had inherited from her grandfather. Margot was clever, vivacious and precocious – far too precocious. It was rare for a child so young to betray such sensuality. Margot at five was, in some ways, like an experienced woman, with those sly glances at the boys, those gestures. Jeanne was thankful that Margot and her Henry had fought one another. She would not have liked to have seen her son attracted by this wicked little Margot as he was by lovely coquettish Mary Queen of Scots. It seemed, watching these children, that Margot at five years old was already deeply involved in a love affair with the Duke of Guise's little boy – another Henry. They were continually creeping away together and returning flushed and excited.

Little Hercule was a pretty boy, though spoilt and utterly selfish. He was four years old – a few months younger than her own Henry.

Yes, there was something unpleasant about this family of children, for none of them seemed quite normal; and when Jeanne saw them with their mother she felt that the strangeness had its origin in her. She seemed to inspire them with awe and fascination, so that they wanted the approval of their mother more than anything, although they so greatly feared her displeasure. Jeanne realised that Queen Catherine was able to inspire strange feelings in those about her – feelings which were quite remote from affection.

Yet, when the children were with their father they seemed normal enough. The madness faded from Charles's eyes; Henry seemed less foppish; Margot would climb on to her father's knee and pull his beard as any little girl might. They were just happy children in the presence of their father.

The Dauphin's wedding was heralded by ceremonies and feasting. Antoine declared his pleasure in being with his wife after their long separations; this, he said, when they watched tournaments, when they danced and feasted, was like a second honeymoon. And Jeanne, looking about her at the discord which existed between most other married people, told herself that she was foolish to criticise the little faults of her husband; she went on to her knees and thanked God for granting her the dearest possession she would ever have – her husband's love.

She was sorry for Catherine, who must see her husband's

mistress take everything that should be hers. Indeed, everywhere one looked one saw the entwined initials D and H – Diane and Henry – not C and H, as custom and tradition demanded. What humiliation! And how patiently it was borne!

'If you were to treat me like that,' said Jeanne to Antoine, 'I would have that woman banished from the kingdom. I would not endure such miserable slights.'

'Ah, my sweet love,' said the faithful Antoine, 'but you are not Catherine de' Medici and I am not Henry of France. You are your sweet self, and for that I am thankful. Why, were I married to the Italian woman, I doubt not that I should cease to be a faithful husband.'

There were occasions when Jeanne fancied she saw Catherine's eyes upon her and that Catherine guessed how she was pitied; and when the prominent eyes met her own Jeanne could not, for some incomprehensible reason, suppress a shiver. There were times when she thought Catherine de' Medici possessed strange powers which enabled her to read the thoughts of others.

The day before that of the wedding a long gallery was erected between the Palace of the Bishop of Paris, where the company had spent the night, to the west door of the Cathedral of Notre Dame; and the porch of the Cathedral was hung with scarlet tapestries embroidered with the fleurs-de-lis. Antoine walked in the procession in a place of honour among the Princes of the blood royal whose task it was to escort the Dauphin to the Cathedral. The King himself followed with Mary Queen of Scots; and Jeanne came after with Catherine and the other attendant Princesses.

At the ceremony few had eyes for any but the bride. Lovely she always was, but to-day her beauty seemed greater than ever. She was robed in white and her crown was studded with pearls, diamonds, sapphires, emeralds – in fact, it seemed that every precious stone that existed was represented among those in her crown.

But Antoine, Jeanne noticed, hardly looked at the bride, and Jeanne believed that for Antoine at least there was only one woman who interested him – his wife. Then she felt as though her heart would burst with its burden of pride and happiness. It was fifteen years ago when, at the christening of this Dauphin, Jeanne had fallen in love with the man who was now her husband.

Jeanne knew suddenly that she wished above all things to embrace her husband's faith and the faith of his family; she wished to lead a good and serious life.

This was a solemn moment for Jeanne. She did not hear the Cardinal of Bourbon make Francis and Mary husband and wife; nor was she aware of the celebration of mass. Later at the wedding banquet she was absent-minded; and when the party left the episcopal palace for Les Tournelles she was still thoughtful.

Now came the climax of her content. The mummers had come into the great hall; and when their entertainment was over the royal children, with those of the family of Guise, rode on hobby horses with back-cloths of gold and silver, and they attached their horses to little coaches while they sang, in their sweet, piping voices, praise to the virtue and beauty of the married pair. Then came the joyful surprise. Into the ballroom were brought six galleons, rolled and tossed by means of ropes which were hidden from sight; and in each galleon sat a Prince, and each Prince sprang from his galleon to choose a lady to be his companion. The Dauphin, naturally enough, chose his bride; but to the delight of Jeanne and the astonishment of everyone, Antoine de Bourbon carried off none other than his own wife; and he was the only Prince, apart from the Dauphin, to do this.

This was a matter for comment, laughter and a little envy among the ladies of the court.

As for Jeanne, she sat in her galleon, with Antoine's arms about her, laughing, reminding him that at this cynical court of France such an action was the last expected of any man who had been a husband for more than a few days.

This was a precious moment which she would remember as long as she lived. She was completely happy; but afterwards she was wont to connect that ride in the galleon with the end of that happy and contented life.

It was just over a year later when, in the château of Nérac, Antoine de Bourbon was making preparations for yet another visit to the court of France. Jeanne was disturbed; she was always disturbed when Antoine left her. She was becoming more and more involved in the Reformed Faith and was deeply concerned at the horrors which were being committed by Catholics and Protestants all over the country. The Prince of Condé, Antoine's younger brother, and his wife Eléonore, with her relations, the Colignys, were looked upon as the leaders of the Reformed Party; they were powerful, but there were others more powerful than they. There were the Guises, the natural enemies and rivals of the Bourbons.

First there was Francis, the Duke of Guise — insolent, arrogant, brutal, the greatest soldier in France. If the nation in general feared this man, Paris adored him. He was attractive in person, and his successes in battle were admired by his friends and enemies alike. *Le Balafré* was the most discussed man in France.

Then there was his brother Charles, the Cardinal of Lorraine, who would, Jeanne had said, 'like to set households by the ears all over France'. Duke Francis was often campaigning and therefore absent from court, and the other Guise brothers were insignificant when compared with the Cardinal of Lorraine. He was clever – the cleverest, the most sly member of his family; amorous in the extreme, he was the handsomest of the Guise brothers, and there was a certain nobility in his features, in spite of his lechery and excesses, which most women found irresistible. He was mean and acquisitive, surrounding himself with luxury and the good things of life, even more than did the English Cardinal Wolsey. He was vain and – extraordinary failing in a Guise – he was a coward.

It was these men of whom Jeanne thought when her husband was summoned to court.

Jeanne watched the preparations for the journey. Antoine was dilatory, one day abandoning plans which the day before he had made with great eagerness.

'Antoine, my darling,' she said, 'there are times when I believe you do not wish to make the journey to court.'

'But why should I, my love, when it means absenting myself from you?'

She could only laugh with pleasure at that, laugh with happiness; she could only suppress those fears which her husband's weak and vacillating nature aroused in her.

She was happier now than she had ever been, she often reminded herself. She had, in addition to her son Henry, an adorable daughter to whom, because the Queen herself had acted as godmother, had been given the name of Catherine. Thank God, thought Jeanne again and again, thank God for this domestic bliss.

There were great celebrations in progress at court. Elisabeth, daughter of the King and Queen, was being married by proxy to Philip of Spain. Jeanne's heart bled for Elisabeth, for it seemed to her that Catherine and Henry were marrying their child to a monster. But such was the fate of royal children. Here was yet another reminder of her great good fortune, for her father had tried to make a match for herself with the man who was about to be Elisabeth's husband. And following on the wedding of Elisabeth was that of Marguerite, the King's sister, to the Duke of Savoy.

'You should have been present at these ceremonies,' she had told Antoine.

'Nay!' he declared. 'There is nowhere I should be but in my own home with my wife and family.'

It was so easy to enjoy this domestic bliss, to forget what was happening in the outside world, forget that, being a branch of the royal tree, it was impossible to escape the reverberations of great happenings.

Antoine was still loitering with his preparations when, one day, messengers arrived at the castle. They had come from the court of France with great news.

'The King is dead!' they cried. 'Long live King Francis!'

It seemed incredible. Only a little while ago, at the wedding of Francis, the King had been in perfect health. It was at the tournament, the messengers explained; he had tilted with young Montgomery, a captain of the Scottish Guard, who had struck the King on the gorget; his lance had flown into splinters, one of which had become lodged in King Henry's eye.

'This was treason!' said Antoine.

'Nay, Monseigneur,' said the messenger. 'The King would not have it so. He had insisted on Montgomery's tilting with him in spite of the young man's reluctance; and he had declared that it was no fault of the young man's.'

The messengers had been given refreshments, and Jeanne and Antoine walked about the castle grounds talking of this dramatic event. Jeanne, with a clear-sightedness which she was rapidly acquiring, saw that it was of the utmost importance that Antoine should go at once to court. This upheaval would have a great effect upon the entire country.

'My husband,' she declared, 'you must not forget that you are a Prince and the head of the House of Bourbon. Next to the royal Valois children, you are first in the land. Francis is sickly; Charles too. And Henry and Hercule?' She shrugged her shoulders. 'Yes, there are many between. But how can a boy of sixteen rule France? Experienced men like his grandfather and his father were faced with a hundred difficulties, had a thousand hazardous decisions to make. Our country is divided and there is bloodshed everywhere . . . in the name of religion. The King will need advisers, Antoine, and you should be one of them.'

'You are right. I must go to Paris with all speed. If it should be necessary for me to stay there, you will join me, my darling?'

'Yes. I will join you with the children. We can be happy in Paris, Antoine, as in Nérac.'

She frowned, even as she spoke. 'I fear the Guises,' she said. 'The new King's wife is their niece, and through her they will have the King's ear. Antoine, I greatly fear that this will mean more persecutions of those who follow the new religion.'

'Never fear, my love. My brother Condé and I . . . with Uncle Gaspard on our side . . . will outwit the family of Guise.'

She kissed him fondly; adoring him as she did, it was so easy to see in him all that she wished he had.

Before he was ready to make the journey, one of the messengers asked that he might have a word with him, and to this Antoine lightheartedly consented.

'Sire,' said the man, 'it has come to my ears that the King of Spain watches your actions. His spies are everywhere – even here in your own land. He knows your feelings for the new faith and he is therefore your sworn enemy. Be warned, my lord. Be cautious. Go to the court of France, as indeed you should, but not in the splendid fashion that you planned. Take only a few followers and go in secret, so that the spies of the King of Spain do not know that you have left Nérac.'

The name of Philip of Spain was one which could terrify many – Antoine not the least. Spain had already annexed part of Navarre which it was impossible to regain, and Antoine lived in terror that one day the Spaniard would decide that the whole territory of Navarre should be his.

It did not occur to Antoine to doubt the integrity of the messengers. Yet he knew that they had been sent from the court of France, and he might have asked himself if the Guises had, by chance, decided who should carry the message to him.

He said a reluctant good-bye to Jeanne and set out northwards for Paris.

## ✤ CHAPTER II ✤

Dressed in a plain black gown and covered from head to foot in a black veil, Catherine paced up and down in her apartments of the Louvre. The room was lighted by only two wax tapers. The walls were covered with heavy black hangings; the same black cloth covered her bed and her *prie-dieu*.

Her forty days and nights of mourning were over, and Catherine was beginning to realise more fully all that the death of her husband would mean to her; she found that she could look forward to the future with eagerness.

There would be no more humiliation, no futile attempts to gain Henry's affections. She would never again watch him make love to his mistress. Henry, who had caused her so much bitterness and humiliation, was now powerless to hurt her. She loved him; she had desired him; his death was a great tragedy; yet freedom was now hers.

She looked back, but fleetingly, for it was not a habit of hers to look back, to those moments when she had watched her husband and his mistress together. She laughed suddenly, remembering that when people made love, wonderful as they might seem to one another, they could appear rather ridiculous to an unseen watcher; and when a woman of nearly sixty and a man of forty behave like young lovers, the unseen watcher – though jealous and tormented – might surely be forgiven a sly snigger. Had she then found a certain coarse amusement mingling with her jealous anguish? What did it matter? It was pointless to look back when there was so much to which she might look forward.

Francis was now King, and Francis was only sixteen years old; he was not very clever, and he was suffering from some poison of the blood which meant that he was continually breaking out in sores. He had, in his formal address to his subjects, asked them to obey his mother. On all state documents he wrote: 'This being the good pleasure of my Lady-Mother, and I also approve of every opinion that she holdeth.'

Such deference was pleasing, but she had quickly realised that it was not so flattering as it seemed.

How unfortunate it was that Henry and Diane should have married Francis to the Scottish girl! That girl now dominated Catherine's dreams, for Mary made Francis obey her in all things; and her uncles, the Guises, cunningly saw that she obeyed *them*.

How I dislike undutiful children! thought Catherine; and, for all his words, Francis was an undutiful son, since he did not obey his mother, but the Guises.

Catherine hated the Guises, and they terrified her. Very clearly the arrogant Duke Francis and the sly Cardinal of Lorraine had shown her that they were the masters. She had tried to placate them while wondering how she could destroy them. She had vowed friendship for them; she had insisted that

Francis issue a statement commanding obedience to the Duke and the Cardinal; and as she had done so, she had wondered how she could betray them. Longingly she thought, as she had thought in the days when Diane had occupied her mind, of the poison closet at Blois; but the people whom she wished to remove were so important, so well guarded, that she had to bide her time. She could only use the contents of her closet, and the fine art which she had gradually mastered, on those who were less significant. At the moment she must go warily, for if she were plotting against the Guises, she could be sure *they* were watching *her* very closely, and one false move on her part would be disastrous to her.

She had already, she saw now, made a mistake by too prompt action. She had brought about the disgrace of her old enemy, the Constable Montmorency, insisting that the young King take from him the seals of office, and, thinking to ingratiate herself with the Guises, had suggested that they be given to them. Francis told the Constable that, in view of his years, these offices were too great a strain on him, but that he should remain a member of the Privy Council. The Constable had retorted hotly: 'Being old and half in my dotage, my counsel can be of little use to you.' And in great rage he had retired to the château of Chantilly. Catherine realised that she had made a dangerous enemy and that the course the ex-Constable would probably take would be to ally himself with the Bourbons.

She could not make up her mind whether or not to make the Bourbons her friends at the expense of the Guises. She had chosen the Guises because Antoine de Bourbon had not been at court when she might have sounded him and thrown in her lot with him. She did not doubt that his prolonged absence might have been engineered by the Guises, but that did not endear him to her; she knew him for a weak and vacillating creature who could not make up his mind on such a simple thing as a journey to court. The Prince of Condé was gallant and attractive; she had always had a pleasant feeling for him; but she did not know enough of him to trust him as an ally in this dangerous game of politics which she was now about to play. Meanwhile, the Guises were at hand, and they seemed all-powerful; and through their niece, Mary of Scotland, they insisted that the young King should take their advice instead of that of his mother. And so, for the moment, Catherine had been forced to take the Guises as her allies.

She drew aside the heavy curtains and looked out on the gardens. The young people were down there, and as she stood watching them, she drew from the observation that delight which watching others, when they thought themselves unobserved, always gave her.

She frowned at those children of hers. There was Francis walking about the enclosed garden with his arm about his wife. Every now and then he would stop to kiss her passionately. He looked like a little old man from this distance. She laughed suddenly, reflecting that he was wearing himself out with the exertions of sport and being a husband. Well, when Francis had worn himself out there would be an end to the easy power of Messieurs the Duke and Cardinal. They would not find it so easy with young Charles. Or would they? But there should be no sly little wife to lure Charles from his mother. She would make sure that over Charles she would have complete domination.

Now there was Charles, sidling up to Mary, trying to take her hand, looking at her in that wild, passionate way of his —

his heart in his eyes. Silly Charles! He was no doubt begging that he might be allowed to play his lute to her or read some poem he had written about her. Catherine must stop this folly of her second son; by the look of young Francis, it might be that he was not long for this world, and, if he were not, Charles would have other things to think about than pursuing Francis's widow. Francis's widow should never become Charles's wife.

She must watch these children of hers, for they were very important. Now that her husband was dead, they were all-important. In them lay her future and all that she could hope for in this land of her adoption.

Margot caught her eye. Margot was sprawling on the grass, and on one side of her was the little Prince of Joinville, son of the Duke of Guise, and on the other the Marquis of Beaupréau, the son of the Prince of Roche-sur-Yon. Margot's wayward eyes went from the dark head of Beaupréau to the fair one of young Guise; and there they rested with a most unchildlike longing. Margot was talking; Margot was always talking, except in her mother's presence. She jumped up suddenly and danced on the grass, lifting the skirts of her dress too high for decorum, while the two Princes tried to catch her and dance with her.

Then into her apartment came her darling Henry, and with him was little Hercule. Hercule had lost his beauty since his attack of smallpox, for his skin was badly pitted; he would never again be known as 'Pretty Hercule'. But Henry in contrast was growing more and more beautiful every day.

She could not repress a fond smile at the sight of him. He had decked himself out in the most brilliant colours; but these colours, though dazzlingly bright, mingled perfectly, for her Henry was an artist. In his ears were sapphire earrings and it was these that he had come to show her. He was nine years old now, and those wonderful dark eyes of his were pure Medici. How ordinary the others seemed in comparison with Henry! They had no subtlety. Francis was foolish; Charles was hysterical; Elisabeth and Claude had been quite obedient girls; Margot, nearly eight years old now, was wild and in constant need of restraint; Hercule without his beauty was a petulant little boy, but Henry, her darling, was perfect. She thought even now as she looked at him: Oh, why was this one not my first-born!

He had come to show her his new earrings. Were they not beautiful, and did she not think that sapphires suited him better than emeralds?

'My darling,' she said, 'they are most becoming. But do you think little boys should wear earrings?'

He pouted. Hercule watched him in that astonishment which was apparent on all the children's faces when they saw the behaviour of Henry towards the mother whom the rest of them feared.

'But *I* like earrings, *Maman*; and if I like earrings I shall wear earrings.'

'Of course you shall, my pet; and I will tell you that if the other gentlemen do not wear them, the more fools they, for they are most becoming.'

He embraced her. He would like a necklace of sapphires, he said, to match the earrings.

'You are a vain creature,' she told him. 'And you have been perfuming yourself from my bottles, have you not?'

Henry was excited. 'This perfume of yours is the best you have ever had, *Maman*. This smell of musk enchants me. Could Cosmo or René make some for me?'

Catherine said she would consider that, in a way which he took for consent. He began to dance round the room, not boisterously as Margot danced, but gracefully, and with the utmost charm. After that he wished to recite to her the latest poem he had composed; and when she heard it, it seemed to Catherine that it compared very favourably with the best of Ronsard.

Ah, she thought, my clever son, my handsome little Italian, why were you not my first-born?

She took him into her arms and kissed him. She told herself, as she had so many times before, that she would use all her power to advance this beloved son. She was as necessary to him as he was to her.

But he wanted now to escape from her, to go to his own apartment and write poetry; he wanted to look at his reflection in his new Venetian mirror and admire the fine garments and the earrings he was wearing.

She let him go, for he was petulant if detained; and when he had gone she felt a distaste for her other children, who were not like Henry.

She did not wish to keep Hercule with her, so she sent him into the gardens to tell his sister Marguerite to come to her at once. Hercule looked startled, for when Margot was not called by her pet name which Charles had given her, it usually meant that she was in disgrace.

'And,' went on Catherine, 'you need not return with her. You may stay in the gardens.'

Hercule went out, and Margot lost no time in obeying her mother's summons.

The little girl stood before Catherine; she seemed quite different from the gay little coquette of the gardens. She curtsied, and her great dark eyes betrayed her fear; Margot was always afraid when summoned to her mother's presence.

She came forward to kiss her mother's hand, but Catherine withheld the hand in displeasure.

'I have been watching you,' she said coldly, 'and I have found your behaviour disgraceful. You roll on the grass like the lowest serving-girl, while you attempt, in your foolish way, to coquette first with Monsieur de Joinville and then with Monsieur Beaupréau.' Catherine gave a sudden laugh which terrified Margot. Margot did not know why her mother frightened her. She did know that this was going to mean a beating, probably from her governess; but there had been many beatings, and Margot had a method of moving out of range of the rod; it was a technique of her own invention which she had taught the others. It was not the beating which frightened her; it was her mother. She was terrified of this woman's displeasure. She had said that it was like displeasing God or the Devil. 'I believe,' Margot had said, 'that she knows in her thoughts what we do; I believe that she sees us when she is miles away from us, and that she knows our thoughts. That is what frightens me.'

'You are not only foolish,' went on Margot's mother, 'you are wanton and wicked. I would not answer for your innocence. What a pleasant thing is this! Your father so recently dead, and you see fit to sport in the gardens with these two gentlemen.'

Margot began to cry at the mention of her father; she remembered suddenly so clearly the big, kindly man with the silvery hair and the understanding smile; she remembered him as a man she thought of first as father, then as King. She could not think how she could have forgotten him when she was trying to make Henry jealous of silly young Beaupréau. Perhaps it was because when she was with Henry of Guise she forgot everything but that boy.

'You, a Princess of France . . . so to forget yourself! Go and tell one of the women to find your governess and send her to me.'

While she waited for the governess to arrive, Margot tried to tell herself that this was nothing; it would merely mean a beating; but Margot could not stop herself trembling.

'Take the Princess away,' said Catherine to the governess. 'Give her a good beating and see that she remains in her room for the rest of the day.'

And Margot, trembling still, went from her mother's presence; but as soon as she was in the corridor with her governess, all her old spirit came back to her; her tears stopped suddenly and she looked slyly up at the poor woman to whom the beating of Margot was a greater ordeal than to Margot.

And in the apartment, with the rod in her hand, the governess tried in vain to catch the small, darting figure; there were not many strokes that found their target on the lively little body. Margot's red tongue popped out now and then in derision, and when the governess was completely exhausted, Margot danced about the apartment, studying her budding beauty, wishing Henry of Guise was there to admire her.

Having despatched Margot, Catherine sent an attendant down to the garden to have Charles brought to her.

He came in trepidation, as Margot had done. He was nine and seemed moderately healthy; it was only after his hysterical fits came upon him and his eyes became bloodshot and there was foam on his lips that he seemed feeble.

'Come here, my son,' said Catherine.

'You sent for me, Madame.'

'I have been watching you in the gardens, Charles.'

Into his eyes there came that same haunted look which she had seen in Margot's. He, like his sister, was terrified of the thought of his mother's watching eyes.

'What were you saying to Mary, Charles?'

'I was asking if I might read some verses to her.'

'Some verses . . . written by you to Mary?'

He flushed. 'Yes, Madame.'

Catherine went on: 'What do you think of your sister Mary? Come, tell me. And tell me the truth, Charles. You cannot hide the truth from me, my son.'

'I think,' said Charles, 'that there never was a more beautiful Princess in the whole of the world.'

'Go on. Go on.'

'And I think my brother Francis is fortunate above all others because Mary is his wife.'

Catherine took his wrist and held it firmly. 'That is treason,' she said quietly. 'Francis is your King.'

'Treason!' he cried, trying to start back. 'Oh no. It is not treason.'

'You cherish unholy thoughts about his wife.' She kept her voice low as though that of which she spoke was too shocking to be spoken aloud.

'Not unholy,' cried Charles. 'I merely wish that I might have been my father's eldest son, and that I might stand in Francis's place – not for the throne, but that Mary might be my wife.'

'These are wicked, wanton thoughts, my son. These are treasonable thoughts.'

He wanted to contradict her, but her eyes were fixed on him and he found that he was speechless.

85

'Do you know, my son, what happens to traitors? I will take you down to the dungeons one day and there I will show you what is done to traitors. They are tortured. You cannot understand torture, but perhaps, as you harbour traitorous thoughts against your brother, it would be a kindness to show you these things.'

Charles cried out in terror: 'No; please do not. I could not . . . I could not look. I cannot bear to see such things.'

'But it is as well that you should know, child, for even Princes may suffer torture if they are traitors to their kings.'

His lips were moving, and she saw the flecks of foam gathering upon them; his eyes were wide and staring, and she saw the pink veins beginning to show in the whites of them.

'I will tell you what happens to traitors,' she went on. 'It should be part of your education. In the dark dungeons of the Conciergerie – you know the Conciergerie, my son – prisoners are kept. They scream in terror. They would faint, but they are not allowed to faint. They are brought round by means of herbs and vinegar. Some have their eyes put out; some lose their tongues or have their ears lopped off. Some suffer the water torture, others the Boot. Those who betray kings suffer more terribly than any others. Their flesh may be torn with red-hot pincers, and molten lead, pitch, wax, brimstone . . . such things are poured into the wounds . . .'

Charles began to scream: 'No . . . no! I won't go there. I won't be tortured. I won't . . . *Maman* . . . you will not let them take me . . . ?'

Catherine lifted the little boy in her arms. That was enough. Perhaps now he would not be so foolish. Perhaps he would think of the torture chambers every time Mary Stuart flashed those bright eyes of hers his way.

'Charles, Charles, my dearest son. My dear, dear boy, your mother is here to protect you. She would let no harm come to you. You are her Prince, her son. You know that.'

He buried his head against her. 'Yes, *Maman*. Yes, *Maman*.'

His hand curled round the stuff of her sleeve as a baby's curls, tightly, for protection.

'There, my little one,' she soothed. 'Nothing shall happen to you, for you are my little Prince, and I shall be proud of you. You would never be a traitor to your brother, would you? You would never be so wicked as to desire another man's wife – and he your own brother!'

'No, *Maman*, no!' He was shivering now. She had averted the fit. That was the way she preferred to do it. It was not pleasant to see him lose his reason.

She soothed him; she laid her cool hand on his forehead; she made him lie on her bed, and she sat beside it holding his hand.

'Have no fear, my son,' she said. 'Do what your mother tells you, and she will see that no harm comes to you.'

'Yes, *Maman*; I will.'

'Always remember that, Charles.'

He nodded while Catherine wiped the beads of sweat off his forehead. She sat beside him until he was calm.

She was thinking what a difficult task lay before her. She must dupe the arrogant Guises and the vacillating Bourbons; but she must not neglect to guide her children's footsteps in the way they must go. She could not guess which task would be the more arduous – the fooling of the rival houses or the controlling of her Valois brood.

87

Francis was preparing for a day's hunting. He was feeling wretchedly ill, but he was happy. He enjoyed hunting when Mary was to be of the party, for whenever Mary was with him he was happy. He never tired of looking at her, of telling her how beautiful she was; and that made them both very happy.

He wished he could escape from his mother and the Cardinal and be alone with Mary all the time. He wished that his father – his dearly beloved father – was alive. He would like to kill the man who had killed his father. He, Francis, did not want to be King; he had been so much happier when he was Dauphin. Then there had been little to do but dance and play and be with Mary. Now that he was King, he was never free from the attentions of his mother and the Cardinal.

He was afraid of his mother; he was afraid of the Cardinal. They were both, he knew, so much cleverer than he would ever be. He had to obey them both, and as they did not always wish him to do the same thing, that was very difficult. The Cardinal sneered openly at him, saying those clever, cutting things which hurt more deeply than Francis would admit. He would have liked to have banished the Cardinal, but Mary called him her darling uncle; and the Cardinal was always thinking of things which would please Mary; he could not banish one of Mary's uncles.

As for his mother, he would have liked to tell her to do everything she pleased, for he was sure she knew much more about governing France than he did. But always at his elbow was the Cardinal, with his thin, beautifully formed features and his cruel mouth letting fall those unkind words.

The Cardinal came in unceremoniously, even as he was dressing himself for the hunt, and with an imperious gesture dismissed the King's attendants. Francis would have liked to protest, but if he did so he would stammer and stutter, and the Cardinal had already mocked stammerers and stutterers, so that Francis was almost afraid to speak in his presence.

'We leave in half an hour, Sire,' said the Cardinal.

Francis said: 'I do not know if the Queen will be ready.'

'The Queen must be ready,' said the Cardinal testily.

'There . . . there is plenty of time,' stammered Francis. 'The Prince of Bourbon shall be met half an hour's ride from the palace.'

'Nay, Sire, we shall not meet the Bourbon, hunting to-day.'

'Not . . . But . . . But he is on his way. I . . . I had heard that he was.'

The Cardinal of Lorraine studied his long white fingers. 'Sire, the Bourbon rides this way. He comes with a humble following because he has some notion that he is important to the King of Spain and it is well that the spies of that monarch should not know of his movements. Therefore he rides to court like a poor gentleman.'

Francis did not laugh. He hated to hear people ridiculed, and Antoine de Bourbon was of higher rank than the Cardinal. He hated the sly, handsome face of the Cardinal; he hated the drawling voice.

'Then we must meet him if he rides this way,' he said.

'Why so, Sire?'

'Why? Because it is courteous. More than that, it is our custom. Do we not always meet those who come to visit us . . . out hunting . . . as if by accident?'

'If the visitor is important, yes.'

'But this is the Prince of Bourbon.'

'Nevertheless, he must learn that he is of no account.'

'I cannot do this, Monsieur le Cardinal. I will not be guilty of such ill manners towards my kinsman.'

The Cardinal sat smiling at his long white hands until Mary joined them. She was flushed and laughing; the young King was enchanted afresh by the beauty of his wife.

'You are ready, my love?' she asked. 'Why do we wait?'

Francis hurried to her and kissed her hands. 'We but waited for you.'

'Alas, dear niece,' said the Cardinal, 'you will not ride the way you chose. The King has given orders that we must ride south to greet the Bourbon.'

Mary looked from her husband to her uncle. She took her cue from the Cardinal as always.

'Oh, Francis, but I did not want to go south. I had made other plans. There is something I wished to show you on the north road.' She grimaced charmingly. 'And the Bourbon! He wears earrings. He is a fop and a fool, and he tires me so. Francis, please, let us pretend we have missed him. Let us ride the other way. Yes, Francis . . . darling . . . to please me.'

Francis murmured: 'We will go where you lead us, my love, my darling.'

And the Cardinal looked on, smiling benignly at his beautiful niece and her little King.

❧ ❧ ❧

Antoine was only a few miles from the Palace of Saint-Germain. He was thinking of the new status which was his since the death of King Henry. He was a Prince of the Blood Royal, and young Francis was only sixteen. In such cases it was necessary to have a strong and influential Privy Council, and naturally he, on account of his rank, should have high office in it.

He thought pleasantly of what he would do for the persecuted Protestants for whom he and his brother felt such sympathy. He felt proud, contemplating that all over the country Protestants would look to him as their leader; they would rejoice when they heard that he was at court. He could almost hear their cries: *'Vive le Bourbon!* Let us make him our leader. All our hopes rest in him!'

He had talked of this with Jeanne before he had left home, for his wife was fast growing in sympathy with the Reformed Faith; she would soon come out into the open. It was not that she was afraid to announce her belief; she did not fear the enmity of the Guises and Philip of Spain; it was the honour which she felt was due to her father that prevented her from making her feelings known just yet.

Oh, Jeanne, he thought, how I love you! How I admire you, my darling! You are more than a woman . . . more than a wife. I am even glad of the profligate life I led before I met you, because my dealings with those light women whom I knew at that time have taught me to appreciate you more.

Jeanne wanted him to lead the Protestants so that they might rid themselves of these perpetual persecutions. In Jeanne's eyes he was already a leader. He would come back to Nérac, to Jeanne and his children; and she would be proud of his achievements.

He said to his attendants: 'We shall be meeting the King's party at any moment now. Be prepared.'

But they rode on, and there was no sign of the King's party; and when they reached the Palace of Saint-Germain, the attendants seemed surprised to see them.

Antoine, furious at this reception, said coldly: 'Take me to my apartments at once.'

'My lord Prince,' was the answer, 'no apartments have been prepared.'

'This is nonsense. Am I not expected? Conduct me to the King . . . no, to the Queen Mother.'

'My Lord, they are out hunting. They will not return until the late afternoon.'

Antoine realised now that this was no accident, but an intentional slight, and he could guess who had arranged it. It could mean only one thing. His perennial enemies, the Guises, were in command.

Even as he stood there, hesitating and uncertain, he knew what Francis Duke of Guise would have done in his place. He would have drawn his sword, he would have shouted curses; he would have demanded that apartments immediately be prepared for him. And the Cardinal? Antoine could imagine the scorn on those cold, handsome features; he could hear the clear, cutting voice which would strike terror into all who heard it.

But Antoine was no Guise. He did not know how to act. He was not physically afraid; his was a moral cowardice, and an inability to think quickly and to know how to act in an emergency. In battle he would be as brave as any – but this was not battle.

His friend the Maréchal de Saint-André came to his rescue and offered him his room at the palace, saying that he would help find lodgings in the village for Antoine's attendants. Antoine accepted this offer with gratitude. He saw now that this had been planned by the Guises, who had decided that he should come to court and find himself in the midst of his enemies with a few – a very few – attendants scattered in the village. He knew that he had been unwise to delay his visit so long and that he should have been at court weeks before, for perhaps at that time the Guises might not have been in such complete power. He should have come in pomp, well guarded by his own men. He had been a fool to listen to evil counsels, and now he knew it. He realised to the full what power was working against him when, on the return of the hunting party, he went into the audience chamber.

King Francis — looking uncomfortable, it was true, but obviously obeying orders — stood quite still and made no attempt to greet him. The Cardinal of Lorraine, who stood close to the King, did likewise. This was a great insult, for Antoine was of higher rank than the Cardinal, and even if the King chose to insult Antoine, the Cardinal certainly had no right to do so. But Antoine was without dignity. Uncertainly he embraced the King and the Cardinal, though neither gave the slightest response.

Catherine was present with the young Queen, and as Catherine watched Antoine de Bourbon she felt a desire to burst out laughing. She had been fortunate in not putting her trust in a Bourbon. He was reduced to the position of a chambermaid, she thought. And how meekly he accepted it! The fool! Could he not see that this was no time for weakness?

He should have demanded the homage of the Cardinal; he could have made the poor little King shiver if he had done so; and the Cardinal also would have realised that he had a strong man to deal with. But no! Antoine had no dignity, no arrogance . . . only meekness.

The Cardinal spoke to him most haughtily, and Antoine smiled, glad to receive some attention.

Poor little popinjay! thought Catherine. Now, there is a man whom it should not be difficult to use.

Antoine had gone back to his wife, and Catherine laughed to think of their reunion. She was no longer jealous of their love for one another, for she was certain that one day Jeanne was going to repent of her marriage. Jeanne was strong, and as a strong woman she must despise weakness; so she must soon despise her husband. It was amusing to think of Antoine's creeping back to his wife to tell of his reception at court, of all he had been able to achieve for the Protestants, whose hope he now was since Condé had been tactfully sent away on a foreign mission – for what Antoine had achieved was precisely nothing.

Condé was in a different class. Condé was not a man to be dismissed as lightly as his elder brother Antoine; but Condé was away, and there was no need to think of him now. This scheming for power was such a difficult task, such an all-absorbing one, so complicated that one could never see more than a few moves ahead.

Still, there was time to reflect that Antoine was creeping back to his wife, his tail between his legs, to tell her a tale of humiliation and defeat. One day Madame Jeanne would be forced to see what kind of man she had married.

Thoughts of Jeanne still haunted Catherine a good deal; she would always hate her, would always see her as a political rival as well as a woman who had been successful in love – though with what a partner! – and a woman to watch in the future.

There was much to think of at home. 'With the help of the brothers Ruggieri and her perfumer René, who had a shop on the quay opposite the Louvre, she had removed from this life one or two minor characters who had made themselves difficult. Such actions gave her a satisfying sense of her power; she enjoyed giving her smiles to her intended victims and assuring them that they were well on the way to gaining her favour; then would come the removal, sometimes swift, sometimes lingering, whichever suited her purpose. This was like soothing ointments on her wounds, those wounds which had been made long ago by Diane de Poitiers and now by the Guises. Sometimes she thought it would be a clever thing to slip something into the wine of Francis of Guise, something which would improve the taste of the wine, for his was a rare palate; at others she thought how she would have enjoyed presenting the Cardinal of Lorraine with a book, the pages of which had been specially treated by René or one of the Ruggieri brothers; it would have made her happy to have given to that dandy, Antoine de Bourbon, a pair of perfumed gloves, the kind which, when drawn on to the hands, produced death. But such would be only a momentary satisfaction. It was unwise to deal thus with those of rank and importance. Moreover, she was beginning to see that the Guises and the Bourbons would be of more use to her alive than dead, for it would be to her advantage to set one rival house against the other. At the moment it might appear that she was siding with the Guises, but she did not always intend to do that. When she had a chance she would let that weak, vain little Bourbon think that she was on his side – secretly, because of the power of the Guises; she would remind him that Francis could not live for ever.

When Francis died, Charles would take the crown; and Charles, hysterical and unbalanced, had been taught to rely on his mother. Yet, pliable as he was, she must not forget that streak of madness in him; there was a hint of rebellion also.

Catherine had seen how, through Mary of Scotland, her son Francis had been weaned from her control.

She decided now to put into action a plan which had long been in her mind. It seemed impossible to banish Mary Stuart from Charles's mind. When Catherine talked to him, rousing that greatest emotion of which he was capable, fear – fear of his mother, fear of torture and death – he was compliant; but when the next day he set eyes on Mary, he would watch her like a lovesick boy.

Catherine sent for two Italians of her suite, two men whom she trusted as she trusted her astrologers.

When they were in her apartments she closed the doors and made sure that there was no one hidden in any cupboard or anteroom. Then she explained what she wanted of them. It was possible to speak frankly – or as near as Catherine could get to frankness – to Birago and Gondi, the Count of Retz; for they, as Italians, must obey the Italian Queen, since they knew that their prospects in France depended on her good graces.

'I am alarmed concerning my son,' she said. 'I do not mean the King, but my son Charles, who would take the King's place were the King to meet with an early death. My lords, the little boy has feelings beyond his years . . . and for his brother's wife. This is not healthy in a little boy. The French . . .' She smiled at them intimately . . . Italian to Italian. 'The French, my lords, see nothing wrong in love between the sexes . . . even in the cases of children. "It is natural," they say. "What a lover he will become!"' She gave a sudden spurt of laughter. 'But at the age of my son, it is more natural, I think, to have a fondness for members of his own sex.'

Her wide, prominent eyes stared blankly before her, and the men watched her closely.

'You think, Madame,' ventured the Count of Retz, 'that it would be more natural were he to indulge in the usual passionate friendships with . . . boys of his own age.'

'How well you understand! I do. Indeed I do. I do not wish to curb his *natural* emotions.' She smiled, and they smiled with her, knowing full well that it was a habit of the Queen Mother's to say what she did not mean. 'I wish him to enjoy friendships with members of his own sex. He is not strong, and I feel you gentlemen could do much for him. Let him not, at his tender age, think of *women*.'

The Italians smiled afresh. They knew that they had been chosen as tutors for Charles because of their perverted tastes rather than for their academic qualifications.

They understood the Queen Mother. The Prince Henry was as dear to her, so it was said, 'as her right eye'. Francis did not look as if he would make old bones, and as yet he had no son to follow him. If it should happen that the little Queen of Scots gave him one, they did not doubt that Catherine would know how to remove that little obstacle. And after Francis . . . Charles. Let the danger of Charles's producing children be made as remote as possible. He was weak and unbalanced; well, it should not be difficult to turn such a boy from his natural inclinations.

Some might have been astonished at this interview with the Queen Mother; but Charles's new tutors were not. They understood perfectly and accepted the task required of them.

Catherine was preparing to set out for Francis's Coronation, which was to take place, as tradition demanded, in the town of

Rheims. How long, she asked herself, would this little King stay on the throne? He had been such a difficult baby to rear. She remembered how in the first year of his life his body had from time to time been covered with livid patches about which the doctors could do nothing, being absolutely ignorant of their cause. There was an obstruction in his nose which it had been thought at one time would kill him; but he had survived to speak with a nasal accent which was not very pleasant to listen to. It had always seemed that he was too delicate for long life, and now, by the look of him, it appeared that he could scarcely survive his Coronation. Watching him, Catherine felt competent to arrange that matters should go the way she wished.

A few days before they were due to set out for Rheims, Catherine was sitting with some of her ladies when the talk turned to Anne du Bourg, whom Catherine's husband, the late Henry the Second, had sent to prison for holding heterodox views. Anne du Bourg was now awaiting his trial, and there was more unrest than ever in the country on account of this man. As they talked, Catherine realised that the ladies about her all had Huguenot leanings – the Duchess de Montpensier, Mademoiselle de Goguier, Madame de Crussol and Madame de Mailly. Catherine was stimulated, for her sense of intrigue warned her that the gathering together of such ladies was not an accident. She let them talk.

'Ah,' she said at length. 'But, ladies, it would seem to me that there are two parties of Huguenots in France to-day: those who devote themselves to their Faith – and these I honour – and those who make a political issue of religion. Nay, Madame de Mailly, do not interrupt me. Some of the party, I have reason to believe, plot with Elizabeth of England. I understand it is their wish to depose my son and put the Prince of Condé on the throne.'

Her thoughts went to Condé as she spoke, and she could not prevent a little smile. Condé! What queer thoughts this man aroused in her! She knew that she would not hesitate to use him, even to slip a little potion into his wine if need be; but she could never hear his name without a slight emotion. That was folly for a woman of her age, particularly as she had no great desire for physical passion. Yet, try as she might, she could not overcome this excitement with which she was filled at the prospect of meeting Condé. He was a man of immense vitality, and his magnetism affected every female who set eyes on him; this must be so if it could touch Catherine de' Medici. She heard that many women were in love with him. He was small, yet enchanting; he was hot-tempered, quick to take offence; and, she imagined, quite unstable. He would need much guidance, but it was said that he got this in good measure from his wife Eléonore, a fervent defender of the Reformed Faith. He was a practised philanderer, this Condé, as was his brother, Antoine de Bourbon. Philanderers both – yet held in check by over-devoted wives!

She had missed a little of the conversation while she had been thinking of Condé, which showed how unlike herself she became at the very mention of the man's name.

'Ah,' she went on. 'You would not expect me to support those who ill-wished my son!'

'Madame,' cried Madame de Montpensier, 'the Huguenots are loyal . . . absolutely loyal to the Crown.'

Catherine shrugged her shoulders. 'There are some,' she went on, 'who wish to have no King at all. A republic, they say they prefer . . . ruled by Calvin!'

'Nay, Madame, you have heard false tales.'

'It may be that you are right.'

And when she dismissed these women, Madame de Mailly remained behind and whispered to Catherine: 'Madame, the Admiral of France would wish to have a word with you. May I bring him to your presence?'

Catherine nodded.

Gaspard de Coligny. She studied him as he knelt before her, and as she looked at his stern and handsome face, it occurred to her that such a man, after all, might not be difficult to use. She knew a good deal of him, for she had made his acquaintance when she had first come to France. He was of Catherine's own age, and his mother had been the sister of Montmorency, the Constable of France. He was handsome in quite a different way from Condé. Gaspard de Coligny had a stern and noble look. Yet in his youth he had been a gay figure of fashion, spending his time between the court and the battlefield. Catherine remembered him well. He had been seen everywhere with his greatest friend, Francis of Guise; now the greatest friends had become the greatest enemies, Francis of Guise being the nominal head of the Catholic Party, while Coligny was the hope of the Protestants. Coligny was a power in the land; as Admiral of France, he controlled Normandy and Picardy. He had been a good Catholic until, during three years' captivity in Flanders, he had taken to the Protestant religion. A quiet and serious man he had become, and he was married to a plain and very wise wife who worshipped him and to whom he was devoted. In the presence of Coligny, Catherine was aware of strength, and such strength excited her as she wondered how she could use it.

When Coligny had risen, she asked him what he wished to

say to her, and he answered that it was the Queen Mother to whom the Protestants were now looking with hope. She smiled, well pleased, for it was amusing to discover how successfully she had managed to hide her true self from the people about her.

'They are aware of your sympathy, Madame,' said Coligny earnestly.

Then she spoke to him of what she had mentioned to the ladies; of plots with England, of plots with Calvin. He in his turn assured her of his loyalty to the Crown; and when Coligny spoke of loyalty she must believe him.

'Madame,' said Coligny, 'you are on your way to Rheims. A meeting could be arranged there . . . or somewhere near. There is much which should be discussed with you.'

'What would be discussed with me, Admiral?'

'We shall ask for the dismissal of the Guises, who hold so many offices; we shall ask for the redistribution of offices; the convocation of the States General. All this would be in the true interest of the Crown.'

'Ah, Monsieur l'Amiral, when I see poor people burned at the stake, not for murder or theft, but for holding their own opinions, I am deeply moved. And when I see the manner in which they bear these afflictions, I believe there is something in their faith which rises above reason.'

'Our people look to you for help, Madame,' pleaded Coligny. Madame de Mailly cried out: 'Oh, Madame, do not pollute the young King's reign with bloodshed. That which has already been shed calls loudly to God for vengeance.'

Catherine looked at Madame de Mailly coldly. 'Do you refer to what took place when my husband was on the throne?'

Madame de Mailly fell on her knees and begged the pardon of the Queen Mother.

Catherine looked from Madame de Mailly to Coligny. 'I think,' she said slowly, 'your meaning is this: many suffered at my husband's command, and you think that because of this a terrible death overtook him.' Catherine laughed bitterly. 'You would warn me, would you not, that if there are more deaths, more suffering, *I* may suffer? Ah, Madame, Monsieur l'Amiral, God has taken from me him whom I loved and prized more dearly than my life. What more could He do to me?'

Then she wept, for it pleased her to appear before Coligny as a weak woman, and both the Admiral and Madame de Mailly comforted her. But as she wept Catherine was asking herself whether or not it would be wise to agree to this meeting with the Protestants. She decided that it would, for she need commit herself to nothing while she learned their secrets.

So she promised that she would see any minister whom the Reformed Church cared to send to her; and Coligny and Madame de Mailly retired very well satisfied with the interview.

When Catherine was alone she thought continually of the Protestants; that led her to Condé; she contemplated his attractiveness, and his weakness. She thought of Antoine and Jeanne; Condé and his Eléonore. And when her women came in for her *coucher* she thought how lovely some of them were. There were two among them of outstanding beauty; one was Louise de la Limaudière and the other Isabelle de Limeuil.

She said, when she had dismissed all but the most beautiful of her attendants: 'Do you remember how in the days of my father-in-law Francis the First, there was a band of ladies, all charming, all good company, great riders, witty, the pick of the court?'

They had heard of Francis's *Petite Bande*, and they said so.

'I have such a band in mind. I shall gather about me ladies of charm and elegance, ladies who will do as much for me as Francis's did for him. Beauty, daring, wit, these shall be the qualifications; and it shall be deemed as great an honour for a lady to enter my *Escadron Volant* as it was to be a member of Francis's *Petite Bande*.'

✤ ✤ ✤

The court had moved to the Castle of Blois on the advice of Ambroise Paré, the King's surgeon. Francis's poison of the blood was particularly severe at this time, and it was thought that the climate of Blois, milder than that of Paris, might be good for the King.

During these uneasy days, Catherine felt herself to be most unsafe. The meeting with the Protestant ministers which she had planned had not taken place, for the arrangements had come to the ears of the Cardinal of Lorraine and he, in his arrogant way, together with his brother, the Duke of Guise, had made it very clear to Catherine that she could not serve two masters. If she wished to throw in her lot with Coligny and the Protestants, she would immediately and automatically become the enemy of the Guisards. And Catherine – with Francis on the throne, and Francis's wife, subject to those uncles of hers, in command of the King – could not afford to offend these men.

If the matter had ended there it would not have been important, but the persecutions of the Protestants had increased. The terrible sentence that he should be burned at the stake had been carried out on du Bourg, and many had watched him die in the Place des Grèves.

The Protestants were murmuring against Catherine for having failed to keep her promise. The French, of whatever class or party, were always ready to blame the Italian woman.

Catherine chafed against her inability to get what she wanted; but the Cardinal of Lorraine and the Duke of Guise had followed the court to Blois. They were on the alert. Catherine knew they watched her closely.

Only the children seemed unaware of the tension. The King knew nothing of what was going on about him. He was only concerned with his happiness in his married life. Mary was happy too, as long as she could dance and chatter and be admired; it seemed wonderful to her to be the most beautiful of all the Queens of France, to be courted and petted by her two formidable uncles.

Charles was not happy, but then how could he be? His tutors bewildered him by the strange things they taught him. He still longed to be with Mary, the Queen and wife of his brother; he wanted to write poetry to her and play his lute to her all day long.

Henry was happy with his dogs and those members of his own sex whom he chose for his playmates; these were all the pretty little boys of the court, not the big, blustering ones, like Henry of Guise, who were always talking of fighting and what they would do when they were grown up; Henry's friends were clever boys who wrote poetry and read poetry and liked fine pictures and beautiful things.

Margot was happy because Henry of Guise was at Blois. They would wander together along the banks of the Loire and talk of their future; they were determined that one day they would marry.

'If they should try to marry me to anyone else,' said Margot,

'I shall go with you to Lorraine and we will rule there together; and perhaps we shall one day take the whole of France and I will make you King.'

But Henry scoffed at the idea of there being any opposition to their marriage.

'Say nothing of this to anyone yet, dearest Margot, but I have already spoken to my father.'

Margot stared at him. 'About *us*?'

He nodded. 'My father thinks it would be a good plan for us to marry.'

'But Henry, what if the King . . .?'

'My father is the greatest man in France. If he says we shall marry, then we shall.'

Margot thought of Henry's father, the mighty Duke of Guise, *Le Balafré*, with the scar on his face which somehow made him more attractive because he had received it in battle. There would be many who would agree with his son that Francis of Guise was the greatest man in France; and if he could give her his son Henry in marriage, Margot herself was prepared to believe it.

And so the little lovers wandered through the castle grounds, talking of the future and the day when they would marry, swearing fidelity, assuring each other that no one should be allowed to stand in the way of their ultimate marriage.

Francis, Duke of Guise, called a Council at the Castle of Blois. He was grave, but his eyes sparkled as they always did at the thought of adventure; for there was nothing that delighted Francis more than a battle – the bloodier the better.

'Mesdames, Messieurs,' he said, addressing the Council, which consisted of the young Queen and the Queen Mother as well as the King, the Cardinal of Lorraine and the leading figures of the court, 'I have news that a plot is afoot. My spies in England have brought me word of this. The King is in danger. A military rising is being planned, the motive of which is to kidnap the King, the Queen, the Queen Mother and all the royal children. These traitors plan that if the King refuses to become a Protestant, another King will be set up to take his place. At the head of these traitors, as you will guess, are the Bourbon brothers. There has been correspondence with Elizabeth of England, who promises them help. Every care must be taken of the King. We must guard the castle.'

After this revelation all were confined to the castle. There were no more ramblings along the banks of the Loire for Margot and Henry of Guise. They did not care; they were happy as long as they were together; and both were of the kind to enjoy the thought of danger's being near to them. Not so Francis and his brother Charles. Charles's fits became more frequent, and he would cry out in his sleep that he was being murdered; he was terrified, on retiring, lest an assassin should be hiding in the hangings of his room. He was becoming more and more nervous. His mother watched him with calculating eyes; it seemed to her that his tutors were having some effect upon him; she was not displeased.

But at present she must turn her thoughts from her children to the bigger issue – the war between the Catholics and Protestants – in which she would not become involved, unless she might effect, by her intervention, a favourable advantage to herself. Sometimes she laughed at the fervency of the people about her. She was the only one who cared not a jot whether Catholics or Protestants got the upper hand, as long as they were subservient to the will of Catherine. Her religion was neither Catholic nor Protestant; she would fight for no cause but that of keeping the Valois Kings on the throne of France, and the Valois Kings under the control of the Queen Mother.

So, while listening to the plans of the Guisards, she was busy formulating her own.

Secretly she sent for Coligny. She had betrayed him once, but she felt that by sending out distress signals she could fool him again. Like most straightforward men, there was little subtlety about Coligny. She wrote to him that she had heard the English were about to attack a convoy of French ships. Now, although Coligny might be in league with England against the Guises and the Catholics, in such a man as he was honour demanded that he must always fly to the help of France; so he came at once to Catherine when he received the message from her. Catherine received him with tears, told him that she was a weak woman completely in the hands of the Guises, and begged him to stand by the King.

'The cause of all this trouble,' said the Admiral, 'is the family of Guise. The only remedy, Madame, and the only way in which a terrible civil war can be avoided is by an Edict of Tolerance.'

Catherine declared that everything in her power should be done to bring this into being; and because it seemed imperative to her to win the confidence of the Protestants, which she had lost when she failed to keep her word with regard to the meetings near Rheims, she issued a decree; it was a decree to stop the persecution of the Protestants; it gave them freedom to worship and contained a promise of forgiveness to all except those who had plotted against the royal family.

Catherine felt that she had handled a delicate situation

rather well; but when, a few days later, Francis of Guise was ushered into her apartments, and the man stood before her, his scarred, handsome face set and determined, those glittering eyes watching her cynically, that cruel mouth smiling a little, she began to realise the mighty force she had to pit her wits against, and her uneasiness returned.

Francis said: 'Madame, we are leaving Blois immediately. I can give you thirty minutes in which to prepare yourself.'

'Leaving Blois!'

The eyes flickered and the one above the scar watered a little, as it did when Francis was experiencing strong emotion.

'Danger, Madame, to the King, yourself and the royal children.'

'But,' she retorted, 'the danger is past. The Edict . . .'

'*Your* Edict, Madame,' said the Duke with unmistakable emphasis, 'will not help us to fight our enemies. We leave Blois for the safety of Amboise. *I* cannot leave the King exposed to danger.'

She realised the power of the man, and that wonderful self-control of hers was ready to meet this situation as it had met many more in the past. She, the Queen Mother, would accept the humiliation of bowing to the will of the Duke of Guise, for, she assured herself as she prepared to leave Blois, it would not last for ever.

✤ ✤ ✤

Francis the King was very frightened. Why could they not leave him alone? He wanted nothing but to be happy with Mary. He did not ask much – only that he might ride with her, dance with her, give her fine jewels, hear her laughter. It was so pleasant to be a young husband in love; so frightening to be a King. There were so many who wanted to rule France: his mother, Monsieur de Guise, the Cardinal of Lorraine, Antoine de Bourbon, Louis de Bourbon . . . If only he could have said: 'Very well, here is the crown. Take it. All I want is to be left at peace with Mary.'

But that could not be done. Unfortunately, he was the eldest son of his father. Oh, why had dearest Papa died? Why had there been that terrible accident which had not only robbed him of a father whom he loved and who had made him feel safe and happy, but had put a crown on his head!

And now there was fresh trouble. Here at Amboise they had been kept like prisoners. The Cardinal sneered at him; the Duke ordered what he should do. Oh, that he might be free of Mary's uncles! Men sought his life, he was told. He must be wary. They had caught some men in the forests surrounding Amboise, and these men had said they would talk to none but the King. He had been lectured and drilled as to what he must do. His mother had told him; the Guises had repeated their instructions. He was to give these men a crown piece each and be jolly and friendly to them while he asked sly questions and found out who had sent them to Amboise.

He knew that while he talked to the men, his mother would be listening through a tube which connected her room and his. He knew that the Cardinal would be concealed somewhere or other and that, if he made a false step or failed to get what they wanted, he would have to face the scorn of the Cardinal, the anger of the Duke, and, worse still, the coldness of his mother, which he dreaded more than anything.

The men were brought in; they bowed low over his hand.

He tried to appear bluff as he had been coached, but it was no good. 'Fear not, my good men,' he said shyly; and he thought that by the sound of his voice it was they who should be telling him not to fear.

He gave them the money.

'Tell me, what were you doing in the forests?'

They smiled and exchanged glances. They liked his youth and his shyness. What was there to fear? If he was the King, he was only a poor, delicate boy.

'We came to rescue you, Sire,' they whispered. It was apparent that the boy was uneasy; it seemed obvious that he would be nothing loth to escape from the rule of the Guises. With his stammering shyness he had won their confidence, and in a little while they were telling him that they had been sent from Geneva and that very shortly their leaders would join them.

The King hoped they would succeed; it was a genuine hope, for he could imagine nothing worse than the captivity he now endured under the control of the Duke and the Cardinal.

'Fear not, Sire,' whispered the leader of the men. 'There are forty thousand men on the way to your help.'

They thanked him for his graciousness; they kissed his hand with affection, it seemed; and Francis was very sorry for them and longed to warn them that they had been overheard.

They were taken as they left the castle, and for weeks afterwards their heads – with those of many others who had been rounded up in the forest – adorned the crenellations of the castle.

All the children, except Hercule, were summoned to the balcony. They dared not refuse to obey the order. They must sit with the ladies and courtiers while they watched the massacre of Huguenots in the courtyard.

Francis felt sick; he could not endure it. Mary covered her face with her hands. Charles watched in horror; later he would go back to his tutors, who would talk of what had happened until he would scream and fall into one of his fits. Margot turned pale; it hurt her to see young and handsome men cruelly pinioned, pale from the dungeons, bleeding from the torture chambers. Margot could not bear to look at the blood, and there was blood everywhere. She wanted to scream: 'Stop! Stop!' Her brother Henry looked on with indifference; he did not care about anyone but himself and his pretty friends. But Henry of Guise was thrilled by the spectacle; he always took his cue from his father, and the massacre of Huguenots was organised by the Guises; therefore it was right.

Francis of Guise exchanged approving glances with his son, the hope of his house. Henry's eyes showed how he adored his father, and there was contentment and understanding between those two. But the Duchess, Henry's mother, disgraced them all by covering her face with her hands and weeping.

'What ails you?' asked the Queen Mother, herself calmly watching the spectacle.

'This piteous tragedy!' cried the Duchess of Guise hysterically. 'This shedding of innocent blood . . . the blood of the King's subjects. Oh, God in Heaven, terrible days are before us. I have no doubt that a great disaster will fall upon our house.'

Duke Francis angrily led his wife away, and Henry was ashamed of his mother.

Later, as the massacres continued day after day, the Duke grew more cruel, as though in defiance of anything Fate could do to him. Everywhere was the sickening stench of blood and decaying flesh; when the children went about the grounds they would be faced with the sight of men's bodies hanging from the battlements. They watched men, fresh from the torture dungeons, tied in sacks and thrown into the Loire.

Neither Catherine nor the Guises attempted to stop the children's witnessing these terrible sights. Duke Francis knew that his son Henry would be hardened by them as he wished him to be hardened; Catherine knew that her Henry was quite as indifferent to the sufferings of others as she was herself. As for the rest of the children, it was to the Guises' advantage as well as that of Catherine that the King and his brother Charles should be weak, and it was in fact Francis and Charles whose nerves were racked by the horrors.

The bloody days went on and it seemed to the children that their beloved Amboise had taken on a new aspect. They thought of the dismal dungeons in which foul things were done; the beautiful battlements could not be dissociated from ghastly corpses which had once been men; the sparkling river was now the grave of many.

Francis cried when he was alone. It hurt him to go out and see how people shrank from him. When he approached he saw startled village women hustle the children into the safety of their cottages.

'Here comes the King!' they cried. 'He is sick, they say, and only keeps himself alive by drinking the blood of babies.'

'They hate me! They hate me!' sobbed Francis. 'They should be told that it is not I who do these terrible things.'

Once, with a sudden spurt of courage, he threw himself against the Cardinal and, when he felt the suit of mail beneath the Cardinal's robes, he knew that this man, too, was afraid.

The Cardinal lived in terror of assassination. He had altered the fashion in men's clothes that it might not be easy to hide weapons about their persons. Cloaks were no longer wide, boots were smaller, that daggers might not be secreted in them.

He is a coward, thought Francis; and he cried: 'It is because of you my people hate me. Would to God you would take yourself away from here!'

The Cardinal only smiled, for if he was afraid of an assassin, he was not afraid of the King.

❖  ❖  ❖

In the little court at Nérac there was great consternation. A letter had arrived for the King of Navarre from the King of France. Antoine opened it and read:

My Uncle, — You doubtless will remember the letters which I wrote to you touching the rising which lately happened at Amboise, and also concerning my uncle, the Prince of Condé, your brother, whom many prisoners accuse vehemently; a belief which I could not entertain against one of my blood.

Antoine's eyes skimmed the page, his hands trembling. He read on:

. . . I have decided to investigate the matter, having resolved not to pass my life in trouble through the mad ambition of any of my subjects. I charge you, my uncle, to bring your brother, the Prince of Condé, to Orléans whether he should be willing or not, and should the said Prince refuse obedience, I assure you, my uncle, that I shall soon make it clear that I am your King . . .'

Jeanne watched her husband as he read, saw the change of colour in his face, and she was afraid for him.

So much had happened during the last year that she had been forced to adjust her picture of him, but he was still her beloved husband, in spite of the occasional bickering between them. Their personalities were quite opposed, one to the other; he was so weak, and he could never make up his mind; she was strong, and once she had made up her mind, for good or ill, she found it difficult to swerve.

She had made him King of Navarre, but she was bold and independent and herself ruled the province. She had sharply reproved him for what had happened when he had gone to court and had been so rudely treated by the Guises. She had explained to him the peril in which he had put himself, herself, their children and their kingdom. She had seen that the Prince who could work with the Queen Mother was the one who would have the largest say in state affairs. He had hesitated, and the Guises had got there before him.

There had been coolness between them for a short while, but the heat of Jeanne's temper always faded quickly; and Antoine, though he changed his mind again and again, was still her beloved husband. They were lovers yet, and if he needed guidance from her, her help in his career, she must only thank God that she had the strength to give it.

Now, as she watched him, she thought of the happiness of their life together here in their own province. She, with her beloved children, teaching them herself, delighting in their precocity at their lessons, could have been completely happy. She drew great contentment from the Huguenot faith, though she had not professed her acceptance of it publicly; yet it was known throughout the land of France – and Spain – that there was refuge for Huguenots in Jeanne's kingdom.

'Antoine,' she said. 'What is it, my love?'

He brought the letter to her and put an arm about her shoulder while they read it together.

Jeanne said promptly: 'You must not go, and certainly Louis must not go.'

'This, dearest Jeanne, is a command. Do you not see that? A command from the King!'

'The King! A sickly boy without a mind of his own. It is a command from the Duke of Guise and his wicked Cardinal brother – a call from the Queen Mother. It means: "Come. Walk into the trap we have prepared for you." '

'You may be right. No. Certainly I shall not go. I shall tell Louis nothing of this, for he is foolhardy enough for anything.'

But Antoine could not remain of the same mind for long at a time.

'A command from the King must be obeyed. I think, Jeanne, that I should go. They would not dare harm us – Princes of the Blood!'

'Princes of the Blood have been murdered ere this,' she reminded him.

The Count of Crussol, the messenger who had brought the letter, assured Antoine that he had nothing to fear. He could give the word of the King on that.

'But the King,' pointed out Jeanne, 'is not allowed to give his word.'

'You have the word of the Queen Mother.'

'Ah!' cried Jeanne, hot and imprudent. 'Might not the Queen Mother keep this promise as she did that other . . . to meet our ministers at Rheims?'

'There are also the words of the Duke of Guise and the Cardinal of Lorraine.'

'Never trust the words of brigands!' cried Jeanne.

And it was Antoine's turn to reprove her.

How impossible it was to continue with the happy life! If they could only live humbly, simply, if they were not of royal blood, how happy they would be! But she must fret against Antoine's indecision and lie against her brusque frankness, and all because they must fear for the children and their kingdom; so they grew angry with each other on account of faults which in a lowlier household would merely have given rise to amusement.

Antoine decided that it was necessary to warn Condé of the King's letter and, on receiving his message, Condé, with his wife, the Princess Eléonore, came to Nérac to discuss the matter.

Condé, fearless, longing for adventure, declared there was nothing they could do but answer the summons. No one should say that Condé was afraid. Jeanne was furious with both brothers.

'It is for your own salvation, Louis,' she cried, 'that I advise you and Antoine to remain here.'

'Dear Jeanne, we cannot stay. It would be said that we were afraid to face the charge.'

Jeanne bit her lips in anger, while the Princess Eléonore, as wise in her way as Jeanne was in hers, added her prayers to those of her sister-in-law; but though the two men agreed to stay, both women knew their husbands well enough to recognise their instability.

'If you do go,' said Jeanne at length, 'you must at least appear before the Princes of Lorraine supported by a force which should compel them to respect the blood of the Bourbons.'

'Louis,' cried the Princess of Condé, 'do you not see that every step you take towards the court will bring you nearer to destruction? In the King's letter there is no attempt to hide their threats. Take men. Take arms. And if you are determined to die, die at the head of an army, not on a scaffold.'

'They are right, Louis,' said Antoine. 'I will go alone to the court. The chief accusation is against you. Let me go alone, test the climate there, and then . . . send you word.'

And while they hesitated, there came another messenger to the court of Nérac with letters from Catherine.

'Advance with fearless courage,' advised Catherine. 'You have nothing to fear if you come with courage. Come humbly, without much state; that will proclaim your innocence.'

'She is right,' said Antoine. 'If we go with an armed force we shall look like guilty men.'

'If the Queen Mother says, "Come humbly,"' said Jeanne, 'then you can be sure it would be wise for you to go fully armed.'

There were more letters. Those from the Huguenot Duchess of Montpensier warned Antoine and Condé not to leave Nérac. Catherine wrote asking Jeanne to accompany her husband to Orléans. 'Bring your little son and daughter,' wrote Catherine. 'I long for a sight of their bright little faces.'

'They at least shall not be exposed to *Madame le Serpent*,' declared Jeanne.

And when, at last, Antoine and Condé set out for Orléans, Jeanne left Nérac for Pau and began to make arrangements for the defence of her realm.

Antoine, King of Navarre, and Louis de Bourbon, the Prince of Condé, were on their way to Orléans. They had sent their chamberlains ahead to announce their approach.

Catherine in her apartments pondered this. She was going to have need of all her subtlety in the next few weeks; she was going to discover whether she had learned her lessons well, whether that self-control, that craft, that method of fabricating miracles, which she had nourished for so long, would work as she had always believed they would.

She remembered well the words of Machiavelli, that protégé of Lorenzo de' Medici: 'A prudent Prince cannot and ought not to keep his word, except when he can do it without injury to himself; or when the circumstances under which he contracted the engagement still exist. It is necessary, however, to disguise the appearance of craft and thoroughly to understand the art of feigning or dissembling; for men are generally so simple and weak that he who wishes to deceive, easily finds dupes.'

That was her policy. She had learned the lesson in her home, the home of her ancestors, in the Medici Palace and the Convent of the Murate, in Clement's Rome; and she would apply it in France. She had not yet enjoyed the full force of her power, she had not yet tried her wings, but she was confident. There was no one in this country who knew her for what she was. There had, it was true, been certain rumours about her from time to time; when the Dauphin Francis, eldest son of Francis the First, had died suddenly, many had believed she had had a hand in his death. But to most she was mild and patient, the woman who had endured over twenty years of humiliation through Diane de Poitiers with such meekness as only a poor, humble creature could show. She had duped them all, and they had been easy dupes.

She went into the little closet adjoining her apartment, locking herself in and then unlocking the door of a secret compartment. Here there were several speaking tubes, and one of these she held to her ear.

Sometimes it was necessary to wait for a long time, but usually she heard what was worth waiting for. These tubes had been, through the ingenuity of René and the Ruggieri brothers, made invisible and inserted into certain apartments of the palace; all were connected with and led to her little room. The one she held so patiently now was that connected with the private apartments of the Duke of Guise.

She knew this would be worth waiting for, since her woman Madalenna had discovered that the Duke had invited young Mary, the Queen, to his apartments.

Catherine thought of the Queen of France as her *bête noire* of the moment. It was infuriating to know that that foolish girl, still in her teens, was the real source of power in France, since, but for her, there would have been no need for the Queen Mother to endure those frequent slights from the intolerable Guises. The foolish Francis and the coquettish Mary were far too important in the land, even though they were merely the puppets and mouthpieces of the House of Lorraine.

Soon she heard the Duke's voice: 'My dear niece, it is good of you to come to my call . . .'

Good of her, indeed! thought Catherine. For was she not the Queen of France? And who was this Duke to summon a Queen in such a manner to his apartment? But he was *Le Balafré*, a man whom many found irresistible, the embodiment of virile French manhood – handsome, dashing, swaggering, with that rare quality in a Frenchman, a calm, cool manner in an emergency. Oh yes, he had fascinated his charming niece as he had fascinated others.

It was not easy to hear through the tube, for it was only possible to catch a word here and there. This was far from satisfactory, but it had sufficed to teach her much, and, until some better method could be found, she would have to be content with a tube.

'The Bourbons are on their way, Mary.'

Then came Mary's high voice: 'Uncle, what is it you wish Francis to do?'

'They threaten our house . . . these Bourbon Princes. They cannot be allowed to live . . .'

Catherine nodded grimly. 'But they *shall* live, Monsieur le Duc,' she murmured, 'for without our little Bourbons, our Princes of Lorraine would be even more arrogant, more intolerable than they are now.'

Then she heard the words which made her face grow pale with anger.

'Continue, Mary, to watch the Queen Mother. Report all her actions . . . however insignificant they may seem. You have done well so far. But continue . . . Contrive to be at her side as much as possible.'

Catherine's eyes had gone blank, her mouth slack. There was about her that look which people must have noticed when they had likened her to the serpent.

So the Queen of France had been set to spy on the Queen Mother!

There could be no greater indignation than that of the spy who knew herself to be spied upon.

Catherine was in the audience chamber when Antoine and Condé came to pay their respects to the King. The Guises were lounging against the wall, and Mary was with them.

Antoine bowed low over the King's hand; he was too humble. Francis, in accordance with his orders, and aware all the time of the fierce eyes of the Duke and the sneer of the Cardinal, ignored Antoine, though he was very sorry for him and hated to be churlish to the uncle of whom he was fond.

Then came Condé.

If the Guises despised Antoine, they feared Condé. Condé was cool and arrogant, showing by his demeanour that, although his life was in danger, he did not forget that he was a royal Prince.

The newcomers went through the traditional address while all courtiers and attendants stood by, tense and waiting.

Then Catherine spoke to Condé. It was an uncharacteristic and impetuous action, but some hidden emotion which she had not fully examined forced her to take it. They were planning to murder Condé, and she wanted to help him to escape; and this was not merely because she wished to use him against the Guises. It was something more, something inexplicable. Was there just a faint tenderness in her eyes as they rested on the gallant Prince?

Condé, alert, knowing himself to be in acute danger, turned to the Queen Mother. Had he one friend, he wondered, in this nest of vipers?

'Monsieur de Condé,' said Catherine, 'there are matters which I would discuss with you before the investigation as to your guilt in the Amboise plot takes place. Pray step along to my privy chamber now.'

The Guises were alert, regarding the Queen Mother with suspicion.

Condé bowed low, his charming face creased in a smile; his eyes said that his journey, his fears, his dangers were worth while if they brought him an interview with the Queen Mother, whom, while he respected her as a Queen, he admired as a woman.

The Guises made no attempt to stop this strange and sudden action of the Queen Mother, and they allowed her to lead Condé to her apartments; but once they had left, quick action was decided on, and it was in the private apartments of the Queen Mother that Condé was arrested.

Condé looked startled when they took him. He was not sure what the friendliness of the Queen Mother meant, and Catherine felt a thrill of triumph. She had the Prince guessing as to her intentions towards him; and that was a position into which she liked to thrust all those with whom she came into contact.

So Condé was in the dungeons and Antoine was confined to the palace, more or less a prisoner.

How ridiculous she had been, thought Catherine, to contemplate any man with tenderness when the struggle for power was more intense than it had yet been!

❦   ❦   ❦

Condé had been removed from the dungeons of Orléans to those of Amboise and condemned to death.

His sorrowing wife had journeyed to Orléans, and she had begged the Cardinal of Lorraine to let her see her husband; but this request the Cardinal had brusquely refused. He and his brother did not like the wives of Condé and Navarre. They were strong women, both of them; upright, moral women, not the kind to interest the Cardinal. He knew what havoc such women could cause. He dismissed Eléonore with threats.

The woman was indefatigable. She even, by stealth and trickery, achieved an audience with the young King, and it had not taken her long to have that little fool weeping with her and assuring her that he felt her sorrow as keenly as she did. But the Cardinal had arrived in time and saved Francis from any great folly.

It was at Catherine's instigation that Condé was removed to Amboise; and here she allowed herself the pleasure of frequent visits to him.

Those hours were some of the most enjoyable she ever spent; for Condé, though he knew himself to be a condemned man, did not brood on this melancholy fact; he was as gallant and charming as he would have been at a masque, and he enjoyed the sinuous conversation of the Queen Mother; it amused him to speculate as to whether she was friend or foe.

As for Catherine, while she sat back on the stool which had been brought for her, and the faint light from the grating shone on the handsome face of Condé, she told herself that she would not let him die. Somehow she would prevent that. This she conveyed to him at great length; he believed her and a very tender friendship was born between them. She was not an old woman. She had never indulged in excesses and she was well preserved and healthy. The widow of a King might mate with a Prince, and if birth were considered, this Prince was of higher rank than she was. The Prince of Condé and the Queen Mother could rule France together.

They were charming fancies, but, like soap bubbles, they could burst and be nothing at all.

Yet it was amusing to ponder and chatter, to make statements which were full of ambiguities, to arouse hopes in the Prince's heart that she would achieve his freedom and give her hand to him. Eléonore? Catherine wanted to laugh aloud at the thought of the meek Princess. A saint, some said. Well, saints were not for this world. Let them get into the next, where they belonged. It would be easy. René or Cosmo? Hitherto murders had gone unnoticed, but she supposed that if such a person as the Princess Eléonore of Condé died, and later the Queen Mother married the Prince of Condé, there would be a renewal of that tiresome gossip which she remembered from those long-ago days when Dauphin Francis had died after drinking a cup of water brought by his Italian cupbearer. That death had made Catherine Queen of France . . . and people had talked. She did not want such talk, yet. Later, when she was secure, all-powerful, she would snap her fingers at the gossips. But at the moment she must remember that it was necessary to disguise the appearance of craft. She must not forget the wise teaching of Machiavelli.

Meanwhile, it was pleasant to talk to the Prince; such a gallant man was not meant to be a faithful husband; but if he were ever married to the Queen Mother he would have to be a faithful husband, for she would endure no more Dianes. There should be no more watching her husband and his mistress together.

And when she recalled that torture, she had less zest for the game she was playing with Condé.

She left him in his dungeon, puzzled and bewildered, vainly trying to understand the strange friendship offered him by Catherine de' Medici; and in the rooms above his dungeons Catherine sought to mould the other brother to her will.

Antoine was easy to handle. It did not need the full force of her cunning to handle this little popinjay. Vain, vacillating, his earrings gleaming in his ears, he walked beside the Queen Mother, who put her arm through his and called him her brother, while she told him she wished to be his friend.

'My dear brother of Navarre, you must not blame me for what has happened to the unfortunate Condé. Rest assured that I did everything in my power to help you both. It was the King who desired this, and kings – though young – must be obeyed.'

All knew that little King Francis had not a will beyond that of his mother and his wife's uncles, yet Antoine found it agreeable to believe in the friendship of the Queen Mother.

'My lord, I have many burdens on these poor shoulders. I fear that my son will not live long.'

'Madame, this is sad news.'

'Alas! But not unexpected. Have you not noticed how this terrible sickness of his gains on him? My poor Francis, he has not many days left to him. But a tragedy to some could be a blessing to others. You love your brother; and it is this son of mine who has sworn that he shall die for the part he played in the Amboise plot.'

Antoine felt a pulse throbbing in his temple; he wished Jeanne was here at Amboise with him; then he could have asked her to help him unravel the meaning of Catherine's advances. But no! Jeanne was suspicious of Catherine. She would say, 'Draw back. Beware. When the Queen Mother tries to win your approval of some scheme, never give your consent to it, no matter how attractive it may seem.'

Catherine pressed his arm; her face was close to his; he looked into the prominent eyes and tried in vain to read what was behind them.

She went on slowly: 'If Francis died, then my son Charles would be King of France, and he is such a young boy to have greatness thrust upon him. Boys of tender years cannot rule a great country, particularly when that country is split by two religious factions. If Charles came to the throne, my lord, there would be a Regency, and you, as a Prince of the Blood, would be expected to play a big part. You know my little Henry and my Hercule are younger than their brother Charles; and the next in succession would be yourself, and after you, Monsieur de Condé.' She gave a sudden laugh. 'I would not care to be the one to have charge of Charles unless his mother were at hand to help me. He is often sick . . . sick in the mind, I mean . . . and at such times none but his mother can manage him. What a tragedy it would be for my son and those who tried to lead him . . . if any but I, his mother, attempted to do that!'

She had removed her hand from his arm. She stood before him, her arms folded across her black gown. She looked unearthly in the cap which she had favoured since the death of her husband, with its point resting on her forehead. Antoine felt himself shudder. There were strange threats in her eyes, and he remembered the mysterious deaths of some people who had come into contact with her. He thought fleetingly of Dauphin Francis, who had died, some said, to make her way clear to the throne.

'What is your will, Madame?' asked Antoine.

And she answered in a manner which seemed straightforward to him: 'That if there is to be a Regent of France, I shall be that Regent. Oh, do not imagine that I am ignorant of your powers, of your wisdom. Far from it.' She put her face close to his and he heard her laugh again. 'I should give you the post of Lieutenant-General and all edicts would be published in our joint names.'

'I see,' said Antoine slowly.

She put her fingers to her lips, and she made of the gesture something almost obscene, unholy. 'A secret, my dear Antoine; a secret, my brother. The Guises would not be made happy by these plans, for, believe me, they are not anxious to see my son Francis in his grave, whither, I fear, this weakening of his blood is leading him.'

'No, Madame,' said Antoine.

'Well, do you agree?'

Antoine's natural indecision came to his aid. 'It is too important a matter to settle quickly. I will think of this, and rest assured that as soon as I have made my decision I shall lose no time in passing it on to you.'

The white hands – her one real beauty – were laid once more upon his arm.

'My friend, do not make the mistake of delaying too long. I am a poor, lonely widow with little children to look after. If I can find no succour from the House of Bourbon – which House it is most proper that I should ask first – there would be no alternative but for me to beg help from the House of Lorraine. My lord, the heads of the House of Lorraine would go . . . to God alone knows what lengths . . . to take from a Prince of Bourbon that honour of Lieutenant-General which I have just offered you.'

Antoine bowed. He felt as though he had been offered the poison cup in order to speed his decision to bend to her will.

Her face was expressionless, but surely her words meant: 'Make me Regent of France on the death of the King. For yourself accept the Lieutenant-Generalship . . . or death.'

Long after he had left her, Antoine's body was clammy with the sweat of fear.

✦ ✦ ✦

Catherine was in the King's apartment. Francis was lying on his bed exhausted. Mary stood up and addressed the Queen Mother.

'Madame, Francis is very tired. He wishes to sleep.'

Catherine smiled smoothly. 'I shall not tire him. Rest assured that I know more of the nature of my son's indisposition than any, and best know how to treat it. I wish to speak to him, and I will ask your Majesty to leave us alone for a little while.'

'Madame . . .' began Mary.

But Catherine had lifted a white hand. 'Leave us . . . for ten minutes only. You will, I am sure, have much to say to your uncle, the Duke. You see, Francis and I wish to be alone.'

'But Francis said . . .'

Francis was feeling ill, and although he wished to please his wife in everything, he was aware of the domination of his mother.

'If you wish me to go, Francis, I will,' said Mary.

'Certainly he wishes it. It is just a little motherly talk, dear daughter. The Duke was asking for you. I should go along to his apartments.'

Mary hesitated for a moment before she bowed and retired.

'Why, she is a little jailer!' cried Catherine. 'I declare she did not want to leave her captive alone with his own mother!'

'It is because she wishes to be with me, to care for me when she knows I am not well.'

'Of course. Of course. Do not rise, dear son. Lie still. What

I have to say to you can be said while you rest. You are looking ill to-day. I must get a health potion for you. Cosmo will mix you something; although I am beginning to wonder whether René's draughts are not more useful. Excuse me one moment.'

She went to the door and opened it. Mary stood there.

'Ah, my dear daughter,' said Catherine with a smile, 'do not stand about in the corridors. They are draughty and bad for your health. Moreover, Monsieur de Guise awaits you. Do not disappoint him.'

Catherine stood watching the discomfited Mary walk very slowly and with some dignity along the corridor and up the staircase to the Duke's apartments.

Catherine shut the door and went back to the bed.

'You are disturbed, my boy. Something worries you. Tell your mother.'

'Nothing worries me, Mother.'

'They try your strength too much . . . these uncles of your wife. Why, what you need is to go away to the quietest of your castles and there rest or walk in the green fields with your wife beside you. You need rest from state duties; you need rest and play.'

'Oh yes!' said Francis fervently.

'I shall see that this is arranged. Your mother will see that you enjoy such recreation.'

'If only it were possible!'

'I promise you rest, my son.' She laid her cool hands on his hot head. How it was throbbing!

He lifted his eyes to her face as he had done when he was a little boy. '*Maman*, there are pains . . . pains in my head . . . in every part of my body.'

'Francis . . . my little one!'

'And oh, *Maman*, I am so tired. Could I not go away . . . just with Mary . . . and the smallest of trains? Could you not arrange that?'

'I will arrange your departure, my son. But first tell me what it is that worries you. Tell *Maman*. What have these uncles been hatching up for you? You hate them, do you not? It is from them you long to escape.'

'*Maman*, the Duke is a very fine gentleman. There is no greater man in France.'

'Ah yes. *Le Balafré* is a very great man. Ask the people of Paris. He is a hero to them. They do more homage to him than to you, my son.'

'Yes; he is a very great man.'

'And the Cardinal, he is also a very great man. Mary says so, does she not?'

'The Cardinal . . .' Francis began to tremble, and Catherine put her lips to his ear.

'It might be, my son, that I could help you. Tell me what it is that they have been hatching up for you?'

Francis swallowed and pressed his lips together. She had not been mistaken, then. She had heard something of this, but the tube failed her again and again, carrying to her alert ears only scraps of conversation; but Francis's demeanour had betrayed his agitation and that he had no liking for this newest plot of Mary's uncles.

'It is something to do with Antoine de Bourbon, is it not?'

He opened his eyes wide and stared at her. '*Maman*, how could you know? Why . . . none knows.'

'There are many things which you cannot yet understand, my son. One day you may understand. Suffice it for the present that I know.'

'*Maman* . . . some say that you are in league with . . . things beyond this world.'

'My son, many strange things are said of your mother. They are going to kill Antoine. That is it, is it not?'

He nodded.

'And how are you, my poor sick boy, to take a hand in this?'

'It is to happen naturally. He is to threaten me, and I am . . . in a fit of rage . . . to strike at him with my dagger. When I lift it, the Duke and the Cardinal with the Maréchal de Saint-André, who will be close at hand, will rush in and do the rest.'

'And how will you get our poor Antoine to strike you, Francis? He loves you. He would never commit such a dastardly action.'

'I am to abuse him and make him angry, to strike him if necessary. He will think I am alone, but a boy, and weak . . .'

'My poor boy! And you will do this?'

She stroked his tumbled hair from his forehead.

'Madame,' he said. 'Madame, my mother, the Bourbons seek to undermine our house. They wish to take the throne from us.'

'My poor Francis,' she whispered. 'Poor Antoine . . . weak, defenceless, helpless. What a terrible thing it is to wear a crown!'

There was a footstep outside the door.

Catherine whispered: 'Obey your conscience, son, but tell no one that your mother knows of this diabolical plot to murder your kinsman . . . a Prince of the Blood.' Mary had come into the room. '*Au revoir*, dear son. Ah, here is your charming wife. Mary, sit beside him. He misses your bright presence. He has been telling me how much you do for him. You have been so quick. Did you find your uncle, the Duke?'

'He was not in his apartments, Madame.'

'Was he not?' Catherine rose and placed her hands on Mary's shoulders. She kissed first one of her flushed cheeks, then the other. 'Thank you, my dear, for all you have done for our dear little King. May the saints preserve you!'

Mary bowed, rigorously correct, as always with Catherine. Catherine smiled at the lovely bowed head.

Spy! she thought. It shall not be long before you find it impossible to spy on me, for you shall not remain at the court of France.

⚜ ⚜ ⚜

Francis was waiting. The palms of his hands were clammy; he was frightened; he fingered the dagger at his belt; he licked his lips. He knew he was going to fail.

He could not forget that they were watching him, despising him. He knew that his lips would tremble and that he would forget what he had to say to Antoine. He would falter, and he would not sound in the least angry or cuttingly cynical. Why did not Mary's uncles carry out their own diabolical plots?

Henry of Guise might look upon this as an exciting adventure if his father had called upon him to play the part Francis had to play. But Francis hated bloodshed; hated death. He wanted to be happy, playing his lute, reading to Mary, making love. That was living a good life. But they would not let him live a good life.

'Sire, the King of Navarre is without and begs an audience.'

'Send him in,' said Francis, and was appalled by the tremor in his voice.

But he must do as he was bid. He dared do nothing else.

And here was Antoine, with a strange, cold glitter in his eyes as though he knew what was about to happen. He approached, and surely there was caution in his manner, surely his eyes were looking round the room for concealed assassins. He was solemn, lacking his usual gaiety; Francis became obsessed by the idea that Antoine *knew*.

One of Antoine's attendants remained stationed at the door.

Francis said: 'You may go. What I have to say to the King of Navarre is for his ears alone.'

The man went, but Francis believed he waited on the other side of the door, ready to run to his master's assistance.

Antoine stood, calm yet alert. He was ready and waiting, for Catherine had warned him of the plot; she had advised him what to do, and the Queen Mother's advice was worth having. If he escaped alive from this trap, he would be ready to throw in his lot with Catherine, he would accept the Lieutenant-Generalship and agree to her becoming the Regent of France on the death of Francis. She must be his friend, for if all happened as she had warned him it would, and he emerged from this room with his life, he would owe it to her.

Francis began to shout in a nervous voice: 'You coward! You traitor! You with your brother have schemed against us. You would set yourself on the throne. You are traitors, both of you . . . vacillating traitors; and you deserve to die.'

Francis waited for the expected indignation, for the protests; but none came, and Francis never knew how to deal with unexpected situations.

He swallowed and began again. 'You traitor! How dare you . . .?'

But Antoine kept his distance; he did not approach the King, but stood midway between him and the door.

'Why don't you speak?' cried Francis. 'Speak! Speak! Why don't you defend yourself?'

Then Antoine spoke. 'There is nothing I would gainsay if my King declared it to be so.'

'You mean . . . you mean . . .' spluttered Francis. He half turned towards the door which led to the antechamber. They were waiting in there for the signal, for the cry he was to give: 'Help! Help! Assassin!' But how could he give it while Antoine kept so far away? It would so obviously be a trick. The man waiting outside the door – Antoine's man – would come in and see what had happened. He must lure him on. But he did not know how.

'Sire,' said Antoine quietly, 'you are distraught. Have I your leave to retire that you may send for me when you are feeling better?'

'Yes . . . yes . . .' cried Francis. And then: 'No, no. You coward! You traitor . . .'

But Antoine had slipped through the door.

'Come back! Come back!' screamed Francis. 'I . . . I didn't get a chance.'

A door was opened, but it was not the one through which Antoine had departed. It was that of the antechamber.

On one side of the King stood the Duke, the terrible scar standing out on his livid face, and the eye above it watering, as it did when he was angry. On the other side of the King stood the Cardinal.

They both carried daggers, and for the moment Francis thought they were going to use them on him, as they could not on the King of Navarre.

The Duke did not speak, but Francis heard the words which came through the Cardinal's thin lips.

'Behold the most lily-livered King that ever sat upon the throne of France!'

✤ ✤ ✤

Antoine had agreed to accept the Lieutenant-Generalship and that Catherine should be Regent of France. Mary Stuart was a spy who was watching every action of the Queen Mother and reporting it to her uncles. So there seemed nothing to be done but wait for the death of Francis; and the sooner it came, the sooner would that power for which she longed be Catherine's.

The poor little King was growing gradually weaker. Catherine herself prepared many potions for him, but these did not seem to improve his health, but rather to make him more feeble. She herself spent much time in his apartment, braving, as she said to some, the jealousy of her little daughter-in-law. 'But,' she would quickly add, 'I understand that. They are lovers, but when a boy is sick it is his mother who should be at his side, and the King is but a boy.'

One day Francis complained of a pain in his ear. He cried out in agony, and then only his mother's herbs and drugs could soothe him. These sent him into deep sleeps which gave him the appearance of a dead man, but it was better that he should be thus, all agreed, than that he should be conscious and suffer such pain.

Mary, frightened, her pretty face marred with the signs of weeping, cried out: 'This cannot go on. These doctors are fools. I will send for Monsieur Paré. He is the greatest doctor of all.'

Catherine took her daughter-in-law by the shoulders and smiled into her face. 'No doctor can help him. All we can do is ease his pain.'

'We must save him,' said Mary. 'We must do everything possible to save him.'

'I will not have Monsieur Paré here. The man is a Huguenot. There will be those to say we plot in the palace.'

'But something must be done. We cannot let him die.'

'If it be God's will, then, my daughter, we must accept it.'

'*I* will not accept it!' sobbed Mary. 'I will not!'

'You must learn to bear misfortune like a Queen, my daughter. Ah, do not think I cannot understand your sufferings. I know full well how you feel. Did I not suffer so myself? Did I not see the husband *I* loved – as you love Francis – did I not see him die in agony?' She wiped her eyes. 'Yet I loved him as you love Francis, but I would not have had him kept beside me to suffer.'

Frightened, and angry at the same time, Mary flashed out: 'He would not have suffered beside you, Madame, but beside Madame de Valentinois.'

Catherine smiled. 'You are right. You see, I suffered far more than you, my child, for your husband has been a faithful husband. I suffered in so many ways.'

Mary looked with horror into the face of the Queen Mother, realising what, in her anguish, she had said. She dropped on her knees and wept. 'Madame, forgive me. I knew not what I was saying.'

'There,' said Catherine. 'Do not fret. It is your anguish as a wife that makes you forget the bearing of a Queen. You need rest. I shall give you something to drink. It will help you to sleep. Wait. I will get it myself, and then I shall hand you over to your women. Rest . . . and perhaps when you wake, our dearest little Francis will be a little better.'

'You are good to me, Madame,' muttered Mary.

And obediently she drank the warm, sweet liquid. Catherine called Mary's women and said: 'See that she rests. She is overwrought. She suffers deeply.'

Catherine sat by the bed and watched her son in his drugged sleep, and as she sat her thoughts moved onwards.

Little Charles on the throne! A boy of ten! Her fingers were ready now to seize the power for which they had been itching during the humiliating years.

How long would Francis live? Another day? Two days?

His ear was puffed and swollen; he was moaning softly. That meant that her drugs were loosening their hold upon him.

❧ ⚜ ❧

Catherine seemed calm, but inwardly she was furiously angry.

Mary had arranged with her uncles that Ambroise Paré should be brought to the bedside of Francis. The Guises were very ready to give their sanction to this request. Paré was a Huguenot, but he was reckoned to be the greatest surgeon in France since he had performed a clever operation on the Count d'Aumale by extracting a piece of lance which had entered beneath the eye and gone through to the back of the neck. This had happened before Boulogne during the war with the English; the Count had lived and regained full health after the operation, and the cure had seemed something like a miracle. The Catholic Guises were ready to overlook Paré's faith, for it mattered not who saved Francis as long as he was saved.

Paré had examined the King's ear.

Catherine said: 'Monsieur Paré, I have the utmost faith in your judgement. I beg of you to tell me privately what you have found.'

'I will know also,' said Mary imperiously.

137

'My daughter, I am his mother.'

'But I,' said Mary, 'am his wife.'

Catherine shrugged her shoulders and had the room cleared until only she, Mary and Paré remained.

'Mesdames,' said Paré, 'the King's condition is grave. I do not think he can last the night.'

Mary covered her face with her hands and began to sob.

He continued: 'There is a malignant abscess in the ear. It is full of evil humours that are entering his blood and poisoning it.'

'Oh, my son, my little King!' moaned Catherine. 'Only a few hours then, Monsieur? Only a few hours of life left to my little son?'

'Madame, if the abscess were lanced . . .'

Mary stared at him wildly; Catherine's eyes glittered.

She said sharply: 'I will not have my son tortured, Monsieur, with your lancings. I will not hear him scream in pain. He has suffered too much in his short life. I would have him die quietly and in perfect peace.'

'I was about to say, Madame, that if the abscess were lanced . . .'

Mary flung herself at the feet of the surgeon and kissed his hand. 'There is a chance? Monsieur Paré, there is a chance to save him?'

'I cannot assure your Majesty of that. I do not know, but it may be . . .'

'You do not know!' cried Catherine. 'You would subject my son to pain when you do not know!'

'It would be a chance, Madame, but it would need to be done at once. Each passing minute carries the poison deeper into his blood.'

'I will not have him tortured,' said Catherine.

'Monsieur,' cried Mary hysterically, 'you must save him. You are the greatest surgeon in France . . . in the world . . . and you can save him.'

'I will try, Madame.'

'Yes. Now! Lose not a minute . . . since every second is precious.'

'Stay awhile,' said Catherine. She began to pace up and down the apartment. 'This needs thought.'

'There is no time for thought!' cried Mary angrily.

'There must always be time for thought.'

'Madame,' said Paré, 'you remember that our great good King, Francis the First, suffered from a similar abscess. Each year it grew big until it burst and let forth its evils. When it did not open, King Francis died.'

'Open it, I beg of you,' said Mary. 'I am his wife. I am the Queen. I demand it.'

Catherine laid a hand on Paré's arm. 'It will be necessary for me to give my consent. I cannot do this in a hurry, and I cannot put my son's life in danger.'

'Your son's life is in danger now, Madame.'

'I cannot bear to have him hurt. If you but knew how he has suffered already!'

'Heed her not,' begged Mary. 'Go and do it . . . now!'

The surgeon looked from the Queen to the Queen Mother. How calm was Catherine; how distrait Mary! Naturally, he must give his attention to the calm Queen Mother.

He began to talk to her persuasively, explaining the nature of the operation. But would he, Catherine wanted to know, take responsibility for the life of the King? Were he allowed to perform this operation and the King died, there would be many to ask if he had intended he should not recover. He was a Huguenot; the King was a Catholic. Would he perform the operation knowing that, if he failed, mighty reverberations might occur throughout the realm? The war between the Protestants and the Catholics was ever ready to break out anew. An operation by a Huguenot surgeon on a Catholic King! Oh, indeed it needed the deepest consideration.

Catherine walked up and down with the surgeon. Mary had flung herself on to a couch and was sobbing in helpless rage against the Queen Mother.

'Passions run high in these times,' said Catherine. 'You are a Huguenot, Monsieur. Oh, do not hesitate to confess it to me. You have my sympathy. Do you not know that? I would not care that you should run the risk of facing such an accusation.'

'Madame, you are too kind, too considerate. When men are sick, I think of all I can do for them . . . of consequences later.'

'But, Monsieur, you are too useful a subject to be lightly lost. Tell me truthfully. You can see that I am a woman who knows how to bear her troubles. I have had enough, I can assure you, during my life. I can bear a little more. My son is sick, is he not?'

'Very sick, Madame.'

'And death is near.'

'Death is very near.'

'And the chances of success?'

'There is just a chance, Madame, a frail chance. As you remember in the case of your father-in-law . . .'

'Ah yes, tell me about the case of my father-in-law. I would hear it all. I must decide whether I can allow my son to face this ordeal.'

Paré talked; and Catherine, hurrying to ask questions whenever he showed signs of stopping, kept him talking. Outside, the December wind howled through the trees, and on the couch Mary Queen of France and Scotland lay sobbing as if her heart were broken.

At length Catherine said: 'I cannot decide. It is too big a thing for me. Oh, Monsieur, was ever mother presented with such a problem? If my husband were only here! Oh, Monsieur Paré, bear with me. Remember I am a widow left with little children to care for. I want what is best for them, for they are more to me than my life.'

Mary had risen from the couch and rushed past them, and Catherine knew immediately whose help she intended to enlist.

'Monsieur,' said Catherine to Paré, 'return with me to the King's chamber, and pray with me that God and the Virgin may lead us to the right decision.'

They were kneeling by the bed when Mary came in with her uncles.

Catherine stood up. She looked at the face of her son and she knew that the intervention had come too late.

The Duke said: 'Monsieur Paré, you can save the King's life?'

Paré went to the bed and looked at the young King. 'Nothing, my lord Duke, can save the King's life now, for there are only a few minutes of it left to him.'

Mary flung herself on her knees, calling to her husband, to look at her, to smile at her, to live for her. But although Francis turned his head towards her, he did not seem to be aware of her.

The Cardinal was bending over him, and briefly Francis

appeared to recognise the man who had overshadowed and spoilt the last years of his life. In Francis's eyes that terror with which he had been wont to look at the Cardinal showed itself for a second or so; and it might have been that, seeing the boy was about to leave this life, the Cardinal was suddenly conscience-stricken; and perhaps he realised that in Francis's mind were lurking the horrors which he had witnessed during the massacre of Amboise and which had, ostensibly, been perpetrated at his commands.

The Cardinal murmured in an urgent whisper: 'Pray, Sire, and say this: "Lord, pardon my sins and impute not to me, Thy servant, the sins committed by my ministers under my name and authority."'

Francis's lips moved; he tried to follow the lifelong habit of obedience; but it may have been that the Cardinal's words bewildered him as they did those others who heard them, for it was the first and only time in his life that the Cardinal of Lorraine had shown that he possessed a conscience.

Francis's head sank back on the pillow, and there was no sound in the room but the moaning of the wind through the leafless trees and Mary Stuart's heartbroken sobbing.

In his dungeon under the Castle of Amboise, Condé sat disconsolately at table, contemplating his fate. The stale stench of the dungeon nauseated him. He thought tenderly of his wife, their two sons and his dear little daughter. Perhaps he would never see them again. What a fool he had been to ignore the advice of Eléonore and Jeanne and to have made the journey to Orléans, to have walked straight into that trap which had been prepared for himself and his brother!

What was the meaning of the Queen Mother's strange friendship? Was she in love with him? Condé shrugged his shoulders. Many women had been in love with him. He smiled reminiscently. Sometimes he wished – as he knew Antoine did – that he had not been blessed with such a saintly woman for a wife. What gaiety there had been in the days before his marriage; always there had seemed to be the light adventure, romance, some different woman to enchant him with some novelty of passion. And yet, how could they – he and his brother, so alike in looks and character – ever be unfaithful to two such women as Jeanne and Eléonore!

He sighed. This was not the time for such thoughts. What was the motive of the Queen Mother? Could she really have him in mind as her lover-to-be? God forbid! That woman! There were occasions when the very thought of her sent shivers even down this brave man's spine. Her way of entering his cell often startled him; one minute she was not there and the next she would be standing quietly in the shadows, so that he had the impression that she had been standing outside, listening to his conversation with his jailers, and had silently glided in like the snake to which some people had compared her.

Oh, he had been gallant; he had been charming. How could it have been otherwise? She could save him, if anyone could. But for what?

He flicked a cobweb off his fine coat. This dungeon disgusted him. He could smell the sweat of others who had lived here before him; now and then he was aware of the unmistakable odour of blood, for his cell was not very far from those shambles they called the torture-rooms. Death awaited him, and his time was short. The Queen Mother had not visited him recently. Had she turned back once more to his enemies, the Guises? They were more useful friends just now than the Bourbons could be.

His thoughts went to Eléonore. One of his jailers, whom he had managed to charm, had told him that she had been to Orléans when he had been there, in the hope of seeing him. Dear sweet wife, the best of mothers! He knew he was unworthy of her.

He was melancholy to-day because he was bored. He needed continual excitement, and now there was nothing to do but await death. Death! He had never thought of it seriously before, although he had courted it a hundred times. Could this be the end, then, of the Prince of Condé? Was this the finale of that tragi-comedy which his life had been, the end of his grandiose schemes for sitting on the throne of France? He was ambitious, and because he had been born near the throne, it had, all his life, stood there before his mind's eye as a possible acquisition.

What was happening above him? He looked at the dismal ceiling of his cell; he looked at the wall down which the moisture trickled. When it was dark the rats came and looked at him hopefully; yet not far from this spot the noble Loire flowed by in sunshine.

One of his jailers passed by the table. He whispered so that the other jailer could not hear: 'Monsieur, King Francis is dead. Your life is saved!'

Condé stared before him, too full of emotion to speak. He thought of the river and the buds on the trees just beyond his prison; he pictured the tears in his wife's eyes and the smiles on the faces of his children. King Francis was dead, and it was King Francis who had condemned Condé to death. Condé went on thinking of all those things which he had believed he would never see again.

✦  ✦  ✦

In his impetuous way, Antoine wrote openly to his wife of what was happening at court:

My darling, — How our fortunes have changed! How delighted you would be to see the position of your husband here at court! The Queen Mother consults me in all things. Why did you ever think that she was not friendly towards us? She is going to urge that the images of the Virgin be taken from the churches. My dear wife, you can picture the consternation in some quarters. The Spanish Envoy, Monsieur de Chantonnay, is furious. He reports this to his master, and one can imagine with what effects! The Queen Mother will shortly pledge herself to full toleration of the Reformed Faith. Think what this means, my love, and what we have achieved. I know you think I should have insisted on sharing the Regency; but, my dear one, I am Lieutenant-General, and that post, I do assure you, is not a small one. I would rather work *with* the Queen Mother as my friend; and surely, in view of all she has done for our Faith, you cannot deny that she *is* our friend?

I must tell you that my dear brother Louis is well and free. How could the brother of the Lieutenant-General remain a prisoner? No! There was nothing to do but free him. He was noble, as you can guess. The King's death meant that it was possible for the Queen Mother to release him, for she says that it was by the will of King Francis that he was made a prisoner — so naturally, with the King's death, our brother was released. But, as I say, he was proud, and at first he would not accept release until his honour was cleared. Is that not like our brother? He was, however, removed to a better lodging than the dungeon he had been occupying at Amboise and at length the Queen Mother arranged for his name to be cleared. She has a very friendly feeling towards Louis, as he has towards her. Ah, my dear wife, at last we Bourbons are getting that respect which is due to us. You would have wept to see Louis and his family together on the day he joined them. The two boys and the little girl threw themselves at him, and all those about them wept, as did Louis and Eléonore, with those little ones. They are now all happy together, and all goes well with the House of Bourbon.

I was glad to hear you had decided to plant the mulberries along the meadow slope where we used to play *Barres*. Ah! How I remember those games of ours!

I hope my little comrade son is in good health, and also our dearest little daughter. Commend me to them.

I will end my note in assuring you that neither the ladies of the court nor any others can ever have the slightest power over me, unless it be the power to make me hate them.

Your very affectionate and loyal husband,

ANTOINE.

When Jeanne read this letter she felt uneasy. What was happening at court? She knew Antoine too well to believe that he could be making a real success there. How was the Queen Mother using him? How long would this benevolence of hers last towards the new faith?

Moreover, was he not a little too insistent on his fidelity? Should that have been necessary if they were all she believed them to be to each other?

❧ ❧ ❧

Little Charles, the new King, did not know whether to be proud or frightened of the new honour which was his. It was startling to find that wherever he went, men and women smiled on him, bowed low to him, treated him with such ceremony as seemed odd when he was reminded that he was only ten years old.

He had to attend many solemn meetings; there were proclamations and declarations to be signed. It was certainly bewildering, when you were ten years old, to find that you were the King of France.

But he had nothing to fear; his mother told him so; for all he had to do was obey her. That was easy, since he had done that all his life. But there were others round him besides his mother. There was his Uncle Antoine, who was very important now; his mother had explained that Uncle Antoine was now Lieutenant-General of France, which meant that, with her, he was the ruler of France until he, little Charles, was old enough to take on that immense responsibility.

Then there were the great Guises. They were very angry because Francis had died and he was now the King. They seemed subdued at present, but Charles was terrified of their watching eyes which never seemed to leave him.

There were his tutors, Monsieur Birago and the Comte de Retz. They had opened up a strange world to him, and it was very interesting to learn so much about life. They wanted him to be more like his brother Henry. He wished he could be, because his mother would have liked him better if he were more like her favourite; but it was difficult to be what you were not. He tried hard, but those tutors of his liked such strange things; they showed him pictures which embarrassed him; they said it was great fun beating each other on the bare flesh. That seemed very strange to Charles as it was what people did when they were angry, or as a punishment. But the Italian tutors said: 'There is much you have to learn, Sire. This is a different sort of beating.'

It seemed a mad world if such was the accepted behaviour. He did not understand them; sometimes he would grow hysterical listening to them; he would have one of those screaming fits during which he did not know what he was saying; then they would have to soothe him with the special drink his mother prepared for him.

He wondered whether these attacks had become more frequent because of his tutors or because he was getting older; and whether they had something to do with the additional strain of being a King.

But there was one glorious thing which, he realised, being a King may have made possible: marriage with Mary. Dear Mary! She was very unhappy now. She was enduring the traditional forty days' seclusion which all the Queens of France must face when they lost their husbands. She was shut up in her apartments at Fontainebleau, and these apartments were hung with black; Mary herself would be in black from head to foot, but that would only make her look more beautiful than ever; her lovely fair hair and glowing skin would show up more against sombre black than they had against her jewelled wedding gown.

Mary was nineteen and he was only ten. That was a great

difference, but there had been greater differences between the ages of husbands and wives.

He had watched his brother Francis. How he had hated to be King, and yet, because Mary was his wife he had been often happy.

I should be happy too, thought Charles, if I could have Mary for my wife.

He broached the subject to his mother.

'Now that my brother Francis is dead – God rest his soul – and his wife is a widow, she will be wanting a husband and I shall be wanting a wife.'

The expression on his mother's face did not change. She said: 'That is true, my son.'

And he was suddenly happy; he saw that what she had called his unholy thoughts about his brother's wife were forgotten, for indeed Mary was no longer his brother's wife; she was his widow.

'Go on,' said Catherine.

He was afraid to look at her; he was so overwhelmed by the thought of all the happiness that might be his that he could scarcely find words to speak of it.

'I thought, dear *Maman*, that it might be my task to soothe Mary's grief for the loss of Francis,' he said eagerly.

He was quite unaware of the fury behind that quiet smile.

So, after all that his tutors had done for him and to him, thought Catherine, he still hankered after Mary; and once let him make this desire known to Mary's uncles – in any case, they probably knew of it already – and they would do everything they could to arrange the little King's marriage with their niece; and then the position of the Queen Mother would be that intolerable one she had endured for the last two years – relegated to impotence while the Duke and the Cardinal reigned through Mary and Charles as they had through Mary and Francis.

Catherine thought: I would see you dead first. And she said: 'I do not think, my son, that Mary would wish to have her thoughts taken from her grief just yet. It would be unseemly to talk of it while she mourns her husband.'

The boy was eager. 'Yes; I do see that. She must mourn her forty days and nights. But they will not last for ever, and . . .'

Catherine laid a gentle hand on her son's shoulder and smiled into his eyes. 'My son, my dearest little King, you know your happiness is all that I desire.'

He buried his head in her lap as he had done when he was a little boy. 'Oh, *Maman*, you will let this be, then?'

'Everything that can be done shall be done. Do not doubt that, my son. But do not forget your dignity as a King. Charles, my dearest boy, you are watched and there will be many to criticise your actions. You must walk with the utmost caution now that you are a King. You must do everything that dear Papa would have had you do.'

Charles's eyes filled with tears at the mention of Papa, whose death had been the greatest grief of his life.

'Papa,' went on Catherine, 'would not have you think of your own pleasure when your brother is so recently dead.'

'No, *Maman*. I did not . . .'

'Ah, but my darling, you did. Did you not? You must not lie to me, you know.'

'But I love Francis. He and I were . . . the best of friends.'

She lifted a finger. 'And yet you so want Francis's wife that, while he is yet scarcely cold, you can think of taking her! Ah, my son, growing up, loving women, being a King — such matters are fraught with danger. Do not think that because you have become a King that you are no longer in danger. Terrible things have happened to kings. One day I must tell you of these things.'

His hands began to twitch and pull at his jacket – the well-known signs of hysteria.

'But I will not do these things. I will not put myself in danger.'

'You have your mother to look after you. And, Charles, do you realise how fortunate you are to have a mother whose one thought is the welfare of her children?'

'I do realise that.'

'Then you will remember that you are a child yet, and that wise children are guided by their parents. Papa is with me in all I do. I feel him near me . . . guiding me. You would want to do what Papa and I know to be wise?'

'Yes, *Maman.*'

'That is a good boy; that is a wise King. You *must* be wise, for if you are not, terrible things will happen to you. Kings have been murdered ere this.'

'No, *Maman, no*! Do not tell me. I know . . . I know these things are, but do not speak of them or I shall have bad dreams to-night, and when I have these dreams . . .'

She embraced him.

'We will not speak of them, but you know, do you not, my son, my little King, that you must be very wise? You have been guilty – ah, yes, I fear you have been a little guilty – of infidelity to your brother, your *dead* brother. What if Francis did not understand and came down from Heaven to haunt you?'

'He would not come to haunt me. I love Francis. I have always loved him.'

'And you loved his wife . . .'

'Not . . . not . . . only as a sister.'

'And you want to marry your sister?'

'Only after a time when Mary has recovered from her grief and I have recovered from mine.'

'Listen, Charles. Go carefully. Not a word of your intentions towards your sister-in-law to anyone. You would not find many to understand as I understand.'

'No, *Maman*.'

'There might be some who would be angry. Now, remember. Why, if this were to reach Mary's ears . . . or those of her uncles, what would they think?'

Charles smiled a little slyly, she thought. 'Oh, I do not think Monsieur the Duke and Monsieur the Cardinal would mind very much. Mary would be the Queen of France if she married me.

Catherine said firmly: 'Now, take heed of this very carefully. If the people of France knew of your evil thoughts concerning your brother's wife, if they knew of your unholy intentions, they would rise against you. And one day when you walked abroad a man would come up to you and . . . you would think he was a friend until you saw the knife gleaming in his hand. Then you would cry out as you felt the cold steel pierce your heart. The pain, my son, would be terrible. I will tell you . . .'

'No, no! I know. You are right, *Maman*. I must tell no one. I will say nothing.'

Catherine put her fingers to her lips. 'Swear to me, my son, swear you will be wise and say not a word of this to Mary and her uncles. This is our secret. No one else whatsoever must know of it. And if at any time you feel inclined to speak, remember cold steel . . . in your heart . . . just about . . . there. You would swoon with the pain, for it is unbearable, but your swoon would not last and you would wake to your agony . . . dreadful agony . . . and the sight of blood on your clothes, and all about you . . . the stench of blood in your nostrils . . . your *own* blood.'

Charles was shaking with fear. 'I will not tell. I will not tell.' He caught her hand. 'But later . . . later, you will help me? You *must* let me have Mary for my wife.'

She put her lips to his forehead. 'I shall do everything in my power, everything for your good.'

He knelt and kissed her hand; she felt the trembling of his small body, the tears on her hand; and, smiling, she thought: I will see you dead before I put that spy back on the throne.

Jeanne was worried. The news from the court of France was too good to be true.

Was it possible that the Guises could have become so weak that they bowed to the greater power of the Bourbons? What of the Queen Mother? How was it that she had suddenly become the dearest friend of Antoine and Louis de Bourbon? How was it that Coligny and the Huguenot leaders were being received at court? Something strange and unhealthy was afoot.

But she was far from the court of France, and she felt that it was better for herself and her family – and perhaps most of all her husband – if she remained where she was, safe in her own province, at the head of an army which was ready for any emergency that might arise.

She had had long discussions with her religious advisers,

and it seemed to her that now the time had come for her to announce her complete conversion to the Reformed Faith.

There was nothing to stop her, and with a new King on the throne of France this seemed as propitious a time as any.

She was convinced that the Protestant Faith was the true one, and she wanted the whole of France – and Spain – to know that from henceforth she would support this Faith with everything at her disposal.

This might be a test as to whether the court of France was sincere in its new tolerance. If the Catholic Guises were really in decline, she felt she would soon know, and that this public avowal of hers would enable her to know the sooner.

Before departing for Nérac, where she intended to stay well fortified, awaiting fresh news from her husband, she went formally to the Cathedral at Pau and there attended Holy Communion in accordance with the Reformed ritual.

Jeanne of Navarre was now acknowledged as one of the leaders of the Huguenots; she was standing side by side with the brothers Coligny and with her husband, Antoine, King of Navarre, and his brother, Louis de Bourbon, the Prince of Condé.

This caused rejoicing among the Huguenot population throughout France. Jeanne was recognised as a staunch leader, even though her husband was suspect. With Jeanne and the Condés and the Colignys, the Huguenot Party felt itself rich in the right sort of leaders, and it seemed to them that a new liberty was beginning to dawn in the political sky. The Huguenots now began to give themselves airs, to become arrogant in their new importance. There were stones of Huguenot atrocities carried out against Catholics. The wheel seemed to be slowly turning.

There were many rumours circulating about the Queen Mother. It was whispered that she was gradually becoming converted to the Protestant Faith and that she would have the royal children brought up in that religion.

But what had happened to the Guises? Was it possible that the death of one sickly little King and his replacement by another, even younger and almost as sickly, had brought about the eclipse of such men?

Letters began to arrive at Nérac for Jeanne, and when she recognised the hand in which they were written, a smile of contempt curved her lips. She would never believe in the sincerity of Catherine. She had seen that quiet smile given to Diane de Poitiers; she had noted the meek expression which seemed to say: 'Stamp on me. Humiliate me. I like it.' Then she remembered that message which had been sent to Diane when King Henry, Catherine's husband and Diane's lover, lay dying: 'Return all his gifts. Hold nothing back. I have noted every one.' All the cunning in the world was hidden behind that expressionless face, and because it was successfully hidden, it behoved one to be the more wary of it.

How was Antoine faring at court? Of what indiscretions was he guilty? How could he – light-hearted, flippant, weak as water – deal with such a sly one as the Queen Mother?

The letters were affectionate. Catherine called Jeanne her 'dear sister'. Jeanne must come to court, for Catherine longed for a sight of her. 'Come, my good sister, and bring your little ones with you, those darlings whom I think of as my own. I have a plan which I should like to discuss with you. It concerns your Catherine, my little namesake. Do not forget that I am her godmother. I would like to arrange a match between her and my little Henry. Such an alliance, dearest sister, would render our union indissoluble. You could not have a more affectionate and sincere relative than myself . . .'

This, from the craftiest woman in the world! What did it mean? What could it mean?

Those were days of great uneasiness at Nérac.

Little King Charles had a new friend. This man had frequently come to the palace since the death of Francis, and now had apartments there.

Such a man, thought Charles, I should long to be.

To be with Gaspard de Coligny, the Admiral of France, was a pleasure; with this man Charles did not feel frightened or bewildered, and this in itself was a strange thing, for the Admiral was a great man, a far greater man than either of the King's tutors.

They walked together in the grounds of the palace; they rode together. People said: 'The King and the Admiral are the greatest of friends.'

Charles talked to the Admiral of the greatest fear in his life – the fear of horrible torture and death.

'One should not fear death, Sire,' said the Admiral, 'for after death comes the life everlasting, the life of joy if it has been preceded by a good and honest effort here on Earth.'

'But, Admiral, if one has committed sins . . .'

The Admiral smiled. 'The sins of a boy of ten years could not be great ones. I think it would be easy to obtain forgiveness for them.'

'I have asked for the intercession of the saints.'

'There are some of us who appeal to God direct, Sire.'

The New Faith! It was exciting to hear of it; and there was nothing wrong in hearing of it, because his mother, it was said, had given her support to it.

How pleasant it was to listen, not only to the Admiral's talking of the New Faith, but to hear him tell of battles he had fought, and of how, when he was a prisoner in Flanders, he had seen what he called 'The Light'! How happy the King felt after these sessions, how stimulated, for when he was with the Admiral, although they often talked of wars and bloodshed, these things were different when spoken of by this man who doubtless knew more of them than did Charles's tutors and his mother.

To fight for a cause you believed in was a glorious thing. Honour mattered more than life; and should you die most miserably, then there was nothing to fear, for, if you died for the right, you were received into Heaven, and there all was good, all was peace. So said the Admiral.

Charles longed to confide his hopes in this man as well as to tell of his fears, but he remembered his mother's injunctions to speak to no one with regard to his beloved Mary.

The Spanish Envoy, watching this friendship between the King and Coligny, wrote home to his master in great anger. The Guises watched and waited while they prepared to put an end to this state of affairs.

Mary Stuart was in despair. To the French court had come men from Scotland, her native land, to claim their Queen. Scotland was a foreign land to her. She had known that she was the Queen of Scotland, but she accepted the Queen of Scots as her title as she accepted that other, Queen of England; she had never thought of it as anything but a title. And now from Scotland had come men to take her there.

They terrified her, these men from Scotland. They were strangers, foreigners – tall, fair-haired and dour. They were not delighted, as she was, with the court of France; they found it shocking. The beautiful clothes, the dainty manners, the charming gallantry between ladies and courtiers – they thought these things wicked, scandalous. They despised the lilting French tongue and they refused to speak it.

Why did not her uncles thwart the plans of these men? To whom could she turn? A little while ago she had only to express the smallest wish and there were many to hurry to gratify it, to count themselves honoured to serve her who, they all agreed, was the most enchanting of princesses.

And now there was no one to help her. She knew why. The Queen Mother had decided that there was no longer a place for her in France.

Mary had wept until she had no tears; she had shut herself in her apartments, declaring that she was too sick to appear. Someone *must* help her. She had not realised when Francis died – and that had been a great tragedy to her – that this greater tragedy must follow. She had thought that so many people at the French court loved her that they would never let her go.

There had been many noble gentlemen who had worshipped her with their eyes; the poet Ronsard had written his verses especially for her. They would have died for her, so she had believed; and now she was to be sent away from them, to a cold and miserable land where there was no gaiety, no balls, no gallants, no poets – only dour men such as these who had come to France, to disapprove of that gaiety and beauty of hers which the French had loved.

She could not believe that it could happen to her – the Queen of France, the pampered Princess. She thought of her arrival in France, of Francis's father, King Henry, on whose knee she had sat and who had loved her, and whom she had loved; she thought of the attention which had been paid to her by Diane de Poitiers, and in those days Diane had been virtually Queen of France. She thought of the fun of playing with the royal Princes and Princesses, of having lessons with them and showing everyone how much more clever, how much more charming she was than they. For years she had thought of this land as her home, and that she would never leave it. How could anyone be so unkind as to let her go? She had loved Francis – oh, not as madly as he had loved her – but adequately. It had been so pleasant to be adored, and she had been truly sorry when he had died; but she had not thought that his death would mean her banishment from the gay land to which she felt she belonged.

There was, however, a ray of hope. Little Charles loved her. Naturally, one did not think of a little boy, not yet eleven years old, as a husband; yet betrothals – even marriages – were arranged between youthful kings and queens.

There were visitors to her apartments – those who came to condole – but she had a feeling that none of them really cared. Her brothers-in-law Henry and Hercule came; but they were too selfish to care what happened to her. Hercule was too young to appreciate her beauty, and Henry had never cared very much for the beauty of women. Margot made a show of crying with her, but Margot did not care and would be glad to see her go, for the selfish creature looked upon Mary as a rival. Margot knew what it meant to be admired, for although only eight she was a true coquette, and she wanted the admiration of the men who admired Mary to be directed to herself; so while she said that it was very sad and that she had heard that Scotland was not a very pleasant place, she was smoothing her dress and patting her lovely black hair, and thinking: When Mary has gone, *I* shall be the most beautiful Princess at court.

As for Charles, she was not allowed to see him.

Why did not her uncles arrange for her a marriage to the new King of France? They neglected her now, and she saw that the attentions which they had showered upon her such a short while ago had not been for herself, their little niece whom they loved, but for the Queen of France, whom they wished to use in order to rule her husband.

She was sick with fright. There was not only the wretchedness of leaving a land which she had come to regard as her home; there was not only the nostalgia which she would feel, she knew, for the rest of her life if she were sent away; there was the perilous sea voyage to be faced, and her terrifying relative who sat on the throne of England had not guaranteed her a safe passage. She was afraid of the red-headed virgin of England, and well she might be, for some said that she, Mary, had more right to the English crown than the bastard daughter of Anne Boleyn.

While she was occupied with these gloomy thoughts, the door of her apartment opened so silently that she did not hear it, and her mother-in-law must have stood watching her for some seconds before she was aware of her presence.

'Madame!' Mary sprang off her bed and bowed.

Catherine was smiling, and the very way in which she stood there, the very way in which she smiled, told Mary that she herself, so recently the petted Queen of France, was of no importance now in the eyes of the Queen Mother.

'My child, you have spoilt your beauty. So much weeping is not good for you.'

Mary cast down her eyes; she could not meet those under the peaked headdress.

'You must not grieve so for poor Francis,' said Catherine maliciously.

'Madame, I have suffered sadly. First I lost my husband, and now . . . they are threatening to send me away from here.'

'Poor Mary! Poor little Queen! But in your great grief for your dear husband, leaving France will not seem so very important to you. I think that God gives us these blows, one following another, in order that we may become hardened to bear them. To leave France – which I know you love – when Francis was alive would have been a tragedy for you. But now, in the shadow of a greater tragedy, it will seem as nothing, for how much more you must have loved Francis than your adopted country! That is so, is it not, my daughter?'

'I loved Francis dearly, yes. And, Madame, I think that, if I were allowed to stay here, I could still, in time, find some happiness in France.'

'Ah,' said Catherine lightly. 'Then what a pity it is that you must leave us!'

Mary went on her knees and took Catherine's hand. 'Madame, you could let me stay.'

Now that Mary could not see her face, Catherine let her expression change. This was the girl who had called Catherine de' Medici 'Daughter of Merchants', had dared to slight her because she had seen others do it. She had taken her cue from Madame de Poitiers. Well, it had not been possible to take revenge on that woman, but on Mary it would be. Not that Catherine cared greatly for revenge for its own sake. If it had been politic for Mary to have stayed in France, she would have forgotten past slights and humiliations. But now she could settle old scores and help her schemes of power politics at the same time. She could allow herself to get full enjoyment from this little by-play. This girl had dared to spy on her!

'*I* let you stay?' said Catherine. 'You over-estimate my power.'

'No, Madame. You are the Regent of France. All power is yours.'

'My dear, I share it with the King of Navarre; and then there is the Council; and the King, though a boy, has his say in affairs.'

'Then I must speak to the King. He will understand. He will help me.'

'The King is indisposed. I could not have him disturbed. As you know, his health is not of the best.'

'Oh, Madame, have you no pity? You would send me from France . . . from my native land?'

'Nay, child. It is the land of your adoption, as it is mine. I doubt not that when you, a little girl of six, heard that you were to leave your home and sail across the seas to France, there to be brought up among strangers, I doubt not that you shed many tears. Well, this is such another upheaval in your life. In a year's time you will be laughing at these tears. You will be loving the mists of your native wilderness as you love our snows and sunshine.'

'Madame, I shall never love any land but France.'

'And you a Queen of Scotland!'

'And a Queen of France, Madame.'

'And a Queen of England!' said Catherine with a malicious

laugh. 'Your cousin in England is not going to be very pleased with you for using that title!'

'You know it was at the wish of your husband, the King, and of my husband, I did not wish it.'

'Yet you seemed very proud, nevertheless – very proud of it. Poor Mary! They are no longer here to answer to the virago of England for their sins. But I am sure she will forgive you and love you.'

'She will hate me. She has always hated me. She has refused me safe passage to Scotland.'

'Doubtless your charming ways will stand you in good stead with her as they did with me. You know how your pretty ways have endeared you to me. I have no doubt that Elizabeth of England will learn to love you as I have.'

Catherine wanted to laugh aloud. She was well aware of the red-headed Queen's feelings towards this girl, this Queen whose existence was a threat to her hold on the throne of England. How would Elizabeth have reacted had she found the girl spying on *her?* Mary would not have got off so lightly as she had with Catherine. She would have had her head off by now.

'Be of good cheer,' soothed Catherine. 'You will grow to love your little kingdom. You will be able to think of us, and we shall think of you.'

'Madame, the little King Charles loves me. If I go, he will be broken-hearted.'

'Nonsense. He is only a child.'

'He is old for his years. He used to say that if his brother Francis had not had the good fortune to marry me, he would have asked to be allowed to do so.'

'He is a precocious boy, that one. Thinking of marrying at his age!'

'It was his love for me.'

'You will no doubt find many to love you . . . in Scotland. And any alliance, as you will see, between you and King Charles is out of the question. You have been the wife of his brother. It would be . . . immoral. You remember what happened when a King of England married his brother's widow. Ask Queen Elizabeth to remind you. *She* will remember.'

Mary cried out: 'Will you not have pity on me? I beg of you . . . I implore you . . . do not send me away.'

Catherine began to walk up and down the apartment. She let herself think back over the past. She saw this girl as a child at her Latin lesson; she remembered the curl of the haughty lips, the whispered words: 'Daughter of Merchants'. She remembered the girl who had quickly learned how wise it was, how diplomatic, to seek the favour of Diane de Poitiers and to treat with indifference the real Queen of France. She remembered also the anguish she had suffered because of her husband's love affair with the Lady Fleming, who had been this girl's governess. But for the coming of the little Scot she would not have had to endure that.

But away with revenge! What did it matter? It was just something to enjoy like the melons of which she was so fond, or a chine of beef which made her mouth water at the very thought of it, or a goblet of rare wine. Revenge was an ephemeral pleasure. The real reason why Mary must go was because, if she stayed and was married to Charles, those arrogant uncles of hers would be in power again, and that situation – against which Catherine had fought with all the means at her disposal, even unto speeding her son along that road to death – that intolerable situation would be re-created.

Mary was indeed a little fool to expect such favours.

'There, my child. Calm yourself. You will be Queen of Scotland, Queen of your native land. I hear the scenery is charming, and that Monsieur John Knox awaits you. I am sure you will have a very lively time. As for your cousin of England, I am sure you have as little to fear from her as from me. Now bathe your eyes. I will send you a lotion to brighten them.' Catherine turned to the door. 'Rest then, and enjoy your last days in France.'

⚜ ⚜ ⚜

And so, a sorrowing girl rode north to Calais. To her it seemed that the procession was like a funeral cortège. She wept bitterly and continually, and the last she saw of the land she loved was through eyes swollen with grief.

She had had one short interview with the distracted King, who had wept with her and begged her to stay and be his wife in spite of his mother, for he loved her. But even as he had talked she had seen the madness in his eyes, and she knew that she could no more hope for help from him than from Queen Catherine.

She had said farewell to her powerful uncles after begging them to let her stay.

'I will live simply,' she had cried. 'I will be merely the dowager Queen of France. I have my dowry of Poitou and Touraine. I will live in France as a simple lady. I will give up everything . . . only do not send me to that wild country. Let me stay here . . . in my home.'

But the uncles had conferred with one another. They were not yet fully cognizant with what had happened at court. There were too many intrigues being conducted. The Queen Mother had seemed like a harmless snake coiled up in sleep, and now she had raised her head and shown her fangs, and those fangs, they knew, were poisonous. They assured Mary that if they could arrange a marriage for her, this should be done, for she could be sure they had her welfare at heart. Let her look upon this as a visit to Scotland, for it was right that she should occasionally visit the country of which she was Queen. Very soon, they doubted not, she would be returning to France for as brilliant a marriage as her first one.

'King Charles would marry me now,' she said.

'He is too young yet. Later . . . we may arrange it. Trust us, niece.'

'Make it soon, I beg of you. Make it soon.'

They assured her that they would. They kissed her fondly, and then she was forced to set out with that miserable cortège.

Although it was April, the weather was bleak, for spring came late that year.

'The whole countryside mourns with me,' said Mary Queen of Scots. 'Oh, Holy Mother of God, how I dread this voyage! I dread it more than death.'

And as they went aboard the ship which was to carry her across the grey, heaving sea, away from the land where she had known such joy, to the land where she was to know great sorrow, she remembered not the last hours of her husband, the tender smiles of the poet Ronsard, the adoration of young King Charles, but the cold, snake-like stare of the woman who could have spared her this agony of exile. She knew now that the woman to whom she had been so indifferent in the past was not the colourless creature she had imagined her to be. She knew now what people meant when they called her *Madame le Serpent*.

She looked back for as long as she could at the receding

shores of France; and as the cold spray touched her cheek she tried to imagine the unknown future which seemed to her already darkened by the shadow of the grim John Knox and the red-headed Queen of England who might even prevent her reaching Scotland.

She was frightened and miserable; she felt that her heart had been broken at the order of a woman whom she had never known until now.

✢  ✤  ✢

It was not to be expected that the Guises would allow matters to go on as they had since the death of King Francis. They realised that affairs had come to this pass because they, like the rest of those around her, had not been allowed to see how strong was the Queen Mother.

In unexpectedly using the Bourbons – playing them off against the Guises – she had caught them at a disadvantage, but obviously this must be changed, and it was decided that the first blow should be one which struck at Catherine's affections. The whole court knew how she doted on Prince Henry; he was to her, it was said, 'like her right eye'. Well, her son Henry should be taken from her, and she should not have him back until she realised who were the real masters of France.

The Duke's plan was simple, and to put it into effect he called in his own son Henry to help him. More than anyone on Earth the Duke loved this eldest son of his, and all his feelings for the boy were deeply reciprocated. Duke Francis saw in Henry of Guise, at present the Prince of Joinville, all that he himself must have been at his age. Their similarity, not only in appearance but in character, was remarkable, even for father and son. Young Henry of Guise would willingly have died at his father's command, and Duke Francis would as eagerly have given his life for his son. Therefore the Duke knew that it was quite safe to tell young Henry of the plot to kidnap the royal Henry.

'We shall do him no harm. It is just to teach his mother a lesson.' But Henry of Guise would not have cared if they *had* done Prince Henry any harm. He had no real feeling for the boy, whom he despised as weak, effeminate and everything that he and his father were not.

'Tell no one of this . . . not even Margot.'

'As if I would!' cried Henry of Guise; and his father laughed, for it was a joke shared between them that women were well enough for the hours of pleasure, but must not be allowed to interfere with the real business of the day. The most endearing thing about his father, as far as Henry of Guise was concerned, was this assumption that he was already a man.

'As if you would!' echoed the Duke, putting an arm about the boy. 'Now listen. You will be playing with Prince Henry. You must see to that, and that the two of you are alone. I and the Duke of Nemours will approach and ask him to come away with us for a little jaunt. The Duke of Nemours will make the suggestion while I am talking of this jaunt to you . . . and it will be as though I do not care whether he comes or not. But you will care, my son. You will talk to him of Lorraine and what good fun it would be if he would come with us.'

'I will do it, Father. When shall we go?'

'At night.'

'But the Prince's apartments are guarded.'

'Never worry your head about that. We'll get him through the window, and a coach will be waiting.'

Henry of Guise laughed with delight. He stood up very

straight and tried to assume the bearing of his father; he greatly regretted that he had not a scar of battle beneath his eye. Sometimes he wondered whether he would make such a scar so that men would say, 'Is that *Le Balafré Père* or *Le Balafré Fils?*'

He was determined to play his part correctly. He was absent-minded with Margot. She reproached him and tried to make him caress her, but Henry of Guise became aloof as he imagined his father would be before some great battle; this was no time for dalliance with women.

At the appointed time he was at his post with Prince Henry, and he so arranged it that they were alone.

He flashed a secret smile at his father, Duke Francis, as he approached with his friend and ally, the Duke of Nemours, just as he had said he would.

Nemours talked to the little Prince while Duke Francis turned away and engaged his son in conversation.

'Good day to you, my lord,' said Nemours.

'Good day,' said Prince Henry. He touched his ears to make sure his earrings were in place.

'And what religion is yours, my Prince? Are you Papist or Huguenot?'

The crafty Medici eyes were immediately alert. He was no fool, this Prince Henry, and he knew very well that all the trouble in the land had arisen through the conflict of religion. At the mention of the subject he was on guard.

He said haughtily: 'I am of my mother's religion.'

'That is well,' said Nemours. 'It shows you are a dutiful son.'

Now it was the turn of little Henry of Guise. He ran to the Prince and said: 'My father is taking me on a visit to our château of Lorraine. Please come with us.'

Prince Henry's Italian eyes went from the Dukes to the boy.

'I do not think,' he said, 'that my mother would wish me to desert my brother, the King.'

Henry of Guise persisted. 'It will be fun in Lorraine. There you will have the first place. Here you are merely the brother of the King. My mother has some beautiful jewels. I doubt not that you would enjoy seeing her sapphires.'

'What sort of sapphires?' asked Prince Henry with interest.

'All sorts. And she has beautiful cloths from Italy. We turn out her trunks and dress up in them. You should come with us.'

Prince Henry's eyes began to shine, for there was nothing he enjoyed so much as dressing up. He wanted to hear more about the cloths and the jewels of the Duchess of Guise.

'Come and see for yourself,' said Henry of Guise slyly.

'Very well,' said the Prince. 'I will come for a short visit.'

Francis of Guise pressed his son's shoulder gently and approvingly; and the two boys ran off whispering together.

The Prince asked suspiciously, when they were out of earshot of the men: 'Why do we go without the consent of my mother?'

'Oh . . . it is but a short visit, and it will be over so soon. There is no need to trouble her.'

'I do not think I should go without my mother's consent.'

Henry of Guise was alarmed, and, seeking to make the adventure more exciting, he whispered: 'It will be the greatest fun. We are going to climb through our windows, and there will be a coach waiting to take us to Lorraine.'

The Prince was thoughtful; he was not so fond of rough, boyish games as his friend was. Henry of Guise was only a young boy; it did not occur to him that such a manner of going could possibly be a deterrent. Prince Henry smelt his perfumed kerchief and studied the rings on his hands. The smile about his mouth was very sly, and he sought an early opportunity of going to his mother.

She embraced him tenderly; there was never any ceremony with her beloved son as there was with the others.

'Mother,' he said, the crafty Medici look creeping into his eyes. 'I am to leave my apartment by the window, go into a waiting coach and be driven off to see the fine cloths and jewels of the Duchess of Guise.'

'*What* is this, my darling?'

'That is what they plan for me.'

'Who, my dearest? What do you mean?'

'Henry told me about it. His father was there, and so was Monsieur de Nemours. They asked what my religion was — Papist or Huguenot — and I told them my religion was the same as yours. They said I should pay them a visit, and we should go through the window and a coach would be waiting to take us to Lorraine. I thought that was a strange way for a Prince to travel.'

Catherine embraced him fiercely. 'Oh, my darling. My wise and clever boy. How right you were to come straight to your mother!'

From then on she could not bear him to go out of her sight. They had terrified her. They had thought to kidnap her dearest boy. What dangerous men these were! And what a perilous position she had put herself in by siding openly with the Bourbons!

When, a few days later, she found herself face to face with Francis of Guise, she realised afresh the strength of this man. He was angry with her because his plot to kidnap the Prince had failed; he distrusted her, seeing her as a different person from the meek woman he had suspected her to be.

He was blunt; the eye above the scar watered freely; the strong, cruel mouth was hard and firm.

'Madame,' he said, 'I and mine have allowed you to become the Regent of France that you might defend the faith. If this is not your intention, then there are others – Princes of the Blood Royal, men of wisdom – who are more fitted to take over the responsibility which is now yours.'

With an impetuosity which was foreign to her, she said: 'Would you, Monsieur de Guise, remain true to me if I and my son changed our faith?'

The Duke answered with frankness: 'No, Madame. I should not.'

'Then you are lacking in loyalty to the Crown, Monsieur.'

'As long as you and the Crown keep to the faith of your forefathers and mine, I will give my life in your cause.'

She did not doubt for a moment that he spoke the truth. She saw the fanatical gleam in his eyes, and during the last few years she had become familiar with that fanaticism. So the mighty Duke, the great disciplinarian, the soldier of France, was as fanatically religious as those men whom she had seen tortured for their religion or burned at the stake.

It was a startling discovery, but it was not an unpleasant one. She considered these fanatics, these people who served a cause. They were weak compared with such as herself whose cause was expediency, who had no religion but that of keeping power. She could change her course so easily, using the winds of fortune; *they* must plough on, whether the wind was with them or against them.

She could see more clearly the way she must take with this man. She feared him. He was the head of the great Catholic Party, and he had a strength and a power which was lacking in the Bourbons. She had been foolish to show too much favour to Antoine of Navarre and Louis of Bourbon, the Prince of Condé, to Coligny and his brothers.

She said softly: 'Monsieur de Guise, rest assured that there is only one faith for me, and that is the faith of your forefathers and mine. How could it be otherwise? Why should I change with these . . . fanatics?'

The Duke spoke coldly: 'It would seem, Madame, that this is what you have done. I hear that you even allow *prêches* to be conducted in the palace. You surround yourself with heretics. It was therefore thought advisable to remove the little Prince Henry from such evil influences.'

'Ah, *Monsieur le Duc*, how you misunderstand me! I am a good Catholic. It grieves me to see this land rent in twain by such disturbances, and all in the name of God. I thought to show leniency to these people. I thought to lead them back to truth by gentleness.'

'They do not understand gentleness, Madame. They grow arrogant under your protection. It was not for this that we allowed you to be Regent of France.'

She came close to him and laid a hand on his arm; she lifted her eyes to his and smiled craftily.

'My object, my lord Duke, was to reform these Princes of Bourbon, to lead them back to the Catholic Faith.'

He was scornful, and he terrified her because he did not attempt to hide his scorn. He was then still very sure of the power his family wielded.

'Is that then the meaning of this great friendship you show for them, Madame? Is that why you are seen so often with the King of Navarre . . . and even more often with his brother?'

Catherine felt a surge of anger as she realised the

significance of his remarks regarding herself and Condé. But the anger was for herself as much as for Francis of Guise. She had been foolish to let this romantic feeling for Condé get the better of her common sense.

But when she spoke her voice was quiet and controlled. 'You smile, Monsieur, but that is because you have not heard my plan. I have a very good plan which I firmly believe will make these two princelings forget the more serious matters of wars and religion.'

'How so, Madame?'

'Think of the King of Navarre!' She made a disgusted noise with her lips. 'Antoine of Navarre, the little popinjay, the vainest man in France! Why is he such a good Huguenot, do you think? It is on account of Madame Jeanne, that wife of his.'

'He was a Huguenot before she was.'

'He could never stay of the same opinion for more than a day or two at a time. The turncoat! That is the man we have to deal with . . . or it would be, but for his wife.' Catherine let out her spurt of coarse laughter. 'Madame Jeanne d'Albret, Queen of Navarre! She has been a Huguenot in secret for years. Oh yes, I know she has just made a public avowal of the fact, but for years she has followed the faith in secret. As for Antoine, he is a Huguenot because his wife says he must be. He is in leading strings. If we would bend Antoine to our will, we must strike at him through his wife.'

'What plan have you for attacking the Queen of Navarre?'

'Oh, I do not mean that we should take an army and march south. That is not my way, Monsieur. That would avail us little. We should have civil war in France, with the Huguenots fighting to free their heroine. No, we strike through Antoine, but we strike at his wife. Did you see them at the wedding of

Francis and Mary? Do you remember the silver galleons and how Antoine selected his wife for his companion? "What a devoted husband!" said everyone. My plan, Monsieur, is to make Antoine a slightly less devoted husband.'

'You think that possible? Jeanne is as strong as granite.'

'And Antoine is as weak as water. That is why we strike through him. Great plans are in my head; I am a poor, weak woman who loathes violence. My plans are quiet plans, but I think they will work as efficiently as your massacres. We will separate Antoine from his wife. It is, after all, unnatural for the man to be such a devoted husband. He was born a philanderer. We will put temptation in his way. We will so anger that saintly wife of his that she will be infuriated with him. The adored wife, the publicly chosen of her husband, will be neglected, forced to see her husband with a mistress whom he adores. And then, where will the leader of the Huguenots be? You know these Huguenots, Monsieur. They are more prim than we Catholics. They do not love adulterers. His mistress will lead him as his wife now leads him; I plan that she shall lead him back to the Catholic Faith.'

Francis of Guise was excited. It was a good plan, and it was not an impossible plan. If the Queen Mother had had this in mind right from the first, he had misjudged her. She was as good a Catholic as he was. She was as much his ally as she had been when Francis was alive.

He looked at her and, smiling maliciously, said: 'And the Prince of Condé?'

She repeated slowly: 'The Prince of Condé.' And she could not help it if her mind went back to those visits to his cell, those conversations that had held in them a hint of tenderness. She shook off such thoughts and looked unflinchingly into the face

of *Le Balafré*. Then she said: 'I had the same sort of plan for
Condé as for his brother. He also, as you know, has a strong
and saintly wife, a woman whom I suspect of leading her
husband.'

'And for him also, Madame, you would suggest a mistress, a
love that will lead him back to the Catholic Faith?'

'That is what I suggest.'

'You think it possible in his case?'

'Monsieur, I do think it possible.'

'And' – the Duke's eyes openly mocked her now – 'and
which lady would you suggest for the seduction of the Prince
of Condé?'

She was ready for him. 'There is one in my *Escadron Volant*.
I do not know whether you have noticed her: Isabelle de
Limeuil. She is a very beautiful woman and, I believe,
irresistible to most.'

'And so, you have selected her as Condé's temptress?'

'I have, Monsieur.'

'And for Antoine?'

'Mademoiselle du Rouet.'

The Duke nodded. 'You have chosen two very beautiful
women, Madame, and very light ones.'

'Those are the qualifications necessary for this particular
task, great beauty and lightness. One would not choose such as
the Princess Eléonore and Queen Jeanne of Navarre for such
tasks, I do assure you.'

The Duke laughed with her, his good humour quite
restored.

'And what of Coligny?' he asked at length. 'That man is
more dangerous than any.'

'He is indeed, for no light and beautiful woman could

seduce him from what he believes to be his duty. When the time comes, we shall have to think of a way of subduing Coligny.'

The Duke came nearer to her, and she saw in his eyes that he was remembering rumours he had heard concerning her. She knew that his thoughts had flitted to the Dauphin Francis, who had died after his Italian cupbearer had brought him water. He was remembering what he had heard of her poison closet at Blois, and waiting to hear what she planned for Coligny.

'When the time comes,' she said, 'we shall know.'

He took her hand and kissed it, reminding himself that it was as well to have the Italian woman working on his side.

As Catherine looked at the proud head bent over her hand she reflected that it was a pity one could not remove from this life the people who made it so difficult; and she was not thinking so much of Coligny as of the Duke of Guise.

❧ ❧ ❧

The ladies of the *Escadron Volant* lounged about their apartment talking together. They had just returned from the hunt, and it had been a strenuous day. The Queen Mother, growing stout as she was, had lost none of her energies.

Mademoiselle Louise de la Limaudière, the daughter of the Seigneur de l'Isle Rouet, was smiling secretly to herself. She was a very lovely woman, and with her friend and confidante, Isabelle de Limeuil, shared the distinction of being the most beautiful in this group of women who were selected not only for the quickness of their wits and their skill on a horse, but for their beauty.

The Queen Mother had talked to Louise this afternoon

when they were in the forest. She had told her what was expected of her. Nothing less than that she should, at the earliest possible moment, become the mistress of Antoine de Bourbon, the King of Navarre.

Louise smiled. Antoine was a charming man. She was not at all surprised by the commission. Every woman in the *Escadron* knew that she belonged to the Queen Mother, body and soul, much as every woman in the *Petite Bande* of King Francis the First had belonged to him. Sooner or later must come the summons to go here or there, to make oneself irresistible to this minister or that, to learn his secrets and pass them on to the Queen Mother. There was danger as well as excitement in the *Escadron;* each member knew that even though she longed to escape, once she was initiated there was no way out. It was, Isabelle had said, like selling one's soul to the Devil. When she had said that her eyes had shone and Louise understood perfectly what she meant. Life under such a mistress – of whom they were permitted a more intimate glimpse than others enjoyed – had its excitements, its pleasures, its intellectual side, its morbid enchantment. All knew that to attempt to escape from the thraldom of the Queen Mother, to pass on her secrets, could end in one way only. They had seen it happen. There had been one girl who had wished to leave the *Escadron*, who had decided to reform and had begged leave to go into a nunnery. 'By all means,' said the Queen Mother. 'If you wish to leave our company, you must go.' And go she did, though she never reached the safety of a nunnery. She had fallen into a decline, her skin had shrivelled, her eyes had sunk into her head and her teeth had broken like glass.

Louise shuddered, yet with a thrill of excitement. *She* had no wish to go into a nunnery; the life of the *Escadron* delighted her.

She was sensual in the extreme. She enjoyed the caress of satin against her skin and anointing her body with the scents which Catherine graciously allowed her own *parfumeurs* to supply to the ladies of the Squadron. There was, Louise knew, some special aphrodisiac quality in those perfumes. She was quick-witted, as all the women were required to be; she delighted in the erotic literature which was so fashionable at the court; she herself composed verses and sang charmingly. Catherine's *Escadron* was very similar to Francis's *Petite Bande*; Catherine desired her women to be clever as well as beautiful, just as Francis had.

Smiling at the ornate ceiling of the apartment, at the naked cupids depicted there with their adorably fat bodies, she thought of Antoine. She had often noticed him with pleasure, and she imagined that he had not been altogether oblivious of her; his gaze had at times rested on her with something like regret, and she guessed that in the background of his mind were memories of his stern wife, Jeanne of Navarre.

Jeanne of Navarre! That woman with the cold, stern face, the new leader of the Huguenots! They were really rather stupid, these stern women who thought themselves so wise. They were so energetic, concerning themselves with *prêches* and edicts; cleverer women achieved their desires by far simpler methods.

Isabelle came to her bed and lay down beside her.

She whispered so that none of the others might hear: 'The Queen Mother spoke to you this afternoon?'

Louise nodded.

'To me also,' said Isabelle.

'And who is your quarry?'

'You'll never guess.'

'I'll swear he is not so exalted as mine.'

'Do not be too sure of that. Mine is a Prince.'

'Mine is a King.'

'A King!'

'Antoine . . . King of Navarre.'

Isabelle began to laugh.

'It is true,' she said, 'that you have a King and I have only a Prince, but my man is the more important.'

'How could that be? Next to the Queen Mother, my Antoine is the most important personage of the court.'

'Only on the surface, my dear. I assure you he is not so important as his brother.'

'So yours is Condé?'

'You are envious.'

Louise laughed, and sang quietly so that only Isabelle could hear:

> Le petit homme tant joli
> Qui toujours chante, toujours rit
> Et toujours baise sa mignonne —
> Dieu garde de mal le petit homme.

'Ah, my friend,' said Isabelle, 'I see that you are jealous.'

'Who would not be? But you will never get him.'

'Will I not!'

'He is devoted to his wife.'

'So is Antoine.'

'Do you think I have anything to fear from that prim Huguenot?'

'But you seem to think that other prim Huguenot, the sainted Eléonore, will keep me from my pretty little man.'

'There is a difference. You know it, my dear. Antoine is the easier.'

'Perhaps, my darling,' said Isabelle, 'that is why the Queen Mother gave him to you. She reserved the more difficult task, you see, for me.'

'Oh, it is not so difficult. It will just need a little more time, perhaps.'

'How fortunate we are! Two such charming men. And of what rank! Good times lie ahead of us.'

'I'm all impatience,' said Louise, springing off the bed. 'I'll wager you I'll get my man before you do.'

'Oh, I think that you may do that, since mine is the more difficult task. Good luck with Antoine.'

'The best of good fortune with Louis. I wonder who will make the better lover.'

Isabelle snapped her fingers. 'There will be little to choose. They have both had much experience.'

'You must remember that they have been in the hands of the saint and the leader for many years. Powers wane and happy tricks are forgotten.'

'We shall have to remind them of better days, my darling.'

They laughed so much that the others looked their way. No questions were asked. All the ladies knew that these two had been singled out for some special task by the Queen Mother that day, and at such times questions were never asked.

❧ ❧ ❧

It was warm in the *salle du bal*. Antoine sat back feigning to watch the dancers, but he was too much aware of the woman at his side to notice them.

It seemed to him that rarely had he seen such a beautiful

woman; she was seductive too; the low-necked gown showed her bare breasts, the nipples delicately reddened to match her lips. The perfume which came from her inflamed his senses; but more enchanting than her sensuous beauty was the homage, the adoration in her eyes.

She was saying: 'My lord King, this is the greatest night of my life. To sit near you, to listen to your talk, that gives me great joy. Often have I watched you from a distance, not daring to approach one of such high rank; and when this night you asked me to partner you in the dance, I thought I should die of delight.'

'My dear lady, you must not continue to worship from afar. You must perform that duty at closer quarters.'

She drew nearer to him and laid her hand on his arm. 'I am bold,' she said. 'There is something within me that makes me bold, something which I cannot control. I beg of you, my lord, do not ask me to come closer, for if I did my feelings might get the better of what is fitting in the presence of one so exalted.'

'It is right, I am sure, that you should come closer,' said Antoine. 'I have no objection to being worshipped at very close quarters by one so fair as you are, my dear Mademoiselle de la Limaudière.'

She smiled wonderingly. 'See how my hands tremble at the touch of Your Majesty.'

'Why so, Mademoiselle Louise?'

'I will be bold and shameless. It is because for a long time I have seen no one at this court but yourself.'

Antoine gripped her hand. 'You are very fair, Louise. I was thinking that of all the beautiful women gathered here in this court, there is not one to compare with you.'

'Such words delight me . . . coming from you, Sire.'

'It would be an easy matter,' said Antoine, 'for me to fall in love with you.'

She lifted his hand and kissed it shyly.

'Ah, if that were so, how happy I should be! There is nothing I would not do for you, my dearest lord.'

'Then . . .' he said; and she leaned forward breathlessly. He frowned, and seizing his goblet drank off his wine. 'Louise,' he went on, 'how enchanted I should be if I might become your lover!'

'My lord, I would give twenty years of my life to be yours.'

She saw the lust in his eyes, the pulse at his temple. She marvelled at the power of Jeanne of Navarre, who had kept such a man faithful to her for so long. She felt a determination to defeat that woman's power over him. She wished not only to do what was necessary and obey the wishes of her exacting mistress, the Queen Mother, but to follow her own desire.

'My lord,' she said breathlessly, 'when?'

Antoine was disturbed. Such adventures as this had been numerous before his marriage, but even as the temptation was here before him, he remembered his wife. He loved Jeanne. She was not, it was true, beautiful as this woman was beautiful. Love between himself and Jeanne had been a serious dedication, the obligation to produce children, and make sure that they could provide heirs to the throne of Navarre. Acts of love performed for such a set purpose held less of pleasure, less of passion than the old erotic excitements which he had known so well. The woman tempting him was very beautiful; but he must think of Jeanne, of the domestic atmosphere of that Huguenot household which she had made for him; he thought of her strength, her rectitude, her decided views. There was no one on Earth like Jeanne, so good, so worthy, so capable of making him really happy in a peaceful home.

He turned his eyes from the woman at his side.

'Mademoiselle,' he said, 'you are very beautiful; you are very desirable. I will not deny that you tempt me. But, I am not a free man. I am happily married to the best of wives, and it is my wish to remain completely faithful to her.'

Louise said with shame in her voice: 'My lord King, I beg of you, forgive me. I have been shameless and I have allowed my feelings to override my respect for Your Majesty. I beg of you to tell me you forgive me.'

'It is I who should ask forgiveness,' said Antoine. '*You* have honoured *me*. Mademoiselle Louise, believe me, it would be the simplest thing in the world for me to love you. Indeed I do already.'

She drew nearer. 'My lord . . .'

'You must know,' he said gently, 'that I am a faithful husband.'

'I would be grateful for one kiss, for one embrace.'

He sighed. 'You are young. You must not talk thus to a man who is married and so much older than yourself.'

'I could talk to only one man thus,' she said with quiet dignity.

He stood up and they danced together; and after a while they left the dancers and went out into the grounds. It was a warm night, and the exotic shrubs which King Francis had, at great expense, brought to adorn the palace gardens filled the air with their scent.

Antoine put his arms about Louise and kissed her. He let his hand rest on her warm bare breast.

'Enchanting!' he whispered. 'Intoxicating! But, my dear, it

must not be. I am a faithful man. A man who owes much to his wife. Why, but for her, I should not be a King.'

'It is she, I am sure, who owes much to you,' answered Louise. 'What is rank? What is position? What is anything compared with love? She has your love, and I would die to possess it.'

He kissed her again, and permitted himself a little freedom with her person. Not very much, he was saying to himself. I must be faithful to Jeanne. What an extraordinary thing that I should be faithful for so long! What an extraordinary man I am! Jeanne is faithful to me, but she is never tempted. Jeanne is cold and I am warm. But she loses her temper with me. She has said some cruel things. She has criticised my actions. Even now, the letters she writes are often full of reproaches. She thinks that I am being imposed upon; she sees me as the tool of the Queen Mother and the Guises. She thinks I have no sense. Whereas this woman – this delightful and passionate woman, this seductive Louise – thinks that every thing I say and do is wonderful. That is how a wife should feel towards a husband; that is the right attitude towards a King.

'Let us walk,' he said; and he put his arm about her as they walked.

'Louise,' he said, 'you are delightful, and my senses long for you. Ah, duty! What a hard taskmaster, my dear! And a man in my position is never free from duty. Always he must think of it. Always he must eschew his pleasure, subdue his desires.'

She turned and pressed herself against him. 'I would rather die than interfere with your duty, Sire.'

He kissed her fervently. Why not? he was thinking. Just once. Just for one night.

But he could not dismiss the memory of Jeanne. If she heard

of any lapse from virtue, she would never forgive him, and it would be the end of their happy life. He must remember that he and his brother, with Jeanne, were putting themselves at the head of the Huguenots. An intrigue with a court beauty would, by their followers, be looked upon with extreme disfavour. Still, who need know? Nonsense! Everybody would know. He was watched wherever he went. No doubt he was being watched now. Their kisses would have been seen. Well, he might as well carry this affair to its natural conclusion, for even if he did not there would be many to say that he had done so.

But he could not bear the thought of Jeanne's steadfast eyes looking at him in horror. Jeanne, for all her wisdom, was a very simple woman. She thought fidelity between husband and wife was natural, not, as it assuredly was, the most unnatural thing on Earth!

And I am a natural man, thought Antoine angrily, kissing Louise again.

Then he told her about his home life and why he could not enter into a love affair. 'My wife is a very wise woman, a great leader and a great Queen . . .'

'Yet she does not understand your needs,' said Louise.

'No. In a way . . . you are right.'

Then he was telling her, not of his happiness with Jeanne, but of their quarrels, their misunderstandings.

'I do not understand how she can bear to be away from you,' said Louise.

'She is a Queen, with Navarre to rule. I must be here to work with the Queen Mother. For people of our rank there is little domestic life.'

'Were I your Queen I would let nothing stand in the way of being with you.'

There were more embraces. Why not? thought Antoine, hesitating; first saying Yes; then saying No.

But when he retired that night, Jeanne's was the victory.

'My darling,' were his parting words to Louise, 'it would be better if we did not see each other. The temptation would be too great, and I must be a faithful man.'

'I would do anything in the world to please you,' said Louise.

And that night, when the palace was quiet, she slipped along to the apartments of the King of Navarre.

His gentleman raised his eyebrows at the sight of her, but she smiled and gave him a nod of understanding.

'I carry no dagger,' she said, 'to kill the King. You may search me.

She was naked beneath her robe.

'I come,' she continued, 'at the invitation of the King of Navarre. Do not attempt to stop me or you will have to answer to him.'

So Louise went through to Antoine's bedchamber. She stood by the bed.

'My King,' she whispered.

'Louise!'

'I could not stay away,' she said.

This is no fault of mine, the King of Navarre told himself.

✤ ✤ ✤

The next day Antoine was remorseful. He had been unfaithful. He was in love. Louise de la Limaudière was the most enchanting creature he had ever known. But he must do without her. He must eschew such love.

He wrote a long letter to Jeanne.

'My dearest wife, — I sigh because you are not here with me. I think of you all the time. Never forget that I am your loyal and affectionate husband. Other ladies have no power to move me. To me they seem ugly. I am bored when I do not see you . . . oh, much more than you can ever know. You must have pity on me . . . for my nights are sleepless and I have grown a little thinner. I shall not revive until I see you . . .'

He wrote on fervently and passionately, assuring himself that he did not *wish* to be an unfaithful husband.

Louise had possession of him now, and the entire court knew it. He disregarded the sly glances and whispers, for he could not do without her. She was so passionate, so loving, and she adored him so blindly; she saw his virtues where his wife saw his faults.

She said to him one day: 'Your brother is a little shocked by our love, my darling.'

'Ah, Louis has a nobler character than I.'

'That I will not believe.'

'Ah, yes. Though in some ways he is another such as myself, though he too needs a woman to love him, see how sternly he sets his face against such solace!'

'Does he?'

'Yes. He sees himself as a leader. He never forgets that he is the Prince of Condé — a man to whom many look as their leader.'

'I doubt that he is as virtuous as you seem to think. I will show you something. Let us give a merry party . . . a small party. Let us give it in your apartments, and let there be none but you and I, a friend of mine and your brother. Shall I tell you a secret? My friend loves the Prince. She is pining for love of him. She feels towards him as I feel towards you. Would you not give him a chance to be happy?'

'No!' cried Antoine. 'He would be tempted, for he is a man who once found beauty irresistible. Who is the lady?'

'You have seen her, my lord. Oh, I beg of you, do not look too closely at her or I shall suffer a torment of jealousy. She rides with the Queen Mother and the rest of the ladies. Her name is Isabelle de Limeuil.'

'A lovely girl.' He kissed Louise. 'Nay, fear not. There is none for me but you, my sweet Louise.'

'You love your brother, do you not?'

'He is a great man, and I honour him. He has my respect as well as my love.'

'Then . . . give him a little fun. There could be no harm in asking him to the party.'

So they planned the party. It would be amusing, thought Antoine, to see how Louis reacted to the proffered charms of Isabelle de Limeuil; and if he too became involved in a love affair he would not be able to look down his handsome nose at his brother Antoine.

It was a successful party; there was plenty of laughter and good wine.

Isabelle had never, thought Louise, looked quite so attractive. Condé seemed to think so too. He was a passionate man and he had been celibate too long; the separation from his saintly Eléonore had made him a ready victim to temptation. He guessed that Isabelle was a spy of the Queen Mother, for he knew her to be a member of the *Escadron Volant*, and he was fully aware of the purposes to which the Queen Mother put these ladies. But the beauty of Isabelle was intoxicating; and the next day he was in no position to reprove his brother.

❖ ❖ ❖

The whole court was now laughing at the affairs of the Bourbon brothers. Catherine's feelings were a little mixed. She was triumphant at Antoine's moral downfall, delighted for more reasons than one. This was the first step in her scheme. What was Madame Jeanne going to say when the news reached her? Would she remember how smug she had been that night when her husband had carried her off in a Spanish galleon that he might make love to her, his wife? Was she going to be quite so haughty now? It would be amusing to observe the reactions of Jeanne. That, however, was a minor issue. The main point was the effect on the Huguenots of what Louise had achieved.

And the other pair? Catherine frowned. Condé in love . . . and with that harlot! What an enchanting lover he must be! She could not help it if she remembered those conversations which had taken place in a dungeon under the château of Amboise. What a fool she was! She was fat; she was getting old; let her compare her grossness with the slender beauty of Isabelle de Limeuil, Isabelle's youth with her age. Isabelle would be wise too in the ways of love. For a moment Catherine thought of those other lovers – Henry and Diane – spied on through a hole in the floor. She would not, for anything, go back to those days of anguish and humiliation. Love? It was not for her. And what did this love amount to? What did it bring but jealous torment, a temporary satisfaction. No, it was not love she wanted; it was power. There was no time to waste, watching Isabelle and Condé through a hole in the floor; she would not bother to listen to their conversation through a tube leading from her apartment to theirs. No! She was done with that folly. She had no time for it.

She sent for Louise, and when the woman knelt before her, she bade her rise and make sure that they were not overheard.

'Now, Mademoiselle,' she said, 'you have done well and I am pleased with you.'

'Thank you, Madame. It is my pleasure to serve Your Majesty.'

'You now have the confidence of the King of Navarre, I believe?'

'I believe so, Madame.'

'How is he with you? His desire, I trust, has not weakened through too much satisfaction?'

Louise was prepared. It was a trait of the Queen Mother that she liked to hear details of the exploits of her Squadron. She took a vicarious pleasure in their experiences through their reports. One must submit to her wishes, enter into her coarseness. Sometimes it was easier than at others; but Louise was half in love with Antoine and did not enjoy discussing the more physical details of their love-making. However, the Queen Mother must be obeyed in all things.

After a while, Catherine said: 'I think that you have his confidence, and now is the time to widen your mission. The King of Navarre is a Protestant, and as such he puts himself in danger. I wish him to become a Catholic. That is your next task.'

'But . . . Madame . . . a Catholic! Change his religion! That will be a very difficult task, Madame.'

'But not one beyond you, I am sure, Mademoiselle.'

The girl looked frightened. How strange these people were!

thought Catherine. Even this harlot was appalled at the thought of discussing religious doctrines between bouts of love-making.

Catherine laughed. 'It will give you something to talk about when you are not in the act of love-making. Holy Mother, woman, would you wear out the poor little man!'

Louise did not smile. 'His religion, Madame, it seems apart . . . a sacred thing. I had not thought. He . . . he is of the Reformed Faith.'

'And you, I trust, Mademoiselle de la Limaudière, are a good Catholic?'

'Yes, Madame.'

'Well then, as a good Catholic, does it not become you to try to turn his footsteps in the right direction?'

'I . . . I had not thought that my duties would lie that way.'

'And now you hear they do.'

'Yes, Madame.'

'You do not seem to relish this task.'

'It is so unexpected, Madame. I had not thought about religion. I . . . I will do my best.'

'I shall demand nothing less,' said Catherine with a smile, and the smile made Louise shiver. 'Now, child,' continued the Queen, 'do not look so glum. You know that I reward those who work with me and for me. Make a good Catholic of your lover and I will see if I can turn him into your husband.'

'My husband! But he is a King, Madame, and . . . married.'

'He is a King – that is true. And far above you in rank, my dear. But I doubt not that if you brought him into a mood in which he wished for marriage with you, he would insist on it; and how could he be refused? He is married, you say. Yes, he is married to the Queen of Navarre. I do not think, my dear, that the Pope would withhold a divorce from a Catholic King who wished to free himself from his heretic wife. Now go and think on what I have said. But remember – discretion. It would be unwise to repeat at this stage a word of anything I have said to you – to *any*. Pray remember that.'

Louise came out of the apartment dizzy with excitement. Had she heard correctly? Had Catherine really held out to her a promise of marriage with the King of Navarre – to her, who was merely the daughter of the Seigneur de L'Isle Rouet? And all she had to do to achieve this was to make him change his religion!

❖ ❖ ❖

When Louise had left her, Catherine sent for the Duke of Guise and the Cardinal of Lorraine.

She was pleased with herself. She had lulled the fears of these men by showing them her hostility to Jeanne of Navarre and the Huguenot cause and supplying two of its leaders with mistresses, so creating a court scandal which must be angering the Coligny brothers whilst it struck right at the heart of the Huguenot Party by bringing into disrepute two of its most prominent leaders.

So far so good; but Catherine did not want this to go too far. She must keep these rival houses of Bourbon and Guise at odds with one another; for if they were to unite and band together against her, she could not hope to hold out against them.

She did not believe for a moment that the beautiful Louise would be able to induce Antoine to change his religion, but it was necessary to make the Guises believe that that was the intention. She thought she understood these fanatically religious people. They never changed. Who would have believed that the cruel and ambitious Francis de Guise could be such an ardent Catholic? They were all alike, scheming, cunning and unscrupulous – except where their religion was concerned.

The Duke and his brother were ushered in. They bowed low over her hand.

'Welcome, Messieurs. What think you of the way things go with the Bourbon brothers?'

'I should enjoy,' said the Cardinal with his sly malicious smile, 'seeing the faces of Mesdames Jeanne and Eléonore when they hear of the frolics in which their husbands indulge.'

'To let them both get caught up by mistresses was a master stroke,' said the Duke with a laugh. 'I myself think that what Antoine does is immaterial. Condé is another matter.'

'Condé,' said the Cardinal, 'is the stronger of the two.'

'But not strong enough to say "No" to Mademoiselle de Limeuil,' added Catherine with her gusty laugh.

'He is soft with women, but a formidable enemy,' put in the Duke. 'Condé must be watched. The greatest mistake that was ever made was to free him after the death of King Francis.' The Duke glared at Catherine with something like his old arrogance as he said this. 'The safest place for Condé's head is on the battlements – not on that elegant body of his.'

Catherine said: 'I like not injustice. Condé defended his honour and it was agreed that he should go free.'

'Not by us, Madame,' the Cardinal reminded her.

She bowed her head in silence, and thought: Of all my enemies, I hate most this Cardinal. Even more than I hate the Duke, I hate him. Would to God I could find some way of despatching him!

'It may be that concerning Condé you are right, Monsieur le

Cardinal,' she said soothingly. 'How can we know? But these Bourbon Princes are popular with the people. I think that had we executed Condé on that occasion there would have been risings throughout France.'

'Madame,' said the Duke, 'the whole question of religion has to be decided sooner or later. It is your behaviour towards the Huguenots which has made them arrogant, too sure of themselves.'

'I think, my lord Duke, I have shown you that I am a true Catholic.'

The Guises were insolently silent, and she could not quell the fear which came to her as she looked at them. The Bourbons inspired no such fear. The Duke was a strong man; the Cardinal was an infinitely cunning one; as a team they were irrepressible, impossible to subdue except by death; and the only death one could consider for such men was a secret, silent stab in the back.

'I asked you to come, Messieurs,' she said, 'that I might give you further proof of my friendship for you, of my loyalty to the faith we mutually hold. I propose to make Catholics of Antoine and Condé.'

'You never will. They are ardent heretics. Their wives would not let them be good Catholics.'

'Their wives would not let them sport with their mistresses if they could help it, Messieurs! But these two gentlemen have, nevertheless, managed to elude the control of their very virtuous wives.'

'But their religion, Madame!'

'Louise de la Limaudière is a very attractive girl, my lord Duke. She is already with child by our little King of Navarre. The Queen of Navarre is not going to be very pleased when this news reaches her. She is going to give our Antoine a piece of her mind, and he, the little coxcomb, flattered and adored by such a beautiful girl as la Limaudière, is not going to relish a scolding from that less beautiful and shrewish wife of his. I do not despair at all of our Antoine's turning his coat. He can never be of one mind for any length of time.'

'A man's religion, Madame,' said the Cardinal, 'is sacred to him. He may change his women, but not his faith.'

Catherine agreed; and it was now necessary to her plans that Antoine should *not* change his religion. But she pretended to believe that he would do so.

'He is weak, my lords. He is like a reed in the wind. Jeanne of Navarre – she is the danger, for although she is the wife and Antoine the husband, it is she who rules. We can do nothing with her except have her branded as a heretic, hand her over to the Inquisition, or have the marriage annulled and our King of Navarre married to a wife more suited to him.'

The Guise brothers were interested now. The Cardinal's long white hands stroked his gorgeously coloured robes; the Duke's eye began to water above his scar.

'And whom have you in mind, Madame, for the King of Navarre's second wife?'

'Your niece, my lords. Mary Queen of Scots. What think you of my choice?'

'An excellent one,' said the Cardinal.

'To that I agree,' added the Duke.

They smiled at the Queen Mother, being once more assured that she was their friend. Catherine wanted to laugh. They were as easily duped as la Limaudière. Did they really think that she would bring back to France their little spy? Evidently they did!

Holy Mother! thought Catherine. How can I fail when these *great* men are such fools!

❖ ❖ ❖

The Spanish Ambassador, de Chantonnay, was a man well versed in the ways of intrigue. De Chantonnay had been trained in diplomacy from his childhood; he had inherited his astuteness and his boldness from his father, Chancellor Nicholas de Granvelle; and Philip of Spain had chosen wisely when, at this time, he had decided that de Chantonnay was the man best fitted to serve his interests in France.

De Chantonnay was not, therefore, unaware of the traps which had been set for the Bourbon Princes, and since the ladies who had lured them into these traps were members of the *Escadron Volant*, and he knew very well what the duties of that esoteric band comprised, it was no great feat of cerebration to determine who had set the traps. The Queen Mother! But whether out of fear or friendship for the Guises he was not sure.

The Guises were the allies of Spain; the Queen Mother, by her prevaricating behaviour since little Charles had been on the throne, had been the subject of many disquieting letters which de Chantonnay had sent to his King. Philip of Spain did not trust the Queen Mother, for he accepted his Ambassador's keen judgment; and de Chantonnay was certain that the waverings from Bourbon to Guise were due to her desire to use their friendship whenever she might need it, and by so doing to keep her own power.

However, de Chantonnay's one object was to work for his master, and for this purpose he was spy and intriguer as well as Ambassador. He had his spies just as the Queen Mother had, and he knew that Louise had been instructed to induce the

197

King of Navarre to change his religion. This suited Spain; but Spain wanted more of the King of Navarre than his conversion.

For this reason de Chantonnay ingratiated himself with Antoine, flattered him, admired him, and made a friend of him. Antoine was the easiest man at court with whom to make friends. Flattery was all he needed, and that was cheap for a Spanish Ambassador to provide.

De Chantonnay talked and drank with Antoine.

'Ah,' said the Spaniard, 'what a great and glorious future might be your Majesty's if you would but play the right cards. I cannot doubt that you will, for I'd wager with anyone that there's a fine head for business beneath those handsome curls. Do you know, my lord King, that there are some who are deluded enough to think that because a man is handsome he is a fool?'

'What great and glorious future do you speak of, Monsieur?'

'My lord King, could we go somewhere where we shall not be overheard? There are too many eyes and ears in this palace, and I should prefer to be out of doors.'

So they walked together in the palace gardens while the Spanish Ambassador unfolded the Spanish King's plans for Antoine.

'Part of the province of Navarre, as your Majesty well knows, is in the hands of my master – won from the sovereign of Navarre in battle.'

Antoine looked sullen. That was a sore point with him. But the Spaniard hurried on: 'What an uneasy thing it is for such a province to belong half to one King, half to another! What if you were offered Sardinia in exchange for Navarre?'

'Sardinia!'

'A wonderful island, Monseigneur. A beautiful climate. A land of beautiful women and great cities. You would be King of all Sardinia. But first it would be necessary that you embrace the Catholic Faith. My master could have no dealings with a heretic. Oh, Sire, do not be rash. Do not be angered. Your soul is in danger. Your future life is in jeopardy – not only in Heaven, but here on Earth.'

'My future here on Earth? How is that?'

'His Most Catholic Majesty, the King of Spain, thinks often of you, Sire. He grieves that you should put yourself at the head of heretics, for that way lies disaster. Give up this new religion and save your soul. And get yourself a triple crown at the same time.'

'What is this? What do you mean, man?'

'If you became a Catholic you could not remain married to a heretic.'

'But . . . Jeanne is my wife.'

'The Pope would let nothing stand in the way of your divorce from one who has publicly proclaimed herself to be a heretic. Moreover, there was a previous marriage with the Duke of Clèves, and this was binding. Oh, Monseigneur, Your Majesty would have no difficulty in divorcing your wife.'

'But I had not thought of this. We have our children.'

'Children who are illegitimate, since the woman you call your wife was first given to the Duke of Clèves! You would have other children – children to inherit a triple crown.'

'Whose triple crown?'

'Your own, for one.'

'But I have that because it was bestowed on me through my wife.'

'We need not let a little detail like that worry us, Sire. Your wife would lose all her possessions, as do all heretics. You would have your own crown – the crown of Sardinia – and in addition the crown of Scotland and the crown of England.'

How so?

'By marriage with the Queen of Scots. His Most Catholic Majesty does not intend to allow the red-headed heretic to hold the throne of England for ever; and when she does not, who should? Mary Stuart, Queen of Scots. You see what glories I hold out to your Majesty.'

'Yes,' said Antoine, dazzled. 'I see, Monsieur.'

'And all you have to do is renounce Navarre and take this beautiful island of Sardinia in its place. Then shall you be married to the heiress of Scotland and England. Her uncles are most willing that the marriage should take place. Oh indeed you are a fortunate man! The triple crown within your grasp, and all you have to do is save your soul and divorce your wife.'

Antoine pondered in silence. Mary of Scots? That little beauty! And such great good fortune! It was enough to make a man thoughtful.

De Chantonnay came nearer and whispered: 'There is a fourth crown that might be yours. But perhaps we should not speak of that yet. The little Charles is not, to my mind, a healthy child. And Henry? And Hercule?' De Chantonnay lifted his shoulders and smiled shrewdly. 'I would not say that those boys have long lives before them. And then, Sire, think what might be yours! This, as you know, could only come about with the aid of His Most Catholic Majesty.' De Chantonnay's face was very near Antoine's as he whispered: 'The most desirable crown of all, Sire – the crown of France!'

200

The Queen Mother was worried. Events were moving too fast and away from her control. She had reckoned without de Chantonnay. So he had offered to exchange Sardinia for Navarre! And that fool Antoine was actually dazzled by the prospect, foolishly believing Sardinia to be all that the Spaniard represented it.

If she were not careful, the Guises would have their niece back in France and the girl would be married to Antoine, for Louise had reported that he was wavering and showing more and more tolerance for the Catholic Faith.

She paced up and down her apartments. Was ever a woman so beset by enemies on all sides? Which way could she turn? To the Guises? To the Bourbons? To the Spanish Ambassador and that shadow which haunted her life, his grim master, Philip of Spain, her own son-in-law? Only for a little while could she turn to any of these, only for a little while walk along beside them in step. She was playing her own lonely game, a secret game; they must never guess what she was planning. She had to work alone, to keep her power, to keep the throne for Henry when the time came. And she doubted not that they were all working against her.

It was she who had, in a misguided moment, suggested Mary Queen of Scots for Antoine. How could she have guessed what such a suggestion would involve? She was beginning to wonder whether after all she was still a novice in this game of politics. She had made so many mistakes.

She must learn by these mistakes. She must prevent Antoine's marriage with Mary Queen of Scots. What a dangerous alliance that would be! The Guises would not rest until they had Mary on the throne of France, and if Antoine became a Catholic they would wish to see him there too.

She had been foolish. She had shown too much favour to the Huguenots. So now the Catholic Party planned to set Antoine on the throne, with Mary Queen of Scotland as his Queen. What of her children – her little Charles, her darling Henry? These children might die. Others had quickly learned the secrets of those poisons which she and her followers had brought with them when they came to France. Was Charles weaker than he had been? Was Henry? It was typical of Catherine that she considered everyone to be as unscrupulous as herself, and that as her thoughts flew so often to poison, she should imagine that other people's did also.

She was not sure which way to turn. But Jeanne of Navarre must be made to come to court. That much was obvious, for if anyone could prevent the divorce of Antoine and his wife, that one must surely be his wife.

She wrote affectionately to Jeanne. How were the dear little children? Did Jeanne not think that a match between her little Catherine, Catherine the Queen Mother's own namesake, and Catherine's own son Henry, would be a pleasant thing? 'How it would bind us together!' she wrote. 'And then there is the match between my daughter Marguerite and your son Henry, which my husband decided on. We should discuss that together and, as you know, such discussions are difficult by letter . . .'

Then Catherine wrote once more to say that Jeanne must come north for the Council of Poissy.

'My dear cousin, you know I am your friend. You know that these differences of faith, which have steeped our country in blood, distress me. I have thought it would be a good plan for members of both sides to get together, to discuss, to try to come to an understanding, this time without bloodshed; for what understanding was ever reached through bloodshed?'

When she had written the letters to Jeanne she summoned the Duchess of Montpensier to her, for, knowing this lady's Huguenot sympathies, she felt she was the one to do what was required.

'Ah, Madame de Montpensier,' she said. 'I am sending letters to the Queen of Navarre, and I think that you should write to her also. It is a very bitter subject, I know, but I am of the opinion that the Queen of Navarre should be made aware of it. It is my belief that if she were here she might be able to rescue that foolish husband of hers from his follies. Mademoiselle de la Limaudière grows larger every day with the King's bastard. I do not like such things to be seen at my court, as you know. The King of Navarre is as devoted to the woman now as ever, and I think his wife should be told. There is another thing. I think that she should know that he is attempting to barter her kingdom for a worthless island. That man is foolish enough for anything. You are the Queen's friend. Write to her and tell her of these things.'

'I will write and tell her of the proposed exchange, Madame.'

'You will also mention that the King's bastard is spoiling Mademoiselle de la Limaudière's slender figure.'

'Madame, I . . .'

'That,' said Catherine, 'is a command.'

The Monastery of Poissy at which the Council was held was not far from Saint-Germain; and to this monastery during those summer weeks came the important figures from the Catholic and Protestant movements. The Council was, as Catherine realised later, doomed to failure from the start.

When people were concerned with religion, they became fanatical. They would not give way. Endlessly they discussed the different tenets. What did it matter, Catherine wondered, how the sacrament was taken? Yet endlessly they must discuss and continually they must disagree on such subjects as the Ordination, Baptism, the Laying on of Hands.

Catherine, as she looked round at these great ones assembled in the monastery refectory, was thinking: Why do they fight each other? Why do they die for these causes, these stupid quibbles?

They were all the same: the crafty Cardinal of Lorraine and the mighty Duke of Guise; Calvin, who mercifully was not present; Théodore de Bèze; Michel de l'Hôpital, that fine Huguenot Chancellor to whose wise judgement she owed a good deal; Jeanne of Navarre and Eléonore de Condé; yes, they were fanatics, every one.

And what did she expect to come from the Council which she had arranged? Nothing – precisely nothing. They would never agree, these two factions. Nor did she wish them to; she only wished to let them think she hoped they would agree. For herself, she had no religion; for her there could only be expediency. But it was good, for her, that others should possess this fanaticism, since it made them vulnerable, while those who did not have to consider a faith were free to turn this way and that, to act not for what was right for their faith, but for what was to their own material advantage.

The excitement brought about by such a Council caused tension throughout the entire country. The Huguenots believed that the Queen Mother was, after all, on their side.

Catherine, worried at the thought of what disaster might threaten herself and her family if Antoine turned Catholic and allied himself with the Guises, now began to show favour to the Huguenots. She wished to be sure of their support, although she realised that a section of the Huguenot community wished to eliminate the monarchy altogether and set up a presidency in its place.

However, the Huguenots were in Paris, Saint-Germain and Poissy in full force; and it seemed that those who rallied to that cause were almost as numerous as the Catholics.

Catherine therefore pretended not to notice that *prêches* were openly held even in the apartments of the palace itself; and when de Chantonnay, in a rage, pointed this out to her, she replied blithely that she had seen nothing of them.

Even the children were aware of the tension.

Catherine's darling Henry was attracted by the Huguenot Faith. It was new, and novelty always appealed to the intellectual set to which Henry belonged. Henry was quick to sense his mother's moods and to follow them; and she listened smilingly while he talked of de Bèze and his wonderful sermons.

There were quarrels in the children's apartments, particularly between Margot and Henry. Henry would make his sister stand in a corner while he preached to her, repeating all that he could remember of de Bèze's sermon. But Margot would not be intimidated.

'I am a Catholic,' she asserted stoutly. 'I belong to the true faith. I and my husband-to-be will always support the true faith.'

'Your husband-to-be is a Huguenot,' retorted Henry.

That made Margot laugh scornfully, for she was as determined never to marry Henry of Navarre as she was to remain a Catholic.

'My future husband is a Catholic.'

'It may be,' teased Henry, 'that you do not know who your future husband is to be, Mademoiselle Margot.'

'Indeed, I do know. We have arranged it between us.'

'What is his name? Tell me that, for I think there is some mistake here.'

'You should know. It is the same as yours.'

'Henry. That is correct. He spent his early days in a peasant's cottage and he drank a peasant woman's milk. That makes a peasant of him.'

Margot tossed her head, throwing back her long black hair. 'You think that I would marry that oaf!'

'I think you will, for it has been arranged that you shall.'

'His hands are unclean. His hair is unkempt. I would not marry a peasant, brother.'

'As that peasant happens to be the future King of Navarre, you will, my dear sister.'

'It is another Henry whom I shall marry.'

Henry laughed aloud. 'Henry of Guise? I tell you, you will have to look higher than that.'

'No one is higher than Henry of Guise. He is the highest man on Earth. His father is the greatest man in France.'

'Treason!' cried Henry.

Margot laughed. 'Everybody is afraid of *Le Balafré*.'

'Henry of Guise is your lover, Margot, and you should both be whipped. He should be banished, and you should be married at once to the peasant with the dirty hands and undressed hair.'

Margot smiled scornfully. 'I would never marry Henry of

Navarre. I hate him. He knows I do, and he hates me. How I wish that he had not come to court with his mother for this Council!'

'You must become a Huguenot, for you are to marry a Huguenot.'

'I will never become a Huguenot; nor will I marry one.'

Henry snatched her prayer-book and threw it into the fire.

'I wonder,' said Margot, her eyes blazing as fiercely as the flames, 'that you are not struck dead for that.'

'Do you? I wonder you are not struck dead for clinging to the old faith. If you do not change, I will have you whipped. I will ask our mother to have it done.'

'She would not dare to whip me, or have me whipped, for such a reason.'

'Do you think she would not dare to do anything she thought fit?'

Margot was silent, and Henry went on: 'I will have you killed, for if your beliefs are wrong you deserve to die.'

'Very well,' cried Margot. 'Have me whipped. Have me killed. I would suffer the worst that could happen to me rather than damn my soul.'

And so the quarrels went on – in the children's apartments, in the monastery of Poissy, and throughout the tortured realm of France.

✠　✠　✠

Jeanne, the deceived wife, the Queen possessed of a husband who was plotting against her, who was planning to give her kingdom away, had arrived in Paris with her two children, Henry and little Catherine.

When she had first heard the terrible rumours concerning

Antoine, she could not believe them. She knew that he was weak, but for all his faults he had loved her. Theirs was to have been the perfect, lasting union. How could he have written those letters assuring her of his faithfulness if all the time he was indulging in a love affair with this Mademoiselle de la Limaudière, La Belle Rouet as they called her? Jeanne would not believe it. He had written only a short time ago to tell her that other women ceased to attract him. Surely he could not be so deceitful.

She was filled with horror at the idea that he could intrigue with Spain. This she would consider even more false than his conjugal infidelities, for with the woman he deceived only her, but with Spain he deceived not only her, but her children, since he was ready to throw away their heritage for his own aggrandisement.

She was bewildered, not knowing to whom to turn for advice and for the truth.

The Queen Mother had offered her apartments in the Louvre that she might be near her dear friend, and that she might often see those little ones whom she thought of as her own, for, said Catherine, she looked upon the bride-to-be of her son and the bridegroom-to-be of her daughter as her own children. But Jeanne had never trusted Catherine, and she preferred to take up her residence in the Palais de Condé.

Here fresh revelations awaited her. Eléonore, who had come to court for the Council of Poissy, received her sister-in-law.

They embraced, and as she looked into Eléonore's face Jeanne realised that she also had her troubles. The forthright Jeanne plunged straight into the subject which was uppermost in her mind.

'Eléonore, you can tell me if this is true: I have heard terrible stories. They say that Antoine is in love with a woman of the court.'

'Oh, my dearest sister, alas, it is true.'

Jeanne's eyes blazed. 'I shall never forgive him for this. I hate philanderers! Is there not enough for us to do . . . our work . . . our cause . . . ? And yet he deceives me. He brings our cause into disrepute at the same time. Oh, Eléonore . . .'

Jeanne covered her face with her hands; she was afraid she was going to weep. She hated to show weakness, but she was so wretchedly unhappy.

Eléonore put an arm about her.

'Dearest Jeanne, I understand your troubles. It is better that you should hear all this from one who loves you and suffers with you. Antoine, you know, has become the lover of that court woman. Jeanne, my dearest, you must prepare yourself for a great shock. Antoine's son was born a few weeks ago.'

Jeanne broke away from Eléonore's embrace.

'I hate him!' she cried. 'I did not know it had gone as far as this. He shall suffer for it. Oh God, to think this could happen to us! We were so happy, Eléonore. I knew that he liked gaiety . . . fun . . . pleasure . . . flattery, but I did not think this could ever happen to us. Oh, Eléonore, I am so miserable, so wretched.'

'I sympathise, my dear,' soothed Eléonore. 'I too am unhappy at this time. You see, Jeanne, I suffer your humiliation — not only yours, but that of my own.'

Jeanne stared at her sister-in-law. 'You mean that Louis also . . . ?'

'Louis too,' said the Princess of Condé. 'Mademoiselle de Limeuil is his mistress.'

Jeanne took Eléonore's hands and pressed them against her

breast. 'And I so wrapped up in my own troubles that I do not think of yours, which are as great! Oh, Eléonore, if I could but be calm as you are!'

'My dearest Jeanne, these husbands of ours are weak men, but we love them. We must forgive them.'

'I shall never forgive Antoine.'

'But you will see when you grow calmer that you must. There are your children to be thought of. We must overlook these lapses. There are more important things to be done than waste our energies on domestic quarrels.'

'But I thought you and Louis were so happy. It always seemed so. As for myself and Antoine – oh, you sit there smiling calmly! You may forgive them; I never will!'

'But you must. Our enemies have brought this about. They have laid the bait and our husbands have fallen into the traps. We must fight for them . . . with them.'

'You may. I never will. I hate Antoine. Not only for his infidelity, but for his lies . . . his hypocrisy.'

'Oh, Jeanne, my dearest sister, how well I understand, but . . .'

'There are no buts.' Jeanne laughed suddenly, but there were tears in her eyes. 'You and I are different, Eléonore. You are a saint and I am . . . a woman.'

❖ ❖ ❖

In the Palais de Condé Antoine faced the fury of his wife.

'So, Monsieur, you have a son. I congratulate you. And what a charming mother! Chief harlot of the court, so I hear. What do you plan for this bastard of yours? The throne of Navarre, or the throne of Sardinia? I gather you have not yet made up your mind what to do with my kingdom.'

Antoine tried soothing her. 'Now, Jeanne, my dearest wife, pray listen to me. Louise de la Limaudière? That is nothing. A lapse, I admit, but that is all. You are my wife, my dearest wife. It is our lives that are important. You have lived too much away from the court of France. Your little courts of Pau and Nérac . . . well, my dear, they are not the court of France.'

'Evidently not, since in them we are old-fashioned and ungallant enough to respect our marriage vows.'

'Why, Jeanne, I care for no one but you. Do you not see that?'

'So then, it is your custom to give sons to women for whom you do not care?'

'It was a lapse – a pardonable lapse. Any but you would see that. I was away from you. I am a man.'

'You are a fool! A conceited popinjay, as easily fooled by a harlot as by a Spanish Ambassador.'

'Jeanne . . .

'Sardinia!' she cried. 'That was a lapse, I suppose. A pardonable lapse!'

She looked at him, and it seemed to her that she looked at a stranger. There he stood, a man of forty-five – not a young man any more – old enough to have some sense, to know when and why people flattered him. His beard was getting grey, but his hair was frizzed and curled; his clothes were more extreme than those of anyone else at court. The sleeves of his coat were puffed with gorgeous satin, and his plumed hat was set with gems. He was conceited in the extreme. He was a fool, an arrogant fool, a deceitful husband; and she loved him.

She stifled the impulse to run to him, to remind him of the happiness they had enjoyed together, the joys of the simple life they had led in the despised courts at Nérac and Pau. Oh God! she thought. Then we were happy. I could have made him happy for ever if I had kept him with me, if they had not made him Lieutenant-General at the court of France, if he had never been important to these unscrupulous seekers after power. But how could this beautiful, elegant creature, who thought more of the line of his coat and the set of his hat than of high politics, how could he resist their flattery, which they would give him as long as they could use him?

She longed for him just as she had in the beginning. She remembered him as a young man at the christening of poor little King Francis. She remembered him in his Spanish galleon at the wedding of King Francis. And now . . . he had betrayed her, betrayed her both as a wife and as a Queen, betrayed her home and her kingdom.

She must not weaken because she loved him. She held him off.

'Do not come near me,' she said. 'You are despicable. Weak and vain. Look at that hat! I should be ashamed of it if I were you. So that is the new fashion, is it? And so that you may preen yourself and mince about the court like a pretty man, a gallant courtier, you would deceive your wife, you would dare to exchange what is not yours for a worthless island. Let me remind you, Monsieur who call yourself King, let me remind you that you owe your crown to me!'

It was the final insult. Antoine would bear no more. He hated criticism. She had sneered at his elegance, his rank. He could deal with an angry wife, but not with a self-righteous Queen.

He said: 'I see it is of no use trying to talk calmly to you. You are determined to quarrel, and I refuse to quarrel.'

He bowed elegantly and left her. He went straight to Louise and told her all that had happened. She soothed him, flattered him; and as she caressed him, Antoine's thoughts went to Jeanne, and it seemed to him that the Spanish Ambassador was right when he had said that it was Jeanne who was standing in his way to greatness. His crown had come to him through her! Well, she should see what the King of Spain thought of her right to that crown.

He embraced Louise, delighting in her youth and beauty. Jeanne was plain in comparison. Louise – *La Belle Rouet* – one of the most beautiful women in France, adored him and had willingly borne his bastard. And Jeanne could do nothing but sneer at him, and all because he had followed that fashion which was surely perfectly natural to a French nobleman – he had taken a mistress.

Jeanne stayed at the Palais de Condé; Antoine kept to his apartments in the Louvre. He had become a Catholic now, and de Chantonnay was his great friend. The two were always together, and the Guises had warmed towards their old enemy. It was known that Antoine was considering divorcing his wife, for how could a good Catholic remain married to a heretic? Spain and Rome had denounced her as such, and together they had destined her for the stake; but this as yet was kept secret, for it was necessary to get possession of the person of the Queen of Navarre before she could be handed to the Inquisition; and she had many influential friends in France who would help her to avoid capture.

The Huguenots were outraged by Antoine's conduct, and even the Catholics despised a man who changed his religion for those reasons which all knew to be behind Antoine's conversion. He was named – slightingly – throughout the country 'L'Échangeur.' Condé, it was known, had been false to his wife; the French understood that, and it was only the more austere among the Huguenots who held it against him; but Condé had never denied his faith, nor, he declared, would he ever do so. He was in love with the beautiful Isabelle de Limeuil, but try as she might she could not persuade him to abjure his faith. Condé, like the rest of the Huguenots, was disgusted with his brother.

As for Catherine, she did not know which way to turn. Antoine had alarmed her by changing so easily, but she trusted Condé to remain firm, and while Condé did so he would be able to provide a mighty force to hold the Guises in check.

Jeanne had arrived too late; the Spanish schemes for Antoine had gone too far for her arrival to turn Antoine back to her. Antoine had been too dazzled by the flattering suggestions of de Chantonnay. All the same, Antoine was not unsentimental, and he still had a great affection for his wife; besides, he was a notorious turn-coat. Might it not be possible to reconcile him with Jeanne? The thought of having Mary Stuart in France again was more than Catherine could endure.

Catherine summoned Jeanne to her presence; she wished, she said, to talk of serious matters with her.

They faced each other, the two Queens, each mistrusting the other. Jeanne, her face pale, her eyes cold, successfully managed to hide most of her misery. Whenever she saw Antoine, on his occasional visits to the Palais de Condé, there were quarrels. He sought quarrels. He accused her of heresy and, worst of all, he threatened to take her children from her. She knew that she was in danger and that there were plots afoot concerning her; her friends advised her to leave Paris as soon as she could and make for her own dominions. She could not do this; she could not leave while this unsatisfactory state existed between herself and her husband. She was terrified that if she made preparations to depart he would insist on her leaving her children behind. She saw little of him, for most of his time was spent with his mistress and with his friends of the court. There were occasions when he would appear at the Condés' home to quarrel with his wife; he would seem sleek, satisfied, smiling secretly as, so Jeanne imagined, he remembered incidents from the previous night's love-making with his mistress. It was an intolerable position for a proud woman, for a Queen to whom − she never forbore to remind him − he owed his kingdom.

Catherine's pale features were composed into lines of sympathy. Having herself suffered from the humiliation of watching a husband's devotion to a mistress, she could guess something of Jeanne's feelings. But how calm *she* had been! She had learned how to smile, to feign indifference. Jeanne's was too frank a nature to be able to hide very successfully what she was feeling.

The foolish Queen of Navarre seemed to think there was some virtue in her frankness; to the Queen Mother of France it looked like sheer folly.

Catherine knew that Jeanne was in acute danger. Not only was she being closely watched by de Chantonnay, but by the Papal Legate, who had arrived in Paris to spy on her and to make plans for her capture if she continued in her heresy. These plans would have to be carefully made and carried out. Jeanne had too many friends for her arrest to be a simple matter. It would have to be carried out by stealth. Both Rome and Spain realised that this outspoken woman was a powerful leader; and one false move on the part of either might bring about much bloodshed and even war.

Catherine knew that Antoine's chamberlain and his physician were spies of the Legate and that every single action, every word lightly spoken, were reported. But Antoine was not regarded with the respect which was accorded to his wife, and for this reason Jeanne of Navarre was in great peril. If she did not take care, in a short while she would be hearing the crackle of wood at her feet; she would be feeling the flames scorch her flesh before they consumed her.

Catherine was indifferent to Jeanne's possible sufferings; but she wished to save her from Spain and Rome, for she was sure that a reconciliation between Jeanne and Antoine could help to counteract the power of the Guises as well as the power of Spain.

'My sister,' said Catherine softly, 'it is with great regret that I hear of your troubles. I remember how fond of each other you and the King of Navarre were in the early days of your marriage, and what an example you set to others. It grieves me, therefore, to see you at variance. Is there no hope that you will be reconciled?'

'There seems none, Madame.'

'Of course, I know that you must stop this ridiculous exchange of territories. You can do so, because nothing can be arranged on that matter without your consent; but do you not think that you might try to appease your husband? Appear to conform to his direction. Be calm. Wait for some more propitious time to mould him to your will.'

'On matters of religion and politics we differ, Madame.'

'You know that the Papal Legate is here, and for what

purpose? You know that de Chantonnay notes everything you say and do and reports it to my son-in-law, the King of Spain? Be wise. Turn to the Catholic Faith. If you do that they cannot harm you. You take away their reasons for doing what they plan. That is the only way to keep your kingdom, that your son may inherit it.'

'Madame,' cried Jeanne vehemently, 'if I at this moment held my son and the kingdoms of the world in my grasp, I would hurl them to the bottom of the sea rather than imperil the salvation of my soul.'

Catherine shrugged her shoulders. Very well. Let her go to the Inquisition. Let her save her immortal soul in the flames of the martyr's death. Others had done it before her. And what was this concern for an immortal soul? Eternal power? So they thought. And Catherine's goal was earthly power. Was one any more selfish than the other? Jeanne was ready to throw away her son's inheritance for the sake of her immortal soul. Her *own* immortal soul. That was where they were weak, all of them. They were as concerned about *themselves* just as she was about herself, but whereas she wished nothing to stand in the way of her earthly power, they were determined to save their souls at all costs.

Fools . . . all of them! And Jeanne was a nuisance too, for she was obviously not going to help Catherine in the least.

'Well,' said Catherine gently, 'you have my best wishes that you may recover from this unpleasant situation and regain your happiness. You know, my dear cousin, that you are close to me and that I regard my little Margot as pledged to your son Henry, and my son Henry to your little Catherine. That should make us close indeed.'

When Jeanne had gone, Catherine sat down and wrote to

the King of Spain. She was very anxious to arrange two matches – one for her daughter Margot and the other for her son Henry. She must look to the future, and little Henry of Navarre's hopes of inheriting the kingdom of Navarre were a little dim at the moment. Catherine wanted Philip's son, Don Carlos, for Margot, and Philip's elderly sister Juana, the widowed Queen of Portugal, for Henry.

She wrote ingratiatingly with the object of trying to assure that grimmest of men, her most Catholic son-in-law, that she was a good Catholic and that the interests of Spain were in truth those of France.

'I wish God would take the Queen of Navarre,' she wrote, 'so that her husband might marry without delay.'

✤ ✤ ✤

The King and Queen of Navarre were the talk of the court. There were open quarrels between them, and Jeanne did not now hesitate to hide her feelings. The King had tried to force the Queen to go to mass. He was by turns cold and quarrelsome, indifferent and abusive.

Louise de la Limaudière, who knew that if the King of Navarre were divorced he would remarry, and saw herself in the exalted position of his wife, gave herself airs.

She was every bit as important, she considered, as the Queen of Navarre. She herself might one day be Queen of Navarre – or Sardinia. The Queen Mother had promised her this reward for having – an unmarried woman of rank – borne the King's bastard.

She grew haughty, and even impertinent, in the presence of the Queen of Navarre herself.

'Why, Madame,' she ventured when there were others

present, 'do you not follow the fashions of the court? A gown such as this would make you look less angular. And that colour does not become you. It makes you look drab, Madame, like a serving-girl rather than a Queen.'

Jeanne turned away; she would not lower her dignity by bandying words with such a woman. But Louise followed her, while all present looked on.

'Believe me, Madame, I know what the King, who is at present your husband, likes in a woman. He has told me often that I possess those attributes.'

'I am not interested in what my husband looks for in a woman,' said Jeanne, 'because, Mademoiselle, I am not interested in my husband, and certainly not in you.'

'Oh, but, Madame, Antoine is such a wonderful lover. I am sure you do not bring out the best in him.'

'He must have seemed so to you,' retorted Jeanne, 'since you besmirched still further for his sake your already foul reputation. Now you may leave me. I have more important matters with which to concern myself.'

'Madame, I have the King's son.'

'You have his bastard, I believe. Mademoiselle, bastards are as common in this land as the harlots who produce them, so that one more or less makes little difference, I do assure you.'

Jeanne swept away, but she was furiously angry.

Antoine was waiting for her in her apartment.

He said coldly: 'It is my wish that you should accompany me to mass.'

'Your wishes, my lord, are no concern of mine,' retorted Jeanne.

She was disturbed to see her son Henry sitting on the

window-seat; the boy laid aside his book to watch this scene between his parents.

Antoine ignored the presence of the boy. He took Jeanne by the wrist. 'You are coming to mass with me. You forget that I am your master.'

She wrenched herself free and laughed at him. 'You . . . my master! Save such talk for Mademoiselle de la Limaudière. Pray remember who I am.'

'You are my wife.'

'It is indeed gracious of you to remember that. I meant, remember that you speak to the Queen of Navarre.'

'Enough of this folly. You will come with me to mass . . . at once.'

'I will not. I will never be present at the mass or any papist ceremony.'

Little Henry got slowly down from the window-seat and approached them. He said haughtily: 'Sir, I beg you, leave my mother alone.'

Antoine turned on his son, and something in the boy's dignity angered him because it made him feel small and despicable.

'How dare you?' he cried.

'I dare,' said Henry, looking, Jeanne thought, like his grandfather, that other Henry of Navarre, 'because I will not have my mother roughly handled.'

Antoine seized the boy and flung him to the other side of the room. Henry saved himself by clutching at the hangings. He recovered himself with dignity. Then he shouted: 'Nothing will induce me to go to mass either!'

Antoine strode over to him and took him by the ear. 'You, my lord, will go whither you are commanded.'

'Whither my mother commands,' flashed Henry.

'No, sir. Whither your father commands.'

'I will not go to mass,' reiterated Henry. 'I am a Huguenot like my mother.'

Antoine gave the boy a violent slap across the face. Jeanne watched proudly, exulting at the way in which the boy stood there, legs apart, glowering at his father. 'A true Béarnais!' his grandfather would have said.

Antoine was by no means a violent man, and he was disliking this scene even as his son exulted in it; he therefore wished to end it as speedily as possible. He was fond of the boy; he was proud of him, for all that he was an unkempt little creature without a trace of elegance; his wits were admirably sharp and there was no doubt of his courage.

Antoine called for an attendant, and when a man appeared he cried: 'Send my son's tutor to me.' And when the tutor came he ordered that young Henry should be severely whipped for his impertinence.

Henry left the room chanting: 'I will not go to mass. I will not go to mass.' His black eyes were alight with excitement, fervour and love for his mother.

The door shut behind the boy and his tutor.

'A pretty scene,' said Jeanne, 'and you, my lord, played the pretty part in it that I would expect of you. My son put you to shame, and I can see that you had enough grace to feel it. What a pity Mademoiselle de la Limaudière could not have been here as witness! I doubt whether her bastard will have the spirit of that boy.'

'Be silent!' commanded Antoine.

'I will speak when I wish to.'

'You are a fool, Jeanne.'

'And you are a knave.'

'If you do not become a Catholic immediately, I will divorce you.'

'How can you do that, my lord?'

'The Pope has promised it. He would not have me tied to a heretic.'

'Divorce me and forgo my crown? That would not suit you, Monsieur.'

'The crown would be mine if I were to divorce you.'

'How could that be? My father left it to me.'

'Part of Navarre was lost to Spain, and the whole of Navarre might be restored to me. Spain does not like heretics, even though they be queens. Spain would like to see me with a wife of my own faith.'

'Mademoiselle de la Limaudière?' she asked, but she had begun to tremble, thinking of that bold high-spirited boy who might grow up to find that, through his father's knavery, he had no kingdom.

'Don't be a fool,' said Antoine.

'It is you who are the fool. Do you not see that these people plot against you as well as against me? They plan your degradation as well as mine. Sardinia! That barren island. And they made you believe it was a paradise.' Her voice trembled. 'Antoine,' she said, 'I think of our children. What will become of them? Your repudiation of me, I can see, will destroy me, but it will also be the ruin of our children.'

And then she did what he had rarely seen her do; she broke down and wept; and once the tears had started she could not stop them. Her tears moved him. He remembered all that she had been to him. Poor Jeanne! That this should have happened to them seemed incredible. It had come about so gradually that he had not noticed its creeping upon them. He thought of all the happiness they had shared, the days when she had been in camp with him, his return to her after the wars. He wavered, as he always wavered. He was not sure, even at this late hour, whether he should give up Jeanne or *La Belle Rouet*, not sure whether he would go on with his conversion or turn back to the Reformed Faith. He was beset by doubts, as he always was. He could never be sure which was the right road for him.

'Jeanne,' he said, 'you had best make this step unnecessary by obeying me and making your peace with Rome and Spain. As for myself, I am undecided which religion is the true one. It is simply this, Jeanne – that while my uncertainty lasts, I am minded to follow the faith of my fathers.'

She laughed with great bitterness. 'Well,' she cried, 'if your doubts on either side are equal, I beg of you to choose the religion which is likely to do you least prejudice.'

She had laughed at him; once more she had mocked. Antoine hardened and swung away from her. It had always been thus. She had never made things easy for him; she would not meet him halfway.

He remembered once more that she stood in his way to greatness.

❧ ❧ ❧

Catherine was terrified. She felt that her first real adventure into foreign policy might cost her her life. She was exposed now, whereas previously she had worked in the dark. She was surrounded by powerful enemies; spies from Rome and Spain. The Guises were against her; the Catholics suspected her of being in league with the Huguenots, and the Huguenots did not trust her. She had tried to follow the teachings of

Machiavelli, but she had not succeeded. The serpent was in the open, uncoiled for all to see, and, realising the poison she carried in her fangs, both sides were ready to crush that cold, inhuman head.

The King of Navarre had joined the Catholic Triumvirate which had been set up to deal with the Huguenot menace; and he had walked through Paris at the head of the Catholic procession and attended mass in public at the Church of St. Geneviève. This meant that he was now openly pledged to the Catholic religion.

Catherine knew that Jeanne was in imminent danger. But what of herself? There were religious riots all over the country. Huguenots were despoiling Catholic churches, breaking up images, setting fire to altars, killing Catholics wherever they could. Catholics retaliated fiercely, surprising congregations and butchering them as they kneeled at prayer, setting fire to Huguenot meeting-places. A mother bringing a child from a christening which had been carried out in the Reformed manner was set upon and her child killed before her eyes. The Council of Poissy, which was to have bred toleration, seemed to have made matters worse. There was dissension everywhere, and the hatred between the Catholics and Protestants was rising to a frenzy all over the country. In Paris — always staunchly Catholic — the Huguenots were persecuted at every turn; but there were towns, such as La Rochelle, where the Protestants were in the majority, and here atrocities were committed against men, women and children in the name of the Reformed Faith.

Catherine listened to the council of the Triumvirate through a tube which hung behind the arras in the council chamber at the Louvre and led into her own apartments.

In clear tones, Francis of Guise said: 'The Queen Mother's interference in matters of state becomes intolerable. It is my suggestion that we get rid of her.'

Listening with horror, Catherine strained to hear everything. She thought of those four men who made up the Triumvirate, now incorrectly named, since Antoine had joined it and made it a council of four. There were the Guise brothers – the Duke and the Cardinal – the Maréchal de Saint-André and Antoine.

'Exclude her from the Regency!' she heard Antoine cry.

Saint-André said: 'Why not rid ourselves of her by drowning her in the Seine? It could easily be accomplished without discovery, for I fancy there is no person in France who would take the trouble to investigate the lady's disappearance.'

Catherine listened to no more. She did not realise that what had been said about throwing her into the Seine had been said jocularly. Had she been in the place of these men, she would have chosen an early opportunity of disposing of an enemy; she imagined that they were prepared to do the same.

She lost no more time, but went to the King's apartment and told him that they must leave for Fontainebleau at once; and this they did, galloping off in secret that night.

Meanwhile, the Council had stopped talking about the Queen Mother, to discuss what they considered a more serious matter, that of Jeanne of Navarre.

'There is only one course open to us,' said Francis of Guise. 'She must be arrested as a state prisoner at the earliest possible moment.'

Listening to this, Antoine turned pale. Jeanne . . . a state prisoner, confined to one of the dungeons! Proud Jeanne! And what then? Turned over to Spain, to the dreaded Inquisition.

Torture . . . the terrible torture of the Spanish Inquisition. He could imagine Jeanne as she faced the Inquisitors. She would never give way. She would suffer the rack, the water torture, any vileness they could think of. They could tear her flesh with red-hot pincers and pour molten lead into her wounds, but she would never give way.

The Cardinal of Lorraine had laid his hand on Antoine's shoulder. 'It sometimes happens,' said the smooth voice of the Cardinal, 'that it becomes necessary, for the sake of true religion, to act in a manner which is repulsive to us.'

Antoine bowed his head. He tried to shut out the picture of a martyred Jeanne. He tried to see himself received triumphantly into Heaven. There would be a good place for him, an honoured place, for he had embraced the true faith, and all would be forgiven once a straying sheep had returned to the fold.

'Then we are all agreed that a warrant must be issued for the arrest of Jeanne of Navarre,' said the Duke of Guise.

Antoine did not speak, and his silence was taken as agreement.

'On a charge of heresy,' added the Cardinal. He then embraced Antoine. 'This, Monseigneur, is an act worthy of you,' he declared. 'May God give you a good and long life.'

'So be it!' said the Duke.

The session was at an end.

Antoine left the council chamber, trying to reassure himself; that was not easy, for he felt like Judas.

It was not long before Jeanne heard that a warrant was being issued for her arrest, for she had many friends at court.

Overcome by this fresh evidence of the perfidy of the man she loved – for she knew that such an order would come through the Triumvirate, of which Antoine was now a member – Jeanne was glad that there was need for immediate action which would prevent her brooding.

'Fly at once,' she was warned, 'for there is not an hour to be lost. You will not be safe until you are in your own dominions. And if you are caught – apart from all the horrors which would await you – what a blow this would be to the Huguenot cause!'

She realised the truth of this and, taking her little four-year-old daughter, set out at once with her attendants.

Since that occasion when her son Henry had defended her against his father, the boy had been taken from her and kept in his father's apartments at Saint-Germain; and as she could not go without Henry, she must journey first to Saint-Germain to see him and, if possible, to take him away with her.

As she rode there her thoughts were bitter. Not content with taking her son from her, Antoine had been callous enough to put him in the care of Vincent Lauro, the Jesuit. Her enemies were determined to rob her of her son as well as her husband.

Her friends had warned her that it was folly to think of calling at Saint-Germain, for she would not be allowed to take the boy; she could depend upon it that he was well guarded, and she would merely imperil her own safety. But Jeanne would not listen. She must see Henry. She must – even if she could not take him with her – have a few words with him, to remind him of his obligations to her and to his faith.

She forced her way to him past his new tutors and the attendants, who were really guards. The little boy ran to her and embraced her warmly.

'Oh, my mother, have you come to take me home to Béarn?'

Antoine, who had immediately been warned of her coming, burst into the apartment; he stood, his arms folded, while he surveyed his wife with cold dislike, his son with sternness.

'You must stay here with me,' said Antoine, answering the boy's question. 'I am your father and you are under my control.'

'But I wish to go with my mother!' cried the bold little boy.

'Try to be sensible,' said Antoine. 'I do not wish to have you punished more than you have been already.'

'Mother, must I stay?'

She nodded, for she knew that guards were in the palace and she could not risk any injury to her son. He was bold and he would, she knew, try to fight them; but he would obey his mother.

'I fear so.' She held him against her breast. 'Henry, my dearest son.'

'Oh, Mother . . . dearest Mother.'

She whispered to him: 'Never forget my counsels, darling. Be true to me always and true to the faith.'

He whispered back: 'Mother, I will. I swear it.'

'Soon all will be well and we shall be together.'

'Yes, Mother.'

'But just for a little while we must be separated.'

He nodded.

'Darling son, never attend mass. No matter what they do . . . always refuse. If you did not refuse, you could not be my son.'

'I know,' he said.

'Then you will be true and strong, my dearest boy?'

'Yes, Mother, I will be true and strong. I am a Huguenot. I will never forget it, no matter what they do to me. I will never forget you and that one day I shall be with you.'

It was so sad to leave him. Again and again they kissed each other. Antoine watched them with some emotion. He had no wish to hurt either of them. He did not forget for a moment his relationship to them both. This was all Jeanne's fault. Why could she not become a good Catholic and set everything to rights?

He rang for the boy's tutor, and Henry, now weeping bitterly, was led away.

Antoine then spoke to Jeanne: 'Do not waste more time here, I beg of you. They are about to arrest you. Fly, I implore you. I beg of you. Your safest way is to make for Béarn via Vendôme. You can rest awhile at my château at Vendôme . . . but do not stay too long. It is your only hope of safety.'

Jeanne stared at him in amazement. 'But you are on their side. Should you not detain me . . . arrest me?'

'Go!' cried Antoine. 'Go before you drive me to it . . . as you have driven me to so much. Your sharp tongue is intolerable. Do not let it drive me to this.'

She said: 'Poor Antoine! That is your great failing. You are never able to make up your mind whose side you are on.'

She took a last look at him, so elegant, so glittering in his fashionable garments. What bitterness was hers that she should still love him . . . even now that he had betrayed her!

She hurried away from Saint-Germain, and at the Paris hotel in which she stayed the night while preparations for her flight went on, the Huguenots gathered under her window, so that those who had been sent to arrest her dared do nothing, with the result that she was able to leave the capital.

But it was not intended that she should reach safety. The Guises, noting the hesitancy of Antoine, suggested that he should be the one to give orders to the citizens of Vendôme to arrest Jeanne when she arrived in their town, for it had not taken them long to draw from him the fact that Jeanne had arranged to call at his château in that town before making the rigorous journey south.

✤ ✤ ✤

After many days of hardship, tired out with the journey, Jeanne came to Vendôme. In the great château which had belonged to her husband's ancestors, she rested and made plans for continuing the journey as soon as possible.

Her little daughter Catherine was a great comfort to her. The child was only four years of age, but old for her years, able to understand that her mother was unhappy and to try to comfort her. Jeanne felt that if only she could have had young Henry with her, she would not have cared very much about anything else. How could she go on loving a husband who had so betrayed her? This was not just a momentary infidelity with *La Belle Rouet*, not just a passing love affair. That she supposed she could, in time, have forgiven. But that he could make himself a party to this plan to destroy her, to take her kingdom, and worse still subject her to the possibility of an agonising death, seemed to her so wantonly cruel that she would always remember this against him.

It was while she was resting in her bed with her daughter beside her that one of her attendants asked for a word with her. He was admitted to her presence – a hardy Gascon, a faithful Huguenot, ready to defend her with his sword against any number of the enemy.

He showed great agitation and without formality addressed her. 'Madame, forgive the intrusion, but we are in acute danger. We have walked into a trap. The King of Navarre has given orders to the citizens that we are not to leave the town, but are to be held captive until forces arrive to take us back to Paris.'

Jeanne closed her eyes. Here was the final betrayal. The trap had been set by the man she had loved, and she had walked blindly into it – perhaps because at that last interview at Saint-Germain she had believed there was still some good in him, that he really meant to help her escape from his friends.

But the truth was that he had lacked the courage to detain her then; he had hesitated once more – and as soon as she was out of his sight, he had given himself wholeheartedly to the plan to destroy her.

'What are your orders, Madame?' asked the Gascon.

She shook her head. 'We can do nothing but wait.'

'The streets are full of guards, Madame. But we could mayhap fight our way through.'

'We are not prepared to fight guards. All my followers would be cut to pieces in ten minutes.'

'But, Madame, shall we be taken without a blow?'

'They will take me,' she said. 'The rest of you will doubtless go free. Take my daughter back to Béarn if that be possible.'

'Mother, I wish to go with you,' said little Catherine. 'I wish to face the Inquisition if you do.'

Jeanne embraced her daughter. Sweet Catherine! What did she know of the torture chambers, of the horrors inflicted by the Catholic Inquisition on those whom they considered to be heretics? What did she know of the *chevalet* and the *autos-da-fé*, of agony and death, the cries of men and women in torment, the odour of burning flesh?

'That,' said Jeanne firmly, 'you shall never do, my love.'

She turned to the Gascon. 'Stand on guard. Forget not my instructions, and remember . . . my daughter.'

He bowed in obedience, but his eyes were fierce. He wanted to fight for his Queen.

All through the long hours of the night, Jeanne lay awake, waiting for the sound of marching feet, the shouts of the troops who would come to storm the château and take her prisoner. They would be her husband's men, she did not doubt; the Guises and de Chantonnay would wish it to be her husband's guards who put the chains upon her and carried her on the first stage of her journey to the stake.

Her daughter had fallen asleep beside her. Jeanne kissed her tenderly. She was so young to be left; she was only four years old. So it was only four years then since she and Antoine had been so happy together over the birth of their child.

And, during that long night, she suddenly became aware of strange noises in the town. She went to her window; the sky was beginning to be red, not with the streaks of dawn but with the reflection of fire. She could smell the smoke; and as she stood there, apprehensively peering out into the gloom, she heard the shouts of men.

She dressed in great haste and, before she had completed this, her Gascon was at her door.

'Madame,' he cried, 'the town is being looted. A band of mercenaries has come into it. The news has just been brought to the château by one who wishes you well. The townsfolk are busy protecting their lives and their property. Now is the time for us to slip away unnoticed . . . for no one will care now whether we go or stay. But there is not a moment to lose . . .'

Jeanne was exultant. All her old energy came back to her.

'Our prayers are answered,' she cried. 'Come, we must

leave here as fast as we can. We must thank God . . . but later. Now, there is no time to think of thanksgiving. First we must be sure that we make the most of this heaven-sent opportunity. We must slip quietly out of Vendôme before the dawn . . .'

She turned to her daughter. 'Catherine, wake up, my darling. We are going now.'

'To the Inquisition?' asked Catherine sleepily. 'No, my love, to freedom.'

Riding south from Vendôme, Jeanne's party were saying that what they had just witnessed was a miracle. God had sent the band of looting mercenaries to Vendôme that the Queen might make her escape. Jeanne smiled tranquilly. She guessed that the Prince of Condé had been warned of her danger, for those mercenaries were Huguenot mercenaries, and their orders had evidently been: 'Occupy Vendôme. Create a diversion all through the night, and keep it up until the Queen of Navarre is too far for pursuit.'

Bravo Condé! He was as wayward as his brother, but he was true to the cause which he believed to be right. She must thank God for her brother-in-law while she wept bitter tears for her husband.

Farther south they went, at the end of each day tired out with hours of riding, each night sleeping deeply from exhaustion; and then on again towards that border which they must cross before they reached safety.

When they reached the town of Caumont it was to discover that the Catholic army under Montluc was only a few miles in their rear. The long and tedious journey, made in such trying circumstances, resting at castles where Jeanne believed she had friends – and how could she trust any, now that he whom she had thought she might trust above all others had failed her? – all this had taxed her strength and she was suffering acutely, not only from physical but from mental exhaustion.

But she must push on without delay, and this she did, reaching her frontiers with only an hour or so to spare; but there she had the joy of finding her loyal subjects assembled in full force to receive and protect her.

The flight was over, and Jeanne had won. Yet, thinking of all she had left behind – the husband to whom she was trying in vain to be indifferent, the son whom she adored – it was an empty, bitter triumph.

## ❧ CHAPTER III ❧

Catherine was filled with rage and terror. Francis of Guise, with the King of Navarre and the Maréchal de Saint-André, had come to Fontainebleau and compelled her and the King to return to Paris, whence they had then been removed to Melun; and, although they were treated according to their rank, it was made clear that they would not be allowed to leave Melun unescorted.

Catherine was exposed in all her dissembling. The student of Machiavelli was unmasked. Letters which she had sent to Condé had been captured and read by the last people who should have seen them, for in these letters Catherine had explained how intolerable was her position and that of little King Charles under the Triumvirate, and begged Condé to rescue her. She had promised him support and, taking her at her word, Condé had plunged the country into civil war – a civil war which, the Duke of Guise continually pointed out to Catherine, had been set in motion by her own duplicity.

He declared that she was no true Catholic. On the one hand she had conspired with them so that Antoine de Bourbon might be turned from the Reformed Faith; on the other hand she was at the same time plotting with Condé, and it was she who had encouraged the Huguenots to such an extent that they had resorted to war.

The Huguenots on their part declared that she had cheated them, that she was a deceitful and cunning woman; and that all the time she was speaking sweet words to them she was plotting against them with the Catholic King of Spain.

In vain did Catherine try to justify herself in the eyes of the Duke and the Cardinal, Antoine and the Spanish Ambassador. Those letters to Condé were not what they would seem, she assured them; they had been written in code. Oh, she admitted that they appeared to contain promises of help, but they were meant to convey something quite different. She became a little coy in her explanations. She had to admit that she cherished a fondness for the gallant little Prince of Condé.

The cold eyes of the Duke were murderous; the thin lips of the Cardinal curled; the Spanish Ambassador did not mince his words and was quite abusive, which alarmed her greatly, for this showed that he no longer considered her of any great importance.

Rumour was now circulating about her and Condé. People said that she was madly in love with him, and that she longed to marry him and make him the King of France at the expense of her children.

Catherine wondered at herself. She had been very reckless in her behaviour to this man, and that was unusual in her. But now that she saw herself and her children in great danger, she had no wish but to see Condé destroyed, with the Guises, Antoine and the rest. What a weak fool she had been to have felt the attractions of the gallant Prince in the first place! What was the excitement of love compared with that which came through wrestling for power?

She waited in terror for some dreadful fate to overtake her. The man who frightened her more than any other was the Duke of Guise. He could not be allowed to live. When Francis had been on the throne he had been the most important man in France, and he was rapidly regaining that position. But how difficult it would be to accomplish his death! It must be done, but not by poison. People would point to her at once if the Duke died of poison; they would whisper about the Italian woman and her poison closet. He must die, though. He was her bitterest enemy, and he now realised that he was not dealing with a weak woman, but a cunning one, whose sly twists and turns were unpredictable.

Meanwhile, the civil war was raging and Condé was triumphant. Orléans, Blois, Tours, Lyons, Valence, Rouen, and many other towns were in his possession. The Kingdom was split in two. The Catholics, in increasing alarm, sent appeals to the King of Spain.

What security was there for Catherine and her children? Neither Huguenot nor Catholic trusted her. She was hated now throughout the country as she had been at the time of the death of Dauphin Francis. She had been unfortunate, she assured herself. She did not realise that she had been cunning rather than clever, that she had misjudged those about her because she judged them by herself.

All over the country the Huguenots were gaining power. They marched on, singing their favourite song, which poked fun at Antoine de Bourbon, who had so recently been one of their leaders:

*'Caillette qui tourne sa jaquette . . .'*

They despised Antoine, the turn-coat; they distrusted the Queen Mother. But while they mocked the one, they hated the other.

✦ ✧ ✦

Outside the city of Rouen, Antoine of Navarre lay sick. He had been severely wounded in the battle for the city. For several weeks the Huguenots had held Rouen against the Catholic army which Antoine led. Even now while he lay on his bed in camp, he could hear the sound of singing inside the city's walls:

'*Caillette qui tourne sa jaquette . . .*'

They despised him; even though they knew he was outside their walls with a mighty army, they made fun of him. Antoine de Bourbon, *L'Échangeur*, the little quail who changed his coat to suit himself.

Antoine felt low in spirit. The pain from his wounds was intense; he lay tossing and turning. His surgeons were with him, one on either side of the bed, and he realised with a sudden flash of humour that it was characteristic of *L'Échangeur* that one of these was a Jesuit, the other a Huguenot.

Was this death? he wondered. Memories of the past would keep recurring. At times he wandered a little. Sometimes he thought the warm winds of Béarn blew upon him and that Jeanne was there, as she had been in the first days of their marriage, discussing with him some domestic detail.

There was a woman in the camp with him, a woman who had followed him and who was nursing him devotedly. She was at his side now, holding wine to his lips. He could smell the perfume she used; he was aware of her soft, yielding body under her rich brocade dress – *La Belle Rouet*. He took her hand and kissed it. She had really loved him after all; it was not because he was a King that she had borne his child. Why had Jeanne not come to see him when he was wounded? It was her duty to have come.

The sweat stood out on his face – the sweat of anger against Jeanne; tears filled his eyes because he had failed, had been unable to live up to the high ideal she had set before him.

The last time he had seen his wife was when at Saint-Germain she had come to see their boy. He had been on the point then – though she did not know it – of throwing away all that was promised him by the Spanish King, of giving up his place in the Triumvirate. Yes, he assured himself weakly, he had all but fled with Jeanne to Béarn. But then he had changed his mind – which was what must be expected of *L'Échangeur*; he had given orders that she should be detained in Vendôme.

She had defied him, he reminded himself. She had gone back to Béarn and had set about bolstering up the Reformed Faith there. She had sent help to Condé's troops. Ah, his brother! What did his brother think of him now? Dearest Louis – they had been close. But religion, as so often happened, had broken the bonds of brotherhood, and they were fighting against each other now.

That was a mean revenge he had taken on Jeanne when little Henry had lain at the point of death at Saint-Germain. Louise had been taking care of the boy at that time. The little fellow had a very bad attack of the smallpox and when Jeanne had heard the news she had been frantic in her anxiety. She had begged Antoine and the Queen Mother to let her have her son with her. But Catherine had refused. She had said: 'It is the only hold we have over the boy's mother.' But Catherine had allowed the child to be sent to the Duchess of Ferrara to be cared for, and that was all the satisfaction Jeanne received. Yet, had he insisted, he could have come to some terms with the Queen Mother; he could have arranged for the boy to be sent to his mother. There had been occasions when he had meant to, but when the Queen Mother had stated her wishes it had been easier to fall in with them.

Tears stung his eyes. He was depressed; he was in pain. His physicians told him that he was not mortally wounded. He would see the entry into Rouen.

'Louise!' he called; and she came to his side at once. 'Let us have gaiety, music, dancing – or I shall go mad.'

She was glad to see the change in his mood. She called in the gayest of the men and women who had followed his army – his court friends. Louise lay on his bed beside him and put her arms about him. There was music and dancing and the latest court scandals were retold. He felt wretchedly ill, but with such distraction he could deceive himself into thinking that he was as much alive as any.

His physicians reasoned with him:

'Monseigneur, you need rest. The wounds must be allowed to heal.'

'Rest!' he cried. 'I don't want rest. Rest makes me think, and I do not want to think. I want to hear laughter and wit. I want to see my friends dance. I want to hear their songs. Be silent, or I'll have your tongues cut out. Let me live my life as I want to.'

So the distractions continued. He kept *La Belle Rouet* with him. 'Why not?' he cried. 'My wife does not come to see me. A man must live. A man must love.'

'Nay, Monseigneur,' begged his doctors. 'Your state does not permit you.'

'To the devil with you!' cried Antoine. 'I'll find my own diversions.'

His army took Rouen. He declared his intention to be carried into the city on a litter, and he wanted Louise carried with him. He wanted to see the fun; he wanted to ask the Huguenots if they would sing *Caillette* now!

He was laid on his litter, but he did not see the inside of the town, for he fell into a deep fainting fit before he reached its walls.

When he recovered he found that he was back in camp.

Lauro bent his head down to him. 'Monseigneur, your Majesty must prepare to meet your God.'

'Is it so, then?' said Antoine; and he began to tremble as the memory of his weakness came back to him. He wished the tent to be cleared of all but the doctors, the prelate and his mistress.

He opened his eyes and looked in bewilderment from one face to another. 'I . . . I . . .' He found it difficult to speak. 'I . . . I am a Catholic by profession, but, now that my end is near . . .'

It seemed to him that Jeanne's steadfast brown eyes were watching him, that she was smiling at him now. It was not my fault, Jeanne, he thought. I loved you. In the beginning, I did. If we had been humble people . . . if we could have lived there in Béarn . . . farming our land together, planting our mulberries, watching them grow, we should have been happy. I should have been the gay one; you the sober wife. You would have kept me beside you. But you were a Queen and you made me a King. The position was too tempting for me. I became greedy for more power. I did not know what I wanted. One moment I was sure, the next I was unsure.

At length he spoke: 'Now that my end is near, my heart returns to the Protestant Faith.'

'Repent,' he was urged. 'Think of your sins, Monseigneur. Repent that you may enter into the Kingdom of Heaven.'

He looked at the man who had spoken, and recognised him. 'Ah, Raphael,' he said slowly. 'You have served me for twenty years, and this is the only time that you have ever warned me of my miserable mistakes.'

Then he began to think of his sins, to enumerate them, and to ask God for forgiveness.

'Oh, Lord,' he prayed, 'if I recover, I will send forth Lutheran missionaries to preach the gospel throughout France.'

He heard someone whisper: 'It is too late to talk thus.'

Ah yes. He understood. It was too late.

'Jeanne,' he moaned, 'why did you not come? You should have made the journey that you might be with me.'

He did not die at once. His brother, the Cardinal of Bourbon, came to him, and Antoine begged him to ask forgiveness for him of that other brother, Louis, the Prince of Condé, whom he had loved so dearly before religion had come between them.

'I will die a Huguenot!' cried Antoine, thinking of Louis and of Jeanne. 'It matters not whether people believe me to be sincere. I am resolved to die in accordance with the Confession of Luther.'

It was decided that he must be moved to more comfortable quarters, and one misty November day he was taken on to a boat and rowed down the Seine towards Saint-Maur. This was not wise, for the rocking of the boat was very painful to him, and when they carried him ashore he knew that his last moments had come.

The Guises had sent a monk to pray for him and, too weak to resist, Antoine listened to his prayers; and when they were over he murmured: 'Amen.'

Because of this the Guises said he died a Catholic, and if he had declared himself a Huguenot when he was dying, well, that was only to be expected of *L'Échangeur*.

In her stronghold of Béarn, Jeanne received the news.

She stared stonily before her. It is nothing to me, she assured herself. I had finished with him. I hated him . . . at our last meeting, if not before. When he refused to let me have my son, I knew I could never feel any tenderness towards him again.

Nevertheless, it was not Antoine the turn-coat, the unfaithful husband, the cruel father, of whom she must think, but Antoine the gay Prince at the christening of King Francis, Antoine the lover in a silver galleon triumphantly seizing his love. It was Antoine, lover and husband, whom she must remember.

And the tears rolled down the cheeks of the widow of the King of Navarre.

Catherine was in residence at her favourite Castle of Blois. Life was a little more secure than it had been a few months ago. The towns which had been taken by the Huguenots were being slowly won back; she herself was no longer a prisoner of the Guises; for she had been their prisoner; she knew it and they knew it, although they had tried so hard to disguise this fact.

Now she had lulled them to a certain feeling of security, and she must keep them thus. She must act with greater caution. She had learned an important lesson, and as she had been learning through bitter lessons all her life, she was not likely to forget this one.

She was glad that Francis of Guise was busily engaged in warfare. She was happier with that man out of the way. At the moment he was fighting for Orléans. Who knew what would happen to him! France's greatest soldier, yes; but Catherine's greatest enemy.

Catherine's thoughts turned from the Duke of Guise to her son Charles, the King,

Charles was growing up. He was only thirteen, it was true, but thirteen was a considerable age for a Valois King. They would have to marry him soon. Catherine smiled grimly. The boy still thought he was going to have Mary of Scotland. But perhaps his memories of her were growing dim by now. He was changing. One expected him to change. He could not remain static. He had to grow up. He was a strange boy, with many sides to his personality. There was a streak – more than a streak – of madness in him and it was widening as the years passed, the unbalanced fits were growing more frequent.

Yet he was clever. He could, at times, be eloquent, but he was too easily moved. She had seen his face work with emotion during a sermon or the reading of a poem which he thought particularly beautiful; she had seen his mouth twitch – though not with madness – and tears stream from his eyes. He himself wrote poetry, and he was modest enough to declare it to be worthless. Ronsard was one of his constant companions. He struck up friendships with his musicians – humble folk like that boy servant of the Duke of Bavaria, just a musician who had a gift for playing the lute; and the King of France would take him for his boon companion. Nor would the King be denied his pleasures; his brow would darken and he would frown, even at his mother, if called from his music and his poetry-reading. He would sit till long past midnight with the writers and musicians, and at such times he would be very happy. Then there would be no madness, only an aloof enchantment. Catherine would look in on him and his friends and find them all together, talking in low, earnest voices while the candles burned low; and he would turn to look at the intruder without seeing her, even though she was his mother, of whom, on all other occasions, he was deeply aware.

His tutors could do nothing with him at such times.

And then that mood would pass and he would be touched with black melancholy. Sometimes he would stay in his bed all day, and this was a sure sign that the madness was on him. Perhaps at midnight, he would be seized with a wild mood of hilarity, and he would awaken his friends – a different set of friends from the poets – and insist that they follow him; he would make them put on masks and carry lighted torches. It was alarming to see him at such times, his eyes glinting through his mask, his mouth working, the madness on him, the lust for violence. He and his friends would creep out of the palace and go to the apartments of one of their friends, whom they would thrash into unconsciousness. This was hardly a suitable pastime for the thirteen-year-old King of France, thought Catherine.

If there was not a flagellating party, he would hunt with such recklessness that none could keep up with him; he would thrash his horses and dogs with the energy which he used on his friends. A more harmless madness was that of imitating a blacksmith and hammering iron until he was exhausted.

Then he would return to normal; he would be gentle, loving, pliable; and it would invariably seem that when he had recovered he would have little remembrance of those terrifying bouts.

What should one do with such a son? Catherine did not have to wonder. She knew. She did not wish Charles to remain on the throne when Henry was ready to take it. Therefore she could look complacently on these fits of madness. Soon the periods of gentleness would grow less; and later they would disappear altogether. And then what would Charles the Ninth of France become? A maniac! Maniacs must be put away; they could not be allowed to breed sons. So much the better, since there was another waiting to take the throne of France.

Charles showed few signs of sexual perversion, in spite of his tutors. He was not voluptuous, nor inclined to amorousness. He was not like Margot – that minx who must be very closely watched – or young Henry of Guise, or that rough little Henry of Navarre. Those three would be lusty and lustful before long. No! He was not as they were; nor was he as his brother Henry. His passion for Mary of Scotland showed a lamentable normality in such matters; and it seemed that even expert tuition in perversion could not achieve the desired result.

Never mind! Charles was growing more and more unbalanced, and each fit of insanity left him weaker, not only in mind but in body.

Her thoughts of the King were broken up by the arrival of a messenger. She saw him ride into the courtyard, for the clatter of hoofs had brought her quickly to the window.

Something was afoot. Guise had taken Orléans. That must be the case, for those were the Guise colours down there. Well, she would feign great rejoicing, for it was very necessary that the Catholics should believe her to be of their faith. She must win back their respect, their belief in her as a good Catholic.

She went down to greet the messenger, but his face was grave; he had no news of victory, that was certain.

'What news?' asked Catherine.

'Terrible news, Madame,' cried the messenger. 'It is my lord Duke. He has been shot. He lies near to death.'

Margot was there beside her mother. The child had no restraint. She ran to the messenger, plucking at his sleeve. 'He is not *dead*! He must not die. Henry could not bear it if he died. Oh, Madame, my mother, we must send . . . send surgeons . . . we must send . . .'

'Be quiet!' said Catherine; and Margot even forgot her anxiety for the father of the boy she loved in her sudden fear of her mother.

'Tell me everything,' said Catherine.

'Madame, my lord Duke was making a tour of inspection before riding back to the castle and his lady wife. He had taken off his armour, for the battle was over. And then, from behind a hedge, there was a shot. My lord fell to the ground senseless. We got him to the castle, but he bleeds . . . he bleeds terribly, Madame.'

'We must send surgeons!' cried Margot. 'At once. Oh, at once. There must be no delay.'

'And,' said Catherine, 'they have caught the assassin?'

'Yes, Madame.'

'Who is he?'

'Poltrot de Méray.'

'All that matters,' cried Margot, 'is that we must be in time to save the Duke . . .'

'I will send surgeons at once,' said Catherine. 'Go back and tell the Duchess that help is on the way. I shall send my best surgeons to save the Duke.'

Margot hung on her mother's arm. 'Oh, thank you . . . thank you. We *must* save the Duke.'

Catherine gripped her daughter's arm so tightly that Margot wanted to scream. But she knew better than to do that. She allowed herself to be led away.

Catherine took her up to her apartment and locked her in an ante-room. Margot lay sobbing. Henry's father was hurt, perhaps dying. She was terrified of her mother, for, having shown her feelings in a way which she knew her mother would consider tasteless, she knew she was going to be severely punished. But for the moment she could think of no one but Henry, whom she loved more than anyone on Earth, of his devotion to his father, of the terrible grief he would suffer if the Duke were to die.

Catherine was talking to her surgeon, talking quietly through half-closed lips. He knew what she wished in regard to the Duke. He was to go and serve him as he knew his mistress would serve that great fighter, if she had his skill and could go in his place.

The man bowed and retired, and very soon he was riding with all speed to Orléans.

Catherine went to her daughter and herself administered the beating.

'Ten years old!' she said. 'And behaving like an ill-bred peasant.'

Margot dared not evade her mother's blows as she did those of others. She lay, accepting them, her body flinching from them, but her mind unaware of them almost, as she prayed silently: 'Holy Mother, do not let Henry's father die. You could not let Henry be hurt like that. The Duke is not only Henry's father; he is the greatest man in France. Holy Mother, save him.'

Catherine prayed neither to God nor the Virgin. But she too was thinking of the Duke; she was thinking of the handsome, scarred face, distorted with pain, the agony of death in those haughty eyes, the eyes of the man whom she had come to regard as her greatest enemy.

✢ ✢ ✢

Riding beside the handsome young boy who was now the head of the House of Lorraine, Margot was weeping silently.

He was so handsome, this Henry of Guise, with his fair curly hair, which seemed such a contrast with his manly face and his well-proportioned figure. Already he showed signs of the man he would become. Margot wanted to comfort him, to tell him that his grief was her grief, and that it would always be so.

'Talk of it, Henry,' she said. 'Talk of it, my dearest. To talk of it will help you.'

'Why should it have happened to him?' demanded Henry. 'Because of treachery, I tell you. I will not rest until I see his murderer dead at my feet.'

'His murderer has died a horrible death, Henry. He has suffered torture. There is comfort in knowing that the man who killed *Le Balafré* lies dead and useless now.'

'My father has not been avenged as I would have it,' cried Henry angrily. 'That miserable, low-born creature was the tool of others. I do not consider that my father has been avenged. You know what he said at the torture. You know whom he accused?'

'Coligny,' said Margot, her eyes flashing. 'Coligny . . . the pious . . . the good man! That is he whom Poltrot de Méray accused.'

'And that villain, that scoundrel, is the murderer of my father. De Méray said Coligny paid him money to murder my father. That is good enough for me.'

Margot said: 'But Coligny has told my mother that it was to buy a horse that he gave the man money, and that it had nothing to do with murdering the Duke.'

Henry dug his spurs into his horse and galloped ahead, that Margot might not see the tears in his eyes. He would never forget how they had carried in his father, his great father, his noble father whom he loved to idolatry. Henry could not bear to think of that once arrogant figure stretched out on a litter, bleeding, unable to speak clearly. Henry had vowed there and then: 'I will not rest content until I see his murderer dead before me. This I will work for. This I will achieve, and until I have achieved it, I will despise myself.' It was a vow; a dedication. And who was his enemy? He might have known. He might have guessed. It was none other than Gaspard de Coligny, the virtuous man, the man who gave Poltrot de Méray money to buy a horse, so he said – not to bring about the assassination of Francis Duke of Guise.

His wily uncle, the Cardinal of Lorraine, had talked to him very seriously. 'Henry, my nephew, remember what this means to you . . . to our house. You are its head. You are vehement; you are young and rash. Gaspard de Coligny is the greatest enemy of our house. He is the leader of the heretics. Henry, my dear nephew, we must protect our Faith; we must protect our house. One day, who knows, it may be a Prince of Lorraine who sits on the throne of France. How do we know, Henry, whether that might not be you, my nephew? Your father was a great man; he was strong and brave; he was the greatest man in France. Shall I tell you why? It was because he was possessed of rare calm, of great discretion; he knew when to act and – what was more important – he knew when not to act. You must walk in his footsteps. You must imitate your father in all you do. And then, nephew, who knows? Valois? Bourbon?' The Cardinal laughed. 'Dear nephew, I wonder whether your opinion of these Princes is the same as mine.'

'My uncle,' young Henry had said, 'you are right; but I have one wish, and that is to avenge my father.'

'You will avenge him best by doing what he would want you to do. Rest assured that when the time comes we shall not spare the assassin of your father. That time is not yet, but I'll swear to you that before the end of your life you shall see the lifeless body of the Admiral at your feet. That foot of yours shall kick him as he lies.'

Henry had covered his face with his hands, forgetting vengeance, forgetting this talk of a crown, remembering only that the one he loved most in the world – more than Margot even, more than any – was lost to him.

Margot rode up to him. 'Henry,' she cried, 'do not mind that I should see your tears. Look! See mine! For I love you, Henry, and your grief is my grief; and when we are married that is how it shall be all the days of our lives.'

He reached for her hand and pressed it; then they rode on together.

'I hate Coligny,' he said, for he was unable to stop talking of this matter.

'I hate him too,' said Margot.

'He admitted that he overheard the plot to kill my father. He admitted that, hearing it, he did nothing about it. Is that not like him? He is so good . . . so virtuous . . . he cannot tell a lie.'

'Hypocrite and heretic!' cried Margot.

'He said: "The words I utter in self-defence are not said out of regret for Monsieur de Guise. Fortune can deal no better stroke of good for the Kingdom and the Church of God; and most especially it is good for myself and my house." Those were his words.'

'He shall die for them,' said Margot.

'He shall! If I wait for years, mine shall be the hand that holds the sword which shall pierce his heart.'

As they rode through the streets of Paris they were recognised. An old market woman called out: 'Long live the little Duke of Guise!'

Others caught up the cry. 'A Guise! A Guise!'

Their horses were surrounded and Margot looked on, smiling proudly. She saw that the eyes of those who watched shone with admiration for the gallant figure of the boy; he had beauty which was beloved of Parisians. Perhaps they thought of their King with his bouts of madness; perhaps they thought of his brother Henry, who might one day be King; handsome, Henry was, it was true, but with long, sly Medici eyes and an Italian way of talking – an effeminate youth with earrings, necklaces and garments of an exaggerated fashion. Perhaps they thought of Hercule, the pockmarked little Prince. These were the children of the Italian woman, and the Parisians could not take them to their hearts, even though they were also the sons of good King Henry. But this boy with his virile, masculine beauty was a boy they could admire and love; besides, he was now a pathetic figure. His father – their idol – had been recently murdered. They were pleased to see him in company with a Princess of the reigning house. With tears in their eyes and love in their voices, they cheered the little Duke of Guise and the Princess Margot.

Henry was sufficiently the son of his father to know how to deal with such a situation.

He doffed his cap and spoke to them:

'Good people of Paris, dear Parisians, who have always shown love and friendship to my house and my father . . .' His voice shook a little, and a cry of 'The good God keep you!' rose from the crowd. 'My father,' went on Henry, 'my most gallant father, now lies murdered; but you must know that I will never let the murderer go free.'

The crowd cheered madly. The excitable Parisians were delighted with their little Duke.

'Power to your arm!' they cried. 'God preserve you. All power to Lorraine. A Guise! A Guise!'

And many came forward to kiss the little boy's hand as though he were the King of France himself.

When he and Margot rode into the courtyard of the Palace, Henry was smiling a little and Margot was delighted; the incident had done something to soothe his grief.

'Oh, Henry,' she cried, 'how they love you! Who knows, one day you and I may be King and Queen of France.'

When Margot went up to her apartments her mother was there.

Catherine was smiling, and Margot did not trust her mother's smiles. It was, however, a smile of pleasure, for Catherine was thinking that her affairs had taken a turn for the better. Antoine of Navarre was dead; Francis Duke of Guise was dead; she had no longer any need to concern herself with these men, and that, to say the least, was a great relief. Montmorency was the prisoner of the Huguenots, and Condé was in the hands of the Catholics. Oh yes, matters were certainly taking a turn for the better. If someone could dispose of the Cardinal of Lorraine and the Spanish Ambassador, all those who had grown to know her too well for her peace of mind would be removed.

'Well, my daughter,' she said, 'did you enjoy your jaunt with the King of Paris?'

Margot did not know what to answer. She expected a punishment, but none came. The Queen Mother was smiling as she continued with her secret thoughts.

✣ ✣ ✣

The court of France was making its royal progress to the Spanish frontier, where King Charles and the Queen Mother were to meet Elisabeth of Spain and Philip's Ambassador, the wily Duke of Alva.

The journey was a slow one; the train consisted of nearly a thousand men and women; great nobles each with his retinue made up the procession. There must be the transportation of household goods, including beds; there must be cooking utensils and food; there must be garments for state occasions. Catherine, with her two sons, Charles and Henry, required extensive *impedimenta*; and young Margot, fully conscious of her person, though still only a child, was already beginning to be a leader of fashion and must also carry a large wardrobe.

Henry of Navarre rode with them, often side by side with Margot. Why, thought Margot, was it not that other Henry, her beloved King of Paris, instead of this boy with the alert black eyes and the untidy black hair which grew straight up from his head in the ungainly fashion of Nérac, who did not care that his hands were sometimes unclean and who now and then broke out into the coarse Béarnais dialect?

Margot looked down her Valois nose at him, but he did not show any resentment. Margot meant nothing to him. He liked girls, but if Margot did not like him, there were others who did. He did not care what class of girls they were – peasant girls, beggar girls, princesses – they were all girls to Henry of Navarre, and if Margot, Princess of France, was not attracted to him, she was one of the few who were not.

Charles the King was quiet on the journey. He was realising that he would never marry Mary Queen of Scots. She was only a memory to him now – beautiful, but distant, almost unreal; and his mother was trying to arrange a match with the Queen of England for him. He did not like the thought of marriage with that woman, for he had heard such tales of her. She was a virago; she would bully him, so he had heard. But his mother had said that was nonsense. He was the King of France, and if he married the Queen of England he would be the King of England as well; it would be for her to live in France with him, and he could command her to do so; they could set a Lieutenant-General over England, so that life would be much the same as it was now, except that he would have two crowns instead of one.

He did not want this marriage, but his mother thought it would be good; therefore it must be so. Sometimes he wondered whether she wanted the throne for his brother Henry. Everything Henry did was right. Henry was the only one who was not afraid of her; she adored Henry; she wanted everything for him. Perhaps she wanted Charles out of the way, settled in England, so that his brother Henry could take the throne of France! Charles did not know, but he was full of misgivings.

He had wanted to protest against this English marriage. The

Queen of England did not seem to want it, nor did her Ambassador, who had such long conversations with him and his mother. As Charles rode in that grand procession, he could still hear his mother's voice, suave and persuasive; he could still see the cold face of the English Ambassador.

'Your first objection is the age of my son. But if the Queen Elizabeth will put up with it, I will put up with the age of the Queen,' said his mother; and Charles had quickly said what he had been told to say: 'I should be very pleased if your mistress would be as pleased with my age as I am with hers.' The English Ambassador said his Queen would never consent to live in France. 'A Lieutenant-General could govern her kingdom,' said Charles's mother. 'The English would not obey a Lieutenant, and Lieutenants grow insolent, says my Queen.' 'Ah,' sighed Charles's mother, 'my good sister Elizabeth already calls herself the Queen of France, but she is so only in name. Through this marriage she could be the Queen of France indeed.' The Ambassador had terrified Charles by turning and speaking to him, with that accent of the English when they spoke French, as though to speak French was somehow comic and shameful: 'If you were but three or four years older, if you had but seen the Queen, and if you were really in love with her, I should not be astonished at this haste.' Under his mother's eyes, Charles had replied: 'But in good sooth I love her.' And at that the English Ambassador had smiled, and, with that bluntness on which the English prided themselves, replied: 'At your age, Sire, none knoweth what love is.' Charles grew hot at the thought of it.

He had been glad to get away from the conference; he was glad to think of the coming meeting with his sister. It was five years since he had seen her. Then she had been sad – sad to leave her native France for a country and a husband she had never seen.

What a tragic thing was this marrying of royal people, though not so bad for a prince as for a princess, for princesses lost their country, their nationality, when they married foreign husbands. His sister Elisabeth was a Spaniard now.

He hoped nothing would come of the negotiations with England. Who knew, there might be negotiations with Scotland one day; then he could truthfully say: 'I love the Queen of Scotland.'

On they went, staying at various castles on the way, where banquets, balls and masques were given in their honour.

Margot was enjoying all this; the only drawback was the absence of Henry of Guise; she could, however, give herself up wholeheartedly to teasing Henry of Navarre. She criticised the way he rode his horse.

'Like a peasant,' she told him.

'I'll ride faster than you.'

'We must race one day.'

'Now,' he suggested.

'I do not choose to do so now.'

'Come, you have said it. Let us put it to the test.'

'And break from the procession! You have the manners of a peasant. Do they teach you nothing of etiquette in Nérac?'

'I learn what is good for me,' said Henry of Navarre, his eyes glinting.

When they rested at the next castle and went hunting in the forest, Henry reminded her of her challenge.

Margot prevaricated, gauging the strength of the boy. He had no gallantry. Henry of Guise would not thus challenge a princess.

'I do not wish to ride against you. I dislike you.'

Henry was angry; he retorted, like the blunt Béarnais he was: 'You will have to learn to like me, for one day I shall be your husband.'

'Do not dare to say such things to me.'

'I shall dare to say what is truth.'

Margot could smile slyly; she knew that one of the objects of this journey down to the Spanish frontier was to renew negotiations for her marriage to Don Carlos, and her brother Henry's to the old widowed sister of King Philip. But Henry of Navarre did not know this, nor did his stern old mother. Margot was not half Medici for nothing; she was an adept at the art of eavesdropping, particularly when she herself was under discussion.

She betrayed nothing of this. Let him think that one day he would be her husband. It amused her. Let him tremble to contemplate the trouble in store for him with the Princess Margot as his wife!

'So you think you will be my husband, then?'

'It is arranged.'

'That remains to be seen. It could not be for years.'

'But the marriages of princes and princesses are arranged when they are young.'

'You should feel honoured, Monsieur of Navarre, to have a marriage arranged for you with a Princess of France, for even if it does not come to pass, it has been arranged, and that is an honour you should recognise.'

'Honour?' he said, the hot blood staining his brown face red. 'If you are a Princess, I am a Prince.'

'My father was a great King. He was the great King Henry the Second of France.'

'My father was the King of Navarre.'

Margot began to chant: ' "*Caillette qui tourne sa jaquette.*" '

At which Henry of Navarre turned to her and would have struck her, had she not galloped off and joined the group about her brother Charles. Then she turned and put out her tongue at Henry of Navarre.

Catherine stepped into the boat which was to carry her across the river, on the other side of which she would meet her daughter. Everywhere about her was the glitter of pageantry, proclaiming to all the importance of this occasion. Leafy arches had been erected, under which the procession passed on its way to the river. The heat was great, and Catherine felt it intensely on account of her heavy figure. She was excited; her face was pale, and her eyes seemed larger and more prominent than usual. This was not so much a meeting with a daughter – now nineteen – whom she had not seen since she was fourteen, as a meeting with the Queen of Spain, the consort of the man Catherine feared more than any on Earth. Her daughter? She did not exactly love her – she loved no one but her son Henry – but she was proud of her, proud of the exalted position she occupied as the wife of the mightiest monarch in the world. Her other daughter, Claude, whom she had visited on her way through France, meant little to her. Claude, a docile, charming girl, was only the wife of the Duke of Lorraine; it was a very different matter, coming face to face with the Queen of Spain.

On the other side of the river were assembled the Queen of Spain and those who accompanied her to the border. Philip had not deigned to come; he had more weighty matters to occupy him; but representing him had come the great Duke of Alva.

The fiery heat of the midsummer sun was unbearable, and several of Catherine's soldiers died of suffocation in their armour before the arrival of the Queen of Spain.

Catherine greeted her daughter warmly; Elisabeth was aloof, solemn, correct; in five years they had made a Spanish lady of the little French girl. Yet Catherine noticed, even in that first ceremonial greeting, that Elisabeth had not entirely forgotten the fear she had once had of her mother.

In great pomp they crossed the river, and the next day they rode into the town of Bayonne with greater magnificence than any in that town had ever seen before. Elisabeth rode between her brother Henry and the Cardinal of Bourbon, with a hundred gentlemen about them. The chief citizens of the town of Bayonne, richly dressed in scarlet, held a canopy over the Queen of Spain as they escorted her to the Cathedral, whence, after listening to music and prayer, she went to the Royal Palace, where little King Charles was lodged. Catherine noticed that the men of Spain who were in attendance were mounted on miserable mules and wore no state dress; she knew by this that Philip of Spain intended to snub her; he was implying by this lack of respect that he did not care for what his Ambassador had told him of Catherine's recent manœuvres with the Huguenot Party.

Little Charles gave his sister, as a present, a horse with a saddle ornamented with precious stones and pearls; other gifts were exchanged, and the tournaments, balls, masques and banquets, which were to last for days, began. The peasants danced their native dances before the royal visitors and their suites; others played on the musical instruments which were indigenous to their particular region. The Provençaux played their cymbals; the Champenois showed their skill with the hautbois, while the Bourgignons joined them; and the Poitevins performed on the bagpipes. Great prominence was given to all things Spanish; music from Spain figured largely in the entertainments; Spanish dances were danced by all; and Ronsard had composed poems for the occasion which were read aloud, and all these praised the greatness of Spain.

But the two parties had not met merely to dance together and to praise each other. Under cover of these festivities they met as opponents in the game of statecraft – Catherine with little King Charles for France, and Elisabeth with the experienced Duke of Alva for Spain.

The Duke of Alva was about fifty-five at this time, a finely made man with all the solemnity and dignity of a Spanish don. His thin face, with its yellowish skin, looked like that of a man already dead, but Catherine was aware of those keen and piercing eyes and all the shrewdness which lay behind them. She knew she would have need of all her cunning, and that King Charles would be of little use to her in their game of wits.

They met – the four of them; and when they did so Catherine felt a momentary anger against the Queen of Spain. She had never liked children who were not docile to her command, and Elisabeth, very lovely now with the abundant black hair which she had inherited from her father, and those black eyes and the dazzling, white skin, seemed more Spanish than French, far more the wife of King Philip of Spain than the daughter of Catherine de' Medici. Elisabeth hated those whom she called 'heretic' as much as did her husband; and it was startling to see her beautiful face grow almost ugly with hatred whenever the word Huguenot was mentioned.

She talked to Catherine of the religious troubles in France, but Catherine did not wish to discuss these matters with one who had become as rigorously Catholic as her royal husband.

'Your husband suspects me of favouring the Huguenots,' said Catherine.

'What cause have you to think, Madame, that the King mistrusts your Majesty?' asked Elisabeth. 'Only evil-minded people could give you such ideas.'

Catherine sighed. Here was some of that deceit of which she herself was mistress. She said: 'Oh, dearest daughter, you have become very Spanish.'

'You are afraid of war with Spain,' said Elisabeth, ignoring the comment. 'If that is so, why do you not talk to the Duke? That is why he is here, Madame – that you may come to terms which will bring peace to our two countries.'

Catherine turned to the Duke and talked of the marriages she wished to arrange. First, Don Carlos and Margot. They could see for themselves what a bright little Princess Margot was, and Don Carlos would be surely enchanted with her. And, second, Philip's sister Juana and Prince Henry. It was true that Juana was a little old for Henry, but in royal marriages a difference of age must not be looked upon as a barrier.

The Duke of Alva smiled his thin smile. 'I notice that you do not mention religion, Madame. And that, I assure you, should be the main subject of our discussion.'

As there was no help for it, Catherine began to talk of all that had happened in recent years in her country – always from her point of view; but Alva insisted on giving his version of affairs, which was a little different from that of Catherine.

'Well,' said Catherine at length, 'what is the remedy which will put an end to our troubles? Tell me that.'

'But, Madame,' said Alva suavely, 'who knows better than you do? Is it not you who should say what has to be done? Tell me, and I will pass on your wishes to my royal master.'

'Your royal master knows better than I do what is happening in France!' retorted Catherine. 'Tell me by what means he proposes to suppress the Huguenots.'

'To take up arms would be useless,' said Alva. 'Strong measures must suffice. Banish the sect from France.'

The Queen of Spain put in: 'Why does not my brother, King Charles, chastise all who rebel against God?'

Charles looked in fear at his mother, who said sharply: 'He does all that is possible.' She saw the fanatical gleam in the eyes of her daughter and in those of Alva. To avoid the subject of religion, she tried to speak once more of the proposed marriages, but Alva stopped her. He dispensed with the customary etiquette and solemnity of Spain and spoke bluntly:

'Madame, we must settle this matter of religion. Give it your consideration, and we will discuss it later. I shall tell you the wishes of my master, and I think you will agree with him.'

And so it was that later, in a quiet gallery of the Bayonne Palace, Alva and Catherine talked earnestly together. It was comparatively cool in the shaded gallery, sheltered as it was from the great heat of the midsummer sun. Alva in his darkly severe Spanish dress and Catherine in her long black robes paced back and forth, their garments flapping as they walked, like the wings of giant birds.

'. . . the heads of Condé and Coligny, Madame, should be severed from their bodies,' said Alva quietly. 'Condé is a man whom many will follow, but he is not a great man. Nevertheless, we shall not be safe from these heretics until he is dead.

The Admiral of France too must die. He is a leader of men, a man who knows how to bind men to him. He is a great soldier; and yet you allow him to lead your enemies!'

'My lord Duke, how could I lay hands on such a man?'

'Madame, Monsieur de Guise was a great man, yet he was shot by a spy of Coligny's. Coligny works fast, while you hesitate. Can this hesitation be due to your fondness for these Huguenots?'

'You have been listening to evil tales concerning me. I have no love for the Huguenots. I am a true Catholic.'

'I wonder how your Majesty can administer justice when it has to pass through the hands of your Chancellor, Michel l'Hôpital . . . the Huguenot!'

'He is not a Huguenot, my lord Duke.'

'You, Madame, must be the only person in France who does not think so. In your husband's lifetime he was known as a Protestant, and as long as he is Chancellor, Huguenots will be favoured. My Catholic King wants to know what you propose to do to remedy these matters. This is the reason why the Queen and I are here at Bayonne.'

Catherine could only reply: 'I am a true Catholic. You must believe this.'

'Your Majesty will have to prove it.'

'That I will do. But . . . in my own way. I will not plunge my country into civil war. These things must be done slowly, cautiously, and over a long time. I have a notion that I might, on some pretext or other, gather in one spot all the most influential of the Huguenots, all their leaders and thousands of their followers.'

'And then, Madame?'

Catherine's eyes shone. 'Then, my lord Duke, I would

suggest that the Catholics should deal with them, take them by surprise.'

The Duke nodded. 'His Catholic Majesty would need to see such evidence before he felt he could have complete confidence in your good faith.'

Catherine went on talking as though she had not heard him. 'It would be in Paris – for Paris is our most loyal city, Paris is Catholic. Yes, some pretext . . . I know not what as yet. For that we must wait. This must not have the air of being arranged; it must happen naturally . . . a sudden annihilation of the heretics by those of the true faith. All the important leaders would surely die – Condé, Coligny, Rochefoucauld . . . every one of them and all their followers, every single Huguenot in the city.'

'I will carry your plans to his most Catholic Majesty.'

She laid her fingers to her lips. 'Never let it be mentioned in despatches. It is a matter for our ears alone and those of his Majesty. I do not know when it will be possible, but I give you my word that it shall be. I must wait for the opportunity . . . the perfect moment. It may not be for years. His Majesty must trust me till then.'

'If this scheme were put into effect,' said Alva, 'I doubt not that his Majesty would recognise you as a friend. He would never wish to make war on such a friend.'

'He shall see,' said Catherine. 'All I ask is patience – patience and secrecy.'

Alva was so satisfied with that conversation that he gave up the rest of the time to discussing the proposed marriages; and at last came the moment for the two parties to say farewell.

Fondly the Queen Mother kissed her daughter. As for Charles, he was so affected by the parting that he burst into bitter tears. It seemed to him that it was indeed a terrible thing to be a princess of a royal house, to marry and to leave your home and country for a strange land, a strange people. He could not restrain his tears, even though he knew that the Spaniards, such sticklers for etiquette, must be very shocked at the sight of them. His mother and his ministers regarded him coldly.

'But I cannot help it,' said Charles. 'I do not care if she is the Queen of Spain. First she was my sister. I remember how I used to love her, and I do not want to be parted from her.'

Charles watched on the river bank while his sister, accompanied by her train, was carried away from him. He wept so bitterly that, afterwards, people said he must have had some premonition that he would never see her again.

✤ ✤ ✤

Catherine was mistaken when she thought that the conversation in the gallery had not been heard by any but herself and Alva.

Young Henry of Navarre had a guilty conscience. He had been separated from his mother for what seemed a long time, but he did not forget her teachings. He was being brought up with the little Princes and Princess of France. There were occasions when he saw his mother; he had seen her as they had journeyed down to Bayonne; he knew how she longed to take him back to Béarn with her and bring him up in their own religion. But this was forbidden; it was forbidden by King Charles, and that meant that it was forbidden by the Queen Mother. Henry was in awe of Catherine as everyone else was, and he kept out of her way as much as possible. She was not unkind to him; in fact, she had implied that she found his quick wits amusing. Sometimes he thought that she compared him with Charles and Hercule, and not unfavourably. 'He is droll, that little Henry of Navarre,' she would say. Or: 'Would that his mother could see him now!' Then she would laugh loudly in that rather terrifying way of hers, so that he knew that he had done something of which his mother would not approve, and he would be unhappy about it until he forgot.

He was, he feared, not a very good little boy. He imitated the Princes; he swaggered about the court; he used oaths, and listened to, and repeated, coarse jests. He had learned a good deal of matters of which he knew his mother would rather he remained in ignorance; and he neglected to learn those things which she would have wished him to learn. Already he knew that there was something about him which made him very attractive to the opposite sex. Women liked to kiss and fondle him; and he was not averse to being kissed and fondled, for the truth was that he liked them every bit as much as they liked him. He longed to be fourteen, so that he could be a real man.

When his mother had last seen him at Macon, on the journey down to the border, she had been more shocked than usual. He had overheard her express her fears to the Queen Mother, who had laughed aloud and said: 'Oh come. Do you want him to be a prude? He is a Prince who will have to live among men and women. Let him grow up. Let him be a man . . . for it is my opinion that that is something neither you nor I will be able to prevent.'

And his mother had said to him: 'Henry, my son, try not to follow in the footsteps of these licentious people whom you see about you. That is not the right way to live. Try to remember always that you are a Huguenot.'

He nodded, very anxious to please her, very sorry that he

was as he was, liking so much those things which it was not good for him to like.

'I am forced to go to mass with the Princes,' he said.

'I know, my son.'

'It is much against my will, but I never forget what you have told me.'

'They can send you to mass, my son, but they can never make you participate in it.'

'They will not. I swear they will not.'

That satisfied her in some measure, and he was determined to show her how he loved her and that he would remember all that she had taught him.

He was an intelligent boy and very interested in everything that went on around him; and he knew there were times when his mother was in acute danger. He knew too that what happened to his mother affected him closely. The times were dangerous, and he was a boy who knew how to keep his ears open.

The Pope had excommunicated his mother, and had wanted to declare Henry and his sister illegitimate on the grounds that his mother was never really married to his father because she had previously been married to the Duke of Clèves. There was yet another plot to kidnap his mother and take her before the Inquisition, to torture her into changing her faith, and then finally to burn her at the stake. This would have been brought about but for the plot's reaching the ears of the Queen of Spain. Elisabeth, Catholic though she was, had been unable to bear the thought of such a near relative's enduring such a fate, and she had warned Jeanne in time.

Henry did want his mother to know that, although he was forced to attend mass and was becoming very like the Princes of France, he never forgot her and was true to the Reformed Faith.

He had seen some of the methods of spying in palaces; and it was not very difficult for a little boy to secrete himself in the great gallery where he had discovered the Queen Mother was to confer with the Duke of Alva.

He was excited by this adventure; imagining, all the time, what would happen to him if he were caught. With madly beating heart, he hid himself in a cupboard, covered himself with old clothes which he found there, and with his ear to the cupboard door, caught snatches of that momentous conversation between Catherine and Alva. As soon as possible, Henry escaped from the cupboard and went to one of his attendants, a man named de Calignon; and he told this man all that he had heard.

De Calignon said that he was a wily little diplomat, and later that day showed him a letter in code which he was despatching at once to the Queen of Navarre.

Henry was delighted. He felt that he could now swear and swagger, kiss and be kissed to his heart's content. Surely a little wickedness might be forgiven such a wily diplomat?

Since she had become a widow, Jeanne had thrown herself wholeheartedly into the cause of the Huguenots. Energetic in the extreme, she needed some such great cause, that she might forget the bitterness of her married life. Now at least she was free from Antoine, free of those continual thoughts of him which had tormented her for so long. All her hopes now were in her children, and Henry, her heir, was the one who caused her great anxiety. He was a delightful boy, but he was his grandfather and her uncle, King Francis the First, all over again. That much was obvious; he was already showing signs of the sensuality which had characterised these men. Had she been able to look after him herself – which was her dearest wish – this would not have worried her unduly. His virile masculinity would have been guided into the right channels. But what could happen to such a child at the decadent Valois court? The cynical attitude of the Queen Mother disturbed her. Catherine would be amused by the boy's frolics, delighted by them, and no doubt she encouraged them.

Her sweet little daughter gave her no such anxieties. Catherine was pretty and clever, yet meek and docile, a lovely little girl of whom to be proud. Jeanne was proud of Henry, of course – proud and afraid on his account.

Jeanne knew that ever since the death of Antoine her danger had been acute. Since there had been a temporary lull in the civil war, other methods had been used to attack her – more sly, more insidious than the sword.

She had been excommunicated. Much she cared! For the Pope of Rome she had nothing but contempt. But when she remembered how nearly she had come to being captured by the Inquisition, she could not help shuddering. She was no coward, but she knew something of the terrible tortures inflicted by those men. Sometimes she dreamed that she was in their hands, that the cruel eyes of the torturers gleamed at her, that harsh hands, wielding red-hot pincers which would tear her flesh, were laid upon her; she dreamed she heard the crackle of faggots at her feet.

There was danger all around her. She had been robbed of her beloved son; her kingdom and his was in perpetual danger. Indeed, had it been in the interest of France to support Spain, she would now have lost her territory; she would have been a prisoner in the dark dungeons of the Inquisition. Catherine, oddly enough, had been her friend in this; Catherine had defended her against Spain; but Jeanne did not for a moment forget that this was a matter of expediency for Catherine, as Catherine did not want to see Spaniards encroaching on more Navarre territory.

Jeanne grew cold now, thinking of the plot to make her children illegitimate, to seize her person and carry her off to Spain. She was never free from the unpleasant attentions of Spain. She knew a little of the character of the tyrant of Madrid, who ruled such a large section of the world. He had once asked the hand of Jeanne in marriage, and the marriage had not taken place. For that slight to his most Catholic Majesty death was too good for Jeanne of Navarre. The same characteristic showed in his attitude to Elizabeth of England. He wished to see the utter destruction of Jeanne of Navarre and Elizabeth of England, for both had been offered the hand of the King of Spain, and neither had taken it.

The plot had failed, but very narrowly. Its object had been to put her in one of the prisons of the Holy Office and her children into a Spanish fortress. When she and they were disposed of, the Spanish troops would seize Lower Navarre. There were many people in this plot apart from King Philip, and one of these was the licentious, crafty Cardinal of Lorraine. Jeanne believed fervently that God was with her, for a certain Dimanche, who had been taking messages to Spain, had fallen ill and in his delirium had disclosed the plot. This had come to the ears of Elisabeth of Spain, who, braving the wrath of her husband – as no one else would have dared to do – had warned Jeanne in time, so that she had been able to fortify her frontiers to such effect that the plot was defeated.

But in what an uneasy world she lived where so many longed for her destruction!

She would win in the end. She was sure of that. Fanaticism had taken the place in Jeanne's heart so recently occupied by her love for her husband and her desire for domestic peace.

Nothing mattered but the Faith; nor did it seem to her of any great consequence by what road she and her followers travelled to their goal, as long as they reached it.

Francis, Duke of Guise, had been murdered. Coligny said that he had not bribed Poltrot de Méray to assassinate the Duke. But what did it matter if he had done so? What mattered such a lie in a good cause? What mattered murder? If Coligny had been instrumental in bringing about the death of an enemy, then all good Huguenots must rejoice.

Jeanne had changed gradually. Her passionate love of sincerity had become clouded over. Bitter humiliation, frustration, misery, danger . . . and her Faith . . . had made of the honest woman a fanatic who could smile at murder.

And now came the report of what her little Henry had overheard in the gallery of Bayonne. A massacre of Huguenots was planned – a greater and more terrible massacre than any that had taken place before.

Jeanne lost no time in writing to Coligny and Condé, warning them of what her son had overheard of the conversation between the Queen Mother and the Duke of Alva. She knew that this was going to rouse fresh trouble. She knew that it was very likely that the bloody strife would break out again.

It mattered not. Nothing mattered but the Huguenot cause. It did not even matter that her son would continue to live at the decadent Valois court, that he would become profligate in his habits. How could it, when he could act the spy with such effect?

✤ ✤ ✤

In the Castle of Condé, the Princess Eléonore was feeling weak and ill, and she knew that her end was very near.

Her husband was no longer a prisoner of the Catholics, and she could send for him, but she did not immediately do so. Sadly she thought of him, of their early life together, of his gay optimism and how he had taught her to be gay. How happy they might have been – as happy as Jeanne and her Antoine might have been – but for their position in this troubled country.

She and her husband had been everything to one another in the early days; it was she who had fired him with the desire to fight for the Faith. She had always known that he lacked her religious instincts, that he was first of all a soldier who must have excitement and adventure; but once he had adopted his cause, he did remain loyal to it. He did not, as his brother had, deny his Faith as well as his obligations to his wife. Poor Jeanne, what she must have suffered! What bitter humiliation had Antoine showered upon her!

There were continual prayers at the Castle of Condé. Eléonore's children were with her, and she prayed that the lives they led would be straight and honourable. She tried to shut out of her mind the thought of Louis with the beautiful wanton, Isabelle de Limeuil.

Why had he not remained faithful to her? How could he have been so weak, knowing all the time that Isabelle was a spy of the Queen Mother's? What charm had this woman to tempt him in such circumstances? It was not as though he were a fool, as poor Antoine had been. Perhaps it was that love of excitement in her husband which had made him such an easy victim of the plots of the Queen Mother – that puckish determination to court danger.

And the Queen Mother had deliberately wrecked the happy home, not only of the Princess of Condé, but also that of Jeanne of Navarre. Poor Louis! He was so attractive, and women had always found him irresistible. It had always been so – more with him even than with Antoine. It was not only his relationship with Isabelle de Limeuil that had set the country talking scandal against the Prince of Condé, for there had been others besides Isabelle. Calvin had written to Louis, protesting; Coligny had begged him to mend his ways. Louis always meant to; he was very sorry for his weakness; but then – a goblet of wine, a gay song and a pair of bright eyes, and he was caught again.

She had been sleepless with anxiety; she had been filled with misgivings; and one morning when she came down from her apartments it was obvious from her expression that a great peace had come to her; she knew that very soon she would be leaving this world's troubles for ever.

She sent a messenger to the Prince to tell him that she could not live long, but she instructed the messenger to break the news gently, that he might not suffer any great shock.

'You must tell him,' she said, 'that I have one aspiration. It is that our spirits may continue to be bound together. Tell him also that I conjure him to keep watch over our children in my stead, that they may be brought up in the fear of God.'

When Condé received the messenger and heard the news of his wife's sickness, he was overcome with grief. Mercurial in temperament, there was nothing for him now but the very depth of his despair. He made all haste to the Castle of Condé, and there he flung himself beside his wife's bed and poured bitter reproaches on himself and his conduct.

'You must live, my love, that I may prove to you that there has never been any in my life but you. You must give me the chance to show how deeply I love you.'

The tears he shed were genuine; but she also knew that what he meant this week he would cease to mean next. Such men were Louis and his brother Antoine, and because they were so, not only must their wives and children suffer, but the great cause of their religion be put into jeopardy.

Eléonore stroked his hair.

'My darling,' she said, 'you have given me great happiness. I would not have you different, for if you had been different, how could you have been my love?'

'I have not loved you as you deserve to be loved. I am a rogue. Tell me so. Tell me you hate me, for I deserve that. I deserve to be unhappy for the rest of my life.'

He was so handsome, with his head flung back and the tears on his cheeks, so earnest in his protestations. But how long would it be before he was swearing eternal fidelity to Isabelle de Limeuil or Madame de Saint-André? How long before they, and others too, would hear from those handsome lips that they were the loves of his life?

Charming Condé, so unstable in his emotions, yet so resolute in battle! Why had these Bourbons, so gifted with their charm and beauty, both been so fickle? Were the characters of these men responsible for the failure of the Reformation in France? They could not resist women, even those they knew to be the spies of the Queen Mother.

But what was the use of regretting now? The end was near for Eléonore.

'Oh, my darling!' cried Louis. 'My dearest wife! Blessed will the moment be when God commands us to meet in eternity!'

'Do not reproach yourself, my love,' said Eléonore. 'Only look after our children and remember that I have loved you. Remember the happiness of our days together. Remember the sober, prim little girl you married and whom you taught to laugh. Promise to look after our children and I shall be well content.'

She had her son brought to her and begged him to honour King Charles, the Queen of Navarre, his father and his Uncle Gaspard. 'Never forget the allegiance to the Faith I have taught you,' she implored him.

The boy was weeping, and she asked her husband to take him away and to leave her for a while. When they had gone she lay back smiling, her lips shaping the words of a prayer: 'Oh, God, my winter is past and my spring is come . . .'

When Condé knew that she was indeed dead there was no stemming his grief. It seemed to him that his infidelities came back to mock him; he remembered so much that shamed him.

'Oh, what a scoundrel am I!' he groaned.

His little daughter came to him and tried to comfort him. He lifted her in his arms and said to her: 'Try, my darling, to be like her. If you are as she was, I shall love you more and more. Girls are said to take after their fathers, but you must try to be like your mother. In her you would find nothing that could not serve as a cherished ideal.'

He stayed in the Palais de Condé mourning for some weeks; he kept his children about him and talked continually of their mother; he longed to have his life over again, he said; he longed to turn back the clock.

But Condé's moods changed rapidly, and this one of remorse had lasted longer than usual. There was work to be done, he declared. He could no longer stay with his family.

Isabelle was waiting for him, more alluring, more beautiful than ever. He told her of his new resolutions to lead a better life. Isabelle listened and commiserated. She knew that it would not be difficult to obliterate those new resolutions of the most charming sinner in France.

Back at court after the trip to Bayonne, Catherine had found that the feud between the Colignys and the Guises was growing dangerous. Young Henry of Guise, whom she had thought of as nothing more than a boy, seemed, with his new position and responsibilities, to have become a man. Youth though he was, he was head of his house, and he could not forget nor forgive his father's death. Catherine saw that such enmity – as seemed always to be the case – was more than the quarrel of one man with another, more than the quarrel even of one family with another; it was once more the quarrel between one religious faction and another, just as the quarrels of Diane de Poitiers and Madame d'Étampes had been in the reign of the first Francis; and in these quarrels were the sparks which set the fire of civil war raging throughout France.

Catherine went to see Gaspard de Coligny in his home at Châtillon, where he was enjoying a life of temporary seclusion with his family. How different Gaspard seemed with his wife and his family and the domestic calm all about him! She realised that these joys in which he was now indulging with such obvious content were what he wanted from life, but he was a man with a cause, a faith; and if he were called upon to fight for it, he must leave everything to do so. Here, then, was another of these fanatics.

Catherine sought an early opportunity of disclosing to Coligny the meaning of her visit. She joined him in his gardens where he was at work. He enjoyed his gardens and he had produced at Châtillon one of the loveliest Catherine had ever seen.

'Monsieur de Coligny,' said Catherine when she found herself alone with the Admiral, 'what trouble you caused us when you had dealings with an assassin named Poltrot de Méray!'

Coligny's face stiffened. Did he, Catherine wondered, arrange to have that shot fired which sent Francis of Guise reeling from his horse to lie senseless on the ground? He was obviously no common murderer, but might he not kill for the Faith? Oh yes, Catherine decided, as long as he could make his excuses with his God, he would kill. 'I did it, Lord, for you . . .' As long as he could say that with what he would consider a clear conscience, he would do anything, she was sure.

'I believed,' said Coligny, 'that the matter had been settled.'

'Not to my satisfaction, I fear. That is what I wish to speak to you about. De Méray was your man, was he not?'

'He was my man.'

'Your spy, Monsieur?'

'He worked for me.'

Catherine smiled, and Coligny went on: 'Madame, what fresh trouble is this? Have I not answered every question satisfactorily?'

'Oh, just a little private interest, that is all.' Catherine wished he would discuss the murder with her. It would be interesting to compare notes on such a subject with such a man. 'You heard this man plotting to kill the Duke and you did nothing about it?'

'I agree to that.'

Catherine nodded. Doubtless he had hinted to de Méray that he wished Guise were dead, but did not care to have the guilt on his own soul. Perhaps he had offered to pay money to this man if he would bear the burden in the eyes of their God. The methods of these people made her want to laugh out loud. De Méray, talking of his plot to kill the Duke and talking of it in Coligny's hearing, had meant: 'Do you approve, master?' And Coligny's silence had meant approval. Perhaps, thought Catherine, as she had thought on other occasions, I and these people are not so very different.

'I did not come, however, to talk of past events, Monsieur,' said Catherine. 'The little Guise is a fiery personality. In him I fear we have another Duke Francis. Young still, but perhaps the more reckless for that. He is declaring open feud between his house and yours, for although we know that you had no hand *whatsoever* in the murder of the Duke of Guise – your very noble confession that you heard the plot discussed exonerates you completely – yet this fiery young fellow will not have it so. Now, you know, Admiral, that these feuds are distasteful to me. I would have peace in this kingdom.'

'What would you have me do, Madame?'

'I cannot have my Admiral suspected of murder. I propose to hold a banquet at Amboise – no, let it be at Blois – and there I wish to proclaim your innocence in this matter. The guests of honour will be yourself and the Guises. I want you to show your friendship to each other, to extend your hand and give the kiss of peace. I want all to know that there is friendship between you, and that the House of Guise no longer doubts your innocence in the unfortunate death of its kinsman.'

'Madame, this is impossible. We have so recently been fighting a bitter war – they in one camp, I in another.'

'That is why it must be done, dear Admiral. I cannot have that rash boy going about speaking of these matters, inflaming his followers. We have peace – an uneasy one, it is true – and we must make it a lasting one. This must be done for the sake of that rash boy, if not for yours.'

'You think that by taking my hand and kissing my cheek he would become my friend, Madame?'

'I wish to proclaim to all that there is no enmity between you. You must do this. I insist. I command.'

Coligny bowed.

'You will be there at Blois to do as I wish?' said Catherine.

'It is your command, Madame.'

High above the village stood the imposing Castle of Blois. Its embrasured windows looked down on the wide stream of the Loire, bounded by the hills and vineyards of Touraine. There was uneasiness in the village; all knew that inside the château the Queen Mother had organised a banquet to promote friendship between the Colignys and the Guises. This was disquieting, for if trouble were to break out in the castle, it would extend to the surrounding villages. Huguenots trembled and thought of the massacre at Vassy, when Duke Francis of Guise had slaughtered Huguenots while they knelt at worship. Catholics told themselves to be ready to rally to the little Duke.

They had seen Duke Henry riding near the castle, handsome and remarkably like his father, so that Huguenots trembled to behold him, while Catholics exulted. The Admiral they had also seen – stern of face, handsome, though in a different manner from the arrogant and dashing Henry of Guise. A great and a good man, it was said; and yet if he had had a hand in the murder of that young boy's father, it could be well understood that there was danger of strife within the castle walls to-day.

Catherine was pleased with the arrangements she had made. Once the two men had kissed in friendship, the young Duke must cease vowing vengeance on the Admiral. The fact that Coligny had come to Blois should show him that the Admiral wished to be friends. And, on his part, when the Admiral took the boy in his arms, he must think of him, not as the son of his old enemy, but as a young boy who had lost his father.

There was one other who occupied Catherine's thoughts on that day – the Prince of Condé, who was now a widower. It was said that the Prince of Condé grieved deeply for his Princess, but he was living as gaily as ever. Catherine felt uncomfortable when she remembered how once she had not been so wise as she was to-day; she had thought a little too often and too tenderly of that man. How easy it would have been to have committed follies on his account! There should be no more folly. At least King Henry had been faithful to one mistress, and Catherine had known who was her enemy.

She felt strengthened in her wisdom. She learned, it was true, often through bitter lessons, but when a lesson was mastered, it should be mastered for life. No more tender feelings, then. Men were made not to love, but to serve her.

These men gathered together here at Blois were here to serve her. It suited her that they should be friends . . . outwardly at least. She wanted no more civil strife, for every time it occurred she and her family were in danger. She should not feel the least regret that Condé was a philanderer bringing disrepute on his party, for Condé's weakness added to her strength. That was how men should be used – not to give a brief erotic pleasure. If she had at one time fancied she would enjoy a lover, she no longer did. She was grateful to her tally of years, for it had brought her wisdom; it had stilled her longing for what was, at best, transient; it had made her grasp with both hands and hold firmly to what should henceforth be the love of her life – power.

In the great hall at Blois were assembled men and women of the highest rank. The light came through the coloured glass of the embrasured windows, shining on the jewels and rich garments of her guests. Catherine had decided that she herself would proclaim the innocence of Coligny before them all, and command that kiss of friendship between the Admiral and Henry of Guise.

There was Anna d'Esté, the widowed Duchess of Guise, keeping close to the side of her son. Surely Anna need not have appeared in such deep mourning! Catherine laughed to herself. Poor Anna! Meek as a lamb. She would be glad enough, if allowed by her ferocious son and her brother-in-law, to accept reconciliation. Anna hated bloodshed. Catherine remembered how she had protested at the Amboise massacre. She could not bear to see men tortured; she could not bear to see them butchered. Hardly the sort of woman to have mated with *Le Balafré*; yet it was said that he had been fond of her for her gentleness, and that theirs had been a comparatively happy marriage. Besides, her rank doubtless compensated the ambitious Duke for her mildness. Yes, Catherine felt sure that it was Anna's son and her brothers-in-law who had insisted on that ostentatious mourning.

There was Duke Henry beside her, already proclaiming to the world, with his arrogant demeanour, that he was head of the great House of Lorraine and Guise – the most feared, the most important in the country. Margot was eyeing him in an unseemly manner for which she should be punished later. When Margot met her mother's eyes she smiled innocently, but Catherine's expression grew a shade colder as she surveyed her daughter, and she knew that she had caused icy shivers to run through that body which, a moment before, had thrilled at the handsome arrogance of Henry of Guise.

There too was the Cardinal of Lorraine, the marks of his dissipation already marring the almost incomparable beauty of his features. It was said that there was nothing sufficiently licentious to please the Cardinal now; his erotic senses must be titillated as regularly as his palate. His mistresses were numerous. In his Cardinal's robes, adorned with magnificent jewels, he attracted every eye, the debauched man of the Church, the Catholic lecher. He bowed to Catherine, and his gaze as he met hers was haughty.

'Welcome, my lord Cardinal,' said Catherine. 'It does me good to see your pious face.'

'May I be so bold as to say that it does me good to see your Majesty's honest one? Madame, you are a light in our court. Your shining virtues are an example to everyone; and above all, your Majesty's deep sincerity puts us all to shame.'

'You flatter me, Cardinal.'

'Nothing, dear Madame, was farther from my mind.'

'Then I will not flatter you, dear Cardinal. I will only say that the whole of France should take as an example the piety and virtue of such a man of God.'

She turned to greet another. She was thinking: One of these days that lecher shall take a goblet of wine, shall eat of roast peacock, or perhaps finger some beautiful jewel – and then, no more of Monsieur le Cardinal!

But what was the use of thinking thus? She must continually guard against her impulse to destroy these notable people. Francis of Guise was dead – let that suffice for the moment – for who knew what the result of his death would be?

If a member of the Flying Squadron became impertinent, if a minor statesman became intransigent, then the procedure was simple; but with these prominent men and women it was always necessary to work in secret, to approach the object by devious roads, along which it was imperative to leave no traces. She would have to postpone dealing with the Cardinal.

Coligny was approaching. Ah, there was a man who was as easy to read as a book. Now he was looking stern, and his cold features said quite clearly: It is no wish of mine to be here. I have no desire for the friendship of the Catholic Guises. I was commanded to come. I gave my word that I would come; so come I did.

'Well met, Admiral,' said Catherine. 'It pleases me to see you here.'

'I but obeyed your command, Madame.'

Catherine tried to infuse into her expression that deep sincerity which had been the object of the Cardinal's jibe. But Coligny, that straightforward, honest man, was not the wily

Cardinal. If the Queen Mother appeared sincere to him, Coligny would not doubt that she was so.

'Forgive a weak woman's desire for peace in her realm, dear Admiral.'

He bowed. 'I have no desire at any time but to carry out your Majesty's wishes.'

He passed on, and Catherine looked about her; she did not see the Duke of Aumale among the assembly, although she had commanded his presence.

She called to the Duchess of Guise: 'Madame, I do not see your brother Aumale here.'

'No, Madame. He is not here.'

'Why not?'

'Madame, he suffers from a fever.'

Catherine's eyes narrowed. 'A fever of pride!' she said angrily. She beckoned young Henry of Guise to her side. How attractive he was! And how handsome! And what a man he would be one day!

'I am grieved not to see your uncle Aumale,' she said.

'I am sorry that your Majesty should be grieved.'

'A fever?' she said.

'Madame, you sent no express command to him.'

'I said I wished your family to be present.'

'Madame, he thought that, as your Majesty wished our family to be represented, you would only need myself and my uncle, the Cardinal.'

'I wished Aumale to be here,' said Catherine haughtily. 'It is no good excuse to plead a fever.'

'Madame,' said the boy, 'it is not pleasant for members of my family to show friendship to their enemies.'

'Have a care, boy,' she said. 'I'll have you thrashed if you give yourself airs. You are not yet a man, you know. A short while ago you were in the nursery. It would be well for you to remember that.'

Many watching eyes noticed the sudden heightened colour of the young Duke.

'My dear Duke,' continued Catherine more gently, 'it would be well for you to remember your youth and the need for obedience.'

Henry bowed formally and left the Queen Mother.

It would not be a good policy, Catherine realised, to have the Colignys and the Guises sitting near each other at table; she had taken the precaution of ensuring that they were separated by other guests. And when the feast was over, Catherine rose to address the assembly:

'Lords and ladies, you know that I have asked you here for a purpose this day, and my purpose is to put an end to evil rumour; for rumour is a foolish thing and when it is without truth it is an evil thing indeed. We mourn the untimely death of our dearly beloved Duke Francis of Guise, our greatest soldier, slain by the hand of a cowardly assassin. That in itself was a foul deed, and we offer to the bereaved family our sincerest condolence while we mourn with them for one we loved as our own brother. But the rumours which have circulated since his death have been as evil as that bloody deed, and there is one man among us here – one of our finest men, a man whom we all honour and revere – who has been accused of complicity in the murder of the Duke.

'Lords and ladies, these rumours are evil. They are proved to be slanders. The assassin has confessed them to be lies; and for that reason I have brought together here my greatly respected Admiral of France and the one who has perhaps suffered more than any of us from this horrible deed. I mean, of course, Duke Francis's son, Duke Henry of Guise, who is now the head of his house and who will, I know, bring it honour and glory as his father did before him. Admiral Gaspard de Coligny and Henry Duke of Guise, come forth.'

They stepped forward slowly towards the Queen Mother: the Admiral pale-faced, his mouth sternly set, the Duke with the rich colour in his face and his head held high.

Catherine stood between them. 'Give me your hand, Admiral,' she said. 'And yours, my lord Duke.'

She placed their two right hands together. Henry's was limp in that of the Admiral; his left hand rested on his sword.

There was silence while the two enemies faced each other and made it quite obvious to all that they had no liking for what the Queen Mother was pleased to consider a reconciliation. But Catherine had little understanding of others. Had she been in Coligny's place, she would have made a great show of embracing Henry of Guise, hoping thereby to assure the spectators of her wish for friendship. If she had been Henry of Guise, she would have accepted Coligny's embrace while she made her plans to destroy him. Catherine's greatest weakness was her lack of understanding of others.

'I would have you show us that you are friends, and that all enmity is forgotten in the kiss of peace,' she said.

Coligny leaned forward to kiss Henry on the cheek, but the young Duke stood up straight and said, so clearly that all in the room might hear it: 'Madame, I could not kiss a man whose name has been mentioned in connection with the tragic death of my father.'

Catherine would have liked to slap that arrogant young

face, and to call to the guards to have him taken down to one of the dungeons where his proud spirit might be broken. But she smiled pathetically as though to say: 'Ah, the arrogance of youth!'

She patted him on the shoulder and said something about his recent loss, and that he had shaken hands, which they would all accept as sufficient proof of his friendly feelings towards the Admiral.

There were murmurings throughout the hall. The ceremony had become a farce. Catherine knew it, but she would not admit it; and, looking at the tall, proud figure and the flushed face of that arrogant boy, she knew that as soon as Francis of Guise had been laid in his grave, there was another, made in his own shape, to take his place, to torment her, to give her cause for anxiety in the years to come.

That murmuring in the hall, Catherine knew, meant approval. It meant: 'The Duke is dead. Long live the Duke!'

The King of France was happy; never in the whole of his life had he been so happy. He was in love, and his love was returned.

He had met Marie on one of his journeys through his realm. She was as young as he was, and as shy. She had not realised when she had first met him that he was the King of France; and that was what was so enchanting about the affair. She loved him, not his rank; and for the first time in his life the one he loved loved him.

Mary of Scotland had become a dream. Marie Touchet, the provincial judge's daughter, was the reality. Marie was delightful, so young, so innocent, so unworldly. She had wanted to run away when she knew that her lover was the King of France.

'Dearest Marie,' he had said, 'that is of no account. It is I, Charles, whom you love, and you must go on loving me, for I need love. I need love as no other man in France needs it.'

It was possible to tell her of his black moods of melancholy and how, when they were over, it was necessary to go out and do violence. 'Now I have you, my darling, it may be that there will not be these moods. I have black fears, Marie — terrible fears which descend upon me by night, and I must shout and scream and see blood flow to soften these moods.'

She comforted him and soothed him, and they made love. He had installed her in the palace. His mother knew of his love for Marie.

'So you are a man after all, my son!' she said with a hint of grim amusement in her voice.

'How do you mean, Madame?'

'Just that, my dear boy. You are a man.'

'Mother, you like Marie, do you not?' His eyes were fearful. Catherine smiled, looking into them; he knew that if she did not like Marie, Marie would not stay long in the palace and he would not long enjoy the comfort and joy she brought him. His hands trembled while he waited for his mother's answer.

'Marie? Your little mistress? Why, I scarcely noticed her.'

'How glad I am!'

'What? Glad that your choice of a mistress is such that she is noticed neither for her wit nor her beauty?'

'Madame,' he said, 'those who remain unnoticed by you are the safest.'

She looked at him sharply, and saw that obstinacy in his face which she had noticed before. He would not lightly let her take his mistress from him. And why should she? What harm could the little Touchet do? She was of no importance whatever. Touchet was safe enough.

'Ah, enjoy yourself, my son,' she said. 'The duties of kingship are hard, but the privileges are rewarding. No woman, however virtuous, can resist a King.'

He stammered: 'You do Marie wrong. She did not know . . . who I was. She loved me ere . . .'

Catherine patted his shoulder. 'There, my son. Your mother but teased you. Go and enjoy your little Touchet to your heart's content, I like her well enough. She is such a mild little playfellow.'

He kissed her hand, and she was pleased with him; he still obeyed her; that was what she wanted.

They had not been able to make a pervert of him. Nevertheless, it was hardly likely that he would procreate offspring. It would be an interesting experiment to let him be tried out on the little Touchet. If there was no child within a reasonable time, it might be safe to get him married and satisfy the people of France.

Henry was growing up. He was seventeen. Young yet for kingship, but in a few years' time he would be ready. She must watch Charles, though. He must not think that, because he took a mistress, he was like other young men. He was not quite sane; he must never be allowed to forget that.

Charles had changed. Marie inspired him, gave him confidence, listened to his accounts of how his mother favoured his brother Henry. 'He is to her as her right eye, Marie. There are times when I believe she wants the throne for him.'

'Then she cannot have it for him,' said Marie with sound provincial common sense. 'Not while it is yours.'

In Marie's company he felt truly a King.

One day his attendants came to him and told him that the Queen of Navarre, who was at court, wished to have a word with him.

He received her warmly, for he was fond of Jeanne, who was so calm and serene; she had the very qualities which he lacked and which he longed to possess. It was true that she was a Huguenot but – and he had determined that none should know this – Marie had confessed to him that she had leanings towards the Huguenot Faith, and though he had bidden her to tell no one, he felt a friendliness for the Huguenots that he had never felt before.

Jeanne was ushered into his presence. She kissed his hand.

'You have something to say to me, dear Aunt,' said Charles. 'Shall I ask my mother if she will join us?'

'Sire, I beg of you, do no such thing, for I would rather talk to you alone.'

Charles was flattered. People usually requested his mother's presence, because they knew that nothing important could be decided without her.

'Proceed then,' said Charles, feeling just as a King should feel.

'Sire, as you know, I am leaving Paris in the next few days to visit Picardy. I have long been separated from my son, and I think that the time has come for him to be presented to his vassals in Vendôme, through which I shall pass. I ask your most gracious permission for him to accompany me.'

'But, my dear Aunt,' said the King, 'if it is your wish, certainly Henry shall go with you.'

'Then I have your permission, Sire?'

He saw the joy in her face, and tears rushed to his eyes. How delightful it was to be able to give so much pleasure by granting a small request! It mattered not to him whether the noisy lustful Henry of Navarre left the court or not.

'You have my permission,' he said in his most royal manner.

'I thank you with all my heart, Sire.' She seized his hand and kissed it.

'Dearest Aunt,' he said, 'I am glad to be able to please you.'

'You have given your word,' she said, 'and I know that nothing will make you break it. May I go, Sire, and give this wonderful news to my son?'

'Go by all means,' said Charles.

She retired, while he sat smiling, thinking that it was sometimes very pleasant to be a King.

⚜ ⚜ ⚜

Catherine walked up and down the apartment while Charles sat miserably watching her – not a King now so much as a foolish boy.

'Have you no more intelligence,' demanded Catherine, for once shaken out of her calm, 'than to let that wily she-wolf come and snatch the heir of Navarre from under our noses? What hope will you have, my lord, of subduing the Huguenots, when you let your most precious hostage go? You *give* him away. No conditions. Nothing! "I want my son," she says, "my little Henry. He needs his *Maman*!" And you, like the little fool you are, say: "You may take him, dearest Aunt. He is only a boy . . ." Fool! Idiot! He was a hostage. The heir of Navarre . . . in our hands! If Jeanne of Navarre had dared threaten us – and I mean you and your brothers – I would have threatened her with the death or the imprisonment of her precious boy. And you, you fool, would give him back! I shall not allow it. The boy shall stay here. And never dare give an order again without my permission. Never grant a request without first asking me if you may do so.'

'But she is his mother, and she asked for him with tears in her eyes. They have been so long separated. I could not refuse her.'

'You could not refuse her! And others have heard you grant this request, I doubt not?'

Charles was silent.

'This was so, was it not?' demanded his mother.

'Yes. Others heard.'

'Fool! To think I should have such a son! Your brother Henry would never have behaved with such folly. But I shall cancel the order. Navarre shall not be allowed to leave the court. His mother shall go alone. Stop stammering and trembling, and sign this order.'

'But I gave my word.'

'You will sign this at once.'

Charles cried shrilly: 'I am tired of being told that Henry would do this and Henry would do that. Henry does not happen to be the King of this realm. I am. I am . . . and when I say . . .'

'Sign this,' said Catherine. She pushed him into a chair and put the pen into his hand. He looked over his shoulder; her face was near his – very pale, her eyes enormous. He trembled more than before. He felt that she saw right through to his soul.

He began to write.

'That is well,' she said. 'Now we can remedy your rash act. Oh, my son, I know you do this out of the kindness of your heart, but always remember that I am here to love and advise you. Never decide such weighty matters without first consulting your mother, whose one thought is to make you happy and' – her face came closer to his – 'and . . . *safe*. Why, Charles, my dear son, what you have done might let loose civil war. And what if your enemies should be triumphant? Eh, what then? What if they took you prisoner? You would not relish lying in a dank dungeon . . . close to the torture-rooms . . . the rats your companions . . . until . . .'

'Pray cease,' whimpered the King. 'You are right. You are always right. Navarre must not go. I have signed it. You will stop his going. You will stop it.'

She nodded. 'That,' she said, 'is my wise little King.'

✤ ✤ ✤

But Jeanne was not so easy to handle as Charles had been. The two women faced each other, and each felt that overwhelming hatred between them which had always been there, and yet at times was greater than at others.

'My dear cousin, I cannot allow you to take the boy away, I look upon him as my own. Moreover, if he is to marry my daughter, he must be brought up with her. You know it has always been our wish to let the young people get fond of each other . . . as these two are doing. It does my heart good to see them together.'

'Madame,' Jeanne replied, 'all that you say is true. But my son has spent so much time at the court, and it is well that he should be reminded of his own kingdom.'

'We will see that he does not forget that. No, Madame. I love the boy too well to let him go.'

'I also love him,' insisted his mother, 'and, but for the fact that I feel he should be allowed to visit his dominions, I should be delighted to leave him in your care.'

Catherine smiled. 'I am going to keep him because, Madame, I know what is best for him. You have only recently come to Paris, and therefore you do not see as clearly as I do what is happening here. I know that it is best for little Henry that he stays with his cousins and learns the manners of our court. I must confess that when he first came to us I was a little astonished. He had the manners of a barbarian. Now there is a great improvement in him. I should not like to see him turned into a country lout.'

Catherine watched the angry colour flood Jeanne's face.

Jeanne said: 'Madame, you need have no qualms on that score. My son would have the best tutors available.'

'But these are more easily obtainable in Paris than in Béarn. My dearest cousin, I insist on his remaining here.'

But Jeanne was wily, and did not allow the matter to rest there.

Later, when Charles and Catherine were surrounded by members of the court, she had the effrontery to bring the matter up again.

'I cannot believe,' she said, 'that any obstacle will be put in the way of my taking my son with me.'

Catherine answered coolly: 'But that, Madame, is a matter which we have settled.'

'The King,' Jeanne persisted, 'graciously promised that my son should accompany me when I left Paris. Many will bear witness to that. I feel sure, Madame, that when you said this promise was cancelled, your Majesty was joking, for I know that it would bring too great a discredit on His Majesty to suppose him capable of breaking his word.'

The King flushed slightly. He felt bold now, surrounded by so many courtiers.

'You are right, Madame,' he said. 'The promise shall be fulfilled, for I made it and it must be so.'

Catherine, for once, had the humiliation of seeing herself defeated. Nor could she protest in such company. She would have liked to kill Jeanne and Charles as they stood there. Instead she smiled calmly.

'So be it,' she said. 'The King has spoken. Madame, I rely on you to ensure that the peace and repose of France shall not be put in danger.'

Jeanne bowed. 'Your Majesty honours me by asking my cooperation in maintaining such a state of affairs. I shall never fail in my devotion to my sovereign.' She paused; then she added: 'Only the peril or destruction of my own house could make me change those sentiments.'

And the next day Jeanne set out from Paris, and riding with her was her son.

✤ ✤ ✤

Catherine proved herself to have been right when she had explained to her son what a foolish thing he had done in giving up to Jeanne their most precious hostage. Civil war had broken out once more in France.

At one time the King and his court had to fly from Meaux to Paris for fear of Condé's troops; Catherine was more shaken by this event than by any that had happened for months. The killing of French Protestants by Catholics and Catholics by Protestants merely made her shrug her shoulders, but the thought of the royal House of Valois in danger always terrified her. Coligny's plan, she knew, had been to kidnap the King and set Condé up in his place.

Those were bitter days for Catherine. The Queen of

England, the Duke of Savoy, and the Marquis of Brandenburg sent money and men to Condé's aid. In despair, Catherine appealed to Spain, but although that country was willing to give aid, Spain never gave anything without taking something in exchange; and Catherine feared Philip more than she feared Condé. Therefore she arranged the Peace of Langjumeaux. But Catherine could not forget her fears of what might have happened if the Huguenots had been successful in capturing the King; and in spite of the new peace there began plots and counter-plots. Catherine plotted to capture Condé and young Henry of Navarre. Condé – now married again – narrowly escaped capture, and orders were given that he should be pursued and that the Catholics should be incited to fresh massacres of Huguenots. The wars started once more; and Jeanne, with her son, Condé and Coligny, had made their headquarters in the Huguenot stronghold of La Rochelle.

There was one great happiness which Catherine enjoyed at this time, and that was due to the reputation her son Henry was gaining on the battlefield. It was the more gratifying because it was so unexpected. Who would have thought that Henry, with his dandyism, his love of fine jewels and garments, always surrounded by those handsome and effeminate young men, would be the one to distinguish himself as a soldier!

Henry was clever. Even his enemies admitted that. He was witty and a devotee of the fine arts. He was very good-looking, though in a way which the French called 'foreign'. His long dark eyes showed clearly his Italian origins; his white, perfectly formed hands were the most beautiful at court, and it was his great delight to set them off with sparkling jewels. And this effeminate Henry was becoming a great general! He was also becoming very ambitious, and already he was waiting impatiently for the throne. He was, like his mother, calculating how long young Charles could be expected to live.

Catherine had suffered a loss recently in the death of her daughter Elisabeth, who had died in childbirth. She had not loved Elisabeth as she loved Henry, but she had been proud of her daughter's position in the world, and it had given her pleasure to contemplate Elisabeth on the throne of Spain. But Henry, that beloved son, compensated her for all else. It was the delight of her life to find that he listened to her as he listened to no other, that he brought all his plans to her and that he rarely acted without consulting her. In all her trials, in all her fears, there was Henry to be a comfort to her.

The mother of Henry of Navarre surveyed her son with nothing like the same complacency. He was just fourteen, but those years he had spent at the French court had, it seemed, already made a man of him. He was popular enough; the citizens of La Rochelle cheered him wherever he went. They could smile at those very qualities which alarmed his mother.

In Jeanne's train there was a young girl, Corisanda d'Andouins, who was not very much older than Henry. This girl had recently been married to the son of the Count of Gramont, a man whom Jeanne greatly respected and whose friendship she felt to be important to her cause. But young Henry, having such little respect for the marriage laws that he could completely disregard them, had fallen violently in love with Corisanda.

He followed the girl everywhere, and Jeanne discovered that secret meetings were taking place. The whole of La Rochelle was discussing this affair between the heir of Béarn and Madame Corisanda.

Jeanne watched in alarm the indications of what her boy was to become. She remonstrated with him. He was good-natured and lazy. He agreed with her quite charmingly, but this, he explained, was love. He lifted his shoulders in an elegant fashion which he must have learned at the French court. His mother was old-fashioned; she was of the country, and she did not understand. Love? Love was all-important. His mother must have no fears for him; he would lead his men into battle; but when it was a matter of love – 'Ah then, my mother, that is a matter between the mistress and the lover.'

Jeanne cried: 'You mean that this woman is already your mistress? You . . . a boy?'

'Not such a boy!' he said, holding his head high.

All Jeanne's puritanical instincts rose in revolt; but when she looked into that vital young face and was aware of that immense sensuality, she knew that protest was in vain. Here again was his father, her father, her uncle, Francis the First. They were men, and whether they were strong or weak in battle, there must always be women to give them what they asked.

'How think you the Huguenot citizens of France will view this licentiousness in their leaders?' she asked him.

He lifted his shoulders. 'The French, be they Catholics or Huguenots, will always understand what it means to love.'

And with that he left her to keep his engagement with the erring Corisanda.

❋ ❋ ❋

Margot was growing up; she had long been aware of this, but others were noticing it now.

There was strife between the royal brothers. Charles was

jealous of his mother's preference for Henry. He never felt safe in Henry's presence. Henry watched him continually. And, as Charles often confided to Marie Touchet, Henry was not a Frenchman whom one could understand; he was an Italian, and Frenchmen were suspicious of Italians.

Henry came home from his victorious campaign, grown more handsome, more ambitious. He noticed his sister Margot and how she had grown up since he had last seen her. He saw too in her something which the other members of his family did not possess. Margot was little more than a child; she was as yet undeveloped; but it was not difficult to see that there was a good deal of sense in that vain little head.

Henry decided to utilise it. He knew that he and Charles would always be enemies, and he decided to have Margot on his side.

He asked her to take a walk with him in the grounds of Fontainebleau, and Margot, sensing the importance of this, since she guessed the matter was too momentous to be discussed indoors, was gratified. She was always ready for excitement and intrigue.

As she walked with him through the green alley of the palace garden, Henry put his arm about his sister's shoulders – a gesture which delighted Margot, for she was no less aware of Henry's position with their mother than Charles was, and the favour of Henry was greatly to be desired on that account. Margot feared her mother more than anyone on Earth, but at the same time she earnestly longed for her approbation. A friendship with Catherine's darling might result in her finding favour with Catherine.

'You may have noticed, dear Margot,' said Henry, 'that, of all my brothers and sisters, I have always loved you the best.'

Margot smiled happily, for if Henry regarded her in that light, so must her mother.

'We have had many happy times together,' went on Henry, 'but we are children no longer.'

'No, Henry. Indeed we are not. You are a great soldier. You have made a name for yourself.'

He pressed her hand and, putting his face close to hers, he said: 'Margot, my power lies in keeping in the good graces of our mother, the Queen.'

Margot agreed with that.

'And, Margot, I am away from the court so much. The wars continue. My brother the King is always beside her. He flatters her and obeys her in everything.'

'But she would never love any as she loves you, Henry. It has always been so.'

He said: 'I have many enemies who might do me harm with my mother . . . when I am not here to protect myself.'

'Charles thinks of little else but making love to Marie Touchet and hunting wild creatures.'

'He makes hate as well as love, and he will not always be content to hunt beasts. One day he will take my Lieutenancy from me and try to lead the army himself. I wish to have someone here at court to uphold my cause with the Queen. You, dearest sister, are my second self. You are faithful and clever. Do this for me. Be with my mother always – at her *lever*, at her *coucher*. Listen to what is said, and find some means of letting me know. Make her confide in you. You understand?'

Margot's eyes were sparkling. 'Yes. I understand, Henry.'

'I will speak to her of you. I will tell her how fond I am of you. I will tell her that you are my beloved sister, my second self. As for you, you must not be so much afraid of her. Speak up when she addresses you. In doing those things for me, you will do much for yourself.'

Henry put his hands on Margot's shoulders and looked into her eyes; he saw there what he wanted. Henry was the hero of the war; and Margot, a young and impressionable girl, was ready to adore him; she was ready to be his slave and to work for him against the King.

Henry took her along to Catherine and told his mother how fond he was of his sister, and of the part he had asked her to play for him at the court. Catherine drew her daughter to her and kissed her on the forehead.

'So you are to guard your brother's interests at court, dear Margot?'

'Yes, Madame.'

'You will have to give up your silliness, your frivolity. You will have to watch your brothers . . . and their friends.'

'That I will do, Mother.'

'Well, my daughter, I shall help you in this. Henry, my son and your brother, is as dear to me as my life. Is he so to you?'

'Yes, Madame.'

Catherine then embraced her son and, as her mother's cold hands touched her, Margot felt that she had become a member of a trinity; and this was none the less exciting because the trinity might be an unholy one.

❊ ❊ ❊

Growing up was an enchanting experience. Margot had other matters with which to concern herself now. She played the spy with all the verve of which she was capable. She was coming to the fore; she was always at her mother's *lever* and *coucher*; she was often in the company of the King; she was ready to continue in her adoration of her absent brother.

But there was one other trait in Margot's nature which both her mother and her brother had temporarily forgotten. If Margot was to grow up, she would do so in more ways than one. She was continually occupied with her dresses; she became the most fashionable lady of the court; she wore a golden wig over her long black hair one day, and a red one the next. All fashions inaugurated by Margot were provocative, designed to titillate the senses of the male.

And Henry of Guise came to court.

Henry too had grown up; they were man and woman now, not boy and girl. He sought the first opportunity of being alone with Margot to tell her of his feelings.

'I always loved you,' he told her as they strolled in the gardens.

'And I . . . you, Henry.'

Margot could not keep her hands from the fine coat or the golden curly hair and beard. Margot was not the only one who thought there was no man in France, or in the world, to compare with Henry of Guise; others said that the Guises made all other men seem insignificant when they came among them.

'We will be married,' declared Henry. 'I know that it can be arranged.'

'It must be arranged,' agreed Margot.

He took her hands, and kissed them eagerly with burning kisses which made Margot's passions flame.

'It will not be so easy as it would have been if my father was alive,' Henry warned her.

Margot was in his arms, all desire and urgency.

'Nevertheless, it must be,' she said.

'Margot . . . I cannot wait for marriage.'

Margot laughed. 'Nor I!'

'Where can we be alone?'

Intrigue was exciting, but passionate intrigue was the most delightful thing in Margot's world. How could she have set such store on spying for her brother Henry when she could be the mistress of this completely fascinating Henry?

It was not difficult for Margot to find a place where they could be together.

And after that there was nothing of any importance for Margot but these passionate meetings with her lover. She was insatiable. She could never have enough of Henry. He was her lover – the only person on Earth, she discovered, who was really important to her. For him she would die. She declared that she would never marry any other man. The meetings grew more frequent, and the more frequent the more necessary they became to Margot. Sensual, passionate in the extreme, she had discovered something which she could not do without.

She was impetuous. She wanted an immediate marriage. Henry was more cautious. He was as passionate, as sensual as Margot – they were as well matched a pair as any lovers could be – but while for Margot there was nothing but love, for Henry there was also ambition. He was the Duke of Guise, head of the mighty House of Lorraine besides being Margot's lover, and his upbringing would not allow him to forget that. And even while he was making passionate love to Margot he could not help remembering that she was a Princess of the House of Valois, and therefore a match with her would be the most suitable he could possibly make.

'We must not be careless,' said Henry.

'Oh, Henry, my darling, what do we care?'

'We must care, Margot; for nothing must stand in the way of our marriage. We can never be completely happy until then. Just think what marriage would mean to us . . . always together.'

She kissed him wildly. 'I will never let you leave me. I will follow you to camp. You do not imagine that I should let you go alone!'

'No,' he said. 'We must never be parted. That must be our aim. Margot, you are so impetuous. We must wait . . . and watch . . . and act carefully. What if people tried to separate us?'

She pressed her body against his. She was not really thinking of anything but the desire of the moment. He laughed, but he was a little uneasy. Margot was an ideal mistress and he adored her; but there were times when he wondered what violence of passion, what sensuality he had awakened. He had never known anyone like this gay little Princess of France with the flashing dark eyes and the eager, sensual lips, the clinging hands, the urgent desire. He was young and virile himself, but he found Margot astonishing.

She would not discuss anything seriously. She wanted him at once . . . this moment. Never mind if they were in the gardens. Who would come to this spot? Who would dare say a word against the Princess Margot and the Duke of Guise?

'My darling,' said Henry, 'I want you as much as you want me, but I want our marriage. I want to make sure of our union. I want it to be firm and secure . . . for the rest of our lives.'

She ran her fingers through his hair. 'But, Henry, of course it shall be.'

'The Queen Mother does not love me; nor does the King.'

'But you are a Prince and I am a Princess; and I will have none other but you.'

'I know. I know. But caution, my darling!'

But she was not listening. She was laughing up at Henry, and he, young and passionate as herself, could not help but find her irresistible.

❖ ❖ ❖

The lovers thought their love unnoticed, but this was not the case; and one of the important people who had seen how matters stood between the Princess Margot and the young Duke of Guise was the Duke's uncle, the Cardinal of Lorraine.

The Cardinal was amused as well as delighted. He himself had known many erotic adventures – in fact, he was at his wit's end nowadays to find some new diversion that could attract him. He was ready to give a good deal to any young and handsome person – man or woman – who could show him a little novelty. But regarding this affair of his nephew and the Princess he was not displeased, although Henry was being a young fool in this, and he thought it his duty to warn him.

He asked the boy to come to his apartments and, making sure that they were unobserved and that there were no means of communication behind the hangings, he told the Duke what was in his mind.

'None of the diabolical instruments of that old serpent the Queen Mother can reach us, nephew, so let us talk without reserve. I notice that you are enjoying a charming interlude with the Princess Margot.'

Henry flushed a little. 'If you mean that I love her, that is so.'

The Cardinal lifted his beautiful white hand and studied the rubies and sapphires which adorned it. 'I wish to congratulate you. What a delightful mistress she must be! You are a fortunate man.'

Henry bowed stiffly. In view of his uncle's reputation, he did not care to discuss Margot with him, or to contemplate those lecherous eyes and read the thoughts behind them.

'I would prefer not to discuss my relationship with the Princess,' he said.

'But that is exactly what we must do. Oh, mistake me not. Do not think I wish to question you as to the most exciting experience you must be enjoying. I can imagine that it is charming – incomparable, in fact – for I doubt if there is, even at this court, a young lady who is so naturally knowledgeable in the greatest of our arts. But you are young, you are sensitive and you are in love; and you do not care to discuss your mistress with a man of my reputation. You see, nephew, I understand. I read your thoughts. Well, let us discuss the practical rather than the romantic. Nephew, I am proud of you. The House of Lorraine is proud of you. If you had made the Princess your wife instead of your mistress, we should be even more proud of you; for what we would like more than anything, dear boy, is to see the Houses of Lorraine and Valois united. The marriage would be an ideal one.'

'It would indeed,' said the young Duke. 'And it is my earnest desire that it should be brought about.'

'I wish to help you in that, but do not imagine that you can go to the King and the Queen Mother and say, "I offer my hand and fortune to the Princess Margot." It is not so easy as that. The serpent has other plans for her loving daughter.'

'I shall do everything in my power to flout them.'

'Yes, yes. But reasonably, sensibly. You must not walk about the court with the Princess, both of you letting your looks and your gestures proclaim to the court what a good time you are giving each other.'

'But . . . we have not!'

'Your faces, your smiles have spoken. They tell us that Margot is a maid no longer. Margot proclaims to the world all that she has enjoyed and all that she intends to enjoy . . . even if you do not. This must not continue. Whether the Queen Mother knows of this yet, or whether affairs of state occupy her too closely, I cannot say; but if she did discover it, I would beg of you to watch your food and wine. Always make one of your attendants taste first. Never buy gloves, books or a garment from any but a man you are sure you can trust. Catherine and her Italians have learned more tricks in their lifetimes than we French have acquired through the centuries. Have a care, nephew. Catherine is negotiating a match for Margot with the Prince of Portugal. She would not therefore at this time be in favour of a match with our house.'

'There have been so many negotiations for Margot. First Henry of Navarre, then Don Carlos, now the Prince of Portugal.'

'That does not mean that one of these may not come to something.'

'I shall never allow that.'

'Now listen, my nephew: it is all very well to be gallant and noble in the presence of your mistress. With your old states-man uncle you must be frank. You want to marry Princess Margot. I, and all our house, will help you in this. Therefore I beg of you to go carefully. Try to hide your intentions for a time, until the moment comes when it is good policy to show them. Dear boy, you are as close to me as though you were my own son – closer, in fact, for are you not the head of our house?

My brothers, your uncles, all have discussed this matter with me, and we have agreed that nothing could advance our house more than this marriage with the Princess. But you must take care. We do not wish to see you in your grave. Your brothers, Charles and Louis, have not your qualities. You must therefore take our considered advice in this matter, which is this: continue to enjoy your mistress; bind her closer to you; but act with more secrecy, and, moreover, it will be as well if you pay court to another lady to divert suspicion. That should not be difficult, for I have heard it said that there is no young man at the court of France who can compare with Henry, Duke of Guise; and there are few women who could resist him. Your success with Mademoiselle Margot, I imagine, did not demand a great effort on your part. My boy, you have charm, you have good looks, you have power and rank. In fact, you have everything. Do not dissipate these assets, but use them to good advantage. Now, the Princess of Clèves watches you, my boy, with languishing glances; she is pining for you. It would not seem amiss if you paid court to her, for she would be a good match.'

'I have no intention of marrying anyone but Margot.'

'Of course you do not wish to marry any but Margot; nor do we wish it. But on account of the Queen Mother and her spies, pay a little court to the Princess of Clèves. Do not let the Queen Mother think that you have hopes of Margot, for I greatly fear that if she did she would not be very pleased. My dearest Henry, it is fatal when the Queen Mother turns those cold eyes upon a man and decides he has become a nuisance to her.'

'Such an affair is repulsive to me.'

'Oh, come come! Are you the head of a great house or are

you a love-sick boy? Explain to Margot if need be. She will not be colder, I imagine, if she thinks you look elsewhere.' The Cardinal laid his arm about Henry's shoulders. 'A great destiny may be yours,' he whispered. 'Look at Catherine's sons: Charles, a little madman; Henry, a pervert; Hercule, that strutting coxcomb! And then . . . Navarre? A lazy good-for-nothing. I have seen in him something which tells me that he will be wax in the hands of women. Condé? Condé will not live long, depend upon it. Either some battle or the Queen Mother will finish him. Ah, my lord Duke, there are many between our house and the throne, I know, but the citizens of Paris love you as they loved your father. I have heard their shouting in the streets. Paris thinks for France, decides for France.'

Henry drew away; he could hear the shouts of the Parisians in his ears. King . . . King of France! And Margot his Queen!

The Cardinal smiled at the flushed, handsome face.

'Why not?' he said. 'A marriage with a royal Valois Princess would doubtless clinch the matter. My boy, do not, in your reckless folly, spoil that chance. Act the statesman even while you act the lover.'

Margot was in a fury of jealousy, and Henry found it difficult to calm her.

How dared he look as he had looked at Catherine de Clèves? She had seen his smile; she had also seen the way the woman had answered it.

He tried to explain: 'Margot, I love you more than anything in the world. I want no one but you. But others have noticed our love, and this must not be.'

'Who? 'Who?' she demanded. 'And what do I care? They will notice that you are playing me false with that creature. I hate her. I will have her banished. I could not believe that you could treat me so.'

It was necessary to make ardent love to her, to soothe her, to assure her a hundred times of his devotion to her alone. Then when she lay quiet beside him he decided to explain.

'My uncle, the Cardinal, knows what is between us.'

'That lecher! That man of God!' she cried.

'I know, my darling. But he has great wisdom. He says it is unsafe for us to show our love.'

'Unsafe? He is a coward. He wears a suit of mail under his church robes. He fears someone may stab him, as he deserves to be stabbed.'

'We must be wise, my Princess, my love. Our hearts would be broken if aught came between us.'

She wept and clung to him.

'Swear to me that you do not love her.'

'I love no one but you, Margot. I must pay some court to her, because to some we have made our love known. We must think of the future. We must marry, but at the moment everything would be against us. Your mother is negotiating for the Prince of Portugal. What do you think would happen if it were known that you and I have already been what we have been to one another?'

'I do not know and I do not care. I only care that we should continue to be that to one another. I am afraid of my mother . . . oh, so terribly afraid. There is something in her that frightens me. But I would brave her anger; I would brave anything for this, Henry.'

He could only caress her, murmur endearments, undying

fidelity, let himself be drawn into more passionate love-making.

'Margot,' he said at length, 'understand me. Our whole future depends on this. When you see me smile at the Princess of Clèves, remember that my heart belongs to the Princess Margot.'

'For every smile you give her, you must give me two. If you ever kiss her hands, you must pay twenty kisses to make up for that.'

She clasped her arms about his neck and strained herself against him. 'Henry, my love, I adore you.'

'And you will understand? You will know that every thing I do is to make our future secure, that I have no thought, no wish beyond my union with you?'

She drew his face down to hers, and her kisses, tender at first, grew warmer and more wild.

'Oh, Margot, Margot,' said the Duke of Guise, 'there was never one like you in the whole of the world.'

She laughed. 'If all women were like me there would be no wars, no politics. There would be no time for anything but love-making. But then, all men would have to be like you to make the women desire them so much – and there is no one in the world like you, my beloved.'

It was difficult to be wise with such a woman; when he was with Margot, Henry forgot that vision of a crown which, by sagacious diplomacy, might be his one day.

Margot, deep in her love affair, had completely forgotten that other Henry, her brother, for whom she had promised to play the spy.

Henry, returning from the wars, found her changed, and he, like the Cardinal of Lorraine, knew the meaning of the change in her. He was angry that she should have forgotten her promises to him, but when he discovered who her lover was, his anger increased to a fury.

Henry was clever enough to understand his sister's nature. Margot made a good spy, but Margot was born to love men. Her lover would be all-important to her; she would betray anything or anybody – even her own brother – for the sake of the man she loved. Henry of Guise was probably already in possession of any secret he cared to know. Margot was the sort who would hold nothing back from the object of her passion.

It was perfectly simple to see what Guise was after. He wanted more than Margot; he wanted alliance with the Royal House. And Margot, the little fool, did not realise that the greatest enemy to the House of Valois was the House of Guise and Lorraine.

Henry sought out his sister.

'You little fool!' he cried. 'You traitress! What is all this of you and Henry of Guise?'

Margot opened her lovely dark eyes very wide and looked at her brother in astonishment. Her lover had made it clear that, as they hoped for their marriage, they must at the moment keep their intentions secret. 'I do not understand you,' said Margot.

Henry took her by the shoulders and shook her.

'You and he have been together . . .'

'What makes you say so, Monsieur? And take your hands from me. Do not bring your camp manners to court.'

Henry was furious; Margot was to have been his creature. Now she was entirely Henry of Guise's.

'You have ignored my interests,' he accused.

'Indeed, there was nothing to report.'

'You were too busy looking into the eyes of Henry of Guise.'

'And you, my lord, have been listening to idle gossip.'

Henry left her and went to his mother.

'You know of this affair between Margot and Guise?'

Catherine knew. She had, through her tubes, heard certain conversations between the lovers. The shamelessness of Margot made her laugh. Her spies had been secreted in certain places and had given her details of what had taken place between those two. It seemed to Catherine that she had a wanton for a daughter, a reckless, passionate girl who pursued Henry of Guise with complete lack of shame, just as she always had done since she was a child.

'My dear son, Sebastian of Portugal will soon be here, and he will be made your sister's husband.'

'And in the meantime you allow her to behave as she does with Guise?'

'It is too late to stop that now.'

'The scandal . . .'

'There will always be scandal concerning Margot. Besides, she goes into a new country where this scandal will not be known. I have made it clear to all those who have spoken of the matter to me that it would be better to remain silent on the subject.'

'So meanwhile our lovers continue to enjoy each other.'

'And never did two enjoy each other more!' Catherine burst into coarse laughter. 'And, my darling, you are back, and it is good to see you.'

'Mother, she should be working for me.'

'My darling, have you not learned yet that there is only one who works for you?'

'I know it.' He kissed her hand and, kneeling, let her fondle his hair. He was thinking of a very charming young man who had come to his notice recently: De Guast. What beauty! What elegance! He wanted nothing so much as to be with his new friend. It was irritating to find that Margot had betrayed him, to have to endure this very possessive love of his mother's.

'Mother,' he said, 'you do not take this affair of Margot's in any great seriousness. Why? The Guises are our enemies. They are too powerful, too ambitious. Duke Henry is Duke Francis all over again.'

'I am watching everything, my dear one. I shall let nothing injure you. I have them watched. When necessary, Monsieur de Guise shall receive his *congé*.'

'For my sake,' said the enraged Henry, 'I beg of you to speed up my sister's marriage with the Prince of Portugal.'

'For your sake, my darling, I would lie down and die.'

He kissed her cheeks. She was happy, as she always was when he gave her a caress for which she had not asked. She smiled at him yearningly. This was how she had felt towards that other Henry who had humiliated her so shamefully with Diane de Poitiers. Loving a son was, she decided, a happier affair than loving a husband. She drew him to her and kissed him fondly. 'Oh, my darling,' she said, 'it makes me happy to have you home.'

'I am happy to be with you, Mother dear . . . And you *will* speed on the arrangements with Portugal?'

'I will, my son.'

Margot was angry, but she did not believe for a moment that the marriage with Portugal would come to anything. Henry would not allow it. Henry and his powerful family wanted their marriage, and the Guises rarely failed in anything they undertook.

Her family were against her. Her brother Henry had now played on the emotions of her brother Charles; and in spite of the fact that she despised Charles, she had to remember that he was the King. It was always easy to work on Charles by telling him he was in danger of assassination. Brother Henry had told Charles some story about Henry of Guise's ambitions to marry their sister and that, being a Guise – the son of *Le Balafré* – he already imagined he had some right to the throne of France. What a King he would make! thought Margot. And what a Queen she would be! The very thought made her clench and unclench her hands with the longing for him. The citizens of Paris adored him. Who would not adore him? All her loyalty was for him. If he wished to snatch the crown from her brother – well, then she would do everything within her power to help him. There was no loyalty for Margot but to her lover. No one else in the world mattered. If she could help to bring him the crown of France for a wedding present, she would be happy, even if, to do it, she had to see her brothers lying dead. It would be but a small reward for all the pleasure he had given her.

Her brothers hated her now. Charles had screamed at her; Henry had been sarcastic about her. What did she care? They could not touch her love.

Charles had cried: 'I tell you I will not have that spy at court. I'll have him killed. I am the King, am I not?'

'It would not seem so, to look at you now, Sire,' Margot had retorted.

She was daring, reckless, but had she gone too far?

Charles foamed at the mouth. 'Have her whipped!' he cried. 'I'll do it myself.'

He ran at her with eyes flashing; he was certainly terrifying in his madness; she must remember that he was the King; he could give an order and have her taken to a dungeon. When his madness was on him he might do this.

She ran to Marie Touchet and begged for her protection.

'Marie, my dear, I have offended the King. Plead with him for me.'

And good-hearted Marie did, soothing the King as only she could soothe him. His sister Margot was but a child. He should remember that. She was so sorry to have offended him.

'She . . . she is a wanton. She . . . she gives herself and our secrets to Henry of Guise.'

'But if she loves, my dearest lord, can we blame her? Do not we also love?'

Margot wanted to laugh at that. Mild Marie Touchet and mad Charles . . . to be compared with her and Henry!

But she had learned her lesson. She must not be so rash. She might put Henry in danger if she were; after all, he had managed to make some people think he was contemplating marriage with the Princess of Clèves.

Her brother Henry was not wild, like Charles, but he was very angry with her. He frightened her more than Charles did, for she knew he discussed her with their mother.

One day Catherine sent for her, and as she entered the Queen Mother's apartments she began to tremble; she felt the sweat in the palms of her hands as she used to when she was a little girl.

'Come here,' said Catherine.

Margot went to her and curtsied. Her lips touched her mother's hand.

'Rise now,' said Catherine. 'No ceremony, my daughter.' Her lids slid down over her eyes. *Madame le Serpent*, thought Margot, waiting, deciding whether or not now is the time to strike.

Catherine started to walk up and down the apartment.

'My daughter, it is time you married. You are no longer a child, and princesses must marry early.' Margot's heart began to pound. 'I have taken a good deal of trouble on your account already, and have, I think, succeeded in making a brilliant match for you.'

Margot began: 'Madame . . .' But Catherine looked at her in astonishment that she should have dared to interrupt, and Margot was immediately silent.

'Sebastian, the King of Portugal, is considering whether he will take you as his wife.'

Margot gulped and tried to speak.

Catherine went on: 'As you know, he is the nephew of the King of Spain, and Philip himself puts no obstacle in the way of the match. I am sure that when Sebastian himself sees you in all your maidenly beauty, he will be eager to make you his wife. Now, my daughter, you will be ignorant of the duties of the married state, and you may need instruction in such matters. Do not forget that I am your mother and that I shall be willing to help you and tell you what you wish to know of such matters of which you, as a maiden, will be ignorant.'

Margot flushed scarlet; she knew that her mother was aware of her love affair. She wanted to show defiance as she had to Charles and Henry, but she was numbed by that cold terror which she always felt in the presence of her mother.

'Speak, my daughter! Speak, Marguerite, and tell me that you are happy because of this match I have arranged for you. Tell me, what is your will in all this?'

The cold eyes held Margot's, and the girl felt as though she were in the presence of a supernatural being, something inhuman and horrible that was threatening death to her love, and life-long misery. She remembered her lover's instructions to be calm, to indulge in temporary deceit for the purpose of winning in the end.

'I . . . I have no will of my own, Madame,' she heard herself say. 'I only have that will which depends on yours.'

Catherine burst into loud laughter. She took Margot's ear and pulled her towards her.

'No will but mine . . . and that of Monsieur de Guise, eh?'

Margot cried out in pain, but her mother gripped her ear the harder. Then she put her lips close to that ear and began to whisper that she knew what Margot believed to have been known only to herself and her lover. All Catherine's coarseness came out now. The loud laugh on her lips, the crude words, made Margot flinch.

'Harlot! Wanton! Do you know no better? It is you who have seduced him . . . not he you. It is you who have importuned Monsieur de Guise to take you to his bed. Marriage! What of that? The Princess of France, for whom I have tried to arrange one of the grandest marriages the world has ever known, is a harlot, begging the favours of the Duke of Guise. "Henry . . . take me . . . take me . . . Now . . . now . . . I cannot wait. I long so for you . . ."' Catherine began to laugh. 'Monsieur de Guise must have found the conquest of the Princess of France the easiest he ever undertook.'

And with these scornful words, Catherine flung Margot

from her; and Margot, who would have been quick-witted, who would have made her escape from any other, lay where she had fallen, as though petrified, unable to move, while her mother, portly and vengeful, swept slowly and majestically towards her.

'Get up!' she cried; and Margot rose immediately.

Catherine slapped Margot's face, her rings cutting into the girl's cheek.

'Ah!' said Catherine. 'That must not be. We must not let your future husband know that we have had to beat you for wantonness with the Duke of Guise.' Catherine pulled Margot towards her. 'And why do you think Guise has made you his mistress? Because he loves you? Because he is as mad for you as you so shamelessly are for him? Never! Because, foolish wanton, the Cardinal of Lorraine told him to seduce you in the hope that, having been his mistress, it would be impossible for you to marry him whom I have chosen for you. That is their scheme. "Henry, I long for you." "And I for you, Margot. And for all that you can bring me. Not your wanton body, you fool, but your name, your rank, for besides being a harlot you are the daughter of a royal house, the most noble house in France."'

'You lie,' said Margot. 'He loves me . . . *me*.'

'You little fool. Monsieur de Guise is not the sort to say "No" when a woman begs so insistently.'

'You lie . . .'

Catherine took Margot by the sleeve of her gown and dragged her to a couch. She pushed her down and bent over her. 'You may well show fear. You dare to tell me, your mother, that I lie! You dare to solicit favours of Monsieur de Guise! You dare to become the mistress of the man who threatens your brother the King and the whole of your family!'

This was one of those rare occasions when Catherine's control broke. She imagined she heard Margot's voice: 'Henry, I long for you.' She imagined she heard the deep, passionate response of Henry of Guise. But it was not these two she pictured; it was another Henry, oh, long ago, loving his mistress as he never could his wife.

In a sudden rush of fury, she tore off Margot's clothes and beat her savagely.

'Not the face this time!' she cried. 'We must not show the King of Portugal that we have a wanton for a daughter. We must beat you where the marks of a beating will not be seen . . . except, perhaps, by Monsieur de Guise.'

Margot lay panting under the fury of her mother, who had picked up a cane with a jewelled handle which Charles used when he left the palace on flagellating orgies. It came down again and again on Margot's body; and all the time it seemed to Catherine that she was watching two lovers through a hole in the floor of the palace at Saint-Germain. It was not, it seemed to her then, Margot who lay there, but Diane.

Eventually her passion was spent. She reflected that it was a rare thing for her to indulge in such emotion. Yet it had been irresistible. Margot had called up too many memories. It had been foolish of her to compare Henry of Guise with Henry of Valois, simply because they both bore the same name.

Margot lay limp on the couch, and Catherine stared down at her bruised body.

'Go,' said Catherine. 'Put on your dress. Later I will discuss with you the arrangements for the greeting of the King of Portugal.'

And while Margot, in her own apartments, was bathing her

wounds, terrified lest some mark should spoil the perfection of her body, Catherine reproached herself for that outburst of fury.

Looking back was something in which she knew it was folly to indulge. There were too many dangers of the moment for past insults and humiliations to be of any importance.

❖ ❖ ❖

Margot was preparing to meet her suitor. Her dress was of cloth of gold; her jewels magnificent; and her eyes were as hard and as brilliant as the diamonds she wore. She was saying to herself: 'I will never marry him. I will marry Henry. There will be a way, and we will find it.'

She had seen Henry of Guise earlier that day. He was constantly in the company of the Princess of Clèves, being so much wiser than she could ever be. He knew of that interview she had had with her mother; he begged her to be calm, discreet. It was for Henry's sake that she had feigned meekness and pretended to submit to her mother's commands.

She had said to Henry when they met: 'I must see you later. I want to come to you in my rich gown and my jewels. I have said I will wear them to greet my bridegroom. You are my bridegroom.'

'It is dangerous,' he said.

But Margot's passion carried her beyond the thought of danger. She *must* see him. It was so long since they had made love. Two days ago . . . It was an age! To-night, after the ceremonial meeting with the King of Portugal, they would meet. Did he know that small chamber close to his own apartments in this palace of the Louvre? She would come to him there, and he must be ready for her. They would spend the whole night together. They must. She would not be put off with a mere hour. They must be together all through the night. It was only with such a prospect before her that she could face the ordeal of the evening's ceremony.

He had agreed to be at the rendezvous, and Margot, having dressed herself with the greatest care, knew she had never looked so beautiful.

'Ah!' said one of her women. 'You look like a Princess who is going to meet her lover.'

Margot embraced her warmly, and the woman knew what that meant.

'Keep my doors locked to-night,' whispered Margot.

'My dearest lady Princess, be careful.'

'Have no fears for me.'

'It is dangerous, my lady.'

Margot laughed; she loved danger if it meant love-making with Henry of Guise.

'Ah, my Princess, I can understand. There is no one like him in the whole of France.'

'There is no one like him in the whole world,' corrected Margot.

She conducted herself with decorum at the ceremony of meeting her suitor, who was deeply impressed with the wild beauty of the Princess. It was true, he concluded, that she was the most fascinating lady at the court of France.

Henry of Guise was there, watching. Margot wondered if he suffered similar pangs to those she felt when he bent his handsome head towards that of Catherine of Clèves.

Catherine watched too. The girl was defiant, but she knew she must obey. During her chastisement she had cringed in a manner which had been quite gratifying. Margot was wild; she was passionate, more desirous – and perhaps therefore more desirable – than a woman should be; but Catherine believed she knew how to manage Margot's affairs with satisfaction.

For Margot the evening seemed endless; the bright lights were too dazzling. She was charming to the King of Portugal and his attendants. She gave the impression that the match would not be distasteful to her; but all the time she was scarcely aware of her suitor; she was only aware of Henry, now talking to the Princess of Clèves, now dancing with her, while the latter – the little fool that she was! – looked as though all she desired on Earth was the smile of the young Duke of Guise.

Margot fretted and waited; and during those long hours of ceremony she yearned for her lover.

At last it was over, and the palace was quiet.

Margot was ready, waiting in her robes of state, for the moment when she should slip out and along to that little chamber where Henry would be waiting for her. Her women ran about eagerly, touching her dress here and there, putting a fold of her gown in place, telling her she was more beautiful to-night than she had ever been; they looked into the corridor to make sure that no one was lurking there; and then Margot was speeding through corridors, up stairs to her meeting with her lover.

She clung to him while they murmured words of love. He told of his jealousy, she of hers. She lit the candles that he might see her in all her finery.

'You were more beautiful than ever to-night,' he said.

'It was because I was coming here to you. If I had not been coming to you, I should have been ugly . . . hating them all. Oh, Henry, shall I ever cease to love you like this?'

'Never,' he said, 'I hope.'

He had made a bed of his velvet cloak; she saw it and laughed. 'We have known so many strange beds. When shall we know our marriage bed?'

'Soon, Margot, soon. But we must be doubly cautious now that this man from Portugal is here.'

The candles guttered out, and they lay in the darkness. The night passed and, when the first signs of the new day were in the sky, Margot regretted its passing.

'The most wonderful night of my life!' she sighed. 'I shall remember it always.'

'There will be many such when we are married. Then we shall have no fear of discovery.'

She was laughing, demanding more kisses. Neither of them heard the door open, so engrossed were they in each other; nor did they see the figure standing there watching them. The door was quietly closed again, and not long after there was a great commotion in the corridor which even they could not fail to hear.

'Keep very still,' said Henry. 'Make no sound.'

He had risen silently, but before he had his coat on and his sword at his side, the door burst open. The King stood there; his clothes had been hastily thrown on; his eyes were bloodshot and his mouth working. Behind him stood several of the attendants of his bedchamber.

He screamed an order. 'Take them to my mother's apartments. With all speed. No delay.'

The lovers were surrounded. Four men were needed to overcome the struggles of Guise. Two seized Margot; and the pair were then hustled along the corridors to the apartments of the Queen Mother.

Catherine, startled out of her sleep, stared at the intruders, but it did not take her long, when she saw who the captives were, to realise what had happened. Charles, the little fool, had once more acted without his mother; by this impetuous act he had exposed the liaison between his sister and the Duke of Guise to the whole court. And Sebastian, the King of Portugal, was in the Palace of the Louvre at this very hour!

Catherine did not know whom she hated more at this moment – her stupid son Charles or her wanton daughter, Margot.

Angry as she was, she did not lose her self-control.

'Monsieur de Guise,' she said, 'your presence is not needed here.'

Henry bowed and left the room. It was the only thing he could do. He flashed a warning glance at Margot, begging her to be calm and diplomatic.

Catherine glanced at all those assembled, and her look said clearly that it would be the worse for them all if they mentioned to any what they had seen this morning. 'All may leave with Monsieur de Guise,' she said. 'His Majesty and I wish to be alone with the Princess.'

When the room was empty but for the three of them, Catherine went to the door and locked it. She signed to Charles to attack his sister, and he, nothing loth, took his stick and approached the terrified girl. Margot ran to her mother, who flung her back to the King. Charles was biting his lips so that blood mingled with the foam there.

'We must try to beat some sense into this little fool,' said Catherine. 'On the very night when she meets her suitor, she keeps an assignation with her lover. Beat her. Let her learn what it costs to bring disgrace on us all.'

Catherine now unleashed her fury. Margot's rich gown was

torn in shreds and, bleeding and exhausted, she begged them to spare her. But she was not to be spared.

Margot had suffered many beatings in her lifetime, but nothing so severe as this. At length she sank unconscious to the floor. Charles kicked her as she lay there; the sight of blood always inflamed him, and a mood of frenzy had come upon him.

Catherine, looking on, considered the possibility of Margot's death. It would not be the first time that a disobedient child had been beaten to death, but Margot's death would be most inconvenient. Catherine's rage had passed. Moreover, the room was light, for the day had now come.

'Enough!' she cried to Charles.

But it was not easy to stop Charles. He wanted to see blood flow. It was always thus when his madness was on him. He wanted to have Henry of Guise's head off.

'Kill him! Kill him!' he screamed. 'Torture him . . . And Margot shall see it all. Let her be there. Let her watch him, naked and sweating under the torture, and see then if she recognises her handsome lover.'

'Silence!' commanded Catherine.

The King's face was distorted as he stared wildly at his mother; his lips were twitching; his glaring eyes were bloodshot; moisture trickled from his mouth. He was prancing about the unconscious body of his sister. He wanted to kick her to death, yet when he recovered his sanity he would be filled with remorse if he had hurt her.

'My dear son,' said Catherine, putting an arm about his twitching form, 'have a care. You know these Guises. What if they turned the tables on you? What if you were naked . . . sweating, eh? Remember who *is* the man you wish to torture.

Remember *Le Balafré*. Remember the Cardinal. Have a care, my son.'

'He must die! He must die!' panted Charles.

'He shall die,' soothed Catherine. 'But *my* way . . . Mother's way . . . not yours. Lie on the couch, my darling, and rest. Leave this to your mother. She knows best. She does not want them to take her darling boy . . . her dear little King, and torture him.'

'They could not. They could not. I am the King.'

'You are the King, and a wise King, because you will do what I say. Rest now, my son, and leave this to me. Am I not always right? I will see that the arrogance of Monsieur de Guise is subdued. I will see that there is no more love-making with your sister.'

Catherine led him to a couch and soothed him; she stroked back his hair and wiped his mouth with her kerchief. He lay back, his eyes closed.

Catherine then unlocked her door and called to her attendants.

'The Princess has fainted. Bring water. We must bathe her. She has had a fall. Hurry . . . I command you.'

They brought the water, and she herself bathed Margot's bruised body, adjusted her dress and helped the girl back to her apartments.

She announced: 'The Princess will rest for a few days. See that she keeps to her apartments. I will make her excuses.'

Then Catherine went back to her bed. She appeared to be sleeping when the ceremony of the *lever* was about to begin, and when aroused she wore her usual calm expression.

328

Catherine spent much time, during the days that followed, with those creatures of hers – the Ruggieri brothers and René, the perfumer, who made such beautiful gloves and sold such exquisite jewels in his little shop on the quay opposite the Louvre.

She had made sure that she was alone in her apartment before unlocking her secret cupboard; she had dressed herself in the garments of a market-woman so that no one would recognise the majestic Queen Mother in the portly woman with the basket on her arm and the shawl which covered her head and half her face.

She left by the secret passage, which she realised must be known to a few besides herself, since it had been in existence long before she had come to France. But she used it frequently, and it provided her with a certain amount of secrecy. She certainly could not leave by the main gates of the palace, dressed in these garments.

As she made her way to the house of the Ruggieri, so conveniently near the river that it was possible to leave by a back entrance and take the boat which was moored there, she could not resist mingling with the market crowds, exchanging a word here and there, trying to get them to speak of the royal house.

'Wars . . . wars . . . wars . . .' said one woman. 'Why should our country be bathed in blood?'

'For the good of the Faith,' said the stout woman in the shawl.

'For the good of the Faith! For the good of great nobles who would snatch power from one another.'

'Oh . . . we shall have a grand marriage soon in Paris,' said Catherine.

'The Portuguese gentleman will be getting a handful, so they say.'

Catherine laughed coarsely and came closer to the woman, 'There are rumours about the little Princess, I believe.'

'Have you not heard? She is madly in love with the Duke of Guise – the good God bless him! – and she has been his mistress for many years . . . since they were in their cradles almost. They say that our Margot is mad for him . . . that she is such another as our great King Francis, her grandfather. There was a man! He couldn't look at a woman without wanting to take her to his bed. They say Margot is such another.'

'Then it is well, is it not, that she should be married quickly?'

'Well for her . . . or for him?'

Catherine passed on. So the rumours concerning Margot had already travelled beyond the palace walls!

The Ruggieri received her with the pleasure which they always expressed when she came to visit them. They took her at once into their secret apartment.

'What I need,' she said, 'is a present for a gentleman. It is a gentleman of the highest rank – fastidious in his tastes. It must be very charming, and most cleverly devised for such a man.'

The brothers looked uneasily at one another, as they always did when asked to help despatch the important enemies of Catherine. They were very happy to assist in the removal of the insignificant who happened to be in their mistress's way, but they were terrified of supplying their wares for use against the great.

'If,' said Catherine, 'it will help you not to know the name of the gentleman, I will not tell it.'

But they knew. Any rumour that had left the palace walls would be sure to find its way into the Ruggieri stronghold; and every market-woman and fishwife, it seemed, was gossiping over the love affair of the Princess Margot and the Duke of Guise.

The Ruggieri brothers were not eager to assist in the removal of a man of such high rank.

Still, their fear would make them subtler; and subtlety was what was needed in such an affair.

'I will give you twenty-four hours in which to think of something. It must be something which will not arouse suspicions. Not a book . . . not gloves. It must be something which has never been tried before. But it must have speedy results.'

Catherine left the brothers trembling at her command. They knew they had been asked to help in the removal of the head of the most powerful family in the country. How could they escape implication? They could not shut out of their minds the sly, clever face of the Cardinal of Lorraine, the power of his family. And the Queen Mother was asking them to help her remove the handsome young Duke of Guise!

Catherine left them and came out into the streets.

She did not notice that one of the women who had been in that group with whom she had paused to chat kept a little way behind her as she made her way to René's shop before going back to the Louvre. For the time she had forgotten that the spy system of the House of Guise and Lorraine was as efficient as her own.

She made her way to the secret passage, where she changed her garments. She came through to her own apartments, unlocked her doors and went along to see her daughter.

Margot was in bed. Fortunately, her face had suffered little damage, but the girl could not move for the cuts and bruises on her body. She lay, pale and wan – very unlike her usual vivacious self. She shrank under the bedclothes at the sight of her mother.

Catherine laid a hand on her brow.

'Ah, my daughter, you are a little better, I think. Let me see how you hurt yourself when you fell in my apartments.' She drew back the bedclothes and pulled up Margot's nightgown. 'Poor child! A pity to spoil your beauty, for you are very lovely, daughter. Is she not?' Catherine turned to the attendants who stood by, and looked from them to Margot, cowering in the bed.

'There is no lady at court more beautiful than the Princess,' they agreed.

'I will send my own special unguents for these wounds. I do not think there is any serious damage done. She will be healed in a week or so.'

Catherine pulled up the bedclothes and tucked them in with the solicitude of a fond mother.

Then she went back to be dressed for the ball which was to take place that night.

Her thoughts were busy while her women dressed her hair and arranged her jewels. She must keep a sharp eye on Charles. He was impetuous. He might easily expose the fact that there was a plot afoot to remove the Duke of Guise. Her beloved Henry, fortunately, had good sense, and he would show the right sort of friendship to Henry of Guise – just enough to allay his fears, and not so much that it would confirm his suspicions. But she could expect no such cleverness from her little madman, Charles.

She went to the King's apartment and, dismissing all his attendants, spoke warningly to him.

'I beg of you, when you see Guise to-night, do nothing rash.'

'No, Mother. But I hate him. He is trying to take my throne. I am sure there will never be peace in this realm while the Guises are so powerful.'

'That is true; but we must take every care. Promise me that you will not shout at him when you see him. For the love of the Virgin, do not let him see that you are thirsting for his blood.'

'Nay, my mother. I am not such a fool as you think.'

'Of course you are not. You are my clever little King.'

'All the same,' said Charles, 'I shall not rest until he has been punished for what he has done to Margot.'

'Rather let him be punished for what he may do to you and your brother, my darling.'

But what was the good of talking to Charles! He was hopeless. He was mad.

And in the magnificent ballroom, when Henry of Guise was announced, Catherine watched with dismay the angry colour flood the face of the King. Before she could prevent him, he was at the door, barring the way of the Duke.

'Whither are you going, sir?' demanded Charles in a high voice which could be heard all over the ballroom, for all had stopped talking to listen.

'Sire,' replied Guise, with excellent restraint, 'I am here to serve your gracious Majesty.'

'Monsieur,' said Charles, with what he thought to be admirable calm, 'I have no need of your services, so you may depart.'

Henry of Guise bowed low and immediately left the palace.

He knew now that he was in imminent danger, and Catherine felt that it would be as well to prepare potions – not only for the dangerous Duke of Guise, seducer of her daughter, but for that little fool who was known as the King of France.

✤ ✤ ✤

In the hotel which was the stronghold of the family of Guise in Paris there was an immediate conference that night.

The Cardinal of Lorraine was there with his brothers, Louis the Cardinal of Guise, Claud the Duke of Aumale, Francis the Grand Prior, and René the Duke of Elbœuf. There were also the young Duke's brothers and sister – Charles, Louis and Catherine; his widowed mother would not move from the side of her son, whom she regarded continually with an expression alternating between adoration and fear.

It was rarely that the entire family was assembled together in this way; but they had come hastily to Paris, summoned thither by the Cardinal of Lorraine, whose spies had informed him that for some time the Queen Mother had marked down Duke Henry as one of her victims.

The Cardinal of Lorraine was speaking. 'At any moment now the blow may be struck. Henry, my nephew, if you have ever been in danger, you are in danger now.'

'I can protect myself,' said Henry.

'You would protect yourself on the field of battle, my boy. You would meet any, I know, in combat, and emerge the victor. But when the serpent slyly coils about you – so quietly that you do not know your body is encircled – what can you do? Take your sword and strike off its head? Do not think of such a foolish thing! The fangs are inserted, and only in the last

334

agonies of death do you see the slimy snake uncoil itself and quietly slip away.'

'You must leave Paris at once,' said the frightened Duchess. 'My darling, you must take horse and fly to Lorraine. I will come with you. I cannot bear that you should leave my sight.'

But Aumale and his brothers shook their heads.

'Flight is no good,' said the Grand Prior. 'Doubtless she has her creatures in Lorraine.'

'What then?' cried the Duchess. 'Would you have him stay here?'

The Cardinal of Lorraine straightened his rich robes.

'No. There is one way out of this and one way only. I must have been inspired when I advised my nephew to pay court to Madame de Clèves. The Queen Mother, the crazy King and his brothers are terrified. They are afraid that Margot will marry Henry in spite of them all. That is why they are determined to remove the cause of their fear. We must show them that their fears are groundless. Show them that, and Henry is no more in danger than he ever was, than any of us are continually. It is very simple. Henry must with all speed relinquish his plan to marry the Princess. He must show he is sincere in this by an immediate marriage with the Princess of Clèves.'

'That I will not do!' cried Henry. 'I have promised to marry Margot, and I stand by my word.'

'Very fine and noble!' said the Cardinal of Lorraine. 'But do we want Margot to marry a corpse? You see, my dear family, how very wise I was in selecting the Princess of Clèves. She is worthy to marry into our family. A marriage with Marguerite de Valois would have been more desirable, but there is only one way now to save our beloved Henry, and that is by his immediate marriage to the lady of Clèves.'

'It is quite impossible,' said Henry. 'I prefer to face any danger than do that.'

'Nonsense! If you do not, you face certain death.'

'I prefer it to dishonour.'

'Oh, come, foolish boy. You are too romantic. The family of the Princess of Clèves will agree to this marriage as eagerly as the lady herself. As for our Princess Margot, well, you will no doubt be able to take your pleasure with her after she has forgiven you.'

'You do not understand, my uncle, what you suggest. You do not know.'

'I have been in love, my boy. I was once young and romantic, even as you are. But love palls; it is like rich fruit, delicious while it is ripe; but it cannot last for ever. But the good of a great and noble house is the most important thing in the life of its members. My boy, it is not of yourself and your love that you must think now, but of your family's honour. We must show the Queen Mother and her sons that she cannot destroy members of our house. We know when to take a step backwards; we know when we must adjust our policy; but we will have no more assassinations. We must not let them think that when we displease them it is easy to dispose of us.'

'I am pledged to the Princess Margot,' said the young Duke. 'I will take none other.'

The Cardinal of Lorraine shrugged his shoulders; the Duchess wept; the Duke's brothers pleaded with him; his sister implored him to save his life; and his uncles called him a fool.

All night they argued with him; and in the early hours of the morning, the gibes of the Cardinal of Lorraine, the good sense of his family, and most of all the passionate tears of his mother, caused the young Duke to give way.

Once he had given his consent, the Cardinal of Lorraine lost no time in presenting himself at the Louvre and asking for an audience with the Queen Mother.

'I have come,' said the Cardinal, 'to ask your Majesty's most gracious consent to the marriage of my nephew Henry, Duke of Guise, to Catherine, Princess of Clèves.'

Catherine did not allow her expression to change in the smallest degree.

'Well, Monsieur le Cardinal, that seems a very satisfactory match. The House of Clèves, I think, is worthy – or as worthy as any could be – of the House of Guise and Lorraine. I am sure my son, the King, will have nothing to say against such a match.'

'Then I have your consent? He may make his arrangements with the lady?'

'With all speed, Monsieur le Cardinal. With *all* speed.'

The Cardinal bowed low.

Catherine went on: 'Let the wedding take place at once. I wish to honour our visiting royalty with as many ceremonies as we can give him. I think that the marriage of the Duke of Guise and the Princess of Clèves should provide us with an excellent occasion for making merry.'

'So be it,' said the Cardinal.

And Catherine dismissed him.

She was pleased. Ruggieri and René were slothful when it came to employing their arts against the great. They could never get rid of the thoughts of torture-chambers; and such thoughts were not conducive to the best work.

And once Henry of Guise was the husband of Catherine of Clèves, this little trouble would be over; and she was the first to admit that one should always take the easiest way out of a difficulty.

The marriage should take place in a few days' time, and all she had to concern herself with now was to make sure that there was no meeting between Margot and Henry of Guise until after the marriage ceremony. That was not difficult. Margot was too sick and wounded to leave her bed just yet. Catherine must warn the girl's attendants – in her own special way of warning – that anyone who whispered to Margot that her lover was about to be married would wish they had not been so rash – if they lived long enough to make such a wish!

A very satisfactory conclusion to a difficult affair!

Catherine came into her daughter's apartment and signified that she wished to be left alone with her.

'Margot,' she said, 'you will make your reappearance to-day, and you are looking as well as ever after your indisposition; but I am afraid that I have news which will be a shock to you, and I feel that it would be better if you learned it through me than in any other way.'

Margot lifted her great dark eyes to her mother's face and waited in apprehension.

'Monsieur de Guise was married a few days ago.'

Margot stared. 'But . . . that is not possible.'

'Quite possible, my daughter.'

'But . . . who?'

'To your friend . . . Catherine . . . the Princess of Clèves.'

Margot was stunned. It could not be. After everything that had happened between them, after all their protestations! She had trusted Henry completely, and he had said that he would never marry anyone but her.

'My child, this is a shock to you. I know your feelings for this young man – indeed, they were most unmaidenly, and they carried you far, I fear, along the road of impropriety. Well, Henry of Guise knows when he must obey the wishes of his family – as you know that you must obey yours – and so he married the lady. By his attentions to her, I should say that he is not displeased. She is a good-looking young woman and as madly in love with him as . . . others have been.'

Margot lay still.

'Now, my daughter,' said Catherine, 'you must not show your feelings or you will have the whole court laughing at you. You have been fooled as far as Monsieur de Guise is concerned. You gave yourself too easily. Now you must show your pride. When you appear to-night, remember that you are a Princess of France. There must be no more retirement, for I have let it be known that you are recovered. See how brave you can be. Show the court that you can snap your fingers at a faithless lover.'

When her mother had gone, Margot called her women to her. Was it true, she demanded, that Monsieur de Guise was married? Then why had she not been told?

They hung their heads. They dared not say. Margot stormed at them; she raged; but she did not weep.

She insisted that they dress her with the utmost care; she had grown thin in the last week or so, but she was none the less beautiful for that. Bitterness, anger, bewilderment had given a new wildness to her beauty.

She was gay to-night, and her mother watched her with approval.

Catherine knew – and Margot knew – that everywhere sly eyes were on her. In the banqueting hall, in the *salle du bal*, all were hoping for some excitement from the inevitable encounter between the Princess and the Duke.

Margot received his wife calmly; she complimented her on her looks and congratulated her on her marriage. Catherine of Clèves was a little frightened of those wild, glittering black eyes, but at the same time she was so happy to have married the man she had loved for so long that she could not care even if the Princess Margot hated her.

Margot coquetted gaily – first with one noble gentleman and then with another. Those wild, provocative glances, which until now had all been for Henry of Guise, were evenly distributed among the handsomest and most eligible of the noblemen.

They were enchanted by Margot, for Margot was completely sensuous; that overwhelming sex consciousness, that adoration of physical love, that promise of what she and she alone could give were irresistible.

Margot knew that Henry of Guise was watching her; and she was glad of that, since the whole performance was for him. She was desperately trying to put hate where love had been, loathing in the place of longing.

In the dance he came near enough to speak to her.

'Margot, I must talk to you.'

She turned her head.

'If you only knew, my love, my darling! If only you would listen to what I have to tell you.'

She shrugged her shoulders. 'I have no wish to speak to you.'

'Margot, darling, give me five minutes alone with you.'

'I have no wish to speak to you.'

'I will wait in the first of the green alleys. Our old meeting-place . . . do you remember?'

'You may wait, for all I care.'

But her voice had broken and he could hear the sob in her throat.

'In half an hour,' he begged.

She could not trust herself to speak, so she turned her head away and shrugged her shoulders.

'I will wait,' he said, 'all night if necessary.'

'Wait all through to-morrow – if you care for such things.'

'Margot,' he implored; and the sound of her name on his lips was more than she could bear. She moved away from him.

She thought of his waiting. Was he waiting? He had said he would wait. But could she trust him to keep his word? He had said he would marry her, that nothing should stand in the way of their love; and, only a few days after that wonderful night they had spent together, he had married the Princess of Clèves.

She must go to see if he waited. I hate him now, she told herself, and it will be just to see if he really is waiting.

She saw him at once – the tall, familiar figure, the handsomest man at the court of France. He came forward with a lover's eagerness. 'Margot, my love, you came. I knew you would.'

She would not give him her hands; she was afraid to let him touch her. She knew her own weakness; and her desire, she knew, would be stronger than her pride.

'Well, traitor,' she said, 'what do you want?'

'To put my arms about you.'

'Shame! And you a husband . . . of a week, is it?'

'Margot, it had to be.'

'I know. You had sworn to marry me, but it had to be Catherine of Clèves. I wish you joy of her – that silly, simpering creature! You could have done better than that, Henry.'

He had her by the shoulders, but she wrenched herself free at once.

'Cannot you see that I hate you now? Do you not understand that you have insulted me . . . humiliated me . . . betrayed me!'

'You loved me,' he said, 'even as I loved you.'

'Oh no, Monsieur,' she answered bitterly; 'far more than that, *I* would never have been led away. I would have faced death rather.'

'Margot, you would have suffered more if I had died. You would not then have had even this pleasure you now enjoy in tormenting me. They planned my death – your mother, your brothers. My family were convinced that the only thing I could do was to marry Catherine if I would save myself. Darling, this is not the end for us. You are here. I am here. It is not what we planned, but we can still see each other, renew all that joy we have in each other.'

'How dare you?' she cried. 'How dare you? Do you forget that I am a Princess of France?'

'I forget everything but that I love you, that I can never know a moment's happiness without you.'

'Then know this also: I hate you. I loathe you and despise you. Never try to speak to me. Never try making your vile suggestions to me again. I have been a fool, but do you not think that I will find others to love me? Do not think that you can desert me, betray me . . . and then, when you want me again, that I shall come back like a . . . like a dog!'

She turned and ran back to the palace.

That evening she danced more gaily than she ever had

342

before. She laughed and coquetted. Her eyes conveyed many a promise, and she was utterly bewitching; but when she retired to her apartments, and her women had undressed her, she threw herself on to her bed and wept so long and so passionately that they were afraid.

At last she fell silent and lay still; and in the morning when her women came to waken her, they found her skin flushed and clammy and her eyes glassy; she was in a high fever.

Catherine and the King thought that the affair of Margot and Henry of Guise had been settled to their satisfaction; the Cardinal of Lorraine and his family thought they had retreated in time from a highly dangerous situation; Henry of Guise had come out of the affair with acute melancholy which would not subside until the Princess Margot was once more his mistress. But the Princess herself lay ill – not caring if she were to die. She tossed and turned in a fever, suffering from that indifference to life which is called a broken heart.

Catherine lay very ill at Metz. She knew that no one expected her to live. She could smile seeing the hope in their faces. There was hardly anyone who would be likely to grieve for her.

As she lay in her bed, she was aware vaguely of the people about her; she was not sure where she was. At times she thought that she was in the Palace of Saint-Germain, and that in the room below, Henry, her husband, was making love to Diane. At others she thought she was riding in the forest near Fontainebleau or Amboise, and that, beside her, rode the King – King Francis, her father-in-law – and the ladies of his *Petite Bande*.

Then she would have moments of full consciousness. She would remember that her beloved son Henry was bravely fighting the Huguenot army, that King Charles was becoming more and more mad and must soon give place to his brother, who was growing more and more worthy of kingship. Then she would think that Margot must be married soon. The marriage with Sebastian had fallen through, as Philip of Spain now wanted him for one of his female relatives; but Margot should be married, for Margot was a wicked, wanton girl. She had taken another lover and scandalous stories were whispered about her; some said that she still had her eyes on Henry of Guise, and that only her stubborn pride prevented her from taking up her relationship with him where it had ceased on his marriage to Catherine of Clèves. They said that Margot took this new lover in order to flaunt him in the presence of young Henry of Guise, and that there was a smouldering passion between these two which must blaze up sooner or later. Catherine's first duty was to find a husband for Margot – and who was there but the boy to whom her father had pledged her when they were little more than babies? Henry of Navarre! It would mean summoning him to court. By all accounts, he was as profligate as Margot, so they would make a good pair. Let them marry and satisfy each other – if satisfaction were possible to either of them.

Margot would be the Queen of Navarre. Well, that had been a good enough title for the sister of Francis the First, and it should be good enough for the present Marguerite de Valois, for wicked little Margot. Catherine decided that if she ever got up from this sick-bed she would start negotiations immediately. Once she had the young Prince of Navarre at court it should not be difficult to change him into a Catholic, in spite of his mother's teaching. She was looking forward to another conflict with Madame Jeanne.

Now her thoughts had turned to another Henry, her beloved son, her 'All'. She knew that there was fighting round about Jarnac and that Coligny and Condé together stood in opposition to her darling. Two men – Condé and her son – were now in danger, and for both of these men she had felt tenderness. She had enjoyed those conversations with gallant Condé, the gay philanderer; she had cherished those moments when his kiss had lingered on her hand. But it was nonsense to think of such things. Who wanted love when there was power to be won?

She might have prayed for her son's victory, but she did not really believe in prayer. There was no God for her; there was only Catherine, the Queen Mother, the power behind the throne. There were no miracles except those performed by clever people like herself.

How hot it was in this room! Her sight seemed to be fading. There were shadowy figures about her bed. Ah, there was the King, her little mad Charles; and with him her daughter, wanton Margot, as yet unwed, yet more versed in the ways of love than many a matron of years' standing. There were others in the room, but she felt that they were too remote to be recognised.

What was happening at Jarnac? The dawn was breaking and the battle would soon begin. There was a cold sweat all over her, and she was afraid.

She wanted to call for Cosmo or Lorenzo Ruggieri. But she was no longer in the sick-room at Metz. She was somewhere out of doors, for she could feel the wind blowing on her face. Then suddenly she heard the voice of her son Henry; it was raised in prayer; then she heard him addressing his men, and she realised that she must be on the battlefield at Jarnac.

'Condé . . . Condé . . . Condé . . .' She heard the name coming to her clearly over the cold air.

'Condé must be killed before nightfall . . .'

Catherine's lips moved. Not Condé . . . not the gallant little Prince. She did not want him for a lover, but he was so agreeable, so charming.

Now she heard Condé's voice. He too was talking to his men; she caught the note of fanaticism which she had noticed so many times in so many people. 'Louis de Bourbon goes to fight for Christ and his country.'

She must have said something aloud, for the sound of her voice had broken the spell and she was back in the sick-room.

'Mother,' said Charles. 'Mother, do you wish for a prelate?'

A prelate? So she was near death. Death! What was death? A beginning again . . . a new fight for power in a fresh sphere?

Then the room faded and she was back on the field of battle. She saw Condé clearly in the light of morning, his handsome head thrown back, a smile on his lips; and then suddenly he was down; she saw him lying on the ground, the blood at his lips, the death rattle in his throat.

'Look!' cried Catherine. 'See how they flee! Condé is dead. He lies in the hedge there. He can never recover. His wound is too deep. Condé . . . ah, Condé . . . he is no more. But Henry . . . my darling . . . Henry is victorious once more. The battle is yours. Condé is dead. Coligny has fled. All honour to you, my love, my darling.'

The King turned to Margot and said: 'She dreams of the battle. She has thought of nothing else since she knew my brother was to fight to-day.'

Margot watched her mother without pity, without love. There was no pity nor love in Margot; there was only perpetual bitterness, a poignant memory, and a deep longing for the man she had vowed to hate.

'Is the end near?' asked the King.

None was sure, but all looked grave.

The end of Catherine de' Medici, the end of the Italian woman! What changes would that bring to France?

But in the morning Catherine was better; and when, a few days later, news of the Battle of Jarnac was brought to Metz, it was thought that to hear of her son's victory would cheer her and help her through her convalescence.

She was sleeping lightly and Charles, with Margot and others, stood at her bedside.

'Mother,' said Charles gently, 'the battle is won. This is another victory for Henry. Condé is dead.'

She smiled serenely; she was her old self now, rapidly recovering from her fever.

'And why should you be so tedious as to awaken me and tell me that?' she demanded. 'Did I not know? Did I not tell *you* . . . as it was happening?'

Those in the room with Charles and Margot exchanged glances. Margot paled; Charles trembled. This woman, their mother, was no ordinary woman, no ordinary Queen; she had strange powers not given to others.

It was small wonder that she could terrify them as no one else on Earth had power to do.

⚜ ⚜ ⚜

After the great news of the victory of Jarnac, a strange gloom fell on the court. The King, more jealous of his brother than of any living person, was thrown into melancholy. 'Now,' he told his little Marie, 'my mother will glorify him more than ever. She longs to see him on the throne. Oh, Marie, I am frightened, because she is no ordinary woman, and what she desires comes to pass. She wishes me dead, and it is said that when my mother wishes a person dead, then he is as good as dead.'

But Marie took the King into her arms and assured him that this was not so. He must be calm and brave and not think of death. He must remember he was the King.

Charles tried; but he hated his brother. He refused to let him have the cannon he asked for, which was foolish and could only lead to trouble; and he knew that if he made trouble like that, matters would be brought to a head and that vague danger which haunted him all the time would come nearer to him.

Margot was anxious. Henry of Guise was fighting with the Catholic army, and she dreaded that what had happened to Condé might happen to Henry of Guise. When he was not at court, it was safe to admit to herself that her passion for him was as strong as ever. If Henry died, she would not wish to live. She prayed hourly that he might come safely home, if only to his wife.

Catherine had her difficulties. She was quite well now, but she was being tormented by Alava, the Spanish envoy; he reproached her bitterly. She had not followed up her advantages; she had been too lenient towards the Huguenots. His Most Catholic Majesty was not pleased with the Queen Mother.

'My lord,' said Catherine, in mock despair, 'what could I do? I no longer have the power that I had. My sons are becoming men, and I am just a weak woman.'

'Madame, you rule your sons, and it is you who have given Coligny the leisure to get an army together.'

'But, my lord, what *can* I do? I am as good a Catholic as you . . . as your master . . . but what can I do?'

'Have you forgotten, Madame, the conversation you had with the Duke of Alva at Bayonne?'

'Not a word of that, I beg of you. Such a plan would be useless if bruited abroad.'

'It must be carried out, and it must be soon. Kill the leaders . . . every one. Coligny must die. The Queen of Navarre must die. They cannot be allowed to live. Madame, I hear you have means at your disposal. You have a known reputation in this art of removal. And yet the most dangerous man and woman in your kingdom – the most dangerous to yourself and your throne – are allowed to live and to build up an army to fight against you.'

'But, my lord, Coligny is not here. He is in camp. The Queen of Navarre would not come if I asked her. I have despatched Coligny's two brothers – Odet and Andelot – the latter in England. Was not that subtle? He dies suddenly, in that austere land. Of what – very few know. I had my friends in his suite.'

'That was well done. But what use destroying the minnows when the salmon flourishes?'

'We shall get our salmon, my friend, but in good time.'

'His Most Catholic Majesty would ask, Madame, when is good time? When your kingdom has been wrested from you?'

She put her head close to that of the Spaniard. 'My son Henry is on his way to me. I will give him something . . . something which I know how to prepare myself. He shall have his spies in the Admiral's camp, and before long, my lord, you will have heard the last of Monsieur de Coligny.'

'I trust so, Madame.'

After that conversation and another with her son Henry, Catherine waited to hear news of the Admiral's death. She had given her son a subtle poison which would produce death a few days after it was administered. Her son's Captain of the Guard had been brought into the plot, for he was on good terms with Coligny's valet. A satisfactory bribe – and the deed would be done.

She waited now for one of her visions. She wished to see Coligny's death as she had seen that of Condé. But she waited in vain.

Later she heard that the plot had been discovered.

Coligny was a man of wide popularity, adored by too many; it was not easy to remove such a man.

Catherine began to grow terrified of Coligny. She did not understand him. He fought with such earnestness; he drew men to him. He had some quality which was quite outside Catherine's understanding; and for that reason she wished to have peace with him. And so she arranged for the Peace of Saint-Germain, in which, so that she might be at peace with this man whose righteousness was so alien to her, she gave way to many of his demands. She had to grant liberty of worship in all towns that were already Protestant; Protestants were to be admitted to office with Catholics, and on equal terms; four towns were to be handed over to Coligny as security for Catholic good faith – Montaban and Cognac as a bastion in the south, La Charité in the centre, and La Rochelle to guard the sea.

The Huguenots rejoiced at all they had won, and Catherine felt at peace temporarily, so that she might turn her mind to domestic matters.

Negotiations for the marriage of Charles were now in

progress. That farcical attempt to make a marriage between Elizabeth of England and Charles was at an end, but Catherine did not abandon altogether the idea of a union with England. She would substitute another of her sons as suitor to the Virgin Queen in Charles's place, and as no satisfactory arrangement had been made for Charles with Elizabeth of England, he should have Elisabeth of Austria.

Charles studied the pictures of his bride-to-be, liking the pale beauty, the meekness of expression.

'I doubt that such a one will give me much cause for anxiety,' he said.

The marriage gave Catherine little cause for anxiety also. It seemed very clear now that Charles would never produce healthy children; nor would marriage and its attendant excitements tend to lengthen the life of such a hysterical and unbalanced creature as this son; and so, on a misty November day in the year 1570, Charles the Ninth of France was married to Elisabeth of Austria.

✤ ✤ ✤

In the town of La Rochelle another but very romantic wedding was taking place. Jeanne of Navarre, preparing herself for the ceremony, thought with friendly envy of her dear friend Gaspard de Coligny, and prayed that he might acquire that rich happiness which he deserved. And he would, she was sure. He was made for such happiness. His first marriage had been ideal. His wife had worshipped him; and Coligny had been one of those husbands of whom women like Jeanne dreamed.

He had suffered bitterly on the death of his wife, but his life was so full and busy, and there was, Jeanne knew, one thing in it which must always come before wife and family, before the consideration of his personal happiness; and that was honour, the long and weary fight for the cause which he believed, with Jeanne, was the only true religion for the French.

It was a simple wedding, after the Huguenot fashion. And how noble was the bridegroom in the dignity of his years and that stern handsomeness that could only accompany a righteous and an honourable nature! Jeanne's eyes filled with tears, as she compared this bridegroom with another – more handsome perhaps in a worldly way, in his gorgeous apparel, the fashionable court gentleman – Antoine! It was so long ago, but it would never be forgotten by her.

Beside her stood her son, handsome with his dark hair and lively black eyes which were fixed on one of the women there in the church; his thoughts were not those which should come to a young man at such a time. The full, sensuous lips were curved into a smile. She tried not to think of him as the young philanderer, the lazy sensualist, but as a man of battle, the son who had sworn to serve the Huguenot cause as his mother and the great Gaspard de Coligny had taught him to do.

The bride was young and beautiful, a widow, earnest and devout, laying such devotion at Coligny's feet as he had received from his first wife; that devotion which, so effortlessly, he seemed to inspire in so many.

She had come from Savoy, this Jacqueline d'Entremont; a widow of great property, for years she had been an ardent admirer of Coligny's. He was a hero to her as he was to so many Huguenot ladies; she had told Jeanne that she had followed his adventures with enthusiasm, and each day her longing to serve him had increased. When she had heard of his wife's death she had determined to comfort him, and against the wishes of her family and the Duke of Savoy, she had travelled to La Rochelle. Here she met Coligny himself and, so great was her love that he had after a little while found that he could not be indifferent to it, and later that he returned it.

'May the Lord bless them both,' prayed Jeanne.

As for herself, she was growing old; she was now just past forty. She should not be so foolish as to feel envious of her friend's happiness.

And how pleasant it was, in the weeks that followed, to see the happiness of these two and to have some share in it. Friendship between Jeanne and Jacqueline grew as once it had grown between Jeanne and her sister-in-law, the Princess Eléonore of Condé.

Then came the letters from court.

These were letters from the woman who represented herself as a poor mother, anxious for the welfare of her country. Now that there was peace in this tortured land, she needed such a great man as Coligny to help her and her son to govern. Coligny must come with all speed to Blois, for she was most eager to consolidate this uneasy peace. The Queen Mother had succeeded in having the Spanish envoy, Alava, recalled to Spain, so there would be no awkward meeting of the Huguenot leader with the emissary of Philip of Spain. Would Coligny not come and help a poor weak woman? Would he not give that advice which was so sorely needed and might result in years of peace for his country?

Coligny read the letters and was excited by them. An invitation to court from which for ten years he had been more or less an exile! What could he not do if he had the ear of the King and Queen Mother? He began to dream of war against Philip of Spain, of an extended French Empire.

When he told Jeanne and Jacqueline what the letters contained, they were horrified. Jeanne was reminded of another occasion, when her Antoine had been called to court.

'It is a trap!' she cried. 'Can you not recognise the insincerity of the Queen Mother?'

'My dearest husband, I beg of you, take care,' cried Jacqueline. 'Do not walk into this trap. They mean to kill you. Remember the plot which was foiled only just in time . . . the plot to poison you while you were in camp.'

'My beloved wife, my dear good friend and sovereign, this is a chance which should not be missed.'

'A chance for your enemies to kill you?' demanded Jeanne.

'A chance to put the case for the Huguenots before the rulers of this land. A chance to bring about the Reformation in France. This is a call from Heaven. I must go to court.'

At length they knew it was useless to try to dissuade him, and the happiness of the bride was clouded with great misgiving. The Queen of Navarre felt resigned; no one, it seemed, understood the deadly quality of the Queen Mother as she did. Catherine was surely behind that plot to poison Coligny in camp. What fresh mischief was being planned in that tortuous mind concerning him?

They would see; meanwhile Jeanne increased her prayers for the Admiral's safety.

With two hundred and fifty men, Coligny rode up the hill towards the Castle of Blois. He was conscious of the tension among his followers. They, like his wife and Jeanne and the people of La Rochelle, thought it folly to ride straight into the trap his enemies had probably prepared for him. He was anxious to calm their fears. There was no good purpose, he said, in looking for evil; when it was found, let them try to stamp it out, but until it was manifested, let there be trust.

There was none to greet the party when they arrived at the castle, and this was ominous. Coligny called to a man who appeared in the courtyard, and asked that he might be conducted at once to the Queen Mother.

When he was eventually taken to her, King Charles was with her. Coligny knelt at the King's feet, but Charles begged him not to kneel. He embraced the Admiral with great friendliness, and lifted his eyes to the stern, handsome face.

'I am glad to see you here, my father,' he said, using that form of address which he himself had given Coligny during that earlier friendship of theirs. 'We shall not let you go now we have got you.'

There was no mistaking the honest intentions of the young King; he had always been fond of the Admiral.

Catherine watched the pair closely. She greeted the Admiral with a warmth which completely disguised her hatred. Her smile seemed as frank as her son's; and Coligny accepted the smile at its face value.

They took Coligny to the apartments of the King's brother Henry, Duke of Anjou.

Henry was in bed; he was, so Catherine had explained to Coligny, slightly indisposed, and for this reason had been unable to greet the Admiral with the ceremony due to him. Henry was clad in a garment of crimson silk, and there was a necklace of precious stones about his neck, which stones matched those in his ears. The room was like a woman's room; an odour of musk hung about it. Seated close to the bed were two of Henry's favourites, very beautiful young men, their garments fantastically exaggerated and almost feminine, their faces painted, their hair curled. They bowed to the King and the Queen Mother, but the glances they gave to Coligny were insolent.

Henry, languidly and with no attempt at sincerity, said that it delighted him to see the Admiral at court. He would be forgiven, he knew, for not leaving his bed. He was most indisposed.

Coligny's hopes were high.

But that evening as he walked from his apartments to the banqueting hall, in a dimly lighted corridor he came face to face with the Duke of Montpensier. Coligny knew Montpensier for a firm Catholic and a man of honour. Montpensier made no secret of his hatred for the Huguenot cause, but his hatred of treachery was equally intense.

'Monsieur,' whispered Montpensier, 'are you mad? To have come here in this manner is folly! Have you no idea of the sort of people with whom we have to deal? You are rash indeed to walk dark corridors such as this one alone.'

Coligny said: 'I am under the King's roof. I have the King's pledge for my safety.'

Montpensier put his mouth close to Coligny's ear.

'Do you not know, man, that the King is not master in his own house? Take care.'

Coligny thought, as he went down to the banqueting hall, that there might be much in what Montpensier said; but he felt that he had received a call from on high; and the Huguenot cause was dearer to him than his own life.

⚜ ⚜ ⚜

The King was delighted to have Coligny at court.

'Such a man as this,' he told Marie, 'I would fain be. He knows no fear. *He* does not care if assassins lie in wait for him. He would meet his death willingly, eagerly . . . if he thought it was God's Will. Would that I were like Coligny!'

'I love you as you are, my dearest Sire.'

He laughed, and caressed her.

'The Huguenots cannot be wicked,' he said. 'Coligny is one, and he is the noblest man I know. Ambroise Paré is the greatest surgeon in France, and he is one. I said to him, "Do you cure Catholics as well as Huguenots, Monsieur Paré? Or when you wield the knife, do you sometimes let it slip . . . when your patient is a Catholic?" And he said to me, "Sire, when I wield the knife, I do not remember whether my patient is a Catholic or a Huguenot. I do not think of faith at such a time. I think only of my skill." And that is true, Marie. There is something fine about such men. I would I were like them. Must I spend my whole life longing to be like others? I should like to write verses as Ronsard does, to be a great leader as is my dear friend Coligny, to be handsome and brave and have many women loving me, like Henry of Guise; and I should like to have won great battles and be my mother's favourite, as is my brother Henry.'

His brow darkened at the thought of his brother. He hated Henry as he hated no other, for he knew that Henry hated him; he was wondering if a plot was being prepared by Henry and his mother, a plot to take the crown from him and place it on Henry's head.

Henry hated Coligny as much as Charles loved the man. Catherine had prevailed on Henry to receive Coligny, but Henry had sulked and pretended to be ill. Henry was obviously dangerous – dangerous to the King and to Coligny.

Charles's friendship with Coligny grew. He would not let the Admiral out of his sight if he could help it. Coligny talked to the King of his plans for a united France, in which he wished to include the Netherlands.

'The Netherlands would then know peace, Sire, and if we made successful war on Spain we might bring the Spanish Indies under the French flag. There would be an Empire – an Empire in which men could worship as they pleased.'

The King listened and applauded. He began to make concessions to the Huguenots. Coligny's presence at court was making itself felt; so was his influence with the King. Some Catholics who had massacred Protestants at Rouen were executed. Coligny only had to request the King's attention, and it was his. The Catholics of Paris were uneasy, while the Guises, during a temporary absence from court, planned the downfall of the Admiral.

Catherine too watched the growing influence of Coligny over the King, but she was not disturbed. Little mad Charles was *her* creature; his tutors, still at their task, were her creatures; and she did not think any man – even such a man as Coligny – could undo so quickly all that she had done over the years. She wished to keep Coligny at court. She had no wish to kill him yet. She hated him; she was suspicious of him, and she would watch him closely, but at the moment he was more useful alive. He was, with Jeanne of Navarre, her greatest enemy; even so, his time had not yet come. For one thing, she liked the idea of this war with Spain. Coligny was a great leader, the very man to lead the French in such a war. He would be invaluable if the plan came to fulfilment. War with Spain! Victorious war! Oh, to be free from the fear of that man of gloom, the Catholic tyrant of Madrid. He was the biggest bogy in Catherine's life, although so many miles separated them. And another reason why she was not ready to get rid of Coligny yet was that she was anxious to marry Margot to Henry of Navarre. If she despatched Coligny, how could she ever lure Jeanne and her son to court? No! All honour must be done to Coligny until, through him, she had brought about this marriage of her daughter and the son of Jeanne of Navarre.

Her son Henry was being a little tiresome over this matter of Coligny. She made excuses for him. It was so difficult for him, so recently at war with the man, to have him here in the palace, to see him fêted, made the confidant of the King. Catherine had neither the authority nor the influence over this spoiled and beloved son that she had over her other children. He sulked and clearly showed his enmity to the Admiral.

So she must have Henry watched; she must spy on her darling; and she had discovered that he was in secret communication with the Guises, who were now at Troyes. They made no secret of their desire for the death of the Admiral; not only was he the leader of their enemies, the Huguenots, but they looked upon him as the murderer of Francis Duke of Guise, and this would never be forgotten nor forgiven.

Catherine was hurt that her dearest Henry should be plotting with the Guises without telling her. She went to him one day and, when they were alone, very gently let him know that she was aware of this secret plan.

Henry was surprised, but he smiled and, taking her hand, kissed it.

'I had forgotten how clever you are, my mother.'

Catherine flushed with pleasure. 'My darling, if I am clever, it is due to my love for you. It is because I watch all your interests with the greatest care. What of this plot?'

'But you know.'

'Tell me. I should like you to tell me all the same.'

'There is to be a fête, a sort of masque, a sham tournament.

We are going to build a fort at Saint-Cloud. I am to defend it and we are to arrange that Coligny shall lead his men to the attack. A sham battle, you see. That is how it will start; and then, suddenly, it will cease to be a sham. We shall, at a given moment, fire to kill. We shall kill them all . . . every Huguenot among them. What do you say to that, my mother?'

She looked into his flushed face, at his petulant mouth. She did not like it at all, but she would not tell him so, for if she did, and this did not come to pass, he would suspect her of having had a hand in stopping it, and be quite cross with her. It was no use; she could not bear his displeasure. She would not therefore explain to him that she hated Coligny as much as he did, and that she had decided on his death – but at the right time. She did not explain that if they killed him now Queen Jeanne would never come to court and bring her son so that a marriage might be arranged between him and Margot; why, if they were to wage war on Spain, this marriage of Huguenot Henry of Navarre and Catholic Margot would be the best thing possible. Catholics and Huguenots would march together against Spain. She could not risk his sulking, so she told him none of these things; she kissed him, admired his new ornaments, told him the plan was a clever one, and begged him to take care of his precious person, which was more dear to her than all else; and in the last statement at least she spoke with sincerity.

Then she went along to the King's apartment and, dismissing all his attendants and taking her usual precautions to ensure that they were not overheard, she revealed to Charles the plot which had been concocted by his brother and the Guises.

Charles was speechless in his horror. There was foam on his lips and his eyes protruded horribly.

'My darling,' said Catherine soothingly, 'there have been times when you have shown a little jealousy of your brother. You have thought that I cared more for him than for you. When such a stupid thought comes to you again, remember this: I know how you love the Admiral; I know of your admiration for this man; and so I am betraying your brother's plot to you, in order that you may foil it and save the life of your friend.'

Charles's body began to tremble and twitch.

Catherine continued: 'Now you will know, will you not? You will not think yourself neglected in future. I love all my children. Their welfare is my one concern. But you, my son, are more than my child – you are my King.'

'Oh, Mother!' he said. 'Mother!' And he began to weep.

She embraced him, and he cried: 'I will have Henry arrested for this! I will have him sent to the dungeons of Vincennes.'

'No, no, my darling. You must not do that. You must be quiet and cautious. You must be clever. Let them build their fort at Saint-Cloud, and then you can give orders that it shall be destroyed, for you have decided to allow no mock battle to take place. You can say you are tired of mock battles and will think of some new masque . . . something of your own arranging. You see, that is clever. That is your mother's way. And all the time they are making their preparations they will be making no fresh plans; you will therefore have the satisfaction of knowing that the Admiral is safe.'

Charles seized her hand and kissed it. Catherine sighed with relief. She had overcome that difficulty. She returned to her apartments to write a letter to Elizabeth of England, suggesting a match between the Queen and Catherine's youngest son, Hercule; and she wrote also to Jeanne of Navarre, reminding her of the match which, long ago, Henry the Second had arranged between her son and Catherine's daughter. She urged Jeanne to come to court with her daughter.

✤ ✤ ✤

How annoying it was to have to deal with recalcitrant children!

'What!' cried the conceited little Hercule, Duke of Alençon. 'You would marry me to the Virgin of England! Why, she is old enough to be my mother.'

'And rich enough to be your wife.'

'I tell you I will have none of it.'

'You will have to be reasonable, my son.'

'Madame, I would beg of you to reconsider this matter.'

'I have already carefully considered it. Have you? Think! A crown . . . the crown of England will be yours.'

He was wild, that boy, conceited, arrogant and a lover of intrigue. She took him to Amboise and kept him a prisoner there. One could not be sure what such a wilful boy would do to wreck his proposed marriage with the Virgin Queen.

'And now that I have my little frog safe at Amboise,' said Catherine to the King, 'I must set about the marrying of Margot.'

When Catherine received Margot in her apartments and told her who was to be her husband, Margot's eyes blazed with contempt and horror.

'I . . . marry Henry of Navarre! That oaf!'

'My dear daughter, it is not every Princess who has the chance to become a Queen.'

'The Queen of Navarre!'

'Your great-aunt was a clever and beautiful woman – the most intellectual of her day – and she did not scorn the title.'

'Nevertheless, I scorn it.'

'You will grow used to the idea.'

'I never shall.'

'When you renew your acquaintance with your old friend, you will grow fond of him.'

'He was never my friend, and I was never fond of him. I never could be. I dislike him. He is a coarse philanderer.'

'My dear daughter! Then you will, I know, have some tastes in common.'

Margot steeled herself to conquer her fear of her mother and to answer boldly: 'I was prevented from marrying the only man I wished to marry. I therefore claim the right to choose my own husband.'

'You are a fool,' said Catherine. 'Think not that I will endure any of your tantrums.'

'I am a Catholic. How could I marry a Huguenot?'

'It may be that we shall make a Catholic of him.'

'I thought I was to marry him because he *is* a Huguenot, so that the Huguenots might fight with the Catholics against Spain.'

Catherine sighed. 'My daughter, the policy of a country may change daily. What applies to-day does not necessarily apply tomorrow. How do I know whether Henry of Navarre will remain Huguenot or Catholic? How do I know what France will require of him?'

'I hate Henry of Navarre.'

'You talk like a fool,' said Catherine, and forthwith dismissed her daughter. She had no serious qualms about Margot's ultimate obedience.

Margot went to her room and lay on her bed, dry-eyed and full of wretchedness.

'I will not. I will not!' she kept saying to herself; but she could not shut out of her mind the memory of her mother's cold eyes, and she knew that what her mother willed must always come to pass.

❖ ❖ ❖

There was a constant flow of letters from Catherine arriving at Jeanne's stronghold in La Rochelle.

'You must come to court,' wrote Catherine. 'I long to see you. Bring those dear children – as dear to me as my own. I assure you with all my heart that no harm shall come to you or to them.'

Jeanne thought of all those years when her beloved son had been withheld from her. What if she allowed him once more to walk into the trap! She could never forget what had happened to Antoine. He had been her dear and loving husband; their domestic life had been a joy; and then one day had come the summons to go to court; he had gone, and soon there were those evil rumours; quickly he had fallen under the spell of *La Belle Rouet*, as Catherine had intended he should. After that he had even changed his religion. It was as though the serpent's fangs had pierced him, not to kill, but to infect him with that venom, that particular brand of poison which she kept for the weak. And Henry, Jeanne's son, was young, and far too susceptible to the charms of fair women. What Catherine had done to the father, she no doubt planned to do to the son.

Jeanne sat down and wrote to the Queen Mother:

'Madame, you tell me that you want to see us – and that it is not for any evil purpose. Forgive me if, when I read your letters, I felt an inclination to laugh. For you try to do away with a fear which I have never felt. I do not believe you eat little children . . . as folks say you do.'

Catherine read and reread that letter.

They were enemies – this Queen and herself. They had been so from the beginning of their acquaintance. Always Catherine was aware of a vague hatred of this woman, which was outside the normal irritation which her character – so different from Catherine's – always aroused in the Queen Mother. Always Catherine was aware of an uneasiness when she thought of Jeanne. She would like to see her dead; she was, in any case, one of those people who the Duke of Alva had declared must be removed; she was dangerous, and her death would give undoubted pleasure to the King of Spain. 'I do not believe you eat little children . . . as some folks say you do.' One day perhaps, Jeanne would see that Catherine could be as deadly as those words implied.

But not yet. The marriage agreements had to be signed, and they must be signed by the Queen of Navarre, for she was the controller of her son's fate.

Well, the bait was surely big enough to bring Jeanne to court – marriage for her son with the daughter of the House of Valois, the King's sister, the daughter of the Queen Mother. Surely that must attract even the pious Queen of Navarre.

But Jeanne prevaricated. There were religious difficulties, she wrote.

'That, Madame,' answered Catherine, 'is a matter that we must discuss when we are together. I doubt not that we shall come to a satisfactory arrangement.'

'Madame,' wrote Jeanne, 'I hear that the Papal Legate is at Blois. I could not, you will understand, visit the court while he is there.'

It was true, for the Pope had sent him; fearing a match between Huguenot Henry of Navarre and the Catholic Princess, he was now suggesting Sebastian of Portugal once more for Margot.

But now Catherine fervently wished for war with Spain; she was fascinated by her dreams of a French Empire, and she wanted Coligny to lead France to victory. If she were to bring Catholics and Huguenots together to fight against Spain, the marriage between Henry of Navarre and Margot would help to bring this about.

'Then come to Chenonceaux, dear cousin,' she wrote to Jeanne. 'There we will meet and talk to our heart's content. Bring your dear son with you. I long to embrace him.'

Jeanne's nights were haunted with troubled dreams, and in these dreams the Queen Mother figured largely. Her very words seemed to Jeanne to suggest sinister intentions. She 'longed to embrace' Henry. What she had in mind was to lure him away from his mother, to draw him into the sensuous life of the court, to get her sirens to work on him . . . to turn him into her creature as she had his father.

But the match with the Princess of France was a good one. Jeanne looked ahead into a hazy future. If, by some act of God, all Catherine's sons died leaving no heir, well then, young Henry of Navarre was very near the throne, and a Valois Princess as his wife would bring him nearer.

So at last Jeanne set out for the court, but she did not take Henry with her. Instead, she took her little daughter Catherine.

She admonished Henry before she left: 'No matter what letters arrive from the Queen Mother, no matter what commands, heed them not. Do nothing except you receive word from me.'

Henry kissed his mother farewell. He was quite happy to stay behind, for at this moment he was enjoying a particularly satisfactory love affair with the daughter of a humble citizen, and he had no wish to leave her arms for those of the spitfire Margot.

❖ ❖ ❖

Margot was dressing to meet the Queen of Navarre.

'That puritanical woman!' she said to her women. 'That Huguenot! I despise them both – the woman *and* her son!'

She painted her face; she put on a gown of scarlet velvet, cut low to expose her breasts. She would do all in her power to drive the good woman back whence she had come.

Catherine glared at her daughter when she saw her, but there was no time to send her back to her room to change her appearance. And when Catherine saw that Jeanne had arrived without her son, she was not sorry for Margot's defiance.

Jeanne bowed low and received the kisses of ceremony. Catherine put her fingers under the chin of her little namesake and tilted the child's face upwards. 'My dear little god-daughter! I am delighted to see *you* at court, although I so deeply regret the absence of your brother.'

Catherine was determined that there should be no discussions on the subject which Jeanne had come to talk about until the ceremonies were over. She was amused to see Jeanne's disgust at the court manners, and the boldness of the women. She was amused to watch Jeanne's contemplation of her prospective daughter-in-law; she was as amused at Margot's sly determination to make herself as unacceptable as possible by flaunting her extravagant clothes and her loose behaviour with the courtiers. Catherine laughed to herself. She knew that Huguenot Jeanne was at heart an ambitious mother, and that for all her piety she would be unable to resist this dazzling marriage for her son. Jeanne would be ready to endure a good deal in order to put Henry a step nearer to the throne.

The weeks that followed were painful to Jeanne, but full of amusement to Catherine, for Catherine delighted in prodding her enemy into anger. It was not difficult. The Queen of Navarre was notoriously frank. She said straight out that she disliked the licentiousness of the court, the masques and plays which were performed; these, Catherine told her, were done in her honour. But the plays were all comedies – for Catherine believed tragedies to be unlucky – ribald or *risqué*; and both the Queen Mother and her daughter slyly watched the effect of them on the Queen of Navarre.

During the weeks that followed Jeanne's arrival, Catherine was constantly urging her to send for Henry; but Jeanne was firmly against this, and would not be persuaded. Moreover, she could not hide her impatience at Catherine's determination not to discuss the matter which had brought Jeanne to court; she could not hide her distrust of Catherine. Catherine smiled calmly at Jeanne's impatience, but her thoughts were the more deadly for her calm.

'Your son would have to live at court,' said Catherine at length, 'and I do not think we could grant him the right to worship in the Huguenot manner.'

'But some people here do worship in that manner.'

'Your son would be of the royal house . . . with a Catholic wife. And when the Princess Marguerite visits Béarn, she must be allowed to attend mass.'

Several times Jeanne was on the point of leaving the court in very exasperation, until she realised that it was the Queen Mother's wish that the marriage should take place, and that it was the mischievous side to her nature which compelled her to tease the Queen of Navarre.

'I do not know how I endure these torments,' Jeanne wrote to her son. 'I am not allowed to be alone with anyone but the Queen Mother, and she takes a delight in plaguing me. All the time she is laughing at me. Oh, my son, I tremble at the thought of this court. There never was such licentiousness. It is not the fault of the King; he has his mistress installed in the palace in apartments close to his own, and he retires early on the excuse that he wishes to work on a book he is writing; but all know that he spends the time with his mistress. Others are not so discreet.'

There was one private interview between Jeanne and Margot. Margot was cold and haughty, expressing no desire for the marriage.

'How would you feel,' asked Jeanne hopefully, 'about a change in your religion?'

'I have been brought up in the Catholic religion,' the Princess said, 'and I would never abandon it. Even,' she added maliciously, 'for the *greatest* monarch in the world!'

Jeanne said angrily: 'I have heard differently. It seems I have been brought to court on false reports.'

Jeanne was made continually aware of the falseness of the court. They did not say what they meant, these people. They were completely without sincerity. They alarmed her, for when they smiled, she knew their smiles hid deadly thoughts.

Coligny could help her very little. He was obsessed by his friendship with the King, with his plans for the conquest of

Spain and the establishment of the Huguenot religion. He was, Jeanne felt sure, too trusting.

Catherine was watching events outside the court, while inside she played with Jeanne. The Guises were growing restive. There was a personal element in the Guises' annoyance. Coligny they looked upon as the murderer of Duke Francis; they had wanted Margot to marry Duke Henry.

They now plotted with Spain. That accursed family! thought Catherine. They were always in the background of her life, foiling her schemes.

France was battered by civil war; Spain was strong. There returned to Catherine that awful fear of Philip which never left her for long; and she knew that sooner or later he must be placated. What was he thinking in his palace in Madrid? His spies would have been watching her closely. They would report that Coligny was at court and that the Queen Mother was planning a marriage for her daughter with the heretic of Navarre! It was obvious to Catherine that she must show Philip that, in spite of outward appearances, she was still his friend.

And so, listening to Jeanne, arguing, teasing, Catherine began to make plans. She would have to throw a very important personage to the King of Spain; she would have to carry out the first part of that pact which she had made with Alva at Bayonne.

Of course, she had always disliked Jeanne. There had always been that uncomfortable knowledge that her existence meant no good to Catherine. Philip would be pleased to see the woman out of the way. He would know with certainty then that the Queen Mother worked with him.

So while she talked with Jeanne her thoughts moved away from and beyond the marriage pact. She pictured the pact signed, Henry of Navarre at court bound to Margot, and then – the end of Jeanne of Navarre.

The Ruggieri? They were too timid. René would be the best man.

She must therefore get the contract signed, tie up the Prince, and make the marriage possible. Then she could proceed with her plans for war with Spain while she lulled Philip's fears by removing the woman whom he recognised as one of his deadliest foes.

Charles would be useful at this stage. His friendship with Coligny must be extended to the Queen of Navarre. Catherine spent much time with the King, explaining to him the part he must play.

Accordingly he was seen a good deal with Jeanne; she was, he said, his dear aunt. He told her of his love for Coligny. He was very useful in subduing Jeanne's fears.

'If there should be any trouble with the Pope,' said Charles, 'we will get Margot married *en pleine prêche.*'

And so, at last, Jeanne of Navarre signed the marriage contract between her son and the Princess Margot; and thus was Catherine free to go ahead with her plans.

⚜ ⚜ ⚜

The court had moved to Paris, and with it went Jeanne of Navarre.

'There must be preparations for the wedding,' said Catherine, 'and you will wish to take advantage of all that Paris can offer you. I myself will take you to my best dressmakers, my own glove-makers, my *parfumeurs.*'

Jeanne suppressed misgivings and went. Coligny assured her that this was a new dawn for the Huguenot Party, and that she could trust her son to adhere to his faith. She must realise that, pleasure-loving as he was, he was not weak as his father had been.

Catherine was delighted to be in her beloved Paris. It was exhilarating to slip out through the secret passage, a shawl about her head, and enter the shop on the quay opposite the Louvre.

René at once recognised her. He was delighted that it was to him that she came. For so long he had been the rival of the Ruggieri brothers.

She asked to be taken into his secret chamber, and thither she was conducted immediately.

'Monsieur René,' she said, throwing off her shawl and putting on her regal dignity, 'I have a commission for you. You must let me know if you are willing to undertake it.'

'My greatest desire, Madame,' he said, 'is to serve your Majesty.'

'Wait before you commit yourself, my friend. The person involved is of very high rank.' She scrutinised the face of the man, but he did not flinch. She went on: 'Her death must be brought about swiftly and subtly. There may be suspicion, however cleverly it is performed. There may be an autopsy. I would not wish you to undertake this until you have considered all that it may mean. I have come to you because I believe you to be more fearless than your fellows.'

'Madame, I shall be fearless in your Majesty's service.'

'How do your experiments go, Monsieur René?'

'Very well, Madame. I have a substance which can be inhaled through the nose or through the pores of the skin.'

'That is not so very novel.'

'But a substance, your Majesty, which, a few days after it is inhaled, will leave no deposit in the victim's body, a substance which will aggravate any disease from which the victim may be suffering, so that if the body is opened after death, it would appear that he, or she, has died of this disease.'

'That is interesting, Monsieur René. And if the victim were not suffering from some disease, what then?'

'Death would come, but it would be impossible for any to find out the cause.'

'That in itself would arouse suspicion. Tell me, have you tested the reliability of the substance?'

'I have buried four serving wenches, all of whom I treated with this substance.'

'And how long was it before death came?'

'A matter of days. Except in one case, Madame. She was suffering from an ulcer. Her death was immediate.'

'So you are sure you can rely on this substance?'

'Absolutely, Madame.'

'It seems similar to your *aqua Tofana*.'

'Similar, Madame. But this substance leaves no trace.'

'Tell me how you have procured such a substance. You know these matters interest me.'

'It is a complicated process, Madame, but similar to that which produces our *venin de crapaud*.'

'Arsenic is one of the most dangerous of poisons, preserving the body as it does. If there should be an opening of the body after death . . .'

'But this, I would tell your Majesty, does not contain arsenic. It is similar to the *venin de crapaud* only in its early stages of production. I have fed arsenic to toads and when the creatures are dead, after a certain period have distilled the juices of the body. These contain the virus of arsenic and, of course, the poisons of decomposition. Then I eliminate the arsenic. Nor is that all. But the process of the details would weary you, and it is complicated and not easy to explain.'

Catherine laughed. 'Keep your secrets, Monsieur René. I shall respect them. Why should others reap the benefit of your experiments?'

'If you would care to step into my laboratory, I would show your Majesty what I have prepared of this substance.'

Catherine rose and followed him through several dark passages until they came to an underground cellar. It was warm in here because of the great fire which burned in the stove, the smoke of which fire escaped through a pipe in the wall. On the benches were skeletons of animals, and on the walls had been drawn cabalistic signs. Catherine was well acquainted with the tools of the trade of such men as René and the Ruggieri. Her eyes glowed as she looked at the bottles which contained liquids of all colours, and the boxes of mysterious powders.

René took a phial of liquid of a sickly green colour which he showed her.

'This, Madame, is the most valuable and deadly poison that has yet been made. In this it is possible to steep some article – a glove, a ruff, a trinket; the article absorbs the liquid immediately and is almost at once dry. The poison will remain in the article until it is placed in a certain temperature. The heat of the body, for instance, would draw the poison out in the form of vapour; it would be absorbed into the body through the pores of the skin.'

Catherine nodded. This was no great surprise. The men of her country were the cleverest poisoners in the world. They guarded their secrets jealously, and it was said that some carried them with them to the grave because they could not bear to share them. No matter what qualities a new poison was reputed to possess, Catherine was prepared to believe in it; she had seen enough in her lifetime to know that these sorcerers from her native land could manufacture poisons, the action of which would seem incredible to the rest of the world.

'It is good that you have such confidence, Monsieur René,' she said, 'for when an eminent person dies, there is much suspicion, and if there should be an autopsy and poison were discovered – well, it might be remembered that the lady called at your shop.'

'That is so, Madame. But I believe in my work. I have tested this substance. Moreover, my wish is to serve your Majesty with my life if need be.'

Catherine smiled. 'You shall not be forgotten, Monsieur René. Now, if this lady comes here to buy gloves, a ruff or a trinket, you could take what she selects and treat it while she is here .. and let her go away with it?'

'I could, Madame.'

'Gloves would be simplest. Now listen. She shall come to buy gloves. You will show her of your best and, when she has selected them, you will treat them. In order to ensure that she wears them immediately, let those she is wearing when she arrives be soiled in some way. You have no doubt means here of doing this. Let her leave them for you to repair, and let her go away *wearing* the new gloves that you have treated. I would not wish the gloves to fall into other hands.'

'It shall be as you command, Madame.'

'That is well. And I should like a little of that . . . substance . . . for my own closet.'

'Madame, it would not be safe. It is not as yet in the perfect form for keeping. When I can trust it, all my stock is at your Majesty's disposal.'

Catherine smiled faintly. She understood René. He was not prepared to lose his sole right to such a valuable discovery.

She came out into the streets, drawing her shawl about her. So far, so good.

The Queen of Navarre lay sick in her room. She could not understand the sudden faintness which had come over her. She had had a pleasant enough afternoon, choosing some clothes she would need for the ceremonies which would follow the wedding. She was not interested in fine clothes, but she did not wish to appear dowdy among the Parisians, who she knew would be gorgeously apparelled.

She had bought a new ruff and new gloves. Catherine had been helpful, telling her where to go, accompanying her to some of the places. And finally she had gone to the glove-maker and *parfumeur* on the quay opposite the Louvre, and there she had bought a pair of those exquisite gloves such as were now worn at court. She had put them on there and then and come back to the palace wearing them, because of some slight accident to her old pair.

And then had come this strange faintness, this nausea. It had been necessary to take to her bed, for there was a violent pain in her chest. She was unable to attend the banquet that day; and the night that followed was passed in a fever of restlessness; a terrible lassitude had taken possession of her limbs, and by morning she had lost the power of them. She could scarcely breathe, and the pain in her chest had become an agony.

Her apartments in the Hôtel de Condé were filled with anxious men and women of the Huguenot Faith. The greatest physicians in the country were at her bedside, but none could discover the strange nature of her illness. Catherine sent her doctors. 'I beg of you,' said Catherine, 'spare no effort to save the life of the Queen of Navarre. It would be terrible if she were to die now that we have settled the arrangements for the marriage in such an amicable manner.'

Jeanne asked that Coligny might be brought to her. She felt, vague and hazy though she was, that there was much she should say to him. She knew that Coligny was in great danger; that the Huguenot cause was in danger; she remembered something of what her little son had overheard in the gallery of Bayonne; but her mind was failing her, and she could not clearly recall what it was.

She knew that she was dying. 'Your prayers,' she said, 'will avail me nothing. I submit myself to the Holy Will of God, taking all evils from Him as inflicted by a loving Father. I have never feared death. My only grief is that I must leave my children, and that they, at their tender age, are exposed to so many dangers.'

She begged them to cease their weeping.

'Ought you to weep for me?' she asked. 'You have all seen the misery of my last years. God has taken pity on me and is calling me to the enjoyment of a blessed existence.'

She longed for death now, longed to escape from the pain of her body. But she thought of her children: her son, Henry, who was in such need of guidance; her dearest little Catherine, who was so young. What would become of them?

Catherine must return to Béarn. She was insistent on that.

'Oh, please, please,' she cried in a moment of acute consciousness, 'take my little daughter home . . . take her far away from the corruption of this court.'

Then she began to speak of her son's coming marriage, and Catherine, who stood by her bed, said: 'Rest, my dear sister of Navarre. Fret not for the sake of your children. I will be a mother to them. Your son is to be my son through marriage . . . and I am the godmother of your daughter.'

Catherine put her lips to the clammy brow of her enemy. This was the woman for whom she had always felt uneasy hatred. Now was the end of the woman. Jeanne had sought to pit herself against Catherine, so now here she lay, a poor weak woman, dying, stripped of all her earthly possessions, of all earthly desires.

The Queen Mother was triumphant.

The Princess Margot looked on at the scene – a humble scene, for the apartment did not look like the death chamber of a Queen. There were no tapers, no priests, none of the ritual which attended a Catholic death.

She looked at the faces of the people in the room; she looked from the dying Queen to the woman who stood by the bed, the woman with the full pale face and large expressionless eyes from which now and then the delicate white hand wiped a tear.

Margot shivered. Death was terrifying, but she was not so much afraid of death as of the woman in black who conducted herself with such calm and sorrowful decorum.

'The Queen of Navarre is dead!'

They were whispering this in the streets.

'They say she visited René . . . the Queen Mother's glove-maker. People have visited René before . . . and they fall into a decline . . . their teeth break like glass on their bread . . . their skin shrivels . . . and then they die.'

'The Queen of Navarre has been *poisoned*!'

The Parisians were mainly Catholic, and they must therefore regard the Queen of Navarre as an enemy; yet they did not care to think that she had been lured to their city to be poisoned.

'It is that woman!' was whispered in the market-place, in the streets, on the quays. 'It is the Italian woman at her tricks again. Was it not her glove-maker to whom the Queen of Navarre went?'

The people of Paris shuddered; they turned horrified eyes towards the windows of the Louvre; they whispered; they spat in contempt; and there was one name which was mentioned more than any other – that of Catherine de' Medici, the Italian woman. 'Italian! Italian!' they hissed. These Italians were past-masters with the poison cup, and the very word 'Italian' was almost synonymous with *'Poisoner'*.

The Guises came riding to court.

The Queen of Navarre was dead. Here was one enemy out of the way. It might be that the Queen Mother, in favouring the Huguenots, had been playing just another of her tortuous, cunning games.

Margot watched them as they rode into the courtyard of the palace, and looked for the figure at their head; Henry of Guise had grown more handsome during his absence.

She was tired of resisting. Soon they would throw her to that oaf of Navarre; and when she thought of his clumsy hands caressing her, her longing for Henry of Guise was more than she could endure.

She met him, as if by chance, in one of the ill-lighted passages near her apartments.

He stood looking at her. She tried then to turn away, but he came swiftly forward and caught her; then she remembered afresh all the enchantment of his kisses.

'Margot,' he whispered, his voice tender and broken with passion.

'Henry . . . they are going to marry me . . . to Navarre.'

'I know, my love, my darling.'

'I will not,' she sobbed. 'I hate him.'

He tried to soothe her. 'My darling, how I have missed you! How I have longed for you! Why do we torment ourselves?'

She shook her head.

He went on: 'It is stupid pride . . . fighting against what we know has to be. Margot, let us take what we can. Let us take what is left to us.'

Memories surged back to him as to her. He caressed her eager body.

'There was never anyone like you, Margot.'

'There is nothing,' she said, 'but this.'

'Do you remember that little room where we were together? We will go there . . . to-night and every night.'

'The wedding is months away,' cried Margot. 'Who knows . . . perhaps it will never be. Perhaps there will be a rising, and you will become King and marry me . . . as we used to plan. You would be all-powerful then, and you would see that nothing stood in our way.'

He stopped her impulsive words with kisses. The walls of the Louvre had ears.

'To-night?' he repeated.

'At midnight.'

'I shall be waiting . . . most eagerly.'

'And most eagerly shall I come.'

'Go now, my darling. Let us not be seen. Let us be wiser than we were.'

There was a last lingering kiss, one more passionate embrace; and Guise went back to his apartments, and joyously to hers went the Princess, who, but a short time before, had been the most miserable, and was now the happiest, woman in France.

✦ ✦ ✦

There was tension in the Louvre. Catherine had realised suddenly what power Coligny had over her son Charles. She had forgotten that he, so malleable in her hands, would be equally so in those of others.

Surrounded by his courtiers, Charles spoke to his mother, his eyes flashing, his mouth working:

'There are evil rumours concerning the death of the Queen of Navarre. It is said that she met her death through foul practices. I command therefore that the body should be opened and examined in order that the cause of her death may be ascertained.'

Catherine felt herself go cold. Her son's gaze was malevolent; and she knew with sudden horror that he, like the whispering women in the streets, believed that she had killed Jeanne of Navarre. That in itself was not so shocking; but that he, though thinking such a thing, should demand an autopsy, was incredible. Did he want to incriminate his mother, the one person who, so she had believed, had dominated his life? Catherine had been outwitted – outwitted by that great, good man, Gaspard de Coligny. He had crept up slowly with his religion and his self-righteousness and had taken possession of the King's feeble mind. Coligny wanted an autopsy, and the King, in spite of his mother, would see that there was one.

She stared into that poor weak face in which the whites of the eyes were beginning to turn red, the mouth to foam. Her voice was cold. She had put all her trust in René, and if René had spoken the truth all would be well.

'My son, if it is your wish that an autopsy should take place, then so be it. To my mind, the Queen's death was natural enough. She was not strong, and she had suffered a good deal; the effort of the journey to court and the strain of arranging the marriage has been too much for her.'

'Nevertheless,' cried the King, 'I will have her body examined.'

He was a man now, twenty-one. Her mistake had been that she had considered him nothing but an unbalanced boy.

❖  ❖  ❖

The doctors were closeted together. Catherine's and the King's physicians were with Jeanne's. At any moment now the result of their examination would be known. If René had failed, thought Catherine, that would be the end of René, and there would be just another rumour attaching itself to the Queen Mother. Already she was hated. What did she care? Let them hate as long as they let her rule France.

Jeanne was dead. Philip of Spain would be smiling – or getting as near to smiling as he was able – into that beard of his. Elizabeth of England would hear the news with concern. Coligny was stricken down in grief. Jeanne's boy Henry would not yet have heard, but soon he would be forced to come to court; he would be delivered into the hands of the Queen

Mother, who would take him under her wing as one of her sons, to be dominated and guided in the way he should go.

There was nothing for her to fear – only hatred and suspicion. She had had her share of them already, and no one would dare harm the Queen Mother of France.

✤ ✤ ✤

In the dim chamber the lovers lay in an enchanted weariness. Margot wept a little. 'For happiness,' she said, 'because I have missed you and longed for you, and there is no one in the world who can take your place.'

Henry of Guise said angrily: 'How happy we might have been, you and I! I shall never forget nor forgive the one who parted us.'

'My mother terrifies me, Henry.'

'I meant your brother. He is the one who has separated us. We might have married in time but for him. I mean your brother Henry, not the King. He is afraid of me – your brother Henry. One day I shall kill him . . . or he will kill me. I shall take my revenge for what he has done to us, and I shall kill Coligny to honour my father.'

'Do not speak of hate when we have love,' said Margot. 'Now we are together let us enjoy it and think of nothing else. Let us not think of your revenge on my brother and Coligny, of my marriage with Navarre. Let us live in happiness while we may.'

She flung herself into his arms once more, but he felt her trembling. He tried to soothe her, but she said: 'Henry, I cannot stop thinking of my mother. Do you think she poisoned the Queen of Navarre?'

He did not answer, and there was a long silence between

them. But after a while they ceased to think of the Queen of Navarre, of Margot's coming marriage and of revenge. They were together, and they had been apart too long.

✤ ✤ ✤

Through the streets of Paris walked a stout woman with a shawl over her head. She joined a group in the market. They were, she knew, talking of the Queen of Navarre.

'So it was an abscess on the lungs,' said one woman.

'So they say . . .'

Catherine said: 'You think then that the physicians may have been wrong?' She drew the shawl about her to hide her face.

'How do we know what devilries the Italian woman is up to?'

Catherine laughed. 'You think then that she can make abscesses on the lungs of her enemies?'

The group laughed with her. 'She is a witch. She is a sorceress. These Italians . . . they know too much about poisons, and the poisons they give leave no signs. We should never have let them come into our country.'

Catherine moved away. She joined another group who were arguing together. Someone was saying: 'The Queen was poisoned. It was the Italian woman who arranged it, mark my words. The Queen went to a glove-maker . . . the *Italian's* glove-maker. The doctors can say what they like. It may be that they dare say no other. If they did, it might be that they too would soon be suffering from some mysterious illness which their friends could not understand.'

Catherine turned away and walked thoughtfully through the streets. Here was another of those occasions like that which had followed the death of the Dauphin Francis, who had died when his Italian cupbearer had given him water.

She was uneasy. The King must be watched. Coligny had too much influence over him. She would have to begin thinking very seriously about Monsieur de Coligny, for there must obviously be only one who was allowed to exercise authority over the King's feeble mind.

She was strong. She would overcome all difficulties. She thought of herself now, and compared herself with the woman she had been on the death of her husband. Then she had had much to learn, and she had learned some of it. She was now in her prime, and in her hands was the power to lead those she loved, to destroy those who stood in her way – and she was fast learning how to use that power.

The Queen Mother drew her shawl closer about her and walked slowly and thoughtfully back to the palace of the Louvre.

# ✦ AUTHOR'S NOTE ✦

*I*n *The Italian Woman* I have endeavoured to portray Catherine de' Medici in the middle stages of her career, when she was no longer the neglected wife and the most humiliated of all the Queens of France, but the powerful mother of kings. At this stage Catherine was not yet the infamous woman she was to become towards the end of her life, but she was already beginning to show definite signs of that ruthless monster.

To a certain extent much of her life must remain a mystery, for no amount of research can tell us whether or not she actually committed all the crimes which have been laid at her door. In this respect the novelist is in a more delicate position than the biographer, for the latter can present a theory as a theory, while the novelist must make up her mind one way or another, since the object of a novel – a work of fiction – is to create an illusion of reality; and the novelist must naturally be in no doubt as to her characters' motives and actions.

In view of Catherine's character as it gradually emerged through acts which undoubtedly she did commit, and through views expressed in her own letters and in the reports of her contemporaries, I do not think that, in *The Italian Woman*, I have been unfair to her. There is no doubt that she was a callous murderess; and even those judges who are clearly biased in her favour have never attempted to exonerate her from responsibility for – for instance – the murders of Coligny and Lignerolles; nor has it been possible to excuse the part she played in that most horrible of all crimes – the mass murders of the St. Bartholomew.

It has become the fashion among modern historians to frown on the more colourful passages of history. We are told that Francis, the Dauphin, died not of poison, but of pleurisy, and that Jeanne of Navarre died of consumption and not through wearing gloves supplied by Catherine's poisoner-in-chief. And yet, Catherine *was* obsessed by her longing for power; and Francis *did* die after drinking from a cup presented by his Italian cupbearer who had come over in Catherine's suite; and by Francis's death Catherine *was* immediately Dauphiness of France, later to be Queen. As for Jeanne, she did die rather suddenly and mysteriously when she was away from home, and she became violently ill after visiting the sinister little shop on the quay opposite the Louvre. Her death did occur *after* she had signed her son's marriage contract, to do which Catherine had lured her to the court; and it must be admitted that her end came speedily after she had served Catherine's purpose. Moreover, it cannot be denied that Catherine was a murderess.

I have studied various opinions – those of her friends and her enemies – including the Catholic and the Protestant point of view, for it is a fact that the religious controversies of her day still echo about Catherine. In my efforts to understand the real Catherine de' Medici, I have gone from one authority to

387

another, and listed below are some of the books to which I am particularly indebted:

*The History of France*, by Guizot.

*National History of France: The Century of the Renaissance*, by Louis Batiffol.

*France the Nation, and its Development from the Earliest Times to the Establishment of the Third Republic*, by William Henry Hudson.

*Life and Times of Catherine de' Medici*, by Francis Watson.

*The Medici*, by Colonel F. Young.

*The Feudal Castles of France*. Anonymous.

*The Favourites of Henry of Navarre*, by Le Petit Homme Rouge.

*Life of Marguerite of Navarre*, by Martha Walker Freer.

*Life of Jeanne d' Albret, Queen of Navarre*, by Martha Walker Freer.

*Henri II*, by H. Noel Williams.

*Catherine de' Medici and the French Reformation*, by Edith Sichel.

*The Later Years of Catherine de' Medici*, by Edith Sichel.

J.P.

ALSO AVAILABLE IN ARROW: THE MEDICI TRILOGY

# *Queen Jezebel*

## Jean Plaidy

The ageing Catherine de' Medici has arranged the marriage of her beautiful Catholic daughter Margot to the uncouth Huguenot King Henry of Navarre. Margot, still desperately in love with Henry de Guise, refuses to utter her vows. But even Catherine is unable to anticipate the carnage that this unholy union is to bring about . . .

In the midst of an August heatwave, tensions run high: the marriage hasn't brought peace between Catholics and Huguenots. Realising her weakening power over her sickly son, King Francis, Catherine persuades him of a plot against his life. Mad with fear, Francis agrees to a massacre that will rid France of its 'pestilential Huguenots for ever'. And so the carnival of butchery begins, marking years of terror and upheaval that will end in the demise of kings, and finally expose Catherine's lifetime of depraved scheming . . .

arrow books

## Order further Jean Plaidy titles
## from your local bookshop, or have them delivered
## direct to your door by Bookpost

| | | |
|---|---|---|
| ☐ Uneasy Lies the Head | 0 09 949248 2 | £6.99 |
| ☐ Katharine, the Virgin Widow | 0 09 949314 4 | £6.99 |
| ☐ The Shadow of the Pomegranate | 0 09 949315 2 | £6.99 |
| ☐ The King's Secret Matter | 0 09 949316 0 | £6.99 |
| ☐ Madame Serpent | 0 09 949317 9 | £6.99 |
| ☐ Queen Jezebel | 0 09 949319 5 | £6.99 |

**Free post and packing**
Overseas customers allow £2 per paperback

Phone: 01624 677237

Post: Random House Books
c/o Bookpost, PO Box 29, Douglas, Isle of Man IM99 1BQ

Fax: 01624 670923

email: bookshop@enterprise.net

Cheques (payable to Bookpost) and credit cards accepted

Prices and availability subject to change without notice.
Allow 28 days for delivery.
When placing your order, please state if you do not wish to receive any
additional information.

www.randomhouse.co.uk/arrowbooks